BY DELILAH S. DAWSON

THE TALES OF PELL
(with Kevin Hearne)

Kill the Farm Boy
No Country for Old Gnomes
The Princess Beard

STAR WARS

The Perfect Weapon (e-novella)
Phasma
Galaxy's Edge: Black Spire
The Skywalker Saga

SHADOW
(as Lila Bowen)

Wake of Vultures
Conspiracy of Ravens
Malice of Crows
Treason of Hawks
Grist of Bees (in the anthology *Death & Honey*)

HIT

Hit
Strike

BLUD

Wicked as They Come
Wicked as She Wants
Wicked After Midnight
Wicked Ever After

Servants of the Storm
Ladycastle
Sparrowhawk
Star Pig
Mine
The Violence

THE
VIOLENCE

THE
VIOLENCE

A Novel

Delilah S. Dawson

NEW YORK

Copyright © 2022 by D. S. Dawson

All rights reserved.

Published in the United States by Del Rey, an imprint of Random House, a division of Penguin Random House LLC, New York.

DEL REY is a registered trademark and the CIRCLE colophon is a trademark of Penguin Random House LLC.

LIBRARY OF CONGRESS CATALOGING-IN-PUBLICATION DATA
Names: Dawson, Delilah S, author.
Title: The violence / Delilah S Dawson.
Description: New York: Del Rey, [2022]
Identifiers: LCCN 2021022272 (print) | LCCN 2021022273 (ebook) | ISBN 9780593156629 (hardcover) | ISBN 9780593499818 (international edition) | ISBN 9780593156636 (ebook)
Subjects: GSAFD: Suspense fiction.
Classification: LCC PS3604.A97858 V56 2022 (print) | LCC PS3604.A97858 (ebook) | DDC 813/.6—dc23
LC record available at https://lccn.loc.gov/2021022272
LC ebook record available at https://lccn.loc.gov/2021022273

Printed in the United States of America on acid-free paper

randomhousebooks.com

2 4 6 8 9 7 5 3 1

First Edition

Book design by Caroline Cunningham

To the survivors.

I used to blame myself for not doing more.

For not leaving earlier. For not pushing back. For not fighting him.

Now I am kinder to the younger version of me.

Now I believe that survival is enough.

AUTHOR'S NOTE

The Violence deals with themes of physical, emotional, and sexual abuse and includes animal death and graphic violence. Some of these scenes may be distressing for some readers. Writing this book—and examining these themes—has been part of my own healing journey.

My relationship with my father was complicated. When sober, he was perpetually disappointed in me, and when drunk, he was emotionally and physically abusive. Chelsea's nights in the kitchen are based on what my mother and I experienced at his hands. He was so well-loved in our hometown that no one believed us. From the outside, things were perfect.

When I was eighteen, my mother and I left, and we met a very special therapist named Betsy. I can't remember her last name or her exact title, only that she's the first person who said, "You understand that this is abuse, right? You are being abused." Until that moment, I didn't understand. I thought my life was normal. She also sent my father to Narcotics Anonymous, which inspired him to stop drinking. To my knowledge, he never drank alcohol again. But that did not stop him from being emotionally abusive—gaslighting, controlling, and manipulative until the very last. As the Narcissist's Prayer goes: That didn't happen. And if it did, it wasn't that bad. And if it was, that's not a big deal. And if it is, that's not my fault.

When we left in 1995, the internet wasn't yet able to answer all our questions, so I'm grateful to the family and friends who helped us—who saved us. Abusers often leave their victims with few resources, but there is help out there. If you're experiencing abuse, please seek support. You are not alone.

THE
VIOLENCE

The first recorded incidence of the Violence occurred as Ruth Belmont of Land O'Lakes, Florida, was putting a tub of mayonnaise in her cart at a warehouse store on Tuesday, April 15, 2025. The peaceful and highly religious grandmother dropped the mayonnaise, reached for a large bottle of Thousand Island dressing, and struck a fellow customer, twenty-four-year-old Melissa Mendoza. Mendoza's toddler sat in the seat of her buggy and watched silently as the elderly woman beat her mother to death with the bottle of dressing. Once Mendoza was dead, Belmont replaced the dressing on the shelf, selected a new bottle, and attempted to continue shopping. As local law enforcement tackled her to the ground, Belmont screamed, cried, and claimed innocence. Store cameras captured the grisly scene. When the Violence was discovered to be a disease, Belmont was released from jail. She is now suing the state for $1.3 million in damages, including a broken collarbone. Later sufferers were not so lucky.

PART I

1.

Chelsea Martin sits in a perfect sunbeam at her perfect kitchen table, staring at the piece of paper that's going to destroy her life.

Insufficient funds? Impossible.

Her husband, David, manages their bank accounts, and he's in finance, so this must be a mistake. She's read the aggressively detached, computer-printed words a hundred times, and an unwelcome sensation roils, deep in her stomach, her coffee threatening to come back up. It's not panic, not yet, but it's not good.

Would David tell her if they were in trouble? She glances at her phone and considers the best way to ask without insulting him. A text would be safest; he hates it when her voice wobbles. He says she cries too easily, that it's impossible to have a conversation with her when she's so emotional.

No, not worth it. He'll come home and see the paper, and he'll handle it. Let him be angry at the bank, not the messenger, and let him be angry later rather than both now *and* later. She unconsciously puts a hand to her throat and swallows hard, dreading what will happen when he gets home from work.

Definitely not worth bothering him now.

She tries to focus on what she was doing before the mail arrived, but she knows logging onto the online portal and watching the mandatory weekly "Let's Sell Dreams!" video will only make her feel worse. When she signed her contract to sell Dream Vitality essential oils, she'd hoped it would give her some small amount of independence, something to do, something to be proud of. Now, staring into the depths of a wooden case filled with tiny purple bottles, all full and unopened and gathering dust, she never wants to smell bergamot again.

A brand-new cardboard box waits in the foyer, her monthly required shipment optimistically labeled DREAM DELIVERY! But after a year of trying to sell a product that's supposed to sell itself, she's ready to admit defeat. She *had* a dream: to start her own business, build savings, and tap into a network of smart, motivated women. Instead, she's alienated friends through the required social media posts, embarrassed her daughters, and outlived her welcome at every party and playgroup, and all she has to show for it is boxes and boxes of product that she can't even sell at cost. Even before the—surely incorrect?—overdraft notice arrived today, she worried that this month's withdrawal would take her over her strict budget, and that when David found it during his account check, things would get . . . bad.

The hardest thing is that her attempt at entrepreneurship has shown her that most of her friends online aren't really friends. There's no support, no sharing, no purchases, no reviews. Everyone just ignores it. The only encouragement she gets comes from a back-rubbing circle of other plucky moms trying to support one another in an online group with good vibes only, and she wonders if everyone else also secretly feels this constant exhaustion, this disconnection, this profound loneliness.

It was supposed to save her, but it just got her in more trouble.

Buck up, bitch, she tells herself. *It's just oil.*

Not that it makes her feel any better.

She runs her hands through what's slowly becoming her mother's hair as her stylist increasingly covers the gray with bleach in a process with a French name that doubles the cost. The perfect pool sparkles outside the picture window, but she can't jump in because it would make her hair as crisp as uncooked spaghetti with a bonus mossy tinge. She looks around at the shiplap, the granite, the Edison bulbs, the seasonal throw pillows. Everything is perfect, but nothing is *right*.

Even the snowy-white dog snoring on a matching dog bed is boutique—a shedless bichon named Olaf that cost more than Chelsea's first car, because David couldn't stand the thought of dog hair rolling along the marble floors like tumbleweeds. Poor, sweet Olaf is terrified of him and spends most of his time hiding in a closet. But then again, Olaf is deeply inbred, a yipping bag of neuroses and surprise puddles of pee.

The big and airy house is the complete opposite of the shitbox apartments Chelsea grew up in. It should be beautiful and relaxing, but it's closing in on her, an avalanche of stuff and the never-ending work it takes to keep that stuff either proudly displayed at perfect angles or hidden from view, to keep everything running. She never imagined that life would be like this, that she would feel so constantly trapped.

Chelsea is pouring another cup of coffee that will barely touch her bone-deep disquiet when the doorbell rings, sending her entire body rigid. She scans the wall calendar, the dates empty of commitments and the top crammed with posed pictures of her family in matching crisp white shirts, but no one is due to work on the house or make a delivery. Between Dream Vitality and David, most of her old friends keep their distance these days, which means only one thing. Her feet already know it and are propelling her backward, away from the soaring foyer and toward the laundry room, where the windows are too high up to tattle on her as she hides. The garage door is closed, after all; there's no way to tell she's home.

And then her phone buzzes in her hand, and the text pops up on the screen.

I know you're in there.

Even the laundry room can't save her. Back in the kitchen, she gulps her coffee and slams the gray ceramic mug down almost too hard, the blond liquid splashing onto the black granite. She hurries to the huge master bathroom, brushing her hair and touching up her lipstick. Her mascara is running, just a little, making her blue eyes pop, and she dabs a tissue under each eye. There's a tiny coffee stain on her shirt, so she throws on a new one and jabs midsized diamond studs into her ears—not so small that they look like all she can afford but not so big that it seems like she's trying too hard.

When the knock comes, it's light and jovial.

Tap tap tap-tap-tap.

It's just little old me, the knock seems to say. *Just a friendly visit.*

If malignant narcissism could knock, it would sound like that.

Knowing that if she doesn't hurry, she'll hear the scrape of the mat being moved aside and the emergency key turning in the lock, Chelsea scurries across the tile, checks the peephole to confirm, and opens the door with the sort of smile that chimps use when they're about to get torn limb from limb by bigger chimps.

"Well, that took you long enough," says Patricia Lane, her own answering smile proper and polite and yet the sort that reflects the stronger ape promising a primordial beat-down with a femur bone. "Eighty-six degrees today. In April! I'm lucky I didn't melt out here."

Witches melt in rain, not sun, Chelsea wants to say but doesn't. *And you've lived in Central Florida your whole life, so move away if you hate it so much.* But, just like with David, talking back only makes it worse.

"Hi, Mom. Come on in."

There is no hug, no posh and affected air kisses, definitely no real kisses.

There never have been.

Patricia straightens the cardigan knotted over her silk shell and looks down her nose at her only daughter before sweeping into the foyer. "I'm not a vampire, darling. I'm family. I'm always welcome."

If she's being honest, Chelsea knows her mother looks more like she's actually Chelsea's older sister. Patricia's hair is blonder, her face is tanner and still smooth, her clothes are neater, and her figure is still so trim that they could trade clothes if they had anything close to the same taste. The diamonds in her ears and on her fingers and wrist don't say, *I'm just the right size;* they suggest that, given the slightest provocation, they would delicately shred you to ribbons while explaining the Mohs scale in the most patronizing manner possible. Chelsea's mother, as David says, puts in the work.

As Chelsea locks the door behind her, Patricia turns a slow circle, raising one perfect eyebrow at the chandelier.

"You have to remind them to dust, dear," she says, almost sad. "Let these once-a-week cleaning services get away with one thing, and soon they'll stop dusting the baseboards and you'll find cash missing. Give them an inch, they'll take a mile."

Chelsea looks up at the chandelier but can't see any dust.

"So what did you need?" she asks, hoping to end the visit as soon as possible while still appearing polite so she won't get another lecture.

Patricia's gaze stops checking the glass over the family portraits for water spots and lands on Chelsea, the older woman's frown going deeper without making any creases in the smoothly filled putty of her face.

"Does a mother need a reason to visit her daughter?" she asks, sounding wounded. "Can I not simply take a loving interest in your life?"

Chelsea smiles as her teeth grind together. "Of course you can. What did you want to talk about? Ella and Brooklyn are doing well in school—"

Patricia sighs the sigh of the sorely aggrieved and swans toward the kitchen, where she plucks a mug from its hook, frowns at its interior, and wipes it out with the kitchen towel before pouring herself a cup of black coffee. She sips it, eyes closed, expectant, then makes a face.

"These beans are burned. I told you: You can't just buy any old bag at the store."

Holding up the twenty-dollar bag of single-origin coffee from a specialty shop, Chelsea presents it for inspection. "I didn't."

Instead of taking the bag or even looking at it, Patricia flaps a hand at it in a gesture that reminds Chelsea of how her mother treats sticky toddlers. "Then you bought the wrong kind. Your generation, I swear. Can't tell you anything."

Patricia's gaze tracks around the kitchen like an airport security dog hunting for more delicious contraband, and Chelsea realizes her mistake the moment her mother goes on point, eyes alight and smile curling up.

"Oh!" She puts down her mug of coffee and saunters over to the wooden cabinet still sitting on the kitchen table. "Are you still doing your . . . little business thingy?" Patricia pulls out a bottle at random and twists off the top, breaking the seal and making Chelsea wince as she sniffs. "Ugh. Thieving Blend? It smells like angry Christmas at the Dollar Store. Do people actually pay for that?"

Chelsea can recite the ingredients, uses, and benefits of the oil by rote, but that would be a mistake, as would be revealing that the simple twist of the cap has cost her twenty dollars that was a problem even before that damn letter arrived today.

"They do, actually. Fifty dollars a pop." She takes the bottle from Patricia's long, slender fingers, re-caps it, and places it back in the cabinet. "It's our most popular product. And it's why none of us got the flu this winter. They say it helps Covid long-haulers, too."

Patricia's nose is all wrinkled up, making her look like a French bulldog. "Well. It's not something *I* would count on, but I suppose you Millennials like to believe in false hope and woo-woo snake oil instead of hard work." She picks up her cup again and sips, gazing into the backyard like she's in a commercial and they're about to have a misty-eyed heart-to-heart about feeling not so fresh. Chelsea is very glad the yard crew came earlier this morning to pick up the fallen branches. "You know, Chel, I worry about you. You have everything you need here, but you're always fiddling around with some little . . . *enterprise*. There was the internet university, which you dropped out of, I believe, long ago. The blogging. You tried to write a book once, and that went nowhere. You sewed face masks. And now the oils. I sincerely worry about you setting yourself up for disappointment. A woman is nourished by her family, not her . . . experiments."

Chelsea loosens her fingers from her fists before that, too, comes under scrutiny. If family was what nourished women, her mother would be a dancing skeleton; she wrote off her entire family when Chelsea was born, probably out of embarrassment, and she only shows up here when she has an agenda or needs to whet her claws.

"I need something to do, Mom. Both girls are in school. I get restless."

Patricia's face attempts something similar to pity, and she sets down her coffee cup and stands before Chelsea, reaching out to arrange her daughter's hair over her shoulders and sighing when it won't cooperate. Chelsea's skin crawls, but she knows better than to flinch.

"If you're so restless, perhaps that energy could be directed inward. A new hairstyle. A Peloton or yoga. Some time at the spa. Get a little work done." She taps Chelsea's forehead with one cold finger. "My doctor is a genius. And diet shakes these days might as well be milkshakes. So rich!"

Rage runs red up Chelsea's neck, heating her cheeks and forehead. She briefly envisions snatching her mother's finger and breaking it in her hands like a pencil. Words tumble through her head a mile a minute, ranging from *If we're the same size, why do I need more exercise?* to *Independence is more important than pretending I'm half my age, not that you'd understand that* to *If I'd married an older man to get rich, perhaps I'd be that complacent, too.* But the thing about her mother's pronouncements is that they are in no way about Chelsea, and Chelsea knows that. Like most things in her life, fighting back only makes things infinitely worse.

"Maybe I will," she says. "The yoga, I mean. Thanks for caring, Mom."

Patricia's eyes close, and she does a sinuous little shoulder shimmy, as if eating compliments could sustain her. The funny thing is that Chelsea remembers how her mother spoke when she was poor, before she set her sights on marrying rich and dropped her southern accent and habit of screaming at people who didn't do what she wanted. This current version of Patricia is a creation, her mother's own little . . . experiment. And it worked, damn her.

"I only want what's best for you, dear. I always have. You must take care of yourself. For the children." Patricia glances at the family calendar, bright with pictures of Ella and Brooklyn at the beach, and frowns. "When was that trip? I don't remember being invited."

But before Chelsea can answer, Patricia has snatched up the overdraft notice from the counter and is reading it as avidly as one of those gossip magazines she hides under her bathroom sink but pretends to hate. She gasps, a hand to her chest.

"Chelsea, what is this? Overdrawn?"

Teeth grinding so hard she's worried she'll bust open a crown,

Chelsea snatches the page back and folds it decisively, stuffing it in the back pocket of her skinny jeans. "Nothing. A mistake. David will handle it."

Patricia licks her lips like a fox and steps forward, a bony hand on each of Chelsea's shoulders. Her signature scent invades Chelsea's nose and mouth, lilies and poisonous white flowers, and she wants to turn away and retch.

"Darling," her mother says, weighty and pitying, her eyes innocently wide. "If you're in trouble, you can tell me."

Not *I'll help you,* Chelsea notes, but *You can tell me.*

"We're fine, Mom." Chelsea shrugs and tries to grin. "Look around you. We're doing fine."

Patricia does look around, but almost as if she's afraid the house will fall down on her.

"Then I'm certain David knows what he's doing. But I should run. So busy. You know how it is."

As her mother swiftly sashays back to the front door, running a finger along the top of the wainscoting and frowning at it, Chelsea wonders if she would even know if she was having a heart attack. Tight throat, aching chest, hot forehead, numb fingers—these are the symptoms of being around Patricia Lane for any amount of time. Thank heavens her mother takes off to her condo in the Outer Banks for major holidays, claiming the children give her migraines. Chelsea wonders if it makes her sad and lonely, celebrating Christmas in a beautifully appointed but empty beach house while her latest husband golfs, but she would never ask such a thing. Her mother might actually tell her the answer.

"Thanks for stopping by," she says at the door.

Patricia turns around, forehead wearing one elegant and rebellious crease. "There was something I wanted to tell you, but I can't remember what it was. Never get old, darling. I swear, my mind is a sieve."

Chelsea smile-grimaces in understanding and opens the door. "Well, you can always text me."

Patricia steps outside, washed over by the sun's glare, her hand shielding her eyes. "Texting is just so cold. I don't understand how the younger generations can eschew real connection."

There is no satisfactory answer to that, so Chelsea cheerfully says, "Bye, Mom!"

Patricia nods once, turns on her kitten-heeled sandal, and marches down the sidewalk before stopping halfway to her car.

"No, I remember!" she calls, not troubling herself to take any further steps back toward her daughter. "There's a news story going around. Some sort of new virus? Not like Covid. People are acting funny. Violent. There was an incident at some value store. Someone died. Beaten to death with off-brand Thousand Island dressing, if you can believe it!"

Chelsea fights for control; her mother is almost gone, and she doesn't want to give Patricia any reason to stay.

"Okay, so check the news and don't go to the store. Got it. Thanks, Mom!"

Patricia takes a single step closer, her eyes pleading. "No, dear. Don't go to *that* store. You can look it up on the internet. Find out more. Maybe wear a mask. Just be careful. For the children."

For me, she means.

Her mother doesn't particularly like her, but she doesn't want to go through the fussy burden of death again, either. Losing her first husband was just so *inconvenient*—her word—especially when his kids got all his money and she had to find a newer, richer husband in time for the country club's summer gala. If something happened to Chelsea or her girls, her mom might have to cancel her standing hair appointment.

Having delivered her message, Patricia spins back around and hurries to her sleek white sedan.

She doesn't wave as she leaves, but she does run over the newly planted begonias.

2.

Patricia checks her makeup in her rearview mirror, deciding that she'll give her next Estée Lauder free gift bag to Chelsea, as the poor girl desperately needs a more expensive mascara and some sort of color on her cheeks. The thing about Chelsea is that she's been weak, sullen, and resentful from the moment she was born, kicking and screaming, but is it really so hard to try a new lipstick? Patricia has always been open to those handy little women's tricks and is satisfied with what she sees in the mirror, although her forehead needs a touch-up. She puts her car in reverse and backs up, letting out a ladylike gasp as the tires bump over something inconvenient in the driveway, probably a hose or a newspaper or something else that should've been put away. If Rosa or Miguel left something like that in Patricia's driveway, they'd get a good talking-to.

Chelsea's neighborhood isn't too horrible, but the gate takes a terribly long time to rattle open. As Patricia drives, other motorists honk behind her for doing something as reasonable as going the speed limit on a curving lakeside road. Annoyed, she switches through radio stations, but they're all shouting and grousing and moaning about that unfortunate incident down at the warehouse store, some sort of violence that's unusual in this kind of area. Not that Patricia would ever be in such a store, fighting over toilet paper and cheese puffs with some overstuffed housewife. That's what the help is for.

Patricia barely misses a green light and is forced to stop her car at a big intersection, and there facing her across the road is a little yellow building, barely a shack. It has a faded sign reading BIG FRED'S FLOORS and crudely built displays out front with ragged versions of what might've once been functional if gauche floor coverings, linoleums and tiles and fake wood. But they're all faded and degraded, and no one in their right mind would be enticed to stop and go into the tiny shop to talk to Big Fred. Jerking red letters tick by on the scrolling digital sign outside.

IF YOU'RE IN THE DOGHOUSE, GET HER WHAT SHE REALLY WANTS. NEW FLOORS!

Patricia raises an eyebrow. Like she needs the doghouse excuse if she wants new floors. She *would* like new floors in the sunroom, actually, but Randall is still complaining about the dust from the last bathroom remodel. She'll have to wait until he's on his next two-week fishing trip to the Bahamas with the boys from the courthouse if she wants to get anything done. And she most certainly won't get her new floors from anything as shabby as a swaybacked shack that resembles all too closely the one-room millhouse she lived in when Chelsea was a baby. She's done her best to forget those days, the struggle and mess and *noise*. She's risen above it. It's over. The shack is simply a grotesque reminder of how hard she's worked to get here.

The light finally, thankfully, turns green, and she's no longer forced to stare at the scrolling words prodding her inelegantly to move forward with her next remodel. Her visit with Chelsea was just too tiresome, so now she's early for her weekly lunch with Randall, but there's always plenty to do at the club, especially now that she's a member of the charity auction committee. Her first husband was a member at Emerald Cove Country Club, too, and so she's enjoyed uninterrupted service here for almost twenty years. Hank waves her through at the gate, and she parks farther away from the clubhouse than she'd like, but at least she finds a spot in the shade. As she walks up the sidewalk, she subtly touches her bracelet, necklace, earrings, hair. She straightens her cardigan and runs a hand down the pleats on her slacks and looks down at her pedicure as she steps onto the curb. Patricia is not a religious woman, but this is her sign of the cross. This is how she blesses herself, how she keeps herself together. If everything is in place, if everything is perfect, then she'll be safe.

The automatic glass doors slide open, and her eyes close as cold air billows over her as if washing off the oppressive heat, sweat, and misfortune of the world outside. Within, everything is just so, and Patricia feels very at home here. Inoffensive artworks in pastels with gold frames line the buttery-yellow walls, and the patterned carpets are always spotless and stainless. Plastic plants never die, never wither, never go brown at the tips—and get dusted daily, unlike Chelsea's chandelier. Barbara Chatham tried to bring a service dog in here once and everyone got so upset that she had to move. That's how clean it is. No wonder she feels at home.

"Good morning, Mrs. Lane," some young person with a fake grin says from the front desk. Patricia lifts a hand the minimum amount and holds her public smile in place. With so many years here at the club, she sometimes forgets she's Mrs. Lane and not Mrs. Worthington. Or, going further back, a young, unwed mother with a greasy plastic name tag that just said PATTY.

The doors of the dining room aren't open yet, and she frowns just a little before pasting her smile back into place and heading for the lounge. She hears the noise before she sees it, the musical murmurs of many women having polite arguments bracketed by *I really just think* and *Wouldn't we rather consider* and *That's how it's going, but of course I'm not in charge, so what do I know?* The little hairs on the back of her neck prickle. Something is occurring in her kingdom without her knowledge. She rounds the corner and peeks in the open French doors to find a conference room filled with familiar faces, led by someone she once considered a friend.

"Patty, is that you?" says an altogether too-triumphant voice. "I was wondering where you were."

Patricia steps into the open space as the room goes quiet and twenty women look her up and down, their eyes crawling over her like ants looking for some vulnerable crack in a castle. She keeps her chin up and smiles that practiced smile, the one that suggests that those in power have never doubted themselves.

"Well, I would've been here if I knew you were throwing me a party, Karen," she all but purrs.

"It's an emergency meeting," Lynn pipes up, sounding somewhat strangled. "About the flowers." Karen shoots her lackey an angry look but doesn't speak. Patricia raises her brows, demanding an explanation. "The florist canceled. So we need a new florist for the auction."

If there were an empty seat, Patricia would sashay in and take it, but Karen has made very sure that's not possible, just as she's made very sure no one has alerted her co-chair to this secret meeting. The histrionic old bat is probably planning to bring in carnations with baby's breath or some other horrific thing.

"That's easy," Patricia says, snapping her fingers and making her diamonds rattle. "Randall's golf friend's wife is a florist. They're playing today. I'll set it up. See? No problem at all. I hope you weren't all inconvenienced by Karen's . . . *little meeting.*" She holds up her wrist and smiles brightly at her new watch. "Well, look at the time! I wouldn't want to be late for lunch with the judge. I'll email you all confirmation of the new florist this afternoon. And I'll make sure they go with our original plan for exotics. Those birds-of-paradise are going to look so classic. Ta-ta!"

Wiggling her fingers at them, she turns her back and sashays out the doors and toward the dining room. It's not actually open yet, but the key to winning these battles is the same as it was when she was young and that bitch named Candy would try to steal her tips at the diner. Get in, go for the jugular, get out. She still has a hank of Candy's hair saved somewhere, a battle trophy that reminds her that the best way to get rid of enemies is to make them regret ever opposing her in the first place.

She's sitting on the settee outside the dining room, listening to the promising clink of silver and china, when her phone rings. She pulls it out of her Birkin and holds it just a bit away from her ear; she saw a Facebook post about how holding it too close causes cancer, and she doesn't like the feeling of her diamond earrings scraping the screen.

"Hello?"

"That you, sugar?" Randall's voice is low and honey-sweet, which makes Patricia frown. She knows what that voice means.

"Well, who else would be answering my phone?" She knows she sounds peevish, and she wants him to know it, too. "Where are you? They're about to open the doors."

"That's just the thing, darlin'. I'm afraid I can't join you today. The depositions are going long—"

Which is code for his secretary is staying in for lunch, which Patricia knows because early in their marriage she tried to surprise him with his favorite chicken sandwich and instead walked in on the trampy little thing scuttling out of his office with smeared lipstick, an unbuttoned blouse, and eyes just bleeding mascara.

"So I'll probably miss dinner, too. You know how it is."

Her smile is a scythe.

"Yes, I do."

"So you just go on with your girls and order some champagne and have a day, okay? Whatever you want."

The doors open, revealing an empty dining room sparkling and ready, fresh flowers on every table and sunbeams streaming in crystal-clear windows that showcase immaculate emerald greens beyond. She knows that if she keeps watching, she'll see men driving golf carts with their wives by their sides, laughing and drinking beer and play-fully taunting each other, and other couples happily power-walking the nature trails with English setters or riding the powder-blue bikes lined up outside the club office. Frank and Emily Lambert walk past her and into the restaurant, arm in arm, laughing, and are seated at the best table in the house, the one Patricia was hoping to secure for their lunch today.

"You have a good day, sweetheart," he recites.

"You, too," she dutifully responds, like the recorded voice box of those dreadful programmed teddy bears her youngest granddaughter loves so much, the ones with the elaborately obscene stuffing ritual at the mall that you're forced to watch, some teenager shoving the furry rag's rear end over a pipe as it fills to bursting with fluff.

The line clicks off, and she holds the phone up for a few moments more as if he'll remember that he didn't apologize at all.

Other women love their husbands, she thinks. But she loved a man once, or thought she did, and look where it got her. Eighteen and knocked up. Abandoned by him, driven away by her family. Destroyed. Every man after that has been merely a necessity, a ladder rung to safety and then, much later, when she'd earned it, to comfort. Her first husband, the contractor, found and secured after Chelsea was finally out of the house at eighteen, brought her legitimacy and respect. Her second husband, the judge, has brought her power and wealth.

Maybe when he dies, rutting with his secretary over his mahogany desk, she'll finally get those new floors.

3.

Ella waits just outside H hall in a little splotch of shadow that only appears between sixth and seventh period. The brick wall picks at the back of her shirt and catches at individual hairs as she leans back, trying to feign coolness, arms crossed to hide the trembling in her hands. If she gets caught out here between classes, she'll get suspended, or at least reprimanded. If her dad finds out she has a boyfriend, he'll kill her.

He'll straight-up kill her.

The door swings open, and Hayden appears, dressed as always in a button-down and khakis, his floppy blond hair riding that perfect line between class president and class clown. He's grinning, and she used to think it was a special grin just for her but now she knows it's because he's anticipating some tongue.

"Hey, angel," he says.

"Hey," she answers.

He drops his book bag with a thump and puts a hand just over her shoulder, flat against the brick wall, pinning her in. She flinches a little and turns her face away, can't stop herself from the reaction. He sees it, and his other hand caresses her face, roughly pulls her jaw around until she's facing him again, and holds her chin so he can dart in for a kiss. She lets him, but . . . well, she's not into it. It doesn't feel like it should, like how it's written in the books she reads, where girls describe good kisses as warm, dry, soft, gentle, probing. She reads those scenes and her tummy flutters, and the first time Hayden kissed her, her tummy fluttered like that, too. But now it twists up, tense, and nothing about his kisses is soft.

His lips are hard, his stubble scrapes, his tongue pushes, his teeth clack. His breath tastes like fake blueberry, and she wants to gag, knowing he's been vaping with Tyler again even though he promised her he wouldn't, even though if his dad found out, he'd be in tons of trouble. His tongue pokes and prods, reminding her of the dentist's professional and practiced onslaught. She opens her eyes, just a little, and his eyebrows are furrowed. She feels him frown against her mouth as he withdraws.

"What's wrong, El?"

"I don't know."

"I mean, why won't you kiss me?"

Something inside her rebels at that, as if he's annoyed that she thought for a minute that he worried about her as a person. He acted like he did, at first. They were friends. They flirted after school every day during drama rehearsals. They would text and chat and send memes and run lines on the bench outside by the parking lot while her friends watched and giggled. But as soon as she agreed to be his girlfriend, as soon as it was established that he could kiss her whenever he wanted to, things changed. He was more . . . businesslike? It doesn't feel much like love, she knows that much.

Sure, he gives her a flower on their monthly anniversary, always in front of a crowd, and yes, they're going to prom, and he's already coordinated colors with her. But she thought there would be something more. Ongoing tummy flutters and deep conversations and inside jokes and nightly texts telling her to sleep well. She thought there would be sweetness.

He's never sweet.

She wants to pull away from him, maybe end it, but he's in drama club, and all their friends are in drama club, and if she dumps him for literally nothing when he's the perfect boyfriend, they're all going to turn on her and hate her like they did with his ex Maddie Kim last year and someone will purposefully trip her in front of the entire school during the next play. Because in public, Hayden treats her like a princess.

He puts her on a pedestal.

She wants to jump off.

"It's just . . . I'm not that into PDA," she finally says.

"It's not PDA. Totally private."

With a snort, Ella gestures to the busy road on the other side of the school's chain-link fence.

"Fuck everybody else. I'm just focusing on us, babe."

He darts in for another kiss, and it's like being dive-bombed by a seagull, like he's determined to take whatever he can from her. His hands begin at her hips, squeezing gently, and run up and down her back a few times like he's going through the motions, and then inch their way around her front, his wide thumbs with their bitten nails probing for the underwire of her bra. She wriggles away from him, hoping he'll take the hint, but he just doubles down, his eager thumbs digging hard enough to bruise her ribs.

"Come on," she says, pushing his hands down and holding them firmly. With the brick against her back, shredding her shirt, she can't pull away. "It's almost time for next period. Did you study?"

He yanks his hands out of hers and checks his phone, his lips twisted up in annoyance as his eyes reflect the screen. "It's fine. I always get A's, anyway."

And he does. She has to study her ass off because her dad said he'd take her car away if she got bad grades, but Hayden just shrugs his way through class and somehow gets near-perfect grades. He's smart, he's in drama, he's on the baseball team. He's everywhere. He's perfect. His dad is a teacher here. And to everyone else, he's this golden boy.

That's how Ella saw him, too, at first. In books, the bad boy is really a good boy who shows his good side only to the girl he loves. But in real life, the good boys are all hiding the fact that they're really bad boys, and no one believes it until it's too late. That's why her friend Kaylin got raped by the assistant basketball coach and had to leave school last year. He, of course, is now the head coach. Because there wasn't any evidence, and when it came down to Kaylin's word versus everyone else, Kaylin lost. Good basketball coaches are hard to find.

As for Kaylin, the basketball team blamed her for the games they lost. After she got mysteriously shoved during a fire drill stampede and broke her arm, she decided to homeschool. She doesn't answer Ella's texts anymore.

"Hey, can you give me a ride home?" Hayden asks. He's a sophomore and won't get his brand-new Jeep for a few more months, but she's been driving her ancient Honda for a year.

"I have to get home and watch Brooklyn," she lies.

"So drop me on the way. I promise I'll be good."

The bell rings, and the door bursts open. Kids hurry in and out, giving her a knowing look that makes her cheeks burn.

"C'mon, babe. Gimme a ride," he pleads, rubbing her arm. "I'll behave."

She doesn't want to, but she's ashamed to admit that she knows damn well she's going to do it anyway.

And she knows damn well he won't behave.

"I have to go." She spins and darts into the crowd, ducking her head and turning sideways to squeeze through spaces where Hayden can't follow.

He knows all her classes and sometimes shows up to joke around with the teachers his dad is friends with. She was impressed at first, but now it almost seems like he's checking up on her. Sometimes it feels like the only place he can't find her is the women's restroom, so that's where she spends her time between classes when she needs some space. The one at the end of F hall is usually quiet, but today, oddly, her friend Olivia is there.

"Did I see you and Hayden sucking face outside H hall?" she asks as she applies slick pink gloss at the mirror. "I swear, he's so hot it's not fair."

"I know, right?" Ella pulls a brush out of her backpack to smooth down the messy effects of the brick wall and Hayden's hands. She never knows what to say when her friends gush about Hayden, but she knows that anything bad she says will get back to him somehow.

That makes one of her friends a bad friend, but she doesn't know who it is, and she suspects all of them would be glad to take her place.

Or at least they think they would.

A toilet flushes, and Sophie steps out of a stall. There are three mirrors, and now Ella is at the center sink with a girl on either side applying makeup and glancing at her in a smiling, measuring way. They're pretty much her best friends, or they once were. They've been tight since middle school and used to do sleepovers all the time, when they were younger, but this feels more like an ambush than a casual bathroom meetup. Olivia and Sophie are always together these days, and Ella usually feels left out. Now, not so much.

"I know what Hayden got you for your three-month anniversary," Sophie sings, glopping on more mascara. "You're *so* going to love it."

"Because you helped him pick it out!" Olivia giggles, her eyes alight. "You didn't answer my texts the whole time you guys were at the outlet mall."

Sophie rolls her eyes. "Oh my God, you know we're just friends!"

Everything is light and playful and sweet, like it's a game to them, but the sort of game that was designed so that Ella would lose no matter what.

"And I know what he wants from you. It's cheap and easy . . ." Olivia clears her throat to get Ella's attention and makes a very specific gesture.

The other girls dissolve in laughter, and Ella's face goes red. That gesture—it's not a thing she's done with a guy, not a thing she wants to do with Hayden, and definitely not a thing she wants to discuss with anyone else.

"I mean, I got him some cologne and was going to bake him a cake, but go off," she says, trying and failing to match the brassy, bold, manic way they talk.

Sophie puts her hand on Ella's shoulder, her perfect eyebrows drawing together. "Okay, but seriously, though, you know guys *expect* that, right? I know Hayden is your first, but . . ." Sophie giggles. "You kind of have to."

Ella steps out from under the other girl's hand. "I don't have to do anything."

Olivia shrugs a shoulder and applies another layer of gloss. "You do if you want to keep him."

If only she knew how unthreatening that threat is. *Take him, if you want him,* she wants to say. But she won't, because by the time he's in her passenger seat this afternoon, he'll be asking her why everyone's saying she doesn't love him anymore.

"You do want to be his girlfriend, right?" Now it's Sophie's turn to swoop in, her brown eyes wide and innocent, like she's only worried about Ella's feelings.

Ella swallows hard; it's like being stabbed in the front and the back at the same time. She remembers when they were younger and actually confided in one another, when they swapped secrets and talked about crushes as these far-off possibilities. When they told one another the truth. She remembers Olivia crying, swearing she would never be like her mother, with a different boyfriend every year, supporting an endless stream of out-of-work losers. Now Olivia has a different boyfriend every month. And Sophie was so angry about her parents' divorce, furious with her mom for cheating with another married man and her dad for just walking out. Now she's spending time with Ella's boyfriend behind her back and proud of it. What happened to them? When did they go from girls to bitches? And why didn't Ella notice it happening?

At that last slumber party, emboldened by their own secrets, Ella told them about her parents, about what her dad did to her mom at night. Even though she could tell neither girl believed her, they hugged her and cried with her and swore she would never be like that, would never let a man have that much power over her.

And she won't. Sometimes it's easier to just go along, but Hayden doesn't own her, doesn't control her. One day soon, he'll dump her for someone else, and then she'll get all the sympathy and none of the catty looks and whispers. Until then . . .

"Of course I want to be his girlfriend." She giggles and applies her own lip gloss. "He's pretty much perfect for me."

The other girls exchange a glance she doesn't quite understand but doesn't like, and Ella checks her phone. The bell is about to ring, which means she needs to hurry to class, as Mr. Harkey hates lateness.

"Can you give me a ride home?" Sophie asks.

"Well, I'm already taking Hayden—"

"Time for more sexytimes!" Olivia croons.

"Ladies?"

The mood in the restroom changes with that one word spoken softly from the hallway. Olivia and Sophie drop their reckless, bold, party-girl personas and are just teenagers again. All three girls instinctively huddle together, nervous and clumsy as antelopes.

"The bell is about to ring," Mr. Brannen says, leaning into the restroom, both hands in his pockets and feet still technically in the hall.

Their vice principal is known for this, for cornering girls in tight spots when they're supposed to be somewhere else. He's blocking the only exit now, and as the bell rings, he looks up at the speaker in the ceiling, knowing and almost apologetic.

"And there it is. Looks like you three are going to be late to class. Unless you have a good excuse."

Mr. Brannen is her dad's age, maybe, with a belly that strains against his shirt buttons. His hair is thinning, and he wears ugly, pointy shoes, and when his flat brown eyes crawl over her, Ella wants to curl up and die. She's heard stories about him, especially since he divorced his wife, but they're always secondhand.

"I'm not feeling so good," Olivia says with an exaggerated sniffle.

"Oh, I bet the boys will still kiss you. I know I would!" Mr. Brannen winks and grins. "But if you need to go to the nurse's office, go on. The health of our student bodies is our highest priority." Olivia shuffles past him, and he knocks out his hip just enough to touch her. "What's your excuse, Miss Gibson?"

"I started my period early." Ella is impressed with how Sophie sticks out her chin and glares defiantly.

"TMI, Miss Gibson, TMI. Did you know the pill can help with regulating your cycle? To avoid unpleasant surprises."

"Yes, sir," Sophie says, hurrying past him. "Thanks to health class." She doesn't even look over her shoulder in apology as she leaves Ella all alone.

Mr. Brannen's hands move around in his pockets like he's playing with loose change. "Miss Martin. One of my favorite students. Good grades, no disciplinary actions. But I've heard a rumor." He steps closer, cups a hand around his mouth as he whispers. "Have you been experimenting with PDA in our humble hallways?" He steps back, grinning like he's pleased with himself. "You know that's not allowed."

"I—no, sir. I won't. I mean I haven't." Ella knows her face is red, knows she's a bad liar, but she can't bring herself to tell the truth.

Mr. Brannen leans back against the wall, his jacket falling open to show a zipper only halfway up. "It's normal for girls your age to experiment. Why, in the Middle Ages, you'd already be married with children." He winks again. "And in some states and cultures, you'd be considered quite a catch at your age."

Ella is stunned and disgusted and can't think of a single reasonable response to an adult man telling her that, much less one who holds her entire future in his hands. But apparently her input is not necessary, as he keeps talking.

"I know it's exciting, but let's try not to break any rules. If I catch you 'macking with your bf,' as they say, you'll owe me a Saturday-morning detention, which happens in my office and at my discretion. You need to learn what happens to girls who break the rules."

Ella swallows hard because the only alternative is dry heaving.

"Are we clear?"

"Yes, sir."

He smiles and nods, calm and certain and pleased. "I always did like the sound of that. *Yes, sir.* One of the many perks of the job. Now get to class, Miss Martin. And if your teacher asks where you were, just tell her you were with me."

Ella can only nod as she hurries out the door, knowing she can't avoid touching some part of him and hoping it'll just be his hip. She's pretty sure that was his hand drifting past her butt, but it was so quick she can't quite be sure. That's how it always is with Mr. Brannen—everything he says feels totally inappropriate and gross, but if it was repeated to the counselor or the police, it could be written off as normal and innocent, as just another girl being histrionic over nothing.

When she gets to class, she doesn't say she was with Mr. Brannen.

She'd rather take the tardy than give everyone something else to gossip about.

4.

It's almost time for David to come home, and Chelsea wonders the same thing she does every day about this time: Will they have a good night, or a bad night?

She never feels small until her husband walks in the door. It's not that he's a big man—he's of average height and resents that fact—but he works out all the time, and there's just something about his presence that makes her shrink down.

Her job, on the surface, should be simple: Be a good wife, a great mom, a loving partner. But there are so many intricate rules she's had to learn over the years. It's like walking through a minefield every night, knowing full well where several old pitfalls lie in wait but also aware that there are new dangers to be discovered. He was such a sweet boyfriend in high school, and then they got married far too early because she had to get away from her mom, and he decided to go to college and bring her along, and her entire life shrank down to being pregnant in student housing and learning how to cook his favorite meals in their tiny cinder-block kitchen without setting off the smoke alarm.

Now, every weeknight, in the time between the garage door grumbling and the kitchen door opening, she wonders if it was a trap all along or just a natural progression that happened so gradually she didn't notice, if she's the frog in water slowly building to a boil.

His car door closes, and Chelsea stands where he can see her the moment he's in the house.

"Girls!" she calls. "Dad's home!"

The only answer from upstairs is rhythmic thumping, punctuated with shrieks of laughter. Brooklyn just got the new dance game for her fifth birthday, and it's so rare the girls play together these days that Chelsea didn't want to disturb them. David prefers it when all three of them greet him at the door, respectful and attentive and polite, lined up like golden retrievers, but . . . well, Chelsea doesn't really want them down here. Not when he finds the letter and sees that their bank account is somehow, impossibly, overdrawn.

The door opens, and David's smile sours. Instead of greeting Chelsea with a kiss, he takes off his blazer and carefully folds it over a chair.

"The welcome wagon's quiet tonight."

"There was an update to their favorite game," Chelsea says, hating how meek and apologetic she sounds. "They're playing together so nicely." She goes up on tiptoe and wraps her arms around his neck, and he drags his nose along her jaw, breathing in the perfume he buys her every Christmas whether she's run out or not. Beautiful, it's called, the same one his mother used to wear. She tried a different one once, something she picked out herself, and he told her she smelled like burned sugar, not at all how a woman should be.

"My day was good," he says, a reminder.

Her arms uncurl from his neck, and she drops down from her tiptoes and steps back. The look on his face is gentle and reprimanding but also somehow pleased to see her mess up. It's the look her mother gave her when she was five and got sent outside to get a switch, as if it was a relief to have a reason to punish her. It makes Chelsea want to make things right, and she hates that. She's always supposed to ask him about his day, but he never asks her about her day unless he's trying to butter her up.

"I'm glad," she answers, aiming for perky. "How's the Hartford account going?"

His frown deepens. She asked the wrong question.

"Not well." He looks around the kitchen, suspicious. "What's for dinner?"

"Chicken Caesar salad." She points to the fridge.

"Rotisserie leftovers?"

Chelsea flinches. "I tried to go to the store today, but it was all roped off. Something happened in the parking lot. Police everywhere, ambulances, yellow caution tape. Probably another shooting."

"If it was a shooting, we would've heard about it already."

God, he sounds like a tired kindergarten teacher when he talks to her like that, like everything she says is juvenile and stupid and disappointing, and she struggles to pick up her line of thought.

"Well, whatever it was, by the time I got out of the parking lot and through traffic to pick up Brooklyn, it was too late to cook. You said you don't mind rotisserie over my Caesar."

He makes a little noise, not quite an agreement, but more of an acknowledgment that perhaps he said that one day to make her feel better when she was gearing up for a pity cry, but they both know the truth.

"I'll have a beer, then."

She grabs a frosty bottle out of the freezer, where she's supposed to put a few at four-thirty every day, and pops off the top. Sipping it, he heads upstairs to the spare room he considers his own private space and goes through his ritual of divestiture, the same one he's observed since college, when they lived in that tiny one-bedroom. His blazer, hung up according to color. His shirt, tossed in the dry-cleaning bag. His slacks, clipped up by the hems to keep them from developing that telltale wrinkle at the knee. His shoes, on the shelf. Everything just so. No one sets foot in that room. No one. The gun safe is in there. His filing cabinets are there, every year's taxes tidily tucked away. After she lost a diamond stud, he even brought up Chelsea's jewelry safe so that he can keep better track of her jewelry wardrobe, offering her the embarrassing process of checking her own things in and out like a librarian until she, as he puts it, learns to act like a goddamn grown-up.

By the time he's back downstairs in sweatpants and his undershirt, the beer bottle is ready to be recycled and Chelsea has caught up to where she should be in his preferred evening ritual. The girls are setting the table, and she's smiling as she puts a new bottle in his hand, the glass perfectly chilled, just the way he likes it. The kitchen is almost silent, and he tells Alexa to play classic rock and sighs as Pink Floyd fills the airy room. Chelsea's body goes tense the moment she hears it; she knows it does not bode well.

Dinner is a quiet affair. Brooklyn picks at her salad, and Chelsea knows that after she's cleared the kitchen and David is safely out of the way, she'll microwave some chicken nuggets and cut up an apple because of course five-year-olds don't want to eat salad.

"When I was a kid, I ate whatever was put in front of me, or else," David says, and it sounds conversational, but it isn't. "You ate what you were given and you were thankful, or you went to bed without supper. I hated green peas, but if I didn't clean my plate, my dad got out the belt."

Ella and Brooklyn exchange looks, and Brooklyn shoves a piece of lettuce in her mouth, failing to hide her distaste. He nods; that's the correct answer. Every time Brooklyn stops eating, he also stops eating and stares at her sternly until she digs in again. Ella is seventeen now, and so well trained at the table that she rarely speaks unless spoken to and always cleans her plate, which is a relief. Chelsea knows her job is to remain silent, although she can practically talk to the girls using just her face. David recently told her that it's actually giving her these unattractive little frown lines that he'd like to see handled before the company picnic. She has learned to hide so much, but she can't stop her microexpressions, can't smooth out those lines to suit him, especially when she knows what's coming.

He wasn't like this when they started dating. He was fun and playful and sweet—or maybe, she thinks now, he excelled at hiding his own true self. When she told him she was pregnant, he was angry at first, but then he warmed to the masculine idea of being a father so early, began treating her like she was a golden egg that might crack if mishandled. On the day that Ella was born, he didn't want to be in the delivery room; he said that if he saw her body doing something that disgusting, he would never look at her the same way again. And when he finally showed up to find her, exhausted and joyful, holding their tiny daughter in the hospital bed, he told her she should put on some makeup for the pictures or he couldn't show them off to his friends. Those were the first cruel things he said to her, and at the time, she wrote it off as a joke. He hadn't gotten much sleep, either.

The cruelties were like that: small and excusable, at first, but then building like snow on branches, slowly but surely weighing them down until they became fragile enough to freeze and crack and break and fall.

That's what Chelsea feels like, sometimes: the Giving Tree, but for a wood chipper instead of a man.

After she's urged the girls upstairs with a bag of cookies to play their dance game again until bedtime, which Ella will handle for her younger sister because she knows what's going to happen, Chelsea clears the table before David can complain about it. He follows her over to the sink, waiting until she's set down the dishes to pin her against the counter with a hand on either side, his beer bottle dangling from two fingers against her hip. She stills like a mouse in a shadow. Knowing something is going to happen doesn't make it any more bearable.

"You know what you need?" he says, a little breathy, just behind her ear. She goes still, the water running over her hands, boiling hot. "A little spa weekend. Brian's wife can tell you which one she goes to. A glass of Chardonnay, a couple of shots to tighten things up, a little waxing, some mani-pedi bullshit. Let your mom watch the kids and just focus on you."

She goes from still to tense, her shoulders rising. Spas cost money. He hasn't checked his desk. He hasn't even seen the bank letter yet. If she mentions it now, he'll blame her for everything.

"I don't know," she says, soft and harmless. "I mean, Botox is just botulism. Do I really need to inject myself with poison?"

He pulls back just a little, and she feels hot breath on her scalp, along her part. "Maybe go a little blonder. Highlights or some shit. That thing that sounds French."

"Balayage." Her voice is tiny. "That's what I already do—"

"You've got to do some self-care," he says, sounding like he's parroting some garbage social media post. "Treat yo self."

She switches off the faucet, and when she looks down, her hands are the raw, angry pink of an Easter ham. He sees it, too.

"And get a French manicure while you're at it. That's what the girls at the office do."

David steps back, tosses his bottle in the recycling, and fetches a new one, popping it open with a smack on the granite countertops he insisted on when they bought the house. It was extra, and she didn't think it was necessary, but he's always been so obsessed with keeping up with the Joneses, with having whatever the guys at the office have. Settling back into the corner of the counter, he watches her, waiting for an answer. She can't give him what he wants to hear, so she turns her back and cleans. Maybe if the sink is spotless and the counters gleam, he'll stop focusing on her as the thing that needs fixing.

Even as she works, she knows that's a lie. Cleaning is quite simply her job, and so is fitting into the impossible mold of Trophy Wife.

"What, I offer you a special weekend and you can't even look at me?" Heat creeps up the back of her neck and cheeks. The beer is gone in several long swallows, and he slams it on the counter, making Chelsea's shoulders jump. "You not even going to acknowledge your husband?"

Chelsea turns to him and swallows like she's trying to get a pill down. She must've lost count of his beers, because he's further along than she thought. She knows full well that her eyes are wide and red, her shoulders up around her ears, her hands red as lobster claws. She's not pretty just now, and she feels so fragile and small, but the way he looks at her suggests that it only makes him want to break her completely. She is reminded of the time they were at the shore and he found dried-out, slightly broken sea stars on the beach and laughed as he crushed each one underfoot, pulling out the dainty white doves and pulverizing everything else to chalk.

"What the fuck are you looking at?"

It's a snarl, somehow, and this time, she can't stop herself from flinching.

It makes him angry, when she flinches. But he likes it, too.

This is how it happens. Bit by bit, even as she does her best to follow the rules and say the right things, she makes him angry and hot, and it feels like being driven farther down a hallway with no escape.

"You said you wanted me to look at you. So I'm doing what you said."

He breathes out, a long sigh, almost a growl. "Why won't you take care of yourself, Chel? We promised each other we'd take care of ourselves. Wouldn't let ourselves go. You think I like going to the gym every fucking morning? You think it was fun getting hair plugs and Lasik, smelling my own fucking eyeballs get roasted? I put in the work. I do that for you. So you need to put in the work, too."

She nods, blinking swiftly. "Jeanie from next door invited me to her kickboxing class."

David snorts as he steps forward, closing the distance and grabbing her wrist. "Little bird bones. Think you can punch somebody with this thing? I said take care of yourself, not waste your fucking time. You wanna work out, use the treadmill I bought you. Swim some laps in your fucking pool. Don't get all bulky and butchy. Jeanie's built like a brick shithouse."

She trembles and glances toward the stairs, checking that she can still hear music playing, even if the girls are no longer jumping around. She sees a shadow move and hopes it's that wretched dog peeing on the banister but knows it's probably Ella. She stares at the blotch of shadow and wills it to move, to go somewhere safe, but it remains firmly in place.

David spins her around and pulls her back against his chest, her back all along his front. He has an erection, prodding her spine, and the hot breath against her scalp is all beer. The world goes unfocused as he threads his other arm around her chest, sliding it up until his elbow perfectly frames her throat.

She's gone from trembling to shaking now, her breath in little gasps. This is the point of no return, when nothing she can say or do will stop him. With his right arm cinched around her throat, he slides his left arm behind her head, grasps his own right biceps, and with infinite care and slowness tightens his grip.

He told her once that his dad called this the Cobra Hold, but she's watched enough MMA with him to know that it's a strangle. Time almost seems to stop. He holds her life in his hands, and she is caught in a moment of infinite horror, unable to move or fight or talk back or look at him or complain. As he slowly pulls it tighter, she can feel the blood in her veins pounding, going thick and sludgy, the world going hazy and dim.

She's looked it up online. He's cutting off blood flow to her brain. He could give her brain damage. Or kill her.

And they both know it.

Just as they know that this, what he does—it doesn't leave bruises. No evidence.

She's almost there, almost out, and she can't stop the tiny little hitch of a breath that signals her giving up. For a moment, there's nothing—no air, no sound, no her, no him, no time. And then, right before everything goes red and then black, he releases her and lets his arm slide down to her waist, a loving hug.

"I'll tell Brian to tell Marissa to text you the place," he whispers into the top of her head, his lips brushing that tender vulnerable place where her hair parts, her scalp now red and prickling as the blood rushes back in and he holds her up so she won't fall.

Chelsea nods, the back of her head against his chest. There's something almost comforting about it, something tender, the way he's supporting her until she can fully stand again, and it makes her feel grateful, and she hates that. "Okay."

He kisses her cheek. "Good. I'll be in the man cave." For a long moment, he pauses, as if expecting something more, but she can't make the words work. "I love you," he murmurs gently, a reminder.

Despite your many failures, she's meant to understand.

"Love you, too," she rasps, throat raw.

Without another look, he heads for the room off the garage, where he closes and locks the door. Chelsea leans into the counter, elbows on the cold granite, and silently cries. That, at least, is one thing she has learned to do exactly right.

5.

Brooklyn already fell asleep with Olaf curled against her on the couch in the playroom, but Ella is on the stairs, huddled down in the shadows, watching the kitchen from between the clean white spindles of the banister. Brooklyn thinks that when they do this, Daddy is hugging Mommy, because Brooklyn is five, just a little kid who still plays with Barbies. She makes Ken hug Barbie like this sometimes, even though their arms can't really bend the right way.

"I love you so much," she says as Ken smashes against Barbie. "So much you turn pink."

But Ella knows exactly what is happening. And she knows what it feels like, because Dad did this to her once, too, when she stuck around too long after dinner on a Bad Beer Night and he yelled at her for getting a C on a math test and she rolled her eyes when he could see it. At first, she thought it was a hug, but when you tell someone to stop, they're supposed to stop hugging you, and Dad didn't stop. He whispered, "Shhhh," in her ear, and then, "I bet you can't escape."

Ella remembers what it felt like, her fingers curling around his arm, pulling gently at first and then desperately, her nails digging in when she couldn't make it budge. She remembers how she wanted to cough but couldn't, wanted to scream but couldn't. She remembers the feel of his curly arm hairs, the way thick muscle shifted against bone in her grasp. She remembers focusing on her mother's face, seeing Mom's eyes all big and bulgy like the goldfish Brooklyn loves in the big tank at the Chinese restaurant; her mind went oddly childish, at the time.

"That's enough," Mom said, more begging than warning.

But Dad didn't stop, and things went very strange. Ella saw colors behind her eyes, dark red and then gray and then black, and she went to sleep, and when she woke up she was on the couch, and Mom had a hand on her forehead like she was sick. Dad didn't apologize, and Mom didn't explain it. They never spoke about it, and Ella figures her mom is probably as embarrassed by it as she is.

"Hurry up to bed," Mom said that night, and then, softer, "Lock your door."

And although Ella felt woozy and strange and her feet were wobbly, and although she felt like some small part of her died and she'd never say the word *Daddy* again, she skittered up the stairs and scrambled into her room like she was still a good girl doing the right thing.

Since that night, she knows: Don't go downstairs when Dad's drinking. And she doesn't let Brooklyn go, either. Sometimes she sits on the stairs like this, both guarding them from her little sister's interest in a bedtime snack and watching to make sure Mom is okay. She knows she can't stop Dad, but somehow watching makes her feel safer. If something really, truly bad happened, she could call 9-1-1 and the police would come. But most of the time, Dad just talks and drinks, and Mom listens and says very little, and eventually Dad sways his way upstairs to bed, and by then Ella has already hidden in her room, her door locked. She knows the sounds of his feet on the steps, though, and she's glad her room and Brooklyn's room are on the far end of the landing instead of right next to her parents' room.

This time, though, it's worse than usual, and Ella has to keep watching. It's like staring at a car wreck in slow motion, waiting for the right moment to run over and help. But Ella feels completely numb as she watches her mother's face go deep mauve and then the sickly white of skim milk. If she called for help, things would only get worse, but if she doesn't call for help when . . . if . . .

She types 9-1- into her phone and then lets her finger hover over the 1, waiting.

Finally, after he lets Mom go, Dad goes to his man cave, but Ella doesn't move. Her mother just stands there for a moment, then doubles over and shakes for a while, then slowly comes back to life like she's been frozen in ice. Her shoulders hunch up, her hands make fists, and she fixes her hair, tucking the blond strands back behind her ears. Muttering softly to herself, she cleans up the kitchen, quietly, swiftly. Once the dishwasher is running and everything smells like lemons, Mom opens her laptop, and her eyes glaze over. She calls this "doing work," but Ella knows how to check browser history, so she knows that her mom is looking at her Dream Vitality numbers and scrolling through the Missed Connections forum of some old website called Craigslist and posting bullshit memes and pics of their great life on social media, which doesn't seem like work at all. Ella asked her about the Missed Connections once, because she thought her mom might be cheating on her dad. But Mom explained that she was always looking for her high school best friend who basically disappeared.

Ella wouldn't blame her mom for having an affair, though. She would almost welcome that if it meant her parents would get divorced. Then there would never be another night like this.

From here on out, nothing will happen. It's safe. Dad will do whatever he does in the man cave until well after midnight. Ella covers a yawn and hurries to her room.

When she wakes up in the morning, her phone is still on the Dialer.

9-

1-

One day, she thinks, she'll have to press that final 1, but for now she just erases everything, almost like it never happened.

Downstairs, Mom stands at the kitchen window, but Ella doesn't think she's looking at the pool. She has the lunches made and breakfast ready. The small trash can they use for recycling is empty of beer bottles. Ella wonders if she actually slept at all. Mom is so pretty, and really young compared with plenty of the other moms, but she does look a little tired. Ella watched some YouTube videos about makeup that could help with that, but she doesn't want to hurt her mom's feelings—especially after Dad's bullshit about how she needs to get Botox and go to a spa and look like Uncle Brian's wife, Marissa, who idolizes the Kardashians.

"Good morning, Smella," Mom says with an apologetic smile.

"Morning, Momster," Ella replies, glad that this little ritual they've had since she was even younger than Brooklyn is still intact. "Morning, Brookie."

When she sits at the table, her mother brings over a stack of pancakes for her, the syrup and butter melted in a mug, just the way she likes it. She almost feels guilty, that Mom has to put up with so much and still takes the time to do nice things. She has no idea how to put this into words, so she just says, "Thanks."

"Mommy, you look sad," Brooklyn says through a mouthful of pancake, and Ella is glad her sister just put it out there, because she's still young enough that it's not quite an insult.

"I had bad dreams," Mom admits with that Sad Mom Smile.

"I did, too!" Brooklyn almost shouts, as if it were a good thing.

"Me, too," Ella murmurs, because it's true.

Mom draws Brooklyn into what must be a very sticky hug and smooths the little baby hairs around her forehead. Ella watches, her face a mask, hating that Mom doesn't really touch her like that anymore but knowing full well she can't help flinching away from anything that intimate.

"Everyone has bad dreams sometimes." Mom's voice is soft and sweet and low. "Just try to think happy thoughts today."

"Can we get frozen yogurt on the way home?"

Mom's sigh suggests that the answer will be no. "I don't think so, sweetheart. All that sugar is bad for you. You don't even get yogurt there—just candy toppings."

"I like the yogurt," Ella can't help adding. But of course she doesn't need Mom to agree; she could just drive there in her car and get yogurt anytime she wanted with her babysitting money.

Mom shakes her head and pulls out of Brooklyn's hug. "Maybe tomorrow. It's time to go to school now."

As they hurry outside, Mom glares up at the sun, frowning, before fumbling in her purse for her big sunglasses. Ella pauses at the door to her car, an older but respectable Honda Civic. She knows she's lucky to have a car, and she knows that it must've sucked for her mom to drive fifteen miles back and forth to her charter school for the year and a half of high school before she turned sixteen, but just now she hates the fact that Brooklyn gets to drive to school with Mom and get all that time with her while Ella has to drive alone.

"You sure you're okay?" she asks, one hand on the door.

Mom gives her a smile, but not a real one. "Of course, honey. Why wouldn't I be?"

And although Ella knows exactly why her mom shouldn't be okay, can't be okay, the words dry up in her throat and she nods and gets in her car.

That day at lunch, the strangest thing happens.

Two boys get in a fight. But something about it is deeply wrong.

One of them, Jordan Stack, is kind of an asshole and gets in fights all the time, so it's no surprise that he's involved. But the other one, Thomas Canton, is a scrawny, dorky kid who can't even run laps without wheezing. He barely speaks in class and when he does, his voice is a whispery mumble, but now he stands, his chair squealing as he pushes back from the table. Ella looks up at him, wondering what's gotten into him, and he jumps at Jordan like a lion leaping on a gazelle—no, no, like a trusted chihuahua launching itself at an unsuspecting toddler, so sudden, so feral, so blindly furious—driving the larger boy to the floor between the tables. Now Thomas is on top of Jordan, straddling his chest, slamming the bigger boy's head into the ground again and again. All the kids gather around them, as keen as sharks smelling blood. The boys start yelling, "Fight! Fight! Fight!" while the girls first command them and then beg them to stop. But they don't.

The sound Jordan's head makes, bouncing off the speckled floor, is like a watermelon being dropped. Red droplets scatter and the sound changes a little, goes squishier, and Ella notices these small details only because she is sitting at the next table over, frozen in place. Some people are recording the whole thing on their phones, but she is doing the same thing she does at home when Dad winds his arm around Mom's neck, just watching, numb, still and silent, in horror.

Mr. Brannen and Ms. Baez show up and pry Thomas off Jordan, who isn't moving. Thomas doesn't attack them, though—he keeps lunging away to get at Jordan, his small white hands curled into bloodied claws. Mr. Brannen carries him out of the room like an angry cat, the boy twisting and thrashing in the big man's grasp. Ms. Baez falls to her knees with a heavy thump, gently tapping on Jordan's cheeks and lifting his head to inspect the bloody spot on the ground as Shelby Miller loudly explains that you're not supposed to move a hurt person's neck. Soon the teachers arrive and herd everyone back to class with their half-eaten lunches to watch nature documentaries as they mechanically chew at their desks.

Thomas and Jordan don't come back to class. Jordan's friend Stevie tells everyone that he's in the hospital in a coma. The evening news talks about it without naming names, and Mom asks Ella a bunch of questions that she obviously doesn't know the answers to about The Boys in Her Class and bullying and drugs and the school's discipline issues.

The weirdest thing, though, is that Ella was right there, sitting with Hayden and Tyler and Olivia and Sophie, and she saw the whole thing herself. Before it happened, the boys weren't talking or even paying attention to each other. Jordan wasn't bullying Thomas, didn't steal his lunch or threaten him or laugh at him or even look at him. He was talking to Stevie and eating a sandwich, just being normal. They were all just being normal. And for all that Jordan is a total jerk, she's never actually seen him go after Thomas; it's like they never even acknowledged each other's existence before that moment. Thomas was reading a book and eating a bag of crackers. He didn't say anything. Nothing was said to him. He just dropped his crackers, stood up, turned, and attacked.

The whole thing makes no sense.

The scariest part, to Ella, was the look in Thomas's eyes.

It was like . . . no one was there at all.

6.

When David finds the letter from the bank, he reacts with an unusual and overly bright calm that Chelsea finds utterly terrifying.

"Everything is okay," he says, crumpling up the paper and throwing it in the garbage. "It's just a mistake. I might need to move some cash around, but this isn't our main account. I'll handle it." And then he pulls a few crisp hundreds out of his money clip to tide her over and tells her not to spend it on "stupid shit."

Like she would dare.

And that's that.

Supposedly.

No matter what David said, she can't quite shake her disquiet, like the rug could be pulled out from under her at any moment. Banks don't just make errors like that these days, and Chelsea knows, because that's David's industry, and she's had to hear about it for years. The memory of David wadding up the letter and tossing it is stuck on replay in her mind, sharp as a pebble in her shoe.

That Friday night, David sends Chelsea off to the spa for a Botox party with Brian's wife, Marissa. He doesn't ask her, just tells her where to be and when and promises not to give the girls too much sugar. Now she's reclining in a heated chair, bare feet bubbling away in hot water tinted an impossible blue. The doctor is injecting poison into her face, tiny pinpricks that would hurt more if they hadn't cheerfully supplied her with a Percocet and a flute of champagne first, which sounds both dangerous and illegal, but to be honest she's grateful for the relief.

Marissa is in the next chair, babbling to her friend Abby about eyelash extensions. Chelsea hates almost everything about this moment and can't believe how excited everyone else is. Six women in heated massage chairs, lined up to solve their problems with a needle. They take turns holding the mirror, turning this way and that, promising one another they look ten years younger even though the doctor clearly said it will take seven days to achieve the full effect and they're all a little pink and lumpy.

"Lot of worry lines here," he says, poking the wrinkles on her forehead that David hates so much. "You'll definitely want to be back in a few months. And if they persist, there are other things we can try. Fillers." He's in his twenties and looks like a cleft-chinned movie star, and Marissa's chest follows him around the room like she's a satellite dish tuning in to a prime channel. Chelsea is all too aware that to a plastic surgeon, she's just a thing that needs fixing, a car that needs some body work, a big pile of flaws clutching her husband's hundred-dollar bills. "That should do it," the doctor finally says, stepping back and holding the needle aloft. "Beautiful."

"Oh my God," Marissa croons, leaning in. "Dr. G, you're a genius. Chel, you look *amazing*."

The doctor grins his thanks and turns to the next chair, murmuring the same combination of compliments before pointing out every delicious flaw on a perfectly normal face. Marissa hands her a mirror, and Chelsea reaches up to touch her forehead. She looks like she's been stung by bees—and has bad allergies. Her face is numb, but she doesn't know if that's the injections or the drugs or this afternoon's crying jag. There's apparently no recovery time, no relief of hiding in bed for a day or a week as things heal—she'll just look stupid for a while. At least it's finally done, one more thing her husband has steered her toward, pushing her inexorably into something she swore she'd never do.

The other night—it was worse than usual. She went all the way unconscious, and when she woke up the next morning, her throat hurt. She made David's favorite dinner that evening, shrimp scampi, and when he led her into the bedroom, she did whatever he wanted, let him shove her to her knees and direct her head with a fist in her hair. She wanted to please him and disappear at the same time, and for a few days, it worked. But then she left a few dishes in the sink, and she didn't buy enough of his favorite beer, and Brooklyn talked back, and he loomed in the corner of the counter as she cleared the table, glaring at her as he lazily tipped back bottle after bottle, and when he sent her out with Marissa to get fixed, she just hoped it would satisfy him more than her mouth could.

When she left this morning, after making sandwiches for his lunch, he smiled at her and told her she was a good wife, and that compliment bloomed like a star in her chest, and she hates that he can do that to her, make her roll belly-up like a kicked dog when she can still feel the bruises his knuckles made in her scalp.

And now here she is, her face numb, her nails gelled long and thick with the tips painted a coy white, her toes on their way to being what David calls "slut red," and she hates herself more than ever even if, deep down, she knows it's David she hates. But there's nothing she can do. She's trapped with him, by him.

It happened slowly, so slowly she didn't even notice it. The sweet crush became the perfect boyfriend became the distracted husband became the college freshman who stayed out too late partying before coming home to his pregnant wife, who was never invited out—for her own good, he said. He insisted they open joint bank accounts and she turn over any money to him, since he's the planner and she sucks with numbers. He's always wanted her to stay home with the girls. He won't let her work part-time, and the essential oils and other attempts at entrepreneurship put her deeper in his debt instead of saving her from him. She has no income, no credit card of her own, no job prospects. No friends. He ran them off, too, jealously insisted he needed her at home, needed her to himself. Told her that was her job—to be his wife. Even Jeanie across the street barely responds to her texts now. There's no one she can turn to.

And her mother?

Well, that would be like running away from a wolf and directly toward a lion.

Somehow, step by step, bit by bit, secretly and silently, he's cut off every avenue of escape. Even if she tries to divorce him, he'll get everything and probably manage to take the girls, considering his best friend, Brian, is an attorney of the vicious kind. No matter what her internet searches say about how mothers generally get custody and alimony, she knows deep down that David would rather see her dead than on her own with the girls and half the money that he considers all his. And her mother would only make things worse, somehow make any relationship problems into Chelsea's failings instead of David's abuse.

But—wait.

Is it abuse?

It must be. He puts her down. Restricts her money. Gaslights her. Strangles her while drunk and then, when he's sober, swears he would never lay a hand on her. Tells her that the bruises are because she's clumsy. Tells her, sweetly, that she's forgetful and silly and stupid and getting fatter every day. Reminds her that his high school best friend is on the force and he knows half the policemen in their hometown.

According to an article she read on the internet, she lives with domestic abuse.

It's hard to call it what it is, but it's impossible to ignore that the violence is escalating. He used to just slide his arm over her throat and hold her there, tight, almost loving, but in the past year, he's strangled her to unconsciousness multiple times. Sometimes she wakes up in bed, unsure how she's gotten there, because her last memory is of a man so drunk he can barely get his own body through the bedroom door.

"Are you watching this?" Marissa squawks from beside her, waving her champagne flute at the big TV on the wall, where a grim-faced blond woman in a jewel-toned blazer reads a prepared statement about the bizarre attacks sweeping across Florida—and spreading beyond it.

The one in the Costco down the street that her mom mentioned was only the first of many, and every day there's a new instance. There was one in Atlanta, another in rural Alabama. A snowbird on a plane from Miami to Philly killed a flight attendant with his bare hands. It's happening in Central and South America, too, but the news anchor gives that only the briefest mention. This explains why Chelsea has seen more people than usual wearing masks, although plenty of people never stopped wearing masks after Covid, assuming the next deadly virus was just over the horizon.

A number flashes on the screen for several moments, and Chelsea is transfixed as the news anchor begs the audience to let the government know if they suspect someone is sick with—whatever this is. Unusual bouts of violence, arising from seemingly nowhere in otherwise healthy people. Anyone attacking someone else right now needs to be quarantined and studied so that scientists can figure out what's going on and hopefully get ahead of the pandemic.

1-555-ALERT-US.

Chelsea wonders where that number goes, if it's a specific branch of 9-1-1, people trained to ask certain questions, or if it's like the phone bank she once helped with when a local kid got lost in the swamp with volunteers taking notes on old hotel stationery. Are the police in charge, or is it the CDC? It's got to be some kind of disease. Doesn't it?

A kid in Ella's class nearly killed a fellow student in the lunchroom, and Ella told her all about it. The poor girl is traumatized from seeing it up close. The school counselor has set up group and individual sessions to talk about it, try to process it, but the kids are all too embarrassed to be seen talking to her.

Like these kids haven't already seen horrible things. In movies, in videogames, maybe in their own homes. Chelsea knows that Ella has seen what David does to her, and that he's choked her, too, that one, horrible time that she's buried down deep lest it tear her apart. They never talked about it, she and Ella, but they have an unspoken system now. When Chelsea can tell it's going to be bad, she raises her eyebrows and tips her head toward the foyer, and Ella hurries upstairs and keeps Brooklyn up there with her. She even taught Ella how to put a chair under her doorknob, just in case. She said it was for staying home alone, but they both knew the truth.

No child should have to do that, have to see that. No child should have to protect her sibling, much less herself. No child should have to lock herself in her room at night. No mother should let it happen.

But that puts all the weight on the wrong person. Chelsea has to turn this around.

No man should do that to a woman.

No one should do it to anyone.

An easy statement to think, but almost impossible to do anything about, in her position.

She's trapped.

If she left, he would find her and punish her. He would cut her off from their money, repossess her car, which is of course in his name. Or use the law to hurt her. Or take the girls away from her. And the girls would live in a broken home, or worse—with him, unprotected— and they would think it was all Chelsea's fault.

"Hon, you okay? This news shit freaking you out? You look like you're going to rip the arms off that chair. Here. Take the remote. It's a massager. It'll relax you." Marissa grabs the remote and presses a button, and the chair begins to knead Chelsea's back in the worst possible way, like fists hellbent on finding the most tender spots on her spine and bruising them. She surges forward a bit, grimacing, angry, and Marissa hands her the remote, tiny gems winking on her long, freshly painted nails. "The harder the massage, the more good it does. You've just got to lean into it."

Chelsea mashes buttons until the chair stops attacking her like waves made of bricks and instead lightly jiggles her, and as an elderly woman squats at her feet and begins the awkward dance of smoothing and trimming and painting her toenails, she sips her champagne and stares at the TV, at that phone number and the list of possible symptoms, and that's when it hits her.

She knows exactly what she has to do to save herself. And her girls.

"There it is," Marissa says knowingly, clinking her glass against Chelsea's. "There's the smile. Now you're gettin' loose."

Chelsea turns her head to face Marissa, and her lips feel lazy and numb. "Thanks for inviting me. This is the best I've felt in years."

Marissa leans in a little. "Just wait until David sees. He's going to go crazy."

"He certainly is," Chelsea says, settling back into the loving, jiggling, massaging arms of her chair.

Because that's the plan.

7.

Three more kids have gone crazy at Ella's school, and the disease finally has a name: the Violence. It doesn't have any symptoms until it happens—until someone has what they call a storm. Two of the kids who got the Violence broke out with it in the lunchroom just like Thomas Canton, and teachers dove on them, dogpiled them, pulling them and their victims apart before they could do much damage. One freshman girl had a storm and attacked a junior in the girls' bathroom on F hall, and when she returned to class without the bathroom pass, covered in blood and specks of pink stuff and completely unconcerned, Mx. Alix went to check and found a dead girl on the floor by the sinks, her face full of shards from the mirror her head had been rammed into a few hundred times. That bathroom is closed now.

Much like with the last pandemic, the president is telling everyone that this new plague isn't a problem, and that if it is a problem, he'll solve it. He sounds exactly like he did when Covid hit during his last presidency, and Ella's political science teacher straight-up said that he hopes he gets impeached again. Tons of kids are staying home, their parents writing strongly worded social media posts about the aftermath of Covid and how many kids already live with permanent physical and psychological damage.

But plenty of kids, like Ella, still have to go to school even though it doesn't feel safe, whether because their parents think it's not an actual dager or it's a conspiracy or because they can't be trusted at home, doing nothing. Ella's dad said she has to go, so here she is, wearing a mask again, on high alert every time someone brushes past her. There are two more police officers roaming the halls, and all the teachers have had to take classes on deescalating altercations. As if that would help. After what she saw with Thomas and Jordan, Ella knows the problem isn't making kids scared of being in trouble or making teachers quicker to act.

The problem is that these kids go as blank as sharks and attack.

It would be like zombies, except zombies don't wake right back up and keep going about their lives despite the blood under their fingernails and the brains spattered on their flowered rompers.

She begged to stay home, but Dad told her she had to keep going to school. It would look bad if his kids stayed home like little pussies, he said. Ella flinched to hear him say that word but didn't bring it up again. She's taken precautions, though. She wears her steel-toed Doc Martens from her emo phase in middle school and doesn't go to the bathroom alone and has rings on all her fingers, big chunky ones with pointy bits she bought on sale at a mall cart. If anyone tries to hurt her, she's going to hurt them back. Or so she tells herself. She's never been in a fight before.

Hayden keeps texting her to meet him at their spot out by H hall, but she's ignoring it. Before, it was kind of annoying, and now it's risking her life. Being alone with anyone is dangerous, and they're not the only kids who use that spot to make out where the cameras and teachers can't see. She feels a little guilty for ghosting him, and with drama club on hold and a return to the no-loitering policies of Covid, she hasn't been alone with him in days. But on the other hand, maybe he'll get mad enough to break up with her. If she breaks up with him, she's a bitch who won't put out, and everyone will believe whatever Hayden says instead of believing her. But if he breaks up with her, she's . . . well, a loser, at the very least, but it won't be quite as much her fault?

She's hurrying out to her car after the last bell when she hears footsteps pounding behind her. She spins, hands up, keys clutched between her fingers like Wolverine's claws, but it's just Hayden. He looks at her like she's insane.

"Uh, what the hell are you doing, El?"

Ella resettles her backpack and holds her keys more normally. "Just being careful. Because of all the . . . stuff going on."

"Well, you look like a spaz when you hold your keys like that."

She stares at him for a moment too long, trying to decide if he's joking.

"Okay. Thanks?"

With a little huff, she turns around and continues walking to her car. Her heart revved up when she heard him running, and it hasn't gone down. He's acting weird. And the texts are getting a little out of hand. And angry. In one of them he called her a slut, and then five seconds later he apologized and begged for forgiveness and called her babe.

"Wait up." He jogs to keep up and walk beside her, his backpack over one shoulder. "You're gonna give me a ride home, right?"

"I can't—" she starts.

But he interrupts her. "Because of your little sister. Sure. You always say that. And then you always give in and give me a ride anyway, so let's just skip the part where I beg and go straight to the part where . . ."

He reaches for her hand and rubs his thumb across her palm. This, too, is described differently in her books. It doesn't feel like a gentle caress meant to make her feel loved and comforted or a sensual touch meant to awaken some latent feeling. It feels like he read about both of those moves in a manual and is now attempting to get them both out of the way.

"What's with all the creepy rings?"

Ella snatches her hand back. "They're not creepy."

"You look like you think you're a witch."

She's at her car now and presses the button to unlock it. She puts her backpack in the trunk, her back to Hayden, wishing he would disappear. When she turns to glare at him, he's grinning like this is all just super fun.

"Hayden, you're being weird."

"No, you're being weird. Stompy boots and witch rings. You didn't dress like this when we started going out."

She's pissed now and can imagine what it would be like to slap him with these rings on, their pointy bits aimed at his freshly shaved cheek.

"And you weren't such an asshole when we started going out."

Reaching past her, Hayden slams the trunk down, making her jump. There's a strange, hungry ferocity about his grin, and a cold trickle crawls down her spine as she realizes that she's seen her dad look at her mom this way. And, once, at Ella herself.

"I'm leaving now," she says.

"C'mon, babe. Don't be that way."

Hayden slides around, pinning her against the car with his hands, down low by her hips. The casual observer would see a couple just playing around, but Ella is suddenly terrified. The parking lot is half full now, but most of the other kids are too busy trying to beat the traffic out the gate to get to their after-school jobs to notice that anything weird is going on. A few people are watching, avid as vultures, and Ella locks eyes with a senior in her trig class named Beth, hoping the older girl sitting on the stairs will ask her if she's okay or step in to chat or something, but Beth's eyes slide down to her phone.

"Hayden, let me go." She hates how high and tremulous her voice is.

"Let you go? We're just talking," he says, smooth and sweet. His eyes are lit up in a way that would be mischievous if he didn't have her pinned and she didn't want so badly to be very, very far away from him.

"Whatever this is, I don't give my consent," she says, remembering what she's been taught, what they talk about in health class.

"I don't need consent to stand here and talk to my girlfriend." He innocently holds his hands up before shoving them in his pockets, but he doesn't move, and even though he's not a lot taller than her, Ella is very aware of his size, of the wiry strength in his muscular arms when he's playing baseball or in the weight room or lifting his partner during the dances in the musical. Her heart is thumping a thousand times a minute, and he just looks so calm and confident, as if nothing could ever touch him.

"Sorry, but I don't think I'm your girlfriend anymore," she says with as much determination as she can muster. "It's not you. It's me." She spins in place to open her door, but she can't, because there's not enough room, nowhere to go. He spins around, too, sliding to lean against the door, his body now blocking the handle.

"Last I heard, it takes two to make that decision," he counters, slouching lazily, eyebrows up.

Her escape cut off, Ella doesn't know what to do. She glances around the parking lot again, desperate for any help, but no one is watching, no one except Beth, who looks like she's low-key recording the whole thing on her phone from the steps.

"Help," Ella mouths silently, but maybe Beth is too far away to see it on the screen, because she doesn't do anything, doesn't say anything or come over to help or tap on her phone to call someone. She just sits there, staring at her stupid screen.

"Help," Ella says, a little louder, not quite a shout, trying to project her voice while sounding calm.

"What did you say?" Hayden hisses. "You're not going to make some embarrassing scene, are you?"

Ella wants to shrink into herself. She squeezes her eyes shut, a million scenarios running through her head, the computations of a prey animal trying to escape.

"Look, do you want to just go somewhere alone to talk about it?"

Hayden's voice is soft and gentle and sweet, and Ella knows that voice all too well.

She's heard it in her kitchen a hundred times.

Instead of turning around or answering him, she takes a deep breath and bolts.

Or tries to.

Instead, one of Hayden's big boots is there, and she trips over it and goes sprawling. Her head cracks into the SUV next door and she barely catches herself on her hands, the asphalt cutting into her palms. Her fallen keys are just a few inches away, and she grabs them, clutching them for dear life. Her vision splinters into little pinpricks, her head reeling and aching and stuffy. Hayden's hand is fisted in the back of her shirt, almost as if he could've caught her but was a second too late.

"Whoa. Are you okay?" he asks. His big hands wrap around her shoulders to help her up, and she's so dazed she lets him pull her to standing. She puts a hand on her car to steady herself. Hayden runs his thumb down her temple, his palm cupping her cheek like it's a basketball. "Poor girl. You're bleeding." But he doesn't sound sorry. "I'll drive you home. Where're the keys?"

Ella shakes her head, her fingers shaking around her key ring. She can't get in the car with him. Everything is wrong.

She steps away from him, one step and then another, but she's slow and clumsy now and he snags her arm easily and yanks her back.

"I told you. I'll drive, we'll talk. Just get in the car." The soft, reasonable tone of his voice is vastly different from the bruising grip he keeps on her arm.

She tries to yank it back, barking, "No!"

He doesn't let go. He leans close, as if they're sharing a secret. "Ella, you're making a scene. People are staring."

"I don't care."

He jerks her arm toward him, grabs her other arm, too, his fingers biting in. "Well, I do!"

Ella is breathing hard now, her heart pounding in time with her head. Her stomach goes cold and her feet want to run. Somewhere in the back of her mind, Mx. Alix is explaining fight, flight, or freeze and an adrenaline drop. Knowing what it is doesn't make it any easier to move. Shaking her head, she wrenches her body away from him with everything she has until she stands on her own.

"I said no!" she shouts. "No! Don't touch me again!"

She hears the slap before she can really process what he's done.

When she puts her hand to her cheek, it stings.

No one has ever slapped her before.

Her jaw drops. Her brain rattles like a maraca. She can feel the tiny balls of stone on her palms from the parking lot asphalt, pressing into her now swelling cheek.

He slapped her.

He *hit* her.

And he must realize the weight of what he's done, because suddenly he, too, looks terrified.

"El, I'm sorry, I didn't mean it. I didn't mean to. It was an accident. I'm sorry, okay? I'm sorry. I can get a ride home from someone else. Or drive you or whatever. Just don't tell anyone. Just don't . . . just . . . you make me so crazy, baby." His desperation raises his voice, makes him seem like a spoiled little boy, and she can't remember why she ever liked him at all.

Ella swallows the lump in her throat and lets her hands drop to her sides. She can't remember if the car is unlocked, so she fumbles for the right button on her key fob. He's not blocking the door anymore, just standing there, so she clicks the button once, gets in her car, closes the door, and locks it.

"I'm sorry!" he screams, his voice high and shredding. "I didn't mean it!" His fist slams into the car roof to punctuate his harmlessness.

The car is on now, and she puts it in reverse and backs up, daring him to stop her. He doesn't, he can't, he just stands there looking much younger and smaller than he did a few moments ago. There's a satisfying thump as she rolls over his backpack.

"I'm sorry!" he screams again, now in her rearview mirror.

As she drives past Beth on the stairs, the older girl holds up her phone and silently points to it.

Bleeding, aching, bruised, possibly concussed, Ella nods and chuckles to herself, a mad, half-sobbing sound.

Some kids at her school have leaked nudes, which spread like wildfire. But if she knows how things work, soon everyone is going to see firsthand what their golden boy did to her.

8.

David was asleep when Chelsea got home from the spa that night, and he was already gone when she woke up the next day. She's fairly certain she recalls him tugging the blanket off her face early that morning, like he was trying to check on her results, but she also recalls savagely yanking it back into place and growling at him. Even asleep, she'd made her peace with what had to be done.

Or so she thought.

She read somewhere that it takes, on average, seven tries for a woman to escape domestic violence. That was embarrassing, in her opinion. You just had to get up and leave.

Until it was her turn.

Chelsea went through seven tries in the first day alone. When she saw David's Post-it requesting steak for dinner and contemplated serving him Publix sandwiches instead. When he came home and told her she looked like shit and the injections weren't working, she wanted to point out how badly his hairline was receding behind his hair plugs. When he asked her why she didn't dust the fucking chandelier, she envisioned snipping through the chains and dropping it on his head.

But she didn't do any of those things. Instead, she made steak—perfectly cooked. She told him he looked handsome and she wore his favorite lingerie. And she dusted the chandelier.

A week passed like that, with Chelsea on her very best behavior, smiling and subservient and painted and plucked, terrified that he would somehow sense her intentions, smell her rage, see the clenched teeth behind her red-glossed lips. And it worked: For that whole week, nothing bad happened. Their life felt as beautiful as the pictures in the calendar. Everyone smiled and laughed and behaved.

And then Olaf pissed on David's favorite shoes, and Chelsea ended up unconscious on the couch. The moment she opens her eyes to find Brooklyn standing over her, asking what's wrong, she knows she has to act.

It has to happen now.

And once it starts, there will be no turning back, no chickening out.

As she moves through her afternoon, Chelsea takes joy in all the small, petty ways she can annoy her husband. For once, the rules are off—or flipped. When he clicks the button to open the garage door, he'll find her minivan parked in his spot. She does that sometimes, when she comes in from the store during a rainstorm, and he says he understands, but she knows he doesn't. He has the nicer car, so therefore he gets to park in the garage. The other side is for their golf cart, obviously, but her minivan doesn't need protection from the elements like his Lexus does. Today there is no rain; she just rolled on in until her hood kissed the tire of David's road bike where it hangs from its hook.

He prefers it when all of his girls hear the garage door opening and greet him with cheerful smiles. But today, no one comes—they're all curled up together, watching a movie in the big bed. Even Ella, usually so standoffish lately, is snuggled under the blanket. Some idiot in the school parking lot almost backed into her, and she dove out of the way and got all busted up, so the poor girl seems happy enough to wear one of Chelsea's fancy face masks and hide in the dark, even if she's not thrilled with the movie selection.

Chelsea hears David slam the door, curse, take off his shoes, and toss them on the rack. She smiles to herself; she stepped in one of Olaf's badly placed hallway poops and the brown smears she didn't clean off the white kitchen tile will infuriate her husband. He sighs, loudly, like an upset child, and she stifles a giggle.

In the kitchen proper, she knows he'll find a cold pizza box open on the counter, a sink full of dirty dishes, and the remnants of one of Brooklyn's DIY projects all over the counter, glitter and googly eyes confronting him instead of the spotless kitchen he demands.

"Hello?" he calls, voice dripping annoyance. "Anybody home? Were we robbed?"

"We're in here," Chelsea calls from the bed, although she doesn't hurry to the kitchen, like he'd prefer. "Watching a movie."

His footsteps are a warning, hard and slow, timeless as the minotaur hunting his maze. Olaf scampers off the bed and runs, whimpering and pissing himself, for Brooklyn's closet. But for once, Chelsea isn't scared of her husband. Let him come. Her blood is humming for this.

When he appears in the bedroom door, he's a furious shadow. Chelsea smiles at him from their bed, snuggled up with her girls in a puddle of pillows and blankets, all three in their pajamas in broad daylight. Ella stiffens beside her, having realized too late that trouble is brewing, but Brooklyn looks up and grins, showing gaps in her teeth.

"Hi, Daddy!" she calls, utterly unaware that his jaw is grinding with rage. "We ordered pizza. And a movie! It's about bears."

Ella says, "Hi, Dad," but she doesn't smile or wave, and no one gets out of bed. Chelsea smiles, too, but they're all wearing those green clay masks that David hates, so it's not like he wants his dutiful kiss.

"Hi, honey. How was work?" she asks, perky as hell.

"Work was fine," he snaps. "But the house isn't much to come home to. Are you sick or something?"

She shakes her head. "Nope. We just decided to have a lazy night. You can heat up some pizza in the microwave. Or eat yesterday's leftovers. It's nice to be lazy, every now and then." The girls are on either side of her, and she gives them a squeeze. Brooklyn giggles and hugs her back, but Ella just watches her father, tense and wary as a cat. She's a sharp kid, even if she doesn't really open up to Chelsea anymore, and she just realized that all the ingredients for a bad night are simmering.

"Lazy," David muses. "Huh. Wish I could do that. But some of us have to work."

"Is Daddy mad?" Brooklyn whispers, but of course he hears it.

Chelsea kisses the top of her head. "Oh, Daddy just needs to relax. Let's get back to our movie."

"I need to do what—?"

And then Chelsea hits PLAY and the room fills with the sound of yodeling bears.

It takes everything she has to keep a straight face. Her stern, angry husband has been interrupted by yodeling.

By yodeling. Fucking. Bears.

David tosses his laptop bag on a chair, turns on his heel, and leaves. Chelsea knows that as his rage builds, he'll hang up his clothes, put on his sweats, and stomp downstairs for a beer. That, at least, won't be a disappointment. She got a case of his favorite local IPA, and he'll most likely start guzzling them down like a dying man in a desert who's just discovered water. The more he drinks, the angrier he'll be. There should be dinner on the table. No dishes in the sink. The floor should be swept, not sandy and poopy. The counters should be spotless. The garage should be empty. His needs should be taken care of.

There are six empty bottles lined up on the counter when the movie ends and Chelsea and the girls wander into the kitchen. It's past their bedtime, but right now Chelsea doesn't care about that, either.

"They should be in bed," David says, slurring a little.

"They're on their way. Just one more cookie." She reaches into the freezer and hands each of her daughters a Girl Scout cookie from his private stash, his last box. It's a petty little fuck you, but it feels good.

"Go to bed!" he roars.

"But Mommy promised to read a story after we washed off our masks—" Brooklyn starts.

"Then she lied. It's past bedtime, and you'll do as you're told!"

Brooklyn flinches away from him, hurt, and he smiles as if gratified to see that he still has that power over someone. As for Ella, she skulks away, out of range. She's watching him so carefully, and Chelsea can't blame her. Before David can yell again, Ella herds her little sister up the stairs and out of sight, shushing her every time she tries to protest. If this is going to work, Chelsea has to get on with it, while they're still awake and alert.

She saunters over and leans back against the counter, right in that corner where David himself generally holds court. She's not even looking at him—she's casually reading the cookie box. *His* cookie box. While she chews a cookie.

His cookie.

"What the hell has gotten into you?" he asks, voice low and deadly.

She looks up, and he scrutinizes her face, now free of the green mud, probably checking to reassure himself that he got his money's worth out of the Botox party. Does he even notice the way she's staring at him, defiant and angry? It's been years since she dared to challenge him.

"Nothing." She smiles. "What's gotten into you?"

And then she shoves another cookie in her mouth.

"Goddammit, those are mine! You know that!"

Relishing every second, she swallows and rolls her eyes at him.

David throws the beer bottle across the room, where it crashes against the cabinet and shatters. Glass rains down, frothy golden beer spilling over his precious granite countertops. Chelsea goes very still, breathing hard, her eyes pinned on him, artificially wide and innocent. Goading.

"I'm just eating a cookie, David. Why are you being so *violent*?"

He slaps the box to the ground and grabs her throat in one hand, his thick fingers digging in as he shoves her head back. Her heart ratchets up with excitement and fear, and she follows his lead. She's just barely tall enough for her head to crack dully against the cabinets, the counter a hard line against her spine. She grabs for his wrist and forearm, scrabbling at him, but it's like fighting a monster, all muscle and bone and primal rage. He's got an erection now, the absolute asshole, and he presses it against her, a threat and a promise. Her eyes drill into his, unblinking, radiating hate.

"You did this, Chel, not me." He pinches with thumb and fingers, pressing in on her trachea, making her gasp. "It's like you want to make me mad."

She tries to shake her head back and forth and can only manage vibration. She's fighting it now, fighting the strangle and the choke, pulling at his arm, trying to get the breath she needs. Her fingers are wrapped around his wrist, trying in vain to pull him away. And then she kicks him with a bare foot, jamming her toes into his shin, freshly painted blood-red nails slicing divots, and he jerks her neck sideways, making her head bounce around.

With frantic suddenness, he lets go, and she drops, barely catching herself, clutching the counter behind her for dear life.

Her hand rises to her throat, her fingertips brushing the aching bruises there with tentative curiosity. She wishes for a mirror, for confirmation. She looks to the stairs, quickly, and sees two shadows watching.

"That was . . ." she starts but doesn't finish, her voice raspy.

"Just don't make me do it again."

He turns back to the fridge for another beer, but what she says next stops his hand in midair.

"I don't make you do anything. You're an adult, David. You're responsible for everything you do, including abusing your wife."

He turns back to her slowly, bares his teeth and growls a warning. She bolsters herself against the counter, unsure if she can stand on her own, shaking as hard as she is. Adrenaline pumps through her, urging her to flee or freeze, but for once she's doing something different. For once, she meets his gaze and doesn't look away.

"What did you just say?" he whispers.

"Wife beater," she hisses. "Coward." She pauses, sneers. "Pussy."

It's like a red curtain comes down in front of his eyes, like any vestige of humanity is tucked away, and David's fist shoots out of its own accord, thudding into her chest, just over her heart. She hears herself make a sound like a dying bird, a squealing, animal gasp.

"You done yet?" he asks, a taunt. "You got anything else you need to say t'me?"

She stands tall, one hand to what she knows will be a nasty bruise, as if she's pledging to the flag. "I always knew one day choking me unconscious wouldn't be enough. That you'd turn to fists like a dumb brute."

This time it's not a fist that strikes her but an open hand, a hard slap to her cheek. She wasn't expecting it, and it rocks her head sideways. Brooklyn's gasp is audible from the stairs. Chelsea spins and catches herself on the counter, her back to him. Her brain rattles in her skull, a flash of copper on her tongue making her wonder if she cut her own mouth on a tooth.

Still she turns back to face him and straightens with painful effort.

"Bully. Monster. Asshole. *Pathetic.*" She enunciates each word. She looks him in the eye. She wants him to know that she means it.

When he hits her this time, she sees it coming but can't dodge fast enough. It's a fist to the jaw, just like in an action movie. She cries out and staggers away, and blood fills her mouth, and when she looks back, he's inspecting his knuckles.

He's more worried about his own pain than hers.

Glaring at her, he shakes his hand as if he's just taken out the trash. "This is your fault," he warns her. "I don't want to do this."

"Funny how you keep doing it, then. Hitting someone half your size. Big hero, there. Your mother would be proud." She sputters a little cough, and glittering red spatters the chest of her sleep shirt. She doesn't bother to wipe it away. She's going to see this through to the end.

David sneers and prods her in the chest with a finger, pressing deep until he hits bone. "She *would* be proud. I'm a good provider. Every problem we have is because of you. I do what I'm s'posed to." When Chelsea snorts her objection, he grabs her, hard, pinning her arms to her sides and holding her in place. His face doesn't look angry and animal now; it just looks cruel and smug.

David leans in close, his lips near her ear. "Remember that trip to Reno? I slept with a waitress. Best tits I've ever seen. She came twice. Howled like a fucking cat. So you call me whatever you want, but know that you're not the one I think about all day. Not even close."

He pulls back to watch her face, like he's hoping for tears, but she hasn't cried yet tonight and that admission won't be what wounds her. Her head drops, and he reaches for her chin, probably to force her head up and make her look at him.

But then she starts shaking, and she looks up at him of her own accord. She's laughing now. Laughing so hard that she's crying. The fact that David is so confused only makes her laugh all the harder.

"What the fuck's so funny?"

"You are," she replies. "You're a fucking joke."

And like a dam breaking, he's done being gentle with her, done being careful. He rears back and punches her as hard as he can, right in the mouth. It hurts like hell, but this is what she wanted, this is what she committed herself to. When he holds up his hand, it's smeared with blood as red as his favorite lipstick.

"Say that again, bitch."

She's not laughing now, but she knows her grin must be a feral thing.

"Thank you," she says through bloodied teeth.

And then she sprints for the bathroom. Before his numb feet and drunk brain can catch up, she's slammed the door and locked it. He yanks on the knob and pounds on the wood, but it doesn't budge.

With trembling hands, Chelsea pulls her cellphone from the pocket of her pajama pants and dials the number that every American knows by heart now.

1-555-ALERT-US.

"Help me," she says, voice shaking as David beats his fists on the other side of the door. "My husband went crazy. He attacked me. I'm bleeding. I barely got away. I'm scared for our children."

She pauses and takes a deep breath.

"I think . . . it's the Violence."

9.

Ella's thumb hovers over the 1 on her phone again, her other hand lost in Brooklyn's full-body hug. Dad is usually quiet when he gets angry, but tonight, there's no way she could keep Brooklyn upstairs with a bedtime story and a closed door. The shouting, the crashing bottle, the slamming door. It's the loudest it's ever been—different, somehow. They're huddled together on the stairs, shaking, Brooklyn's face smashed against her, and Ella remembers what it felt like to be small, afraid to go downstairs after dark because then she'd have to run back upstairs feeling like something was going to grab her ankle. Her fears were so different then.

She can't hear what her mom says in the bathroom, but she must've said something unforgivable, as her father smashes his fists against the door and screams, "Chelsea, you bitch, that's a fucking lie and you know it!"

He yanks at the knob and looks frantically around the room, running his hand through his sweaty hair. Whatever he's looking for, he doesn't find it. But he does find her.

His eyes move to the stairs, flying wide and then narrowing like a killer robot locking in on a target. Ella stands and shoves Brooklyn up the steps without taking her eyes off her dad.

"Hurry, Brookie. My room."

Brooklyn whimpers but obeys, scrambling up the carpeted stairs on hands and feet like a dog. Ella follows, herding her, making sure she doesn't stop to look behind them, doesn't make some crucial, babyish error. They skid through the door, and Ella slams and locks it, sliding the chair under the doorknob like Mom taught her. Brooklyn crouches on the bed, hunched down in the farthest corner, as their father's footsteps pound up the stairs. He says nothing, which is scarier than saying something. The door jumps as he yanks on the knob.

"Ella, honey? Can we talk?"

She's seen enough Lifetime specials and horror movies to know that this is a ploy. She triple-checks the chair under the doorknob and hurries to the bed with Brooklyn, tucking her sister against her side. There's a big knife under her pillow, one her mom threw away because it wasn't sharp enough, but Ella's not ready to reach for it. She turns her phone back on, finally presses that last 1 for the first time, then hits CALL. The phone shakes in her hand, and she hates how she questions whether this is a good enough reason to call 9-1-1, like someone might be mad that she bothered them.

The door quivers like a toy prodded by a curious cat. Either her dad doesn't know how to unlock it with something as simple and common as a nail or a bobby pin, or he's so drunk or angry that it's made him forget.

"Nine one one, what's your emergency?" The woman's voice is a weird mix of kindness and exasperation.

"My dad hit my mom, and now he's trying—" Ella's throat has gone bone-dry, and she clears it. "He's trying to get in my room."

The woman's voice changes, all business now. "Address."

Ella recites it, whispering, barely stumbling. The woman confirms that her phone is a good callback number, asks for her dad's full name and her mom's full name, and asks if the front door is unlocked.

"I don't think so. I brought my little sister upstairs, to my room. There's a chair under the door, but he's trying—" She looks at the door. It's not moving anymore. She doesn't see a shadow underneath it. "He was trying to get in. I don't know where he is now. He's drunk."

When the woman takes too long to respond, she uses the magic word, the one she's been taught since she was three, the one that will get her whatever she needs. "Please. Please."

In the background, she hears the woman speaking to someone else, urgent, her voice muted. Then she's back. "What's your name, honey?"

Ella usually hates it when people call her honey, that saccharine old man's reward for being young and female, usually employed around the time someone tells her she should smile more. But now, she doesn't mind it. It softens her, reminds her of . . . well, not *her* grandmother. But the grandmothers in movies and books, the ones with warm kitchens who make biscuits with jelly jars and care about their families.

"My name is Ella."

"Ella, you're doing real good, okay? Just stay with me. I've got people coming to help you. But you need to stay with me, okay?"

"Okay."

"What's going on?" Brooklyn asks. She's got a death grip on Ella's other arm but is otherwise burrowed under Ella's covers.

"Someone's coming to help us."

"Are we in trouble?"

"Of course not. Just be quiet."

"Can you hear anything else going on?" the woman asks.

Ella eyes the door but isn't willing to go anywhere near it in case her father is finding a nail or preparing to bust through it like a rhino.

"No. There was a lot of shouting and banging—"

"Is there a gun involved?" the woman asks sharply.

Ella gasps.

What if he's getting a gun?

"I haven't heard any shots, but . . . we have guns. In the safe. In his room."

"How many guns?"

Ella swallows, her mind spinning. He could be turning his key in the lock of the gun safe right now, pocketing bullets and coming back to make sure this door opens. Or the one downstairs.

"Lots," she whispers. "Lots."

She hears the woman's voice switch over to the other half of her job, and she sounds competent and confident and not at all chill as she barks orders at someone else. To Ella it sounds like Charlie Brown's teacher, wah-wuh-wah wah wah. Somewhere outside, a siren wails. As if in response, there's a loud bang downstairs, harder than fists could make.

He's trying to beat the bathroom door open with . . . something.

Bang.

Bang.

"Look, bitch, you'd better open up!"

"He's trying to bust the door open," she tells the woman, her voice a whisper now in case he can hear her. Not that he should be able to hear anything—not through whatever he's slamming into the door downstairs. A golf club? Her old softball bat? "Downstairs. My mom's in there."

"Just stay put," the woman reminds her. "Stay safe, okay? The police are almost there. They're going to help you. But I need you to stay out of the way. Can you do that?"

"Yeah, okay."

"Just stay on the line."

The woman's voice clicks over as she talks to someone else, and Ella's phone bings with a message. She doesn't pull it away to look at what it might be. Bing. Another message. Bing. Another one. She glances down quickly and sees that it's Hayden.

Come on, baby. I said I'm sorry.

He is the least of her problems now, and she doesn't care if he's sorry.

She snort-sobs and touches her cheek, surprised to see that she's crying. The sirens are louder now, and she wants to go to the window and see what it looks like when the cavalry comes, but Brooklyn's still got her in a death grip, and the animal deep inside Ella refuses to budge, as if holding completely still is the only thing that can save her, can save them all.

The banging stops, and she exhales as if she'd forgotten how to breathe.

"Okay, bitch. You don't want to open up? Let's see if the doors upstairs are up to it."

Her dad's feet on the stairs is her least favorite sound in the world. When they watched *Halloween* at some stupid slumber party, she didn't need the scary music and mask to feel her heart in her throat; just the way Michael Myers walks is too much like her father when he's angry.

A shadow falls under the door. If she leans over, she can see his bare feet.

"Ella, this is your father. Open this door right now."

He says it breathless, slurring, commanding.

He says it like he wants a reason to break the door down.

"Daddy, no!" Brooklyn screams, and Ella drops the phone and slaps a hand over her sister's mouth.

"Ella, are you there?" The woman's voice is tinny and far away, the phone lying on the blankets.

"Brookie, sweetie, can you come open the door for Daddy?"

Her mouth still covered, Brooklyn frantically shakes her head—that's Ella's special name for her, and the fact that Dad is using it is utterly chiling.

And then he hits the door with something much harder than his fists.

The door shakes, and he hits it again, and the sirens are loud now, probably right outside the house. Red and blue and white lights flash through the blinds. Brooklyn is shaking and crying, Ella is holding her close, the woman on the phone is calling her name, her phone is buzzing with Hayden's stupid texts, and the entire world has shrunk down to a grown man testing the strength of a plastic door.

Until there's an even bigger slam downstairs, the front door rammed open.

"Drop the weapon, put your hands up and step away from the door!" someone barks, and the banging stops.

Something heavy and metal drops to the ground outside in the hall.

"You don't understand," Dad slurs.

And then everything happens very fast.

Ella hears it all, wishes she could stop Brooklyn from hearing anything. Dad shouts and curses and threatens and fights the police. They have to Taser him. He thumps and writhes on the ground, and feet pound up the stairs to collect him and drag him away. They don't ask Ella to open her door, though—she won't do that until her mom is there.

As they take her dad outside, Ella picks up her phone again. The woman is still there.

"They're here," she says. "Thank you."

10.

There is a fruit fly floating in Patricia's glass of water and her waitress has disappeared.

This is not why Randall pays the club an exorbitant fee every month, and she will definitely be having a little chat with the manager. It won't go well; she's already in a terrible mood.

She has just hung up from another unapologetic phone call that could've very easily occurred before she went to the trouble of getting done up and arriving at Emerald Cove for a late dinner.

An unexpected meeting, Randall said.

Order champagne and dessert. Treat yourself.

Ha.

Patricia has chosen to stay and dine alone because to do otherwise would suggest that she's been stood up or is suffering some other unfortunate occurrence. Unfortunate occurrences would not dare befall Patricia Lane. She's at the very best table in the clubhouse, but she has her back to the window to monitor the room. Instead of ordering the champagne Randall suggested, she is waiting on a very dry, very distinguished Cabernet and a Cobb salad. Champagne is for celebrations. Champagne is ordered by a man and delivered to the table with its own stand to chill in a silver bucket. Champagne is not a consolation prize for neglected wives who are already dealing with dead flies.

The silly man. Does he not know her at all? *Champagne and dessert.* If she partook in champagne and dessert every time life disappointed her, she wouldn't still be a size four.

She dabs at her lips, careful not to upset her lipstick. Her mouth is numb, so numb she can only feel her teeth grinding together. She thinks of them as robot teeth, those gleaming, expensive, foreign objects screwed into her jaw when her own teeth finally crumbled after all those years of poverty, bad eating, and rage. These teeth are more substantial. These teeth could bite through glass.

Patricia berates her waitress, receives her salad, picks at it without really tasting it, and barely sips her Cab, which is drier than an attic floor—and comped in apology for the fruit fly. She does not enjoy anything about the meal.

Her smile is in place as she stands and saunters out of the room, giving little parade waves and exchanging compliments with everyone she passes.

New earrings, Denise. Lovely!

Oh, Bob, where is Sharon tonight? And who is this? Mm. Your niece. Charming.

We missed you at tennis, Dawna, but you're just glowing.

I know you, she tells them with each backhanded compliment. *I know your secrets. I know your fears. I know your pride.* It's like a spider spinning a web, binding them all together. She knows who's having an affair, she knows who's seeing which doctor for which tightening up. She knows who's mistreating their aged parents in which home. She knows that redhead is not Bob's niece.

The façade holds until she's in her sedan, hands at ten and two. Her head falls forward as she exhales. It's exhausting, all this work. But it's necessary. If you start to let go for one little minute, you end up like Chelsea, adrift at sea with neither captain nor anchor. Patricia's life is a well-run ship, and even if things get windy, she will not be battered about. Not again. Never again.

It takes her longer than usual to get home, thanks to a messy car accident on a two-lane road. A rough-looking policeman waves her around, and she can't help staring at the bright-red speckles painting the crushed door of the cheap white Ford, lurid in the patrol car's high beams. Ambulance people huddle around someone on the ground, their backs turned to the road and their energy tense and frantic, but she rolls past without being able to see too much. At least it's not near her house.

Homer waves from the neighborhood guardhouse, and Patricia waves back. She always feels better the moment the tall iron gates swing shut behind her. It's safe here, everything carefully planned and kept up. The nice thing about this neighborhood is that the sidewalks don't start until you're inside the gate. There's no public thoroughfare encouraging just anyone to linger outside, and if anyone tried to walk in, Homer would keep that from happening; they even gave him a gun. Cars can't piggyback in, like they can in Chelsea's neighborhood. You're on Homer's list or you're not, and strangers have to show their ID. You quite simply can't get in unless you're supposed to get in.

She's not such a fan of the speed bumps, but she knows they, too, serve their purpose.

Their house is in a cul-de-sac just the right distance from the club-house, which is nowhere near as nice as the one at Emerald Cove but still functional enough for throwing a perfectly respectable bridal shower for someone else's daughter. She smoothly pulls into her side of the garage and stops when the tennis ball touches her windshield. Everything in the garage is exactly where it should be, the shelves and racks Miguel installed perfectly hung and painted just the right shade of white, not too crowded with ugly garage things.

Once inside her echoing home, she steps out of her mules in the mudroom and does a quick walk-through of the downstairs to make sure Rosa is keeping up with her duties. Unlike her daughter, she knows how important appearances are, and for all that Rosa has been decently paid and loyal for years, it's easy for anyone to get a little lazy when they're not being watched. She can't find a speck of dust, a dropped penny, a single petal fallen from the all-white arrangement on the foyer table. It's almost disappointing, having nothing to complain about.

But then she spots the backyard.

All the lights are on, and it's an utter wreck, as if a tornado has torn through.

The patio furniture is tossed about, the cushions just lying on the ground in the dirt. Some of the flowering bushes—she doesn't know what they are, Miguel handles that—are crushed and tumbled over, broken branches and fallen flowers everywhere. There are shattered ceramic pots and dented candles, and—well. Someone is in big trouble.

As if on cue, movement outside catches her eye. It's Rosa, carefully closing the pool house door behind her and locking it. She's a tall, thickly built woman in her fifties, and she charges over to the patio furniture and jerks up each chair, setting them upright and dragging them back into place. Patricia watches from behind the curtains, almost fascinated. What on earth has happened here? Was there some sort of break-in? As Rosa fights to get the table upright, Patricia hurries to her bedroom and checks her furs and purses, finding everything exactly where it belongs. There are no broken windows, no stolen televisions, no sign of anything wrong inside the house. When Rosa has all the big furniture back in place, Patricia opens the patio doors and goes outside.

"Oh, Mrs. Lane! I didn't know you would return so soon," Rosa says, looking back at the pool house where she and her husband Miguel live. It's only two bedrooms, but having them available around the clock has been an utter godsend. Rosa does all the housework, laundry, and cooking, while tiny, wiry Miguel handles the yard and fixing things.

"Well, it is my house, so I consider myself free to come and go." Patricia says this with a little smirk, as if they're friends sharing a joke. "What happened back here? And why isn't Miguel helping you?"

"There was . . . a lot of wind. Very windy night." Rosa looks down. She's a terrible liar, which is one of the reasons that she's a terrific housekeeper. "Miguel hurt his back trying to clean up. I called our son to come help."

Patricia feels that little rumple form on her forehead. Annoyance.

"You know Mr. Lane doesn't like it when Oscar parks in the driveway, Rosa."

Rosa flinches and nervously glances over her shoulder, back at the pool house. "I'll make sure he parks around back, Mrs. Lane."

Which, honestly, Randall doesn't love, either, but at least there aren't as many windows on that side of the house, where the driveway extends around to the pool house, so no one has to see his beat-up old truck.

"You know, Rosa—"

Before she can finish explaining that this is Not How Things Are Done, the pool house door bursts open, hard enough to make it bounce off the siding. Miguel barrels out, moving faster than a sixty-six-year-old man has any right to move.

"Go inside, Mrs. Lane," Rosa says, daring to put hands on Patricia's arm, gently, and push her toward the house. "Please. Lock the doors."

Before Patricia can offer a sharp rebuke, Rosa spins around and catches Miguel as he charges. She must weigh nearly twice as much as her husband, but he struggles in her arms like a mad cat, a belt wrapped around one wrist. Something about the way he's behaving hits Patricia like a slap across the face—this is not normal. Miguel is a calm, quiet, competent, dreamy sort of man. He slowly plods through his day, singing old songs under his breath, taking twice as much time as he should on basic tasks. She's never seen him move faster than a thoughtless amble. He can take an hour to eat an apple. But now he's writhing, kicking, clawing, and it's all Rosa can do to keep him contained.

"Shhh," she croons to him. "Stop now." Rosa turns to look over her shoulder at Patricia, who can see where he's gouged bloody strips down his wife's cheeks with his fingernails. "Please, Mrs. Lane. Please. Inside."

Patricia's brain flips the switch from anger to fear, and she hurries for the door, goes inside, and fumbles with the lock. For a moment, she stands there watching through the glass as Rosa struggles with the crazed man, trying to capture his arms against his sides so he can't scratch her again. He looks through Patricia as if he doesn't even see her.

The rage she sees there—the fury, the hate, the absence of humanity—it makes her step back and clutch her heart.

A man looked at her that way once, a long time ago. He slapped her.

Once.

And she slapped him back and called him every foul name she could think of and smashed in his precious TV with the broom, and then she walked out of his tidy white apartment full of pictures of Jesus, penniless and alone and pregnant with his child. But there's no reason for Miguel to hate her like that, to see through her, to have that look that says he wants nothing more than to tear her apart for what she's done to him—or not done for him. She hasn't defied him or denied him something he thinks he's due, hasn't belittled him or emasculated him.

She takes good care of Miguel, pays him well enough. Sure, it's all under the table because the Estrellas are undocumented, but Randall has some plan in place to help them become citizens one day when there's a president who supports that sort of thing. Miguel should be *thankful*.

And that's when it clicks.

The Violence.

Patricia has heard things, here or there, but honestly, who has the time? She's not going to spend all day poking at a computer like Chelsea, looking for things to worry about. If it was important, Randall would tell her to worry, but so far everyone around the courthouse seems to think it's all a bunch of baloney, people without means using some nonexistent disease as an excuse for getting up to trouble. Randall got into one of his grooves the other night, after a few bourbons, comparing the Violence to some odd old occurrences where everyone thought laughter or dancing was contagious and therefore just spent days or weeks laughing or dancing.

People are stupid, he often reminds her. *That's why I have a job—because someone smart needs to send them to jail to pay for their stupidity and get them off the street. When the president is worried, I'll consider worrying. And he ain't worried.*

Rosa is carrying Miguel now, step by step across the yard, back toward the pool house. He's still fighting just as hard, kicking and scratching and punching, and her arms are just torn to ribbons, bruises already showing, but Rosa isn't stopping. If he were a bigger man, the situation would be far more dire.

Patricia touches the lock again to make sure it's engaged and picks up her phone to get some information about this Violence thing. The first search result is for the CDC's website about it, and it lists the symptoms.

Sudden, violent rage.

Attempts to hurt one particular target that, if unstopped, will result in their death.

Constricted pupils.

High heart rate.

Fever over a hundred degrees.

Excessive salivation.

Well, Patricia can attest to only two of those symptoms, but it's good enough for her.

She dials 1-555-ALERT-US as Rosa disappears into the pool house, dragging Miguel with her.

It's the patriotic thing to do, after all.

11.

Chelsea sits on the front porch step, a throw blanket tossed over her shoulders despite the fact that it's a warm spring night in Florida and she's sweating. One of the EMTs awkwardly wrapped the blanket around her after they checked her out. They took a million pictures, asked a million questions, put tiny Band-Aids on her cuts, looked inside her mouth, assured her that if she stuck to soft foods for a few weeks, her loosened teeth would resettle in her jaw. All that tender care took place only after the officers cuffed David and wrestled him out of the house, kicking and screaming, drunk and slurring and threatening Chelsea in a hundred ways that were now recorded on the cops' bodycams.

"I'm gonna kill you for this, you lying bitch!" he'd shrieked. "You did this!"

Like he hadn't been promising to kill her for years.

But it didn't count if he was drunk, he always said. That wasn't him. That wasn't who he was.

And he wouldn't talk that way, anyway.

David always brings up how much he respects women.

"What's that?"

Ella sits on the stair beside her and points to a card that's apparently been in her hands for some time, turning over and over between her French-manicured nails under the moth-ringed porch lights. Chelsea looks down at it, a clean rectangle, whiter than white, with contact information for the government's Violence Task Force. The disease has changed how they do things: Now they can drag people off and ask questions later. They said she could call in a few days, after David has been processed, if she wants to know which quarantine center he's been sent to.

Like she cares.

Chelsea might be a beaten dog, but she doesn't plan to lick that hand again.

She's pretty sure the cops and EMTs all knew it wasn't actually the Violence, that it was just regular old domestic abuse, but no one questioned that part of the story. She could see the pity in their eyes—well, except maybe for the older cop, who looked like he wanted to grind her under his boot. It's a shame, that these people have seen enough situations like hers to assume that she'll run back into his open arms, that she's already planning for him to return home again.

She crumples it up and shoves it in her pocket.

"Someone's business card."

Ella hands her a cold seltzer from the fridge, and for a moment, they just sit that way, together in the dark, not quite touching, the night lit by streetlamps and passing cars and the cracked blinds of curious neighbors. Chelsea sips her seltzer, swatting at the mosquitoes as they land on her hand. One leaves a fat red smear, and she flicks it away and stands up. She's seen enough blood for one night.

Chelsea drifts inside, and Ella follows and locks the door behind them. The house feels big and empty. All the lights are on—they did that, when they broke down the door—and Chelsea flicks the switches until things seem less revealed.

It's funny. How many times has she imagined this moment over the years, what it would feel like to finally do something about David, to speak the truth about his violence, to have witnesses and evidence? She'd always imagined it in the daytime, somehow, even though nighttime is when his monster comes out. A bright-blue day, airy and cool, and she would twirl in the foyer like Maria on that Austrian hillside in *The Sound of Music.*

But it's dark and hot and humid, and the quiet is a beautiful thing except for the part where she feels like she needs to fill it.

What does she say to her daughter about what happened tonight? How much of the truth is necessary? How does she apologize for everything that came before?

And does Ella know that the Violence was just an excuse?

"So that was exciting," Chelsea says, keeping her voice low so she won't wake up Brooklyn, who crashed out on the couch when the boring part of the law process began.

Ella is vaguely orbiting her, not touching or making eye contact, but hovering. "Yeah."

"I bet I look terrible."

At that, Ella looks up, probing and . . . hurt? "Mom, a guy just beat the shit out of you. How else would you look?"

Chelsea glances in the hall mirror, the same one her mother rubbed a thumb over just a few weeks ago, and can't help but stare, judge. She does look like shit. It's scary, how bad she looks. Bruised and tender and fragile. The little butterfly Band-Aids, the dark smudges, the swollen, bloodstained lips. She touches them, gently, and flinches, and then the tears finally come. First it's sniffles, as if she's trying to catch the tears one by one and suck them back down. But soon it's great, whooping sobs, each one shuddering through her, racking her body as water sheets down from her eyes, locked in the mirror. Ella's arm is around her shoulders, but it's not enough, so she pulls her daughter close, and Chelsea can't remember the last time they hugged like this, plastered down the front, clinging like they're holding on to that door in *Titanic*, frightened by the cold realities of life and terrified to be adrift outside of this fragile connection.

For a moment, Chelsea isn't sure who is the child and who is the parent, and that only makes her cry all the harder for the burden Ella's been forced to bear.

"Mommy, what's wrong?" Brooklyn asks, just her eyes and the top of her head visible over the sofa. "Does it hurt?"

Chelsea turns, automatically producing that reassuring mother's smile that says everything will be okay even when it won't.

"A little, baby. But I'm going to get better." Just saying it makes her smile more real.

He's gone. The house is quiet. For the first time in forever, she doesn't feel fear.

And then the doorbell rings.

Ella looks to her, both of them gone from calm peace to high alert. No one really rings doorbells out of the blue these days, not in a neighborhood with a gate, and it's too late for Patricia to be out randomly looking for someone to torture. Maybe it's one of the neighbors, checking to see if they're okay? Maybe it's Jeanie, the only person with any inkling of what Chelsea's been dealing with.

She peeks through the peephole and feels the strangest combination of shifting feelings.

It's a cop. Is that bad?

No. Cops helped her out. They must have more questions. It's okay. It's safe.

No.

Wait.

It's a cop she knows. One of David's high school friends.

"Open up, Chel. I know you're in there."

And she has to open up, doesn't she, because he's a cop?

"Take Brooklyn upstairs," she whispers to Ella. "Try to get her into bed."

Ella nods and swoops Brooklyn off the couch, carrying her like a koala as the younger girl sleepily asks questions, the same questions that Chelsea is asking herself.

Who is it?

Is Mommy in trouble?

Are they going to take her away like they did Daddy?

"Shh," Ella says. "We have to be quiet and brave."

"You always say that," Brooklyn complains, one fist rubbing her eyes.

Once the girls are safely upstairs, Chelsea opens the door.

"Hey, Huntley," she says, hoping her exhaustion is obvious.

"That's *Officer* Huntley." It comes out crisp, and he's wearing re-flective sunglasses despite the fact that it's pitch black outside. "Can I come in?"

Chelsea steps back. "Of course." Because Huntley's been here be-fore. He comes over with David's old high school crew to watch the fights on their huge TV, and he comes to their Fourth of July barbe-cue, dragging his miserable wife, Laura.

Huntley—his first name is Chad, but his friends don't call him that—steps inside, takes off his sunglasses, and looks around like he's in a James Bond film, like he's never been here before despite the fact that he once barfed Jell-O shots into one of Chelsea's decorative vases. As she watches him tuck his glasses into a front pocket and walk around, chewing his ever-present cinnamon gum, she can't help glancing at the open front door and wondering if this is an official visit. Did she have to let him in? She's known him for almost twenty years, but in that friend-of-a-friend way. David doesn't like to hang out with the boys and girls together; they always separate off into the women and the men. Most of what she knows about him she's heard from Laura over the years, and Laura is the kind of woman who fades into the background and laughs too loud at everyone else's jokes.

"I heard your address over the radio. Tried to text David but didn't get an answer. They said you said it was the Violence."

He turns to face her, and his eyes are small and sun-creased, nar-rowed in suspicion. He looks her up and down, sneering a little. Chel-sea has always gotten the idea that he either hates women or doesn't care to take the time to understand them, and now she stills like a rabbit in a hawk's shadow, knowing that this kind of attention from Chad Huntley is definitely not a good thing.

"Thing is, Chel, I've seen folks with the Violence. Pulled a ten-year-old girl off the crossing guard yesterday, and thing is . . ." He steps closer, so close she can smell his cinnamon gum and a whiff of dan-druff shampoo clinging to his high and tight. "That crossing guard was a big man, and that girl was a little bitty thing, and the crossing guard looked a hell of a lot worse than you do right now. But David's so much bigger than you. And you don't look so bad."

Chelsea swallows hard, and he snatches her chin, fingers digging into her jaw. He turns her face this way and that, and she feels every aching place where David left a bruise. "See? You look okay. Some women who look like you do right now? They tell me they fell down the stairs. You fall down the stairs, Chel?"

She's shaking now, trying hard not to yank her face away as his fingers dig in where a tooth is loose. But he only holds her harder.

"Answer me, Chelsea."

"No."

"No what?"

"No, Officer Huntley, I did not fall down the stairs." Her voice shakes, and she hates that. But what she hates even more is that she's been made to feel this way twice in one night by two different men who should be protecting her.

He lets her go almost as if he's throwing her face away, and she works her jaw, hoping he hasn't made it worse.

"Does David really have the Violence, Chelsea?"

He's talking in that way men do when they're angry and want it to be very clear that they're containing the anger, almost as if it's a favor. He paces the foyer, hands on his hips, one right by his gun. He looks down at a blood spot on the floor, one the other officers took pictures of, and rubs it away with his shoe.

"Well?"

She has to choose her words carefully.

"David was violent. He hurt me. He scared me. I ran into the bathroom and slammed the door before he could do worse." Every word of it is true. Chelsea does not consider herself a good liar.

"Does. He. Have. The. Violence?"

Each word grinds out. It's meant to make Chelsea feel like a little kid in school who's too stupid to produce the easy, obvious answer. But it just makes her angry.

"That's for someone else to decide. My daughter called nine one one because my husband was trying to kill me." She looks up at him, sullen. "Has he ever seemed violent to you, Chad?"

He's been running his fingers over some dents and cracks in the bathroom door—hits from Ella's old softball bat, which they took as evidence—but now his attention jerks back to her. "When I'm on duty, my name is Officer Huntley, and you will respect the badge."

"Is this an official visit, Officer Huntley?"

For a long, long moment, he chews his gum hard, staring daggers, and then smiles brightly, in a studied way, although it doesn't quite touch his eyes.

"Of course not. Just checking up on my buddy's house. And his sweet little wife." He squeezes her upper arm like they're pals and takes a few steps toward the door. "I'll be checking in with my old pal David, make sure he's all right. You and your girls'll want to be careful, though." He hooks his thumbs in his belt loops and looks up at the chandelier. "Three women, alone in the world. Lot of scary things can happen."

"Something scary happened tonight."

Again, that overbright smile. "I'm sure it did. You know, Chel, sometimes people make mistakes."

Now her smile is overbright. "They sure do, Officer Huntley. For years, sometimes. Years and years. Here's to hoping things go right for once. Thanks so much for stopping by. To check in on us." She walks back to the front door and holds it open, still mirroring his smile. "Unless there was anything else? Give Laura my love."

For just a second, he drops the lie, baring his teeth and working his jaw, but then the smile comes back like a mask, and Chelsea realizes that this is a skill he's honed over the last fifteen years as a police officer, that it's simply part of the job. And he's not very good at it. She's just never seen it before because when he comes here, he's with David and their cronies, and no one ever questions their authority.

"And I'll give David yours. I'll be speaking with him shortly."

Chelsea yawns, clumsily covering it with a hand. "Sorry, Officer Huntley. I'm so exhausted. I just hope they can find a cure to this meaningless violence."

He's outside now, on the doorstep. She could slam the door in his face, but that would mean he'd won, wouldn't it?

"We do need a cure," he says, thumb playing over the little snap that holds his gun. "And then we'll see who really needs to apologize."

Chelsea laughs, light and silly, like it's nothing. "I'm guessing the ones who need to apologize won't be the ones with a busted lip, huh? What a crazy world."

"What a crazy world," he echoes. He walks backward off the steps, and right before he leaves the circle of porch lights, he points two fingers at his eyes and then at Chelsea, that old threat.

I'm watching you.

In a fit of what can only be considered suicidal exhaustion, Chelsea rubs at the tenderest bruise on her jaw with her middle finger.

She watches him drive off in his squad car, making a mental note not to speed for the foreseeable future, not to do a single thing that could land her in jail. Seeing goofy little Chad Huntley act like this tonight—it was like watching a terrier suddenly go into attack mode. She'd thought his wife was just boring and stupid, but now she wonders if the poor woman just lives her entire life in fear of what her husband will do if she embarrasses or defies him.

All those years David halfheartedly threatened Chelsea with his "friends on the force," she'd had no idea those friends were exactly the same thing as David.

Predators, hiding in plain sight.

When his taillights have disappeared, she closes the busted-up door, engages the chain, and sets the alarm. With David gone, the house felt safe. But with a brief, five-minute visit, a family friend—a policeman sworn to serve and protect—destroyed that feeling.

Chelsea walks around the house, closing curtains and locking doors and turning off lights. Her phone is still sitting on the bathroom sink. There are two texts. One is from her mother, reminding her to be careful. The other is from David's best friend, Brian. The lawyer.

He's going to take everything, you bitch. I'll see to it.

All the masks, she realizes, are coming off.

But that works both ways, doesn't it?

12.

Ella knows Uncle Chad. She's known him all her life. He's the youngest of her dad's friends and the one who gets into the most trouble when he's been drinking. She saw him smash a beer bottle on his own head once and laugh as he shook off the shards. In the past couple of years, Chelsea's firmly ordered Ella to stay upstairs whenever Dad's friends are over, and Ella has been more than glad to comply. These men she's been told to call Uncle since she was tiny—Uncle Brian, Uncle Chad, Uncle Jimmy, Uncle Gavin—well, she doesn't like the way they look at her now. She hates it when they tell her she's pretty, like she owes them something in return.

She especially hates it when Uncle Chad asks her if she has a boyfriend.

As she listens from the top step, the same old rage rises in her chest. He's so obviously threatening her mom, and he so obviously doesn't care that Dad was straight-up beating her when Ella called 9-1-1. The people who showed up—the Violence Task Force, the EMTs—they all seemed to care. They were kind and moved slowly and spoke softly around the family, like they didn't want to startle anyone. But Uncle Chad sounds like a villain in a movie, and the moment he's gone, Ella lets out a deep breath that she didn't even know she was holding in. At least Brookie is asleep, flopped out across her bed with Olaf curled against her side. At least Brookie didn't have to see what Uncle Chad really is, under his sunglasses.

The door closes, and Mom moves around the house, closing it up tight like they're leaving for vacation. Ella thinks about going downstairs to talk to her, but she doesn't know what to say. It's almost like she's the mom sometimes, like Mom secretly wants her to fix things, or at least do everything that needs to be done to keep Dad from exploding. Ella's life is all about responsibility. For Brooklyn, for Mom, for the babysitting and petsitting jobs she started picking up when she was thirteen because it was easier than asking Dad for money, for her grades and her car and her chores. She's exhausted most of the time, and then when she tries to sleep, it's like her brain won't turn off.

So she goes back to her room and puts the chair that was recently underneath her doorknob back by her desk where it belongs. She fixes her bed where she and Brooklyn mussed it up. She picks up her phone, and—

Holy shit.

Her phone blew up.

There are fifty-seven messages, not to mention hundreds of hits on social media. And most of the messages are from numbers she doesn't even know.

OMG, girl, I'm so sorry.

Forget him. He's a loser.

Bless, queen!

Ah.

Looks like Beth decided to post the recording from the parking lot. And then *everybody* decided to share it.

Ella finds it on YouTube, squinting like it's a horror movie that she has to watch but doesn't really want to see. Damn, Beth's phone is good. The video is crystal clear, and it leaves no doubt whatsoever that Hayden was being a total dick. The way he blocks her door, the way he obviously trips her, the bite of his fingers around her arm, and then . . .

God, he really did hit her hard.

Ella winces, watching it happen. Her fingertips brush her cheek, remembering.

That's enough.

She clicks off the video and scrolls through her texts, wondering how everyone got her number, wondering how she's going to figure out who's interrupting all the pity and sweetness with things like *If you talked that way to me, I'd hit you so hard you couldn't get up* and *Take it, bitch*. Most of it is under the usual anonymous and burner accounts; no one uses their real names for social. The first familiar account she comes across is Lindsey, her science lab partner from last year. *I hope you press charges*, she says, which is sweet but not helpful. Everything is running together. It's just too much.

Ella keeps scrolling until she finds Hayden's name in her texts. His first messages came in before the video hit, back when she was on the phone with 9-1-1. It feels like it happened weeks ago, but it was hours ago.

Baby I'm so sorry.

Please. Let's just talk.

Let's go somewhere private and talk.

Why won't you answer me?

Well fuck you, too.

Baby, please. I didn't mean that. I'm sorry. Let's talk it out.

Circles and circles and circles.

Coaxing, begging, commanding, insulting, apologizing, coaxing again.

And the thing about circles is that you get trapped inside them.

His texts changed when the video hit.

Who'd you tell? Who saw that? Was this a setup?

Tell Beth to take it down. Say it's not what it looks like

It was the Violence I would never do that to you

I was out of control I'm sorry

My mom is freaking out pls baby do something

The police are here

This is on you

Mom told them it's the Violence

They're gonna take me away

You did this

Ella jerks back from the phone as if it could bite her.

Those are the same words her dad said to her mom when he had her by the throat.

You did this.

Ella is totally certain she did not make her boyfriend be an asshole who pushed her around and hit her in the school parking lot. She's very certain her mom didn't make her dad get drunk and beat her. Why is it that when men act out it's always someone else's fault?

She puts her phone down on her bedside table and stares at it. It buzzes, and she picks it back up and disables notifications because at this rate, she'll never get to sleep, and if she does, she'll dream of bees. The messages just keep coming.

This is . . . a lot.

She feels utterly helpless. Can't help her mom. Doesn't know how to respond to anyone in her texts. Can't help Hayden, not that she's sure she wants to.

Can't help herself.

As she curls up in bed, her hand creeps under the pillow, making sure that the knife is still there. Her father is gone, but he's not the only dangerous man in the world. She sleeps lightly, tossing and turning, dreaming of a long, dark tunnel she can't escape.

When her alarm goes off the next morning, she silences it and holds very still, listening in the dark. The house is utterly silent. By this time, Brooklyn is usually already awake, and she and Mom are downstairs chatting over the crunch of cereal and the clink of spoons. But no one is awake, and Ella doesn't really want to go to school today and face . . . everything. Or everybody. So she curls up facing the wall and falls back to sleep almost immediately.

She wakes up again in a patch of sunlight and stretches like it's a lazy Sunday. Now she hears her mom and Brooklyn, and she checks her phone briefly before remembering that it's just a bunch of work. There's a grunt down by her feet, and she finds Olaf looking at her reproachfully, like she's interrupted the world's most important nap. He's so cute for an idiot, snowy white and soft with soulful eyes, and she likes snuggling him as long as he's not covered in piss.

The dog follows her downstairs, and everything smells like lemon cleaner. Mom's done her usual wipe job on the kitchen, hiding any evidence at all that something went wrong last night. The blood splotches are long gone, as are the beer bottles in the recycling bin. Only the marks of the aluminum bat remain, pockmarking the bathroom door and denting the wall beside it. That damage isn't so easily erased. They took the bat away as evidence.

"Morning, honey." Her mom smiles from one of the barstools at the kitchen counter, and Ella pauses. There's something different about her mom besides the fact that her face and neck are mottled with bruises and bandages.

She's . . . relaxed. Her smile is genuine. Ella realizes that for the last several years, her mom has been tense, like a human fist, her shoulders up around her ears and little lines of tension crumpling around her eyes and mouth. But now she looks like a mom in a commercial, like she always looks on their first day at the beach, before Dad starts growling and Brooklyn starts whining. She looks . . . well, if not happy, then as close as she's been in a while.

Ella smiles back, a little tentative. "Hi. How are . . . I mean . . ." God, the right words don't exist. "Are you okay?"

Her mom's fingertips brush her jaw, where the biggest bruise is. "I'll be okay." Her brows scrunch down, the tension back. "How about you? That must've been scary."

Ella's fingers now hover around her own biggest bruise, and she's about to answer honestly when she remembers that her mom doesn't even know what happened to her in the parking lot with Hayden— she lied about that. Her mom is asking something else entirely.

To think: Two huge, earth-shattering, terrifying things happened yesterday, and yet here she is at the breakfast table, pouring a bowl of Cocoa Pebbles. And here the earth is, not shattered, everyone outside their house just going on as usual. Well, except for the new pandemic.

But her mom is asking about last night, and she's waiting for an answer as Brooklyn happily munches and watches a cartoon on her tablet.

"Yeah, it was scary. Dad's never . . . I guess . . . he hasn't done that before, right?"

Mom's eyes flicker to the bathroom door. "No. Not like that."

They both know he's done other things. They've lived through them and watched them happen, and if they've never spoken about it before at length, not really, then now's probably too late.

"How long is he in jail? Or, I mean . . . is he in jail?"

Everything she says sounds like a question, but that's because she has no idea how any of this works. The Lifetime movies show the woman getting abused and fighting back, and then they skip to the part where she's powerful and beautiful and running her own business and finding new love. They don't linger on the day after, when there are new holes in the wall and everyone is waiting to hear bad news.

"I don't actually know." Her mom looks down at her phone. "They said he would go to a county facility. For the Violence. I don't think there's a test yet, but they want to keep these people isolated so it doesn't spread." She doesn't look up as she says it.

And Ella knows why. It's because her mom knows her dad doesn't have the Violence. What she doesn't know is that Ella also knows this because Ella has seen it firsthand and her mother has not.

"So what do we do?"

God, her mom looks so young sometimes. Ella knows she was born when her mom was only twenty, which means she's only thirty-seven now, which is a lot younger than all the other moms at school. Her mom glances around the kitchen as if looking for answers, as if she's lost.

"I don't know. You guys can stay home from school today. Mental health day. Three-day weekend. We'll figure it out by Monday, I guess. We can just . . ." She smiles, and it reaches her eyes. "Chillax."

But it's awkward, the concept of chillaxing. They finish breakfast and put their dishes in the sink, and Olaf eats his food like a fucking weirdo, picking up one piece at a time, dropping it on the floor, and then eating it. He's always done that, and they have no idea why. He's just super inbred, but Brooklyn loves him. When he's finally done eating, Brooklyn picks him up like a baby and carries him over to the couch, where Mom is queuing up a Disney movie from under a cozy blanket. Ella kind of wants to join them; they see these movies in the theater without her, these days, but she never wants to admit that she'd like to come along, too. She pauses near the stairs, hoping for a clear invitation.

"I'll make some popcorn," Brooklyn says, sliding out from under the blanket; she can never sit still. Ella and her mom exchange a look; microwave popcorn is the only thing Brooklyn knows how to cook, and they're not hungry, but it looks like they're about to eat popcorn. Olaf is being a little douche, growling at Mom and lunging like he's trying to attack the remote.

"Ouch! Cut that out, you little—"

Ella is walking over to help when her mother leaps to her feet. Olaf flops off the sofa and scrambles on the floor with a yelp, but Ella's attention is on her mother.

She's—something is wrong.

Ella has seen this look before.

Cold seeps down her spine.

"Mom?"

No answer. Ella is half hidden by the open bathroom door, and she watches, frozen and terrified, as her mother's pinprick eyes focus on the ground at her feet. As if in slow motion, she raises her foot and slams it down. Ella's grateful that she can't see what's happening on the other side of the couch as her mother stomps again and again. The sound is terrible, the snap of bones and the thud of meat. Olaf only gets one whimper out before he goes silent.

"Mommy, is Olaf okay?"

Shit.

Ella was so busy watching her mom that she forgot about her little sister making popcorn in the kitchen on the other side of the room divider. Luckily—luckily? *Luckily?*—her mom is still stomping on what's left of Olaf, so Ella darts around the door, her sock feet slipping on the tiles, and uses the island to propel herself toward Brooklyn. She grabs the little girl with one arm and bolts for the door to the garage, flinging it open and immediately realizing her error.

The garage door is closed.

And her mom has the Violence.

Not like her dad or Hayden, but the actual disease. Whatever it is. The *real* Violence.

The kind that left chunks of brain and skull all over the F hall bathroom.

Ella presses the garage door button, but it catches, because it always catches, and she knows that any moment her mom is going to tire of stomping on the dog and look for something bigger to kill.

"Ella, what's wrong? You're hurting me."

Brooklyn squirms in her grasp, and Ella lets her down easy on her feet. She pushes Brooklyn behind her and grabs for the old rake, stepping backward as the garage door slowly ratchets upward.

"Climb under the garage door and wait for me by the mailbox," Ella says, her voice rough.

"Why? What's going on? Where's Mommy? What's wrong?"

"Just do it!"

"But I'm not supposed to go near the street—"

"Go, Brookie! Now!"

She never raises her voice to her sister, not ever. Brooklyn's voice catches on a little sob of betrayal, and she scurries under the garage door and into the yard. It's a gray day, just a little drizzle, and Ella backs into the rain, holding the rake, waiting for whatever has taken over her mother to run outside, thirsty for blood.

A few moments later, her mom appears, one hand to her head, looking confused.

"Honey, what's going on? What's with the rake? I thought we were going to watch the movie?" Mom stands in the door, her sock feet coated in blood and gore, and crosses her arms over her chest with a little frown. "It got chilly, didn't it?"

"Mom, are you in there?" Ella asks, rake at the ready.

"In where?"

"Are you . . . normal?"

Chelsea chuckles and runs a hand through her hair. "Yeah, why wouldn't I be?"

Ella lets the rake fall to the ground and points at her mother's feet.

13.

Chelsea sits at her perfect kitchen table, staring into her box of Dream Vitality bottles. They were supposed to solve everything. That's what she was promised. For a while, she believed it. But now, there is no sunbeam, no perfect cup of blond coffee, no sense of aspirational perfection overlaid with swoopy, feel-good cursive like in the ads she reposts. No matter what her sales leader tells her to say in the daily email blast, she knows that taking Dream Vitality oils internally and loading her house with their airborne molecules can't stop the Violence. She takes her oils every day, and look at her. Look at what she's done. Nothing can stop the Violence—she knows that now. Hell, it's like she wasn't even there when it happened.

This is the last thing she remembers: She was sitting on the couch under a blanket, holding the remote control, a little bored about seeing the same movie for the fiftieth time but just so happy she could relax, so relieved that David wasn't going to burst in and yell at her or chide her or demand a sandwich. She was fast-forwarding through the ads, and Olaf was being nippy, and then—

Nothing.

She blinked, and then she was standing in the door to the garage, staring at Ella, who was holding a rake like she was about to fight off the monster from a horror movie. And then Chelsea looked down at her feet and saw blood and bits of pink guts, and her first thought was that she'd killed Brooklyn.

Brooklyn, her precious baby, whom she loves more than life.

The relief that flooded her when she saw that it was Olaf made her feel like a sociopath. At least it wasn't one of her daughters.

It was bad, but it could've been so much worse.

No wonder Huntley knew she was bluffing. What's left of the little dog is unrecognizable. If David truly had the Violence, Chelsea now has no doubt that she would be a small, unsightly smear, a red tinge in the grout with a few bleached-blond hairs stuck in it.

She turned around and left Ella in the garage, went to see what sort of mess she'd made. She threw up when she saw what was left of Olaf. There were no words of comfort she could offer Brooklyn, and no child should ever see what was on the living room rug, so she put the blanket over it and sent the girls upstairs. She told Ella to take Brooklyn to her room and lock the door until Chelsea texted her that it was safe to come out.

It will never be safe again, really, but things are relative.

Cleaning up the mess was the first thing she had to do. She'd never felt this guilty, this vulnerable, this helpless. She finally just pushed the couch back and rolled the rug up tightly around the body and the ruined blanket and dragged it out into the garage.

What's happened to her—she has to hide it. And she hopes Brooklyn never finds out what she did, because Ella said she kept her little sister away from the whole thing. Shame burbles up. She can't hug Brooklyn right now, which makes her heart ache, but she also is spared the gargantuan task of facing Brooklyn and answering all of her questions. About what happened, about where Olaf is, about why Mommy won't touch her again and why they couldn't just watch the movie and enjoy some popcorn. The whole time she was tugging the big rug away, hoping nothing damning and bloody fell out of it, the air smelled like hot butter and the movie played in the background, princesses singing about their hopes and dreams in a beautiful world the Violence will never touch.

Next, Chelsea gathered everything she needed to function for a while and dragged it all into the master suite. She brought in her laptop, David's laptop, his pile of mail and his bag and all his files that aren't locked up, her phone, tons of chargers, the man cave mini-fridge, all the food she knows her girls won't touch. She went through her closets and bathroom and cleaned out everything that could be used as a blunt-force weapon, all the way down to her hair dryer and all her pumps with the pointy heels. There's a big pile of garbage bags in the garage on top of the rug, and her bedroom looks like the world's coziest jail cell, all puffy duvet and throw pillows, no bedside tables or scale or mirror. They say that scientists around the world are working around the clock to understand the Violence, and until they figure it out, she has no choice but to go into hiding in her own home.

With David gone and the real Violence in her blood, there's nothing else she can do. If she turns herself in, her kids will have nowhere to go—except her mother's house, and there's no way Chelsea will let that happen. She has no sisters, no cousins, no close friends, no one she trusts enough to make any decisions for her girls, not when the world is working the way it should and definitely not in the midst of a mystery pandemic that's making the entire government seem pointless. She'll have to figure out how to set the kids up to do remote learning again before Monday. Plenty of people have stopped sending their kids to school, Ella tells her. So now she'll do her parenting through a sturdy door.

No one knows what triggers the Violence. No one knows how it's transmitted. She has to be there for her girls while firmly physically separated from them. They must stay together, but they must stay apart.

What she needs is a plan, and in order to make a plan she has to do a thing that David has always told her was unforgivable: She has to snoop. She needs to know where their money is and how to access it, because her account is almost drained and David isn't here to top it off. She needs to know if he ever bothered to add her name on the mortgage like he promised he would. She has to figure out how to keep paying for electricity and water and Wi-Fi and insurance, because without those things they're all fucked.

She stands, running a hand over the solid wood of the kitchen table, her French-manicured nails dragging over the grain. This table made her so happy, once. It was expensive and sturdy and perfect and real in a way past tables weren't. Now it means nothing, and she can imagine a more honest sort of apocalypse in which she's healthy and trustworthy and strong, hacking the table to bits with an ax to burn as fuel. But this is no zombie outbreak, no nuclear fallout, no meteor or volcano that claimed the dinosaurs. This isn't a cut-and-dried situation, an us-versus-them, live-or-die, end-of-the-world scenario. This is mass confusion with constant nonsense mumbles from the president about caution and preparedness and how nothing is really wrong except that part where the stock market dropped a thousand points after some trader on the floor killed the man next to him with his bare hands.

What will happen, she thinks, if she's overcome with the Violence while utterly alone? It's known that those suffering focus on a living target and beat it to death in the most brutal, hands-on way possible. No guns. Just bottles of salad dressing and wastebaskets and staplers and fists. Will she catch herself in the bathroom mirror and bash her own head in? Will she break through the big, arched window in her bedroom and jump out to go hunting for prey?

That's one of the oddest things about this disease, or whatever it is—no one who suffers it remembers it, and no one with them generally survives.

For a moment, she stares at her beautiful nails and her beautiful table, thinking about how useless beauty is when you're just trying to survive, but then she remembers that no one knows how this disease is spread. Her girls could already be infected. She could be leaving germs all over the table, all over everything she's touched or breathed on. She snatches back her hand and hurries to her room, shutting the door and locking it with grim finality.

I'm locked in my room, she texts Ella. *Wear a mask. Don't let Brooklyn downstairs until you've hit everything with sanitizing wipes and turned up the AC. I could be contagious.*

k, Ella texts back. *how do we make sure you can't get out?*

Chelsea considers the door. The person on the inside can put a chair under the doorknob—she showed Ella that trick a while back, a thought that now floods her with shame. She should've done something about David a long time ago, but that's an easy thought when the thing has been done and the fear isn't pressing down like a boot on your neck. But to keep someone *inside* a room?

Barricade me in, she texts. *Couch, chairs, table. Whatever you can drag over.*

k. love you.

Love you, too.

As tentative footsteps stutter down the stairs and the quiet shushing of disinfecting wipes moves around the kitchen, Chelsea starts opening the mail, looking for answers. Looking for something, anything she can control.

14.

Patricia places the perfectly rolled cocktail dress in her suitcase, nestling it carefully between two cashmere cardigans. Sure, she could give Rosa a list and have her do the packing, but she knows that even with the sternest reminder, Rosa won't do it as neatly as she will. These things don't belong to Rosa, so of course Rosa wouldn't give them the attention that they deserve. This dress costs more than they pay Rosa in a month, but Rosa doesn't care.

Just now, Rosa doesn't really care about anything. She's leaving food in the disposal to rot, ignoring streaks on the windows, letting blooms fall to the yard and turn brown. It will be good for her to be alone for a while, and it will be pleasant for Patricia to be somewhere she won't have to watch her housekeeper sulk. Ever since the police dragged Miguel away, the whole house has felt like a funeral.

It's no way to live.

"Any word, Mrs. Lane?" Rosa asks, peeking in nervously from the hall.

She's lost weight, Patricia notices, and it will serve her well once she gets her cheerful attitude back.

"I'm afraid not," she responds, rearranging things in her suitcase so she won't have to see the tears in Rosa's eyes. "The judge still doesn't know where he's being held. We'll let you know the moment we hear anything."

"Thank you. I worry for him. I just . . . we've never been apart . . ." Patricia looks up sharply, and Rosa cuts herself off. "Thank you, Mrs. Lane." She scurries away, and Patricia sighs and zips the suitcase shut.

She can't wait to leave, can't wait to be somewhere fun again, somewhere people still go shopping and out to dinner without wearing masks and acting terrified when anyone gets too close. They don't know much about the Violence yet, but they do know one thing for certain: It's only happening in tropical places. Any incidences up north can be easily traced back to travelers who've recently come from sunny climes. Dr. Baird suggested that if they wanted to get out, they should hurry before the airlines get picky about that sort of thing. And so they're headed to Deer Valley in Utah, where Randall will see her installed in a luxurious suite and enjoy a long weekend of golf and hot toddies before heading back to the office next week. She may stay a week, she may stay a month. Who knows? So much is up in the air just now.

She almost calls Rosa back to roll all her cases to the foyer, but, honestly, Rosa is exhausting right now. Of course they don't know exactly where Miguel is, but Randall knows he's not in a county holding facility. Like so many immigrants, Miguel has disappeared, and he may resurface one day in Mexico, but then again, maybe he won't. It's an ugly system, but there's nothing they can do, even if they were willing to spend the bribe money to find him. And Patricia will not be the person to tell Rosa that, and so she'd like very much to be out of Rosa's presence.

She is also not unaware that if Rosa, like her husband, has the Violence, she herself is at risk of being brutally beaten to death. Rosa is a much larger woman, and Patricia has felt more comfortable out of her orbit these past few days. With Randall at the office from dawn until dusk, the women are often alone in the house together. Over the past ten years, Patricia has gotten into the habit of ignoring the help, but that's hard to do when the help feels like a looming threat.

There's a list downstairs of everything that will need taking care of while they're out of town. Rosa will have extra duties, with Miguel gone, and Oscar can help pick up the slack. The Lanes travel frequently, so this is old hat.

Soon the town car will come, and Randall will hold open the door for her, and she'll climb daintily inside and accept whatever wine he offers her, and it will taste like blessed relief.

There's no reason to stay behind when Florida feels like the epicenter of the pandemic, the beating heart of the Violence, where it began and where it continues to spread and kill. With her friends likewise fleeing and the auction on hold, there's no excuse to remain. What's the point of Randall's millions if they can't avail themselves of an escape?

When she considers whether she's forgotten anything, not a single thing comes to mind.

She has to get out while she can.

She has to take care of herself.

PART II

15.

Days pass, then weeks, then months. Chelsea feels like she's twenty years older. Her bruises heal and her teeth tighten back up in her jaw, just like the EMTs promised. She orders groceries online and watches movies with the girls on FaceTime and texts constantly with Ella and orders workbooks with David's Amazon account to keep Brooklyn occupied. It's a relief when school ends and Chelsea no longer has to direct the girls' remote learning from the other side of a door. Ella's grades fall, but she has the credits she needs for when the pandemic subsides. Together they decide to keep Brooklyn on the same schedule but call it Learning Camp—she needs the routine, and they need to keep her occupied.

Stuck in her bedroom, Chelsea is bored and exhausted and anxious. She has her own daily schedule to keep from going insane that includes yoga, online aerobics, walking on her treadmill, and strength exercises with a towel around the doorknob. Exercise makes her feel conflicted—she needs it for her mental health, but she hates that in getting stronger, she makes herself a more dangerous predator for the sickness hiding inside her.

She doesn't think she's had another flare of the Violence, but she hasn't been tempted to venture beyond her room and act like things are back to normal, either. She would give everything in the world to feel Brooklyn's weight in her lap, but she loves her baby too much to risk it.

According to the internet, things are bad outside and only getting worse. As spring moves into summer, the disease has spread well beyond Florida, popping up in other states, clustered around the South. It's in other places around the world, Brazil and Vietnam and Nigeria. Someone finally connected the dots and figured out that it's spread by mosquitoes—hence why it's in all the hot places—but they don't yet know what triggers the violent outbursts. Most sufferers have their first attack shortly after being infected, but after that, it's anyone's guess. With the return of the same bumbling politicians who botched the Covid response, everything is being mishandled and sometimes even touted as fake news, especially in places where mosquitoes can't spread the sickness. It turns out that most people still want freedom more than communal safety. The smartest thing to do, for the infected and uninfected alike, is to stay home.

Chelsea's worry now is that she'll become symptomatic near her daughters, not that she'll give them the disease. She orders their food online, has it delivered, and grabs what she needs while the girls are locked in Ella's room. Once a week or so, they order pizza, which is left on the doorstep. It feels a lot like the early days of Covid, except that no one is posting about dolphins in the Italian canals or the lifting of smog over the LA freeway. Nature is not returning, not in that sweet, touchy-feely way. This is the dog-eat-dog sort of nature, and everyone is still too exhausted from the first pandemic to be altruistic and kind.

Her mother sends obnoxious emails about how the Violence is a hoax, and then how it's real, then how she's at a spa in Utah, and lastly how she's home briefly but will soon be jetting off for Europe. Patricia doesn't ask any questions about how they're doing, so Chelsea doesn't have to lie. She can only assume that with as much money as her mother has, she can buy her way out of any real problems.

Her own money is getting short, but Chelsea hasn't told Ella that. She has some cash—basically useless now since she can't leave the house—what little is left in the bank account, and David's secret emergency credit card. Since her name isn't on it, she doesn't care about maxing it out. Every time she clicks the ORDER button online, she waits for that card to be rejected. Their main credit card is already shut down.

Because that's the thing: As far as she can tell, they really are broke.

Apparently David made some investments, and they didn't turn out so well. Their savings are drained and their main checking account is only barely afloat because David had amassed so many vacation hours that his work has to keep paying him while he's on leave, plus the payments are on a two-week delay. Chelsea suspects the most recent paycheck that landed was the last one she can count on. David is still gone, and she has no idea where he is or when he might return. She dug that business card out of the trash and called the number to find out, but all she got was a recorded message about how the system is overburdened and families will be contacted as information is available.

Each long day that passes is one day closer to David coming home.

As she's yet again trying to guess the password on his laptop, the doorbell rings, and the house goes silent.

Pull back the barricade, go upstairs and lock yourselves in your room, Chelsea texts Ella.

k, her daughter texts back.

The couch and chairs and tables outside her door scrape away one by one, and then footsteps patter up the stairs. Ella texts her, *we're in here.*

Chelsea looks in the bathroom mirror. She's a mess. She's still showering, but she's not doing her hair or makeup, and she pulled off her gel nails, leaving a ragged pink mess. Her bruises faded weeks ago and her cuts healed, but she's grown accustomed to the feeling of not being looked at. She's in her house uniform, yoga pants and a hoodie. Seeing the cop car in the driveway through her bedroom window, she assumes it's Huntley. Funny that she could spend her entire life being good, following rules, driving the speed limit, hands at ten and two, and now she's going to have to lie to a woman-hating cop who'd love nothing more than to destroy her life for sending her abuser to jail.

The doorbell rings again, twice, a little pissy, and she slips her phone in her pocket and hurries to push past the door and out into the living room. Not that having her phone is going to help her—Chad *is* the police, and he knows all the local officers, and according to the internet dialing 9-1-1 doesn't always get a response these days. Everyone's just too busy with too many emergencies.

"Took you a while there, Chel," Huntley says when she opens the front door. It's still all busted around the locks that no longer function, but it's not like she has the money to get it fixed. Ella is supposed to put a kitchen chair under the knob every night. A chair, a chain, and the security system are all that stand between Chelsea's girls and whatever new horror the world might send their way.

Chelsea steps outside and softly closes the door behind her, hoping he won't come inside and see the wreck the girls have made of the house and the huge pile of damning junk outside her own bedroom door. The barricade the girls built is pretty pathetic, but they all know that if Chelsea tries to break through it, the girls are supposed to run and not stand around to check out the success of their handiwork.

"Can't be too careful these days," she responds.

Huntley smiles big around his cinnamon gum, showing his bright white teeth. "No, you can't."

His frown quickly returns, and his sunglasses show twin images of her, looking lean and frazzled. And angry. She tries to make her features settle into the gentle smile she developed to placate David. Not big enough to seem like she harbors thoughts of superiority, not small enough to make her seem ungrateful. Soft. Compliant.

"So I've got good news. Took me a long time to find him, but David's in a county facility. I been keeping an eye on him, making sure they're taking care of him, and he's doing fine. In case you're worried." He pauses, chewing his gum like cud, waiting for a kowtowing response.

"Of course I'm worried. I'm so glad he's okay. Thanks for checking up on him. No one else has contacted me—"

"Naw, we're a little too busy trying to save lives to have little chit-chats. But here's that good news I was talking about. There's finally a test for the Violence, and a truck full of test kits is gonna show up any day this week, and David's one of the first people on the list to get swabbed. If he doesn't have it, I'll be bringing him home myself."

Chelsea's stomach drops to somewhere around her feet, and she feels numb and woozy but fights through it. "Well, that's great news!"

Even she can hear that the exclamation point at the end is a lie. Huntley looks gratified at her lack of enthusiasm, like it's just confirming what he already knows about her—that she's a shitty wife.

"So you'll be real glad to see him, huh?"

"Of course!"

But what she's really thinking is that if there is a God, he'll let the Violence strike her now and punish this bullying little shit for showing up to make her impossible life even harder. Because he expects a victim of domestic violence to kiss the feet of the man who abuses her instead of being grateful every day that he's gone. The only reason she's playing along is because Chad can take her away for any reason, plant drugs on her or say she got violent or Violent, which would leave her girls all alone.

"And he's getting vaccinated, too," Chad says as if he's remarking on the weather.

Chelsea's head jerks up, and Huntley smiles smugly at finally having her full attention.

"Vaccinated? There's a vaccine?"

"Oh, yeah. You haven't heard? They announced it this morning. Big press conference. Some college kid figured it out. Price is crazy high and only selling to rich people right now, but Brian's covering the cost. You know, our good friend Brian—David's lawyer? He's been building a case, too. Talking to our people at the lab, looking at evidence, all that. It'll be real interesting if David doesn't have the Violence, won't it? One of these days, when the truth is out there, it's gonna be a crime to turn someone in for the Violence if they don't have it."

"A man attacked me with a baseball bat," Chelsea starts, her voice wobbling.

"A little girl's softball bat," Huntley corrects. "And he didn't hit you with it, did he? He says he went for it *after* you locked yourself in the bathroom and started telling tales. People with the Violence don't do that. They don't leave their prey and run off to get weapons."

"They don't run off to get bigger weapons to inflict more damage, huh? So what kind of person *does* do that?"

With his sunglasses on, she can't tell if he's staring at her, can't tell what he's thinking. She just sees that tight, stubbled jaw working at the pink gum, the now nauseating scent of cinnamon rising in the heat of the afternoon.

"It'll be real interesting," he repeats. "Take care, Chel."

"Will do, Officer Huntley."

She watches him saunter to his car and look over her yard with a frown like he's a big, important man who doesn't approve. The yard is overgrown now, as they don't have money to pay the landscaper, but the HOA letters stacking up are the least of her concerns. As she looks up and down the street, she's not the only one. Plenty of yards are ragged, one house is half burned down and abandoned, and one flower garden has an upside-down car settled in the center of it. Nobody really wants to be outside like a sitting duck for Violence sufferers and Violence-carrying mosquitoes, so anyone doing outdoor work has raised their prices significantly to cover for the added risk.

From what she's been reading online, the economy is changing, almost like Covid on steroids. No one is going to restaurants anymore, so the restaurants that want to stay open are doing a steady delivery service. Online business is brisk, and almost everything gets delivered in brown boxes or specialized grocery bags by desperate people in branded T-shirts. The mom-and-pop stores in the cool areas downtown are closing up due to a lack of foot traffic. Rich people like her mother are fleeing north, hoping for fewer mosquitoes, or barricading themselves in behind fences and walls and gates in their tropical paradises, going to ground in their mosquito-sprayed compounds and hiring guards and having their prescriptions delivered by drones. Everyone has to adapt or die.

And that's what Chelsea has to do, too, because she can't be here when David gets home. Either he'll kill her or he'll take the girls and throw her out, and if he finds out she has the Violence, he'll take immense joy in the process of sending her to her own government facility and knowing she won't pass the test and receive the gift of vaccination from a friend.

There's only one thing she can think to do, and . . . God, she doesn't fucking want to do it.

She goes back inside, back into the stale room where she's lived a tortured, fearful, truncated life for the past few weeks to keep her girls safe. Funny, how her gilded cage got even smaller. She takes a long shower, fetches the blow dryer from the garage to smooth her hair, does her makeup. Even puts on pastels and nice sandals, glad that she's been keeping her toenails painted in all the non-red colors that David hates.

You and Brooklyn need to shower and get dressed nice, she texts Ella.

We're going to visit Nana.

16.

Patricia sits at the breakfast table with Randall, poking at Rosa's attempt at an egg-white omelet as her husband rambles on about their plans. Oh, how she misses the food at the lodge.

She absentmindedly rubs the top of her arm, hating that she's going to have another scar to rival the clumsy one from the smallpox vaccine when she was a little girl. Randall's longtime physician, Dr. Baird, showed up at the house a few days ago to administer the vaccine for the Violence—they chartered a jet from Utah to get it as soon as possible. Patricia knows she should be grateful that Randall is so wealthy and well connected that they were able to receive the vaccination before the rest of the world even knew about it, but . . . well, honestly. A scar. And the ID card with her vaccine number printed on it has absolutely the worst photo of her she's ever seen. She looks like she's seventy and has jaundice in it.

"Are you even listening, Patricia?" Randall asks, sounding like a schoolteacher with a wayward and annoying student.

"You were saying we'll have Rosa vaccinated," she parrots.

Randall nods and squints, his jowls waggling and his belly dangling between his knees as he leans over. No one loves a breakfast steak like the judge, even if it's been clumsily cooked to leather.

"That's right. Only way to keep the help around without getting attacked. We pay for her vaccination, and in return she signs an ironclad contract committing her to ten years of service. With Miguel infected and sent off to wherever, she'll jump at the chance." He smiles fondly at her. "You did good, sugar, calling the hotline when you did and getting him off the property."

Patricia smiles tightly and nods. Making the call was a lot easier than watching Rosa afterward, crying on the ground and muttering in Spanish and beating her fist on the perfectly cut grass. She'd hoped Rosa would come to terms with her loss and cheer up while they were gone, but instead she's been in an even deeper sulk since they returned, which is preposterous—while they were in Utah, she had *so* little to do. And when Randall flew back and forth for work, he stayed at the hotel downtown by the courthouse, so it's not like Rosa had to take care of him. But now, even her food tastes sad. The omelet is inedible. Patricia pushes it away and focuses on her bowl of fresh berries. One of the raspberries slips off her fork and falls to the shelf of her cleavage. She fusses with it, her mind elsewhere, and ends up with a bright-red streak of berry juice across her white silk shell.

Randall watches her, one eyebrow up. He's not a handsome man, and he's been steadily gaining weight the whole time they've been married, but he could be called distinguished in the right light and he's surprisingly fastidious about his wardrobe and toilette. Fifteen years older than her and richer than God, with fingers in every pie downtown and friends tucked away in every position of power, he's a man so well known that all she has to do is mention the judge and she gets whatever she wants, from tables at the best restaurants with complimentary champagne to a policeman's tipped cap as she drives away from what would've been a speeding ticket. Being married to Randall makes everything easy.

Well, everything except living with him.

"And I'm the one who will deliver this news to Rosa?" she asks as she inspects the stain.

"Of course. You handle the help. That's your job. And I'll handle my job." He leans over and dabs at her bosom with his napkin, fussy and in no way sexual. He's never come to her for such things; that's what secretaries are for. "Sugar, that's gonna stain. You should be more careful with silk."

He gets up for more coffee, and Patricia's rouged cheeks flush hot. She remembers another stain, bright red against stark white, another time she was told to be more careful. She didn't know what it was at the time, didn't even know it had happened. She was getting ready for church on Easter morning as a girl, and the tiny rented millhouse was already hot for spring, and her mother called her over and made her spin around to check that she looked good enough for the upcoming service.

"What the hell is that?" Mama barked, skinny hands on her hips in a plaid dress she'd found at the thrift store in the nicer next town over.

Patricia—Patty back then—had no idea what she'd done wrong but was already shrinking into herself. It was better when Mama didn't notice her at all.

"I don't know." She looked back over her shoulder but didn't see anything, and when Mama marched her over to the long, cracked mirror, she saw the red splotch on the back of her special dress, the one they'd bought new since she was in the Easter pageant. "Did I sit on something?"

She did feel a bit sweaty down there, but that was nothing new, as they had no air-conditioning and the day was already in the eighties with all the windows closed. She tried to think of what she could've sat on that was that color, but there was nothing in the house, not even ketchup, and—oh Lord.

"Is that blood? Am I dying?"

She hurried to the house's only bathroom, closed the door and pulled down her underwear, and found yet more blood, everywhere, everywhere, starting to dribble down her legs. She dabbed at herself, but that was bloody, too.

"Mama, I'm dying!" she shrieked through the door.

"You're not dying, stupid. It's your monthly."

"My monthly what?"

Because no one had ever told Patty about menstruation, had they?

There she was, crying in the nicest dress she'd ever owned, now ruined, and she thought she must be dying, her blood leaking out of her like she'd been stabbed.

"It'll happen once a month until you get knocked up. If it stops, you're knocked up. Don't you get knocked up, Patty! Only bad girls do that. Now take off that dress and put on this one and let's go. You got to be more careful."

Patty had so many questions, but Mama was always in a bad mood, and this one was worse than usual. She couldn't get the dress off without help, so she opened the door and turned her back. Mama's quick fingers undid the fake-pearl buttons, and Patty kept her back to her mother as she slipped off the ruined dress. Mama took it and shoved an old tweed sheath dress and a new pair of underwear through the door.

"There's rags under the sink. Fold one into thirds and put it in your pants," Mama said. "Goddammit. Ruined this dress. Do you know what it cost?"

"Yes," she'd murmured under her breath as she followed Mama's directions and emerged looking frumpy and rumpled in the itchy, heavy dress that was made for an older, taller, curvier woman, waddling with her legs clenched together as she tried to get used to the bulge of cloth. "What about the Easter pageant?"

Mama looked at her, disgusted, the cigarette dangling from her dry lips. "Pageant's for little girls, and you're not a little girl anymore. You're a woman now, full of sin. So you'll just sit in back and don't mess up that dress, too." Then she leaned close and poked a bony finger into Patty's chest to punctuate her words. "A woman, so you'd better get used to it. No more playing around. Don't be a whore, or I'll kick you out." She leaned even closer. "And don't you dare start looking at my dates. Just keep your goddamn mouth shut and do what you're told."

Everything had changed that day because of one unexpected stain. Patty had not, in fact, been a whore, but she had taken Mama's words to heart. She'd kept her goddamn mouth shut, she'd done what she was told, and she'd been fine, right up until four years later when the preacher's son told her to do something else she didn't expect, something else she didn't really understand, and that knocked her up. Even then, she kept her mouth shut. Because that was what good girls did.

"Did you hear me, Patricia?"

She looks up. Randall is staring at her, and she shakes her head and smiles at him. "Lost in fond memories, I'm afraid. Remember that lovely little hotel in Paris?"

"Yes, sugar, but I was talking about Iceland," he says with cloying patience. "Got to get away from all these fools and skeeters in the hot weather. Just because we're vaccinated doesn't mean they are, and Utah's warming up. Paris is, too. Now that court's all virtual again, we're free to head on out. We leave next week. All the boys are going. And their wives," he adds, almost an afterthought. "I'll have Diane email you a shopping list. Coats and all that. Probably best to do it online. If Rosa signs, she'll stay here and hold down the fort, like usual."

"And if she doesn't sign?"

He lifts one meaty shoulder. "Can't make her do it, I reckon. But she knows we've got her over a barrel. Undocumented, all that unfortunate mess. There'll be plenty of people willing to sign papers to get that vaccine. Can't believe they found a loophole to keep it privately owned so they can charge so damn much. I've been working up all sorts of contracts, you know—for companies willing to offer vaccines in return for service. Folks are gonna be desperate for it, for themselves and their kids. Vaccine's thirty thousand dollars right now. Most folks these days have never seen that much money in one go. Idiots."

Patricia huffs a little sigh, remembering a time when she'd never seen that much money in one go, never bought groceries without running the numbers in her head and putting something back after the cashier had rung it up. By the time she met Randall, she'd dropped Patty like a cicada shell and become the far more vibrant Patricia, and he doesn't know about that part of her past. They've simply never discussed it. They're not actually that interested in each other as people, but they both need something the other can provide. She makes his life beautiful and easy and respectable, and he provides the money for her to make that happen. And she also looks away when he hires, fires, and woos endless young brunette secretaries, like twenty-two-year-old Diane, who'll be sending an email later with an annoying and somehow knowing smiley face at the end of it.

Randall places a folder on the breakfast table, points to the signature tab with one fat finger. "It's all marked where she needs to sign."

It looks a lot like the endless, ironclad prenup she had to sign herself, but she nods amicably. "Of course, Randall. I'll take care of it."

He pats her on the head like a dog. "Good girl. You got the flowers, didn't you?"

He sends her so many bouquets that she forgets which one is in which room.

Oh yes. The sunny-yellow tulips in the powder room.

"Yes. So cheerful. So thoughtful."

"Sugar, I'm sure you understand I'll be more busy than usual, once we get to Iceland. The world is changing around us, and the law itself is having to change with it. Damn inconvenience, this Violence business."

A *damn inconvenience.*

That's the same phrase he uses when the neighbors' gardener uses a leaf blower before noon on a Sunday. She smiles up at him and nods agreement, feeling like one of those stupid dolls Brooklyn wanted for Christmas, a plastic thing that blinks and talks and wets itself and, thanks to technology, takes basic orders. Stand up. Sit down. Say mama.

As if any child ever were that biddable. Chelsea certainly wasn't, and her older granddaughter is following in those same rebellious footsteps. Brooklyn, at least, is reasonable and does exactly what she's told.

"Have a good day, sweetheart," she calls as he waddles out the door.

"You have a good day, too, sugar. Stop dabbing at that stain and just order yourself a new blouse."

There is no discussion of love or even fondness. There never has been. It's probably better this way.

As soon as Randall's car is gone and the garage door closed, Patricia changes her blouse and picks up the contract he left on the table. As she walks out to the pool house, she notices the yard isn't quite as nice as usual; Miguel may take his time, but he's very thorough, whereas his son, Oscar, does things quick and sloppy. The boy isn't here now, at least. Every time he's seen Patricia since Miguel was taken away, the boy has glared daggers at her and muttered in Spanish under his breath.

Their backyard is large and beautiful, but it's noisier than it used to be. The mosquito trucks seem to run day and night, and drones buzz erratically overhead as they deliver prescriptions and light sundries. That's one of the benefits of being wealthy and living in an enclave like this during such a dangerous time—very few strangers can get past the gate, and the rules around deliveries now are stricter than ever.

She gives Rosa the courtesy of knocking on the door of her own pool house and hears movement within. She doesn't often come out here, preferring to give the help their own space, but it seems like a gesture of trust, meeting Rosa on her own ground instead of commanding her to appear in the big house via text.

"Mrs. Lane?" Rosa blinks in the bright light, her tight bun coming undone. Once husky, she now looks gaunt and gray, her polo shirt hanging off her shoulders.

"Might we speak? I have an exciting offer for you."

Rosa nods and steps outside, closing the door behind her. Patricia caught the quickest glance inside, and the space is torn apart and messy, completely unacceptable. But now is not the time to mention it.

"Judge Lane has drawn up a contract for you." Patricia hands Rosa the papers, noting the woman's ragged nails and torn cuticles. "There's a vaccination for the Violence, and we'd like to provide it for you."

English is not Rosa's first language, but she's competent enough. Her brow draws down as she flips through the contract, touching a line here and there with a fingertip.

"What about Miguel?"

"That's out of our purview, I'm afraid. We were able to shelter him here as long as no one knew, but we can't get him back, not with the courts like they are now."

Rosa clears her throat and points at the contract. "Servitude for a period of ten years, and then you will *consider* helping me become a citizen?"

Patricia peeks over Rosa's shoulder. She didn't see that part.

"Yes. The judge will do everything he can—"

"He told us that five years ago, and he has done nothing."

Rosa goes quiet, and Patricia can feel her rage, building like thunder.

So this is why Randall gave her this job. Because it's not a pleasant one when the contract isn't fair.

Patricia knows what it feels like, signing one of Randall's contracts.

"Well, if you sign here, you'll have it in writing—"

"Mrs. Lane, *consider* is not worth signing my life over. I will sign only if you change it. Five years, and you will sponsor me for citizenship. Miguel, too, if he returns."

"You know I don't have that power, Rosa," Patricia says, softening her voice. "But I can guarantee you employment and protect you from this horrible illness—"

"No, Mrs. Lane. No. This contract does not *employ* me. It is slavery. There is no mention of payment. What is the cost of this vaccination?"

Patricia steps back a little. "Around thirty thousand dollars."

"Ten years. For thirty thousand dollars. That is three thousand dollars a year, Mrs. Lane. And that is no life. What about sick days? Vacation? Food? Clothes?"

"It says uniforms and basic necessities will be provided . . ."

Rosa roughly closes the folder and hands it back to her. "Slavery," she hisses. "I know you think I am stupid, but I am not that stupid. No, thank you."

Much to Patricia's surprise, Rosa goes into the pool house—Patricia's own pool house!—and slams the door in her face.

All the way back into the big house, she isn't sure how to feel. Fury with Rosa at her ingratitude or fury at Randall for asking her to deliver papers that apparently offer little more than modern-day slavery.

Most of all, she's angry at herself. She has failed them both.

17.

Ella hates this baby-blue—ugh, prairie dress?—but her mother in-sisted. They're dressed up like it's Nana's yearly Easter brunch, Ella's hair blown out soft and shining and Brooklyn dolled up in her favorite pink dress with ribbons in her curls.

"What are we doing?" Ella asks as they pile into the car.

Her mom looks so nice that she's beginning to feel nervous, and she was already nervous because at any moment her mother could go crazy and try to kill one of them or crash the minivan into oncoming traffic. So whatever they're doing, it must be really important. Mom hasn't left her room in over two months—not without making the girls go upstairs and lock themselves in. And she knows how Ella feels about her grandmother.

"We're going to visit Nana," Mom says with a creepy calm.

"Yeah, you keep saying that, but you won't tell us why."

"Because it's the right thing to do."

In the back of Ella's mind, some dark part of her unfurls and stretches out feelers like a spider testing life beyond the shadows and wonders if Chelsea is hoping she'll go all Violent on Nana and end . . . whatever their relationship is. It's obvious they hate each other, and Ella's pretty sure her grandmother stopped liking her and possibly even loving her when she was old enough to say no to the dresses and ribbons and speak her mind. She doesn't even know if Nana is okay, much less if she's been checking in with Mom, but probably not. Most likely Nana hasn't thought about them at all.

The past couple of months have been fucking terrible, actually. Ella's entire life has shrunk down to doing busywork, teaching her sister, babysitting her sister, feeding her sister, cleaning the house, scanning the internet for updates on the Violence, and reading Hayden's long emails from the county holding facility. They took his phone, but they let the guests—not inmates, not infected, but *guests*— use a makeshift library once a day if they behave well during their manual labor, and he apparently makes a beeline to send her emails, for some reason. He doesn't apologize anymore or make excuses or whatever. He just tells her about his day, even though she never answers. Like she's his fucking diary.

Again, like she's just . . . a thing.

A vessel for his thoughts, a witness to his ongoing suffering.

Hayden is housed with other boys ages five to seventeen in the abandoned shell of an old Kmart. They have army cots and mildewy Goodwill blankets, and they have to do all the work to maintain their life on their own, from cooking and cleaning to taking care of the younger kids. Almost every day, the older kids get bussed out to pick up trash or clean public buildings. There are guards in camo with huge guns, but nobody really talks to the boys at all unless someone comes down with a case of the Violence. Then, according to Hayden, the National Guard guys run in and yank the afflicted away from whoever he's trying to kill and put him in what's basically a giant dog kennel. Hayden says it looks like something from that first Hannibal movie. If the kid in question can't chill, they shoot him with tranqs, and then he sleeps it off and wakes up confused. It hasn't happened to Hayden yet, because as they both know, he doesn't have the Violence.

The whole thing is more like a bad boarding school than a hospital, and Hayden is stuck taking care of these younger kids and cleaning toilets. Ella is grimly amused by the fact that because of the Violence, she can no longer earn money babysitting while Hayden is forced to babysit for free—plus his charges occasionally go totally feral on him. One little six-year-old tried to bash his brains in with a dictionary. He used to make fun of her for having to do so much for Brooklyn—and yes, she's with Brooklyn 24/7 now—but maybe Hayden is finally beginning to understand what it's like, actually having responsibilities.

Ella doesn't really care what Hayden is going through, but she is slightly interested in the whole setup, since her mom legit has the Violence and her dad is supposedly in another county facility. She can't believe Hayden is even getting these messages out, but then again, he likes to call himself a hacker, and he once got into the school system and anonymously sent everyone an email of the nudes he found on the now ex-principal's server, without getting caught.

She also can't help wondering if her dad also has access to a computer, and if so, if he's been talking to Mom. Mom hasn't said anything about it, but then again, she's been locked in her room for months. He hasn't sent Ella anything, but why would he? They're not close. They don't talk. He doesn't even know her email address, and she blocked him on Facebook two years ago when she posted a happy, innocent beach pic in her bikini with Olivia and Sophie and he gave her a drunken lecture on not being a slut. Either way, Hayden probably hacked something like an idiot who doesn't understand that when you're under government quarantine during a weird pandemic, you shouldn't hack shit, especially not to talk to someone who's glad you're gone.

The trip to Nana's is weird. There aren't many cars on the road, not since everyone realized that people who have a Violence flare while they're driving tend to purposefully ram other vehicles at full speed. The schools are closed for summer now, and most of the rich and wannabe rich people have driven up north to cold places where mosquitoes can't live. Ella read an article online about how prices for hotel rooms, rentals, and homes in cooler climates have skyrocketed, and it's almost impossible to find an open bed north of the Mason-Dixon Line now. The only people left in the hot, humid South are those who can't afford to leave and those who live behind strong fences—and, she figures, people who have the Violence and are hiding it by avoiding the public. Considering her family is still down here and her mom harps on her to keep the AC at seventy-four and turn off the lights in empty rooms, she's starting to think they might be among those who have money problems.

They get caught at a red light even though not a single car is waiting to turn. Ella's in the back with Brooklyn, and directly ahead of the car is a little building she's never noticed before because she's usually either driving or checking her texts at the light. It's a small yellow house, maybe the size of a large bathroom, and the big sign on the roof says BIG FRED'S FLOORS. A scrolling digital sign is shouting something about how what women really want is new carpet, but that's not nearly as eye-catching as the splotch of red on the other side of the front door. It's at head height and in a big . . . splurt. What looks like a body in a plaid shirt is slumped on the ground underneath it, a concrete block resting where the head should be.

Mom must see it, too, as she guns it and runs the red light. Good. Ella didn't want to look at the little yellow house with its plaid-covered lump for another moment. Luckily Brooklyn is directly behind Mom's seat and totally enraptured by the princess movie on her tablet.

At Nana's gate, the usual guard, Homer, is wearing badly fitting riot gear. He shuffles over to check Mom's driver's license and lets them through. Mom heaves a big sigh of relief, and Ella realizes that she hasn't seen another adult, other than Uncle Chad, since she got the Violence. Did she think Homer was going to swab her and throw her in jail?

It's definitely different in Nana's neighborhood. The yards are all perfect and green like Astroturf, summer in full bloom. The palm trees and flowers provide bright pops of color against the imposing mansions, their fountains spouting sparkling water. No one is outside on the sidewalks, none of the usual power-walkers in Lululemon or upright old women proud of their tiny poodles or sleek hunting dogs. There aren't even any golf carts or golfers. The perfect green hills with their perfect little flags are utterly empty of angry old men. It's a beautiful, shiny ghost town. A mosquito spraying truck slowly crawls up the road, pumping poison into the air despite the fact that mosquitoes can never be completely eradicated.

"Do you even know if Nana is home?" Ella asks.

Her mom doesn't answer immediately, and when she says, "No," it's almost a question.

In the back of the car, Brooklyn kicks her feet along with whatever song the tablet is piping in through her kid-sized, cat-eared headphones.

"Mom. Seriously. What's going on? Please tell me. I don't . . . It's just . . ." Ella huffs, almost a whine. "This is hard, you know?"

Chelsea parks the minivan in Nana's empty driveway and looks into the rearview mirror to make eye contact, as close as she'll get to her daughters in the tight space. Ella usually prefers to sit up front. But not now.

"I know it's hard, honey. It's hard on all of us, and it wasn't exactly easy before." Her crooked smile is the saddest, smallest apology for marrying Dad and sticking with him, and it does not spark an answering, understanding smile in Ella. Mom frowns again and in a cracking, defeated voice, says, "Uncle Chad said Dad's going to be home soon. We need options."

And then she's getting out of the minivan and making an effort to look upbeat and happy and nice and in firm control. It's an all-too-familiar sort of look, and Ella hates it but knows well enough how to follow suit. Like Dad, Nana is nicer to her when she's smiling and silent.

"Come on, Brookie." She snaps her little sister out of her tablet coma and they follow Mom to the front door. Brooklyn skips and sings about what might currently be in Nana's candy dish. She only really comes to Nana's house for parties, and she spends the parties either splashing in the pool or playing croquet with Nana's nice old gardener, Miguel. She loves the pastel dresses Nana buys for her and the shiny black shoes with lacy socks. Nana makes her feel like a princess, which is exactly what she wants. It would be so much easier to be five right now and have no idea what was going on.

Mom rings the doorbell, and after a long time, Nana answers it herself. She doesn't hide her annoyance and distrust as she glares at them.

"What a surprise," Nana says, and not in a way that suggests it's a good surprise.

"Hi, Mom. Can we come in?"

Nana glances up and down the sidewalk and waves them inside. "How unlike you to seek me out."

They don't visit often, and never without a clear invitation, which is always more like a summons. This is the first time Ella can remember Nana answering the door herself since she married Grandpa Randall and moved in here. It's always smiling, friendly Rosa in her polo shirt, so tall she has to duck through the front door but always glad to see them. Or acting like she is.

"Where's Rosa?" Brooklyn asks, and Nana's frown makes Ella very glad she wasn't the one to ask.

"Rosa and Miguel are no longer with us. Brooklyn, sweetheart, why don't you go investigate Nana's candy dish." Nana is already gliding toward the kitchen, no hugs or questions about how they're doing. The house is spotless, and a fresh bouquet of white flowers sits on the hall table. Brooklyn skips off to the sunroom to raid the shiny crystal bowl that's always full of sweets.

"How's Randall?" Mom asks.

Nana stops at the kitchen island and turns to face them, her acrylic nails tapping on the marble. "The judge is very busy."

"That's good."

"It is."

Because that's Nana logic. The world is upside down and people are dying but as long as her husband is busy and making more money, it's good.

Ella fights the urge to fidget as her mom and her grandmom face off wearing masks of cold politeness. There is no silence like the silence in Nana's house. No pets, no TV in the background, no loud appliances, just the ticking of Grandpa Randall's grandfather clock in the all-white dining room that they're never allowed to enter.

"Did you need something?" Nana finally asks, as formal and flat and cold as if they were strangers knocking on her door to sell her cookies she doesn't want.

"I need to ask a favor."

Nana's lips curl up like a Disney villain. "I'm sorry, darling, I didn't quite catch that. Could you repeat it?"

Mom huffs in annoyance, her mask slipping. "I said I need a favor."

"And what might that be?" Nana crosses her arms and leans back against her kitchen island looking young and lively and smooth, like she's nourished by groveling. It's so odd to Ella that her mom is only twenty years older than her, and Nana is only eighteen years older than her mom. She has friends whose moms are older than her grandmother. She is determined not to continue the pattern.

"I need to borrow money for the vaccine."

Nana's perfect eyebrows shoot up, her forehead barely wrinkling. "Oh? Money? I thought David handled the money and you were just *flush* with cash. Isn't finance his 'thing'?"

Ella is not a fan of her dad, but still her hands curl into fists at her sides while her mom breathes through her nose. She knew Nana was kind of an asshole, but she's never seen it this out in the open.

"Yes, finance is his 'thing.' But it turns out he made some bad investments. I found out after they took him away for the Violence. I have no money." She smiles, the kind of smile you give when you have nothing left to lose. "So there it is. Are you happy? I married a bad man who cheated on me, beat me, and lost all our money, and now I'm destitute. Just what you said would happen. Just what you always wanted."

Nana's eyes get big and fake-pitying, and she steps forward and brushes Mom's hair back, cups her cheek. Mom does a good job of holding still, but Ella imagines this is how she would stand if a venomous snake was crawling over her foot.

"Oh, darling, I never wanted you to suffer. I wanted you to have a better life than mine."

Chelsea steps back. "Don't pretend you aren't enjoying this."

"How could I ever enjoy my child's unhappiness?"

"I've asked myself that question for years and never could figure out an answer."

Nana steps back, too, her eyes narrow and sly. She arranges the fruit sitting out in a ceramic bowl, moving around the apples and oranges and bananas that Ella is pretty sure no one ever eats. "The vaccine costs *quite* a lot of money, you know."

"I know. I'll pay you back."

"Ninety thousand dollars for all three of you. You're going to pay me back ninety thousand dollars, starting at zero today in the midst of a recession sparked by a pandemic, when you don't even have a profession?"

"That's a lot of words to say no, Mom."

Brooklyn chooses that moment to dance back into the kitchen. She's already managed to get candy stains on her dress, bright streaks of red and purple. "I like your jellybeans, Nana!" she says. "Did you know Mommy had to send herself to her room and not come out?"

Mom and Ella exchange glances. Mom goes pale under her foundation.

"Oh really?" Nana bends over, hands on her thighs, and gives Brooklyn the brightest, chummiest smile Ella has ever seen her use. "Tell me more."

"Nothing to tell," Mom says, swooping over to pick up Brooklyn and hug her close. "I had the flu, and it turned into bronchitis. You know, how I always do."

But Brooklyn loves being the center of attention, and she's been locked up with only Ella for weeks, and there's no way to stop her. She twists in Mom's grasp to face Nana, who's now upright, arms crossed. "No you didn't! You got mad because Olaf ran away and we had to put the couch against your door."

Nana shakes her head at Mom like a disappointed teacher. "Chelsea. You're infected, and you didn't turn yourself in? Why, that's against the law. Thank goodness the judge isn't here."

Ella slides closer to her mom. Up until now, she was scared that her mom would suddenly go feral and try to kill her, but now she's more worried about what her grandmother is going to do with this information.

"I just want my girls to be safe," Mom says, head hanging over Brooklyn's shoulder as if the hope has drained out of her. "David's getting out of quarantine soon, and we need . . . we can't be there when he comes home. He came after us with a baseball bat."

A good grandmother, a kind grandmother, the kind of grandmother

other people all seem to have would now invite them to stay with her in her huge mansion behind the tall gate and pay for their vaccinations and fix things.

But that is not the kind of grandmother Nana is. Her smile curls in again, and she runs a hand down Brooklyn's back.

"How would you like to stay here with Nana, sweetheart?" she coos.

"That would be fun!" Brooklyn nearly shouts. "Could I swim in the pool? And watch movies? And eat candy?"

Mom turns to the side so Nana is no longer touching Brooklyn. "How long can we stay with you?" she asks, skittish as a wild cat.

Brooklyn wriggles and fights in Mom's grasp until Mom has to let her down. She runs over to Nana and leans against her hip, and Nana puts a protective arm around her.

"Well, you'll need to go find a job, won't you, darling? I'll take care of the girls while you get yourself back on your feet. You can stay in the pool house, now that Rosa and Miguel are gone." Her eyes light up with glee. "You could even take on their responsibilities. Cleaning, cooking, yardwork. You were doing most of that for David, weren't you?"

Mom is shaking now, her hands in fists. "I will not be your . . . your . . . servant!"

"Oh, so you're too proud to do work?" Nana strokes Brooklyn's hair, the gentleness of her touch the complete opposite of the venom in her voice. "Not like me at your age, working my fingers to the bone on double shifts, slopping hash at the diner to take care of you? You don't love your daughters enough to debase yourself with menial labor, like I did?"

"I love them more than you ever loved me!" Mom hisses, clearly trying to keep her cool for Brooklyn's sake and very nearly failing. "But I won't give you the satisfaction of having me under your heel again. Your criticisms, your sharp words, your undermining. I didn't leave an abusive husband just to fall back under the thumb of an abusive, narcissistic mother."

The words hang in the air, one more thing that can't be taken back.

"Well, if that's how you feel," Nana starts with grim finality. She pauses and looks at Ella as she continues to stroke Brooklyn's hair, and Ella takes a step closer to her mother, wishing she were young enough to hide behind her, because whatever Nana is thinking is not good.

"If that's how you feel, how about this. I'll vaccinate the girls, but you have to leave them with me. I'll do my best to fix whatever garbage nonsense you've put in their heads." She frowns down at the jellybean stains on her khaki shorts. "And teach them the basics of hygiene. We leave for Iceland next week, so they'll be perfectly safe."

"And what about me?" Mom asks, sounding lost and young and . . . God, hurt. So hurt. Ella wants to hug her mom as if she were the bigger one.

Nana's eyebrows go up. "You? You're infected. Unsafe. You said you could pay me back, so go out and earn your own vaccine. I offered you a job, and you turned it down. Find someone else with a better opportunity. *That's* how finance works."

Mom closes her eyes and tries to hold herself together, and it's embarrassing and sad, watching Nana gloat as Mom falls apart.

"That's not fair," Ella says, the words falling out before she can stop herself.

Now Nana turns the full power of her coldness on Ella. "Oh, isn't it? Tell me, would you like to go home and live with an infected mother and an abusive father, or would you rather go to Iceland with your well-off grandparents and enjoy a real education and proper medical care?" Nana sighs dramatically. "And of course it's not fair. Life isn't fair. Surely you know that much by now."

"What's Iceland?" Brooklyn says, pulling away from Nana to look up at Ella, who's been answering a thousand questions a day for her these past few months while shielding her utterly from the news.

"It's a country in Europe," Ella tells her. "A very cold place. They eat lots of fish."

Brooklyn's nose wrinkles up. "Ew. I don't like fish. Unless it's crunchy fish sticks with ketchup."

"They don't even have passports," Mom says, desperate.

But Nana just swipes a manicured hand through the air. "The judge has friends who can get what we need. We're living in difficult times, darling."

"Mom, you can't be considering this," Ella says, wanting to hug her or touch her but knowing on an animal level what her mom can do when she loses control.

"Sweetie, I—"

"Before things get maudlin, I think I need to remind you that you're currently breaking several laws," Nana says sweetly, sliding her phone from her pocket and gesturing with it. "You should be in quarantine, not gallivanting around with children, not driving, not visiting the elderly. You're a danger to us all."

"Mom—" Ella starts.

Before she can say anything, Mom lunges for her and pulls her into a tight hug and whispers, "If I don't say yes, she's going to turn me in."

When her mom steps away, Ella feels like a little kid who's been abandoned.

"She can't," Ella says at a normal volume.

"She can, honey. She will."

And Ella knows it's true, and yet she doesn't want to believe that people can have this kind of power over each other, that money can make this sort of thing possible. She doesn't want to believe that a mother could treat her own daughter so badly. She can't understand why Nana even wants them; she's never seemed to care about them before, except as decoration. Her grandmother must be powered by pure spite.

"It's rude to talk about someone as if they're not there," Nana chides before gaping at them all. "Don't you dare look at me like I'm some kind of villain. I'm the only one thinking clearly here, the only one with any concern for safety. And I'm the only one with resources. I'm doing what's best for us all."

"Bullshit," Chelsea growls.

"Call it whatever vulgar thing you wish, but you know that I'm right. And if you don't, then I suppose that's why I'm forced to make this call."

For a long, tense moment, they all just stand there, but then Brooklyn fidgets and says, "I have to go peepee before we go to Ice World." She runs off for the bathroom, and as soon as she's across the house,

Mom lets out a big, sucking sob and starts crying. Violence or no, Ella runs to her and hugs her, fighting her own tears.

"Fine, I'll do it. I'll live in the pool house—"

"I've reconsidered that offer." Nana looks down her nose, cold as a Disney villain. "I don't think it would suit. I've spent enough of my life trying to help you help yourself, trying to guide you in making good decisions. This time, you really are on your own."

"No!" Ella shouts into her mother's shoulder. "No, you can't make her leave!"

"It's okay, baby," Mom whispers. "This is temporary. I'll find the money, I'll get vaccinated, and I'll come back for you. I promise it will be okay."

"You can't promise that because no one can."

"Too bad. I already did."

A few feet away yet a world away, Nana says, dismissively, "Chelsea, if you can just go home and get their things and maybe drop them by on your way out."

Mom looks up, her red face a mass of snot. "On my way out?"

"Well, there's no way to earn money *here*," Nana says. "Florida's a wreck. The job market is awful. I imagine you've got to go north and find something. The food and hospitality industries are bustling in the cool, overburdened areas where there are no mosquitoes."

Mom is almost panting, and Ella wonders if she's going to get Violent again. "How can you be so cold? So callous? Do you even have a heart?"

Nana steps forward, almost close enough to touch her daughter. She reaches out, then pulls her hand back as if Mom is surrounded by a force field. "I have a heart. But more important, I have a brain. And unlike you, I recognize that what's most important is keeping these children safe, even if it's from you."

Mom sticks her chin out. "Let me talk to Brooklyn first."

Nana just rolls her eyes, mutters, "If you must," and goes to the fridge for a glass of unsweetened tea.

When Mom heads for the bathroom, Ella follows her. Brooklyn is inside with the door cracked, singing a handwashing song and splashing around; she loves Nana's fancy, flower-shaped soaps.

"Come here, baby," Mom says, and there's a grim finality in it. Brooklyn dabs her hands on the lavender towel and rushes directly into a hug. She's just like that—dancing through life, living for hugs and cozy things. Not like Ella, who's always been shy and standoffish and prone to question things in a way that adults find annoying.

"Mommy, are you crying?" Brooklyn asks.

"Sweetie, you're going to stay with Nana for a little while. You and Ella. Ella's going to take care of you, okay? So you have to do what she says."

"I like it better with Nana when Ella's not here," Brooklyn pouts.

"Yes, because then there's no one to tell you no when you eat too much candy. But, baby, promise me you'll be good, okay? I'll be back soon."

Brooklyn cocks her head, ponytail swinging. "So for the weekend?"

"For the weekend," Mom agrees, kneeling to pull Brooklyn into a hug, and Ella shoots her a questioning glance. That's one lie she's not looking forward to explaining, but Mom doesn't look like she can take on another burden right now.

"I'm going to run home and get your pajamas, okay?"

"The pink unicorn ones! And my pillow! And Green Blankie! And—"

Mom closes her eyes and buries her face in Brooklyn's neck, smiling through her tears. "I know, baby. I know everything you need."

When Brooklyn starts squirming to get out of the hug, Mom stands and wipes at her face. She pulls Ella into a hug, and Ella clings to her like she's drowning, breathing in her shampoo and perfume, squeezing hard.

"Text me what you need from home," Mom whispers, which hurts, because she should already know.

"I love you, Momster."

"I love you, too. I'm so sorry—"

"Don't. I just can't right now."

They don't have enough time for all the things Mom should be sorry for and all the ways Ella can tell her it's okay even though it still won't be true.

Mom goes quiet, and they keep hugging until Brooklyn tries to push between them, laughing like it's a game and squealing, "It's just a weekend, goobers!"

Clearing her throat, Mom nods as she turns. She dashes away her tears, stands taller, goes from soft to hard as if she's poured all her sweetness into the hugs and has nothing left. "I'll be back soon. Text me with anything you need. Take care of each other." She meets Ella's eyes, and the utter desolation there strikes Ella to the core—Ella feels it, too. "And no matter what you do, don't let her hurt you."

Ella can only nod through the tears, and then her mom is gone.

18.

Chelsea doesn't speak to her mother as she hurries for the door. What else is there to say? When someone is driving the knife into your heart without a single iota of mercy, nothing else seems to matter. Chelsea can't give her orders for taking care of the girls like it's just an innocent weekend sleepover, and if she tried, her mother would just say something so infuriating that she's afraid she'll lose control. And not in the way of the Violence. What her mother is doing brings such a wide, deep sea of fury to the fore that she can easily imagine her digging her fingernails into those cold blue eyes.

For her part, Patricia likewise says nothing. She stands at her kitchen island, a marble statue of a woman, perfect fingers wrapped around a glass of iced tea, mouth pursed like she's spotted a roach skittering across the floor and is trying to decide whether to call the exterminator or just get a flamethrower. Her phone is right there, ready to make the call that will put Chelsea away if she attempts any kind of fight or argument. At least this way, she has a chance.

So she leaves.

Just walks away from her daughters and gets in her minivan, hands clenched on the wheel, willing herself not to have a full-on meltdown where one of them might see it through the curtains. She holds on to a picture in her head, her two daughters in Iceland riding fat ponies, vaccinated, fed, safe, happy. She knows her mother is a narcissistic black hole of a human, but at least the girls won't have to see their father again for a long time.

Oh God. What if he gets home and files for divorce and custody? He would hate having to spend that much time with the girls—he's never been a fun dad who enjoys their company—but would he do it just to spite her?

Just as her mother has done this to spite her?

Definitely.

If he can't strangle her with his hands, he'll gladly do it with his lawyer.

He has always enjoyed hurting her, and she can see it so clearly now that he's been forced to stop.

On the way home—well, back to the house, as she shouldn't keep calling it home if she can't live there anymore—she gets stuck again at that same goddamn light, staring at what she's pretty sure is a corpse, but this time there are other cars behind her and around her, so she doesn't turn on red even though she wants to. She thinks about calling 9-1-1 to let them know there's a body, but since she's infected with the Violence and being harassed by a cop, she's not willing to take that chance.

Even when life seemed good, she hated this light. She hates the little yellow building, hates imagining what it would be like to stop here and go inside, the structure so tiny and cramped that she knows it would smell like twenty years of body odor and probably the off-gassing of a thousand cheap carpet samples. Whoever Big Fred is, the sign for his store has always infuriated her.

ALL I WANT FOR CHRISTMAS IS YOU . . . TO BUY ME NEW FLOORS.

CUT A RUG WITH YOUR BEST GIRL. WE'LL SELL YOU ONE CHEAP! THE RUG, NOT THE GIRL!

HOP ON IN FOR EASTER SAVINGS AND SHE WON'T MIND THAT YOU BEEN FISHIN'.

GIVE HER WHAT SHE REALLY WANTS: NEW CARPET!

She hates it because every message assumes that women are powerless and have to wait for some big, strong man to come along and provide something as basic as a floor covering. Because it's assumed that women are screeching fishwives who must be appeased with lino-leum. Because every message is a joke between men about how ma-terialistic and easily manipulated women are.

Whoever hurt Big Fred, they really did a doozy on him.

Literally, she thinks as she stares at the plaid-marked body under the eaves, the bloody splatter on the yellow wall right at head height. It's not a kind thought, but she hopes it was a woman that took Big Fred down.

Give her what she really wants: a cure for all this violence against women.

Lower-case *v.*

The light turns green and she's on autopilot. She passes by her gro-cery store, noting that there are very few cars there. When the Violence first broke out and people thought it was contagious, they repeated their coronavirus scare and bulldozed every shop for hand sanitizer, disinfecting wipes, and toilet paper. Once they realized it wasn't con-tagious but that anyone could randomly break out in a Violence storm, those who could stayed away from public places—and other people—as much as possible. It's almost funny, how America didn't take Covid seriously because it was "just like the flu," but now that a pandemic could result in being beaten to death, they're a lot more willing to stay home.

New delivery companies have sprung up overnight, tough guys and adrenaline junkies and the truly desperate eager to make money by turning grocery runs into something from an Indiana Jones movie. Those who can afford it wear protective gear and helmets, carry tacti-cal batons and other not-quite-illegal weapons. The government has been overrun with concealed-carry permits. Everybody wants to be a hero while forgetting that they could randomly and for no reason be-come the villain.

Her girls, at least, will have what they need. She saw the bottles of water and blocks of toilet paper stockpiled in her mother's mud-room. Now that they'll be well supplied, she can take what she needs from the house, fill up the minivan like she's going on a road trip. Because . . . shit. Where is she going? What's she supposed to do? Find a job in a dead market and a place to live in a time when no one trusts anyone at all? If there was more than six hundred bucks in the checking account, if it was as robust as David had always promised her it was, she'd buy a little RV and live out of there for a while. Instead she'll be stretched out in the backseat of her minivan in a nest of pillows and blankets, her neck crumpled up and her feet scrunched under the front seat, if her guess is accurate.

At home, she breathes a sigh of relief as soon as she opens the door and David isn't there. Knowing the way her luck has gone lately, she half expected to find him sitting at the island holding one of his guns, waiting for her. She hurries to her room to pack her bags, heart jittering at the knowledge that David could still appear at any moment. His car is sitting out front, and she knows where he keeps his spare keys, so she collects them all and tosses them in her bag. Might as well slow him down as much as she can, because once he finds out she's gone, he'll enlist every ally he has to find her. Huntley will take to it like a mad dog finally let off the leash. She's got to make it hard for David to focus on her.

She already has his laptop and phone, even if it's locked and out of juice, so she loads those in the car, too. She pushes the barrier away from her door and takes all her underwear and bras, the part of her wardrobe that's easy-care and folds down small, tons of yoga pants, clean socks, several pairs of sensible shoes, plus a few nice but easy and professional dresses. She needs a job, but in this odd new world, she can't imagine putting on a pencil skirt and heels and becoming some awful man's receptionist. She could be a barista or waitress— how that would make her mother laugh. She fills backpacks and then garbage bags with her things, then tops everything off with her only coat, scarf, and hat, shoved to the back of her closet because even the coldest days in Tampa aren't really that cold. But if her mother is right and real life is still happening up north, she might need to stay warm if she's still there come fall.

As Chelsea walks through her home—ex-home?—it feels like the set of a TV show she used to watch religiously but hasn't seen in years, one that hasn't aged well. All these objects and views are so familiar, but they are not for her. She does not take the wooden box of Dream Vitality oils. No matter what her upstream managers promised her, those little bottles didn't change her life. They didn't keep her safe. They didn't guard her health. They didn't cure her. If she had time, she would break every bottle.

The beautiful kitchen table in its sunbeam is just a heavy piece of junk. The Edison bulbs are just glass and wires. The shiplap is just someone else's old wood. The only real thing here is the bathroom door, pockmarked with indentations from a little girl's bat. The blood has been scrubbed away, but those divots don't lie.

Chelsea's phone buzzes in her pocket, and she finds several texts from Ella that she's missed while she worked. A list of things her daughter wants—far longer than what she has time to deal with, plus more requests from Brooklyn. She trudges upstairs, glancing nervously out the front windows, and does her best to get what they'll need. She thinks about tossing in some gloves and their coats, but she knows full well her mother will want to buy much more expensive versions to show them off on their trip, as if her girls are just fancy little dolls. She collects Ella's clothes, plus chargers and all the junk in her bathroom she needs to survive. She finds Brooklyn's favorite stuffed animals and Green Blankie. Her van is full of garbage bags, their contents partially visible through the stretched white plastic. The girls' bags are in the trunk, and Chelsea's bags are where the girls should be sitting right now.

She's about to head out when she remembers that she never had time to fully ransack David's office when the girls were home and in danger. She's even happier she remembered this step when she finds over a thousand dollars in cash stashed in his dresser, not to mention the folded hundreds in his wallet. She can't get into his locked safes, can't access her jewelry, but she is the one who keeps track of the passports, birth certificates, Social Security cards, and even their marriage license, and she takes everything with her.

It breaks her heart, the thought of handing the girls' documentation over to her mom, but she knows Iceland is the safest place for them right now. There are zero cases of the Violence in Iceland because there are zero mosquitoes there and a hardy quarantine program. The girls don't have passports, but her mother said Randall can take care of that easily, considering his money and friends. God, the smugness on that woman's face as she parades around her privilege in front of someone suffering—it's disgusting.

Chelsea slides into her van, every inch of it stuffed with garbage bags and backpacks. And that's when she breaks down. Just completely fucking breaks down. Great, heaving gasps, sobs that rack her body and make her shoulders and spine ache. Her eyes burn, her throat is numb and heavy, and she's crying so hard that her bra is soaked from the tears and snot running down her chest.

When her phone rings, she takes a deep, shuddering breath and prepares to act totally normal and explain to Ella why it's taking her so long.

Much to her surprise, it's Jeanie.

"Hello?"

"You okay, kid? I can see your van shaking from here."

Chelsea checks her side mirror and sees Jeanie standing in her driveway across the street, phone to her ear. David always said Jeanie was built like a brick shithouse, but Chelsea sees her more like some sort of ancient mother goddess, like those carved stones they find that are all breast and butt with tiny little feet. She might look fat from the outside, but she's slabbed with muscle and sturdy as hell, and whether she's at kickboxing or Zumba, she's graceful and strong. Jeanie is a PE teacher who usually spends her summers running a local outdoor camp, and Chelsea wonders what she's doing to make ends meet now that the schools and camps are closed.

She's a scrapper, Jeanie.

"Yeah, I'm fine."

Jeanie snorts at the lie, and Chelsea gives a sad chuckle.

"Okay, no, I'm not fine. Everything is a complete mess. But I'm just crying. Nothing dangerous."

"You safe?"

Chelsea glances at her mirror. Jeanie's in the driveway now, approaching the car. "I'm not sure how to answer that question."

"You got the Violence?"

She must wait too long to answer, because Jeanie barks her belly laugh and says, "Yeah, me, too. Hard to say it out loud the first time, isn't it? Don't worry, kid. As long as you're not currently feeling it or inhaling pepper, we should be good. Open up."

Jeanie's outside the car door now, and she's grinning because Jeanie is always grinning. Chelsea opens the door and steps out, flicking off her phone. They haven't spoken in months, not since she ignored Jeanie's text about going to kickboxing. Jeanie turns off her phone, too, but something she said is bothering Chelsea.

"Wait. Why pepper?"

Jeanie's eyes go wide. "Girl, you haven't heard? They announced it today. Big press conference and everything. Pepper is the . . . what'd they call it? I don't know, but if you're infected, it makes you storm. It triggers the Violence. Caps-something, some molecule, I don't know. All the stores are pulling it from the shelves. Black pepper, salsa, jerky, pepper spray."

Chelsea glances back at her kitchen, so quick, but Jeanie catches it.

"Yeah, go inside and get some, if you want. Better self-defense than a bulletproof vest, these days. Looks like you're packing out. I don't blame you. David finally hit critical mass?"

Chelsea takes a deep breath. It's a long story, and she doesn't really have time to tell it now.

"I called the Violence hotline on him . . ." she starts.

And of course Jeanie connects the dots. "Oh shit! So they took him away. What've you been doing since then?"

"Keeping inside."

"Oh. Because now you've got it. Why didn't you call me?"

Chelsea looks down and away, and Jeanie puts a hand on her arm. "Honey, it's not your fault. You know that, right? So don't you start feeling bad about it. I would've texted you, but David caught me at the mailbox and told me to leave you the fuck alone, or else. His exact words. I didn't want to make it worse. Didn't know if he had access to your phone. And I looked for you outside, but . . . well, it's a hell of a time, isn't it?" Before Chelsea can answer, Jeanie keeps on talking. "Wait, where are the girls?"

Every question brings a new flush of shame and rage, but Jeanie is the closest thing to a real friend that she has left, and anyway, what does she have to lose, telling the truth? "My mom's going to take them for a while. Get them vaccinated. I have to find a job."

Jeanie frowns at the mounds of bags barely visible through the van windows.

"So you're just leaving?"

Chelsea takes a step closer to the van. Every moment now means something it didn't before.

"There are no jobs here. I've got the sickness. I need to go up north, where it's cold." She squints up at the sun; it's already in the mid-nineties in Florida. "Colder. I need to make enough money to . . ." She cuts herself off. She doesn't have time to get into the thing with her mom and money and vaccinations. "Support the girls. But I need to hurry. David could be coming home any moment. So I guess this is goodbye."

She looks up at Jeanie, wondering if theirs is more of a hug friend-ship or just a nodding sort of thing, at this point. They used to have coffee, go to neighborhood Bunco, do Zumba. When she was selling Dream Vitality, Jeanie was the only person who bought any, even if it was just a bottle of lavender and a diffuser, and then Jeanie was the only person willing to tell her to back off about the oils, already. But in the last few months, David had gotten bitchier about Jeanie, and Chelsea couldn't take it anymore, so she just stopped answering.

Oddly, Jeanie isn't frowning, not even that polite sort of social frown people use when they don't know what to say. Jeanie's dark-brown eyes are alight and crinkling in the corners like Santa Claus.

"What is it?" Chelsea asks.

"You're going to think this is crazy, but I've got a lead on a job. Jobs, plural. Pays really well. And they don't care if you're infected because they're promising vaccination."

"What is it?"

Because Chelsea will do anything for her girls, but . . . there are some jobs she just can't do.

Jeanie pulls out her phone and shows her an email. A flyer, really. As Chelsea realizes what it offers, she shakes her head.

"The Violence Fighting Ring?"

Jeanie nods. "Sounds badass, right?"

"No way. That's insanely dangerous."

"No, it's not. You have to keep reading."

Chelsea waves a hand and steps back toward the van. "You can't be serious. When we're storming, we're just gone. Monsters. If you have it, you know that. We can't fight each other. We'd *kill* each other."

Jeanie pulls back her phone, chuckling. "You didn't read it all. It's like pro wrestling. It's all made up. You just pretend to fight. Costumes, props. They'll train you."

"If it's just like pro wrestling, then why aren't they using pro wrestlers?"

"Because they want it to seem real. Real people, people you don't expect. No steroids, no insane bodies. Regular folks, caught in the throes of the Violence and battling it out on the stage."

Chelsea backs into the van's open door, sits on her seat, and chews her lip. "Why?"

"Because it's all bread and circuses! The people are scared, and they need entertainment. Didn't you watch that old show, *GLOW*, about the underground women wrestlers? This is like that. We could get in on the ground floor. Tryouts are in Deland through Sunday. I was going to leave tomorrow morning, but maybe we could head out tonight, if you need to hop town." She shoves her hands in the pockets of her jean shorts and rocks back on her heels in her flip-flops. "No prior experience needed. Girl, I've been shopping and making deliveries for rich assholes for weeks—for crappy tips—and I'm ready to make some real money, do something fun. And get vaccinated. It'd take years to get it, otherwise, at the going rate. Don't you want to get the hell out of . . ." She waves her arms at Chelsea's house. "Don't you want to get away from this?"

"Not from my girls," Chelsea says, oddly breathless.

"Oh, it's only Deland. Just two hours away. Come with me. Make a bunch of money. The pay is good; a hell of a lot better than the delivery shifts I'm picking up. Believe me: Nobody here is hiring, and nobody up north wants a new employee with a Florida tan. You need that vaccine. And it sounds like your mom will keep them safe."

Chelsea isn't so sure about that, but it's also the best idea she's come across. She hates the thought of driving north into a place she's never been with no real destination in mind, all alone, knowing every moment that she could run out of money or pop a tire or snap and kill someone. She understands that the delivery services don't pay enough to survive, and she knows she's not qualified for much, considering she has a high school diploma and no references. David cut off every ray of hope, every avenue of escape. Did he do it on purpose, or is it just a side effect of his shitty, controlling ways?

"I have to leave today, Jeanie. I can't be here if he—"

Jeanie puts a hand on her arm again, squeezing gently. "I know. I know you can't. I just need to finish packing, and we could go. Might be good for you, y'know?"

Chelsea feels like she's standing on a precipice, like she's staring down into an abyss that's endlessly dark and yet somehow welcoming. She had no options, and now she has one. Even if it's insane, at least she won't be alone. At least she'll have hope.

"I need to take this stuff to my mom's house. The girls' things."

Jeanie nods, her grin widening. "Sure. Do what you've got to. I can be ready in an hour. Or you can park in my garage overnight and David won't have a clue. So you're in?"

Chelsea steps out of her minivan and looks up and down her street. This neighborhood should be a haven, but it's a prison. This is a place where instead of reaching out to help their less fortunate neighbors, the HOA mails letters detailing every step out of bounds. Who is hiding in their house, hoarding food and paper goods, and who has left, and who is sick or hurt or dead? There's no way to tell. From the outside, everything is fine. If not for the high grass, that overturned car, and the one pile of blackened rubble, it could be any day here for the past ten years. She would've thought a group of people living behind the same high fence and gate would bond together, reach out to help one another, but here they are in a crisis, more separated than ever.

No, she will not be sorry to leave this place.

She's almost tempted to set the house on fire herself, leave David just as adrift as she feels now because of him.

But she can't. Once everything is back to normal and the courts and insurance companies catch up, that house will represent all the money they have, and she needs whatever resources she can find for her girls, even if David will fight like hell to keep her from getting what's hers.

Yes, Brian is a good lawyer, or at least a cruel, scrappy one. But for the first time, Chelsea thinks that maybe she can get to a place where she, too, can have a lawyer who believes in her rights.

"Sure. Yeah. I mean, why not? I'll be back in an hour or so."

Jeanie does a little wiggle of happiness. "Good. I'll go make a playlist and put together snacks."

As she drives to her mom's house, Chelsea lets herself hope. She considers what it will be like, leaving with Jeanie, under no threats from David. Singing songs, eating hamburgers and fries and milkshakes, playing trivia games. If she thinks of it like a road trip, it's easier somehow. Less permanent. Less real.

She doesn't want to fight anyone, but then again, she doesn't really want to do anything except hug her daughters.

When she gets to her mother's neighborhood, Homer doesn't wave and open the gate. Instead, he steps out of his little guardhouse, unsnapping the holster where he keeps his gun.

"Sorry, Ms. Martin, but you've been removed from the list. I can't let you in."

Chelsea's heart drops, her cheeks burning. "But my girls are in there!"

Homer frowns like a basset hound with bad news. "I can't do anything about that. I'm just doing my job. Mrs. Lane said you could leave their things with me, and she'd take possession of them later."

Yeah, that sounds exactly like something her mom would say.

Chelsea holds back another flood of tears as she helps Homer unload the garbage bags and backpacks containing the clothes and blankets and toys she gave her girls, remembering each item and how it came into their lives. Brooklyn's favorite hoodie, bought to keep out the cold on a chilly night at Disney World. Ella's pillow in the soft, faded, ragtag cover they sewed together on a Girl Scout retreat. Memories on memories, stuffed into bags like so much trash. She leaves them piled behind the perfect little guardhouse and drives away.

Of course. Of course she won't get to see her girls one more time.

Her mother always has to get in the last word.

A strange new rage builds in her chest like a fire smoldering.

Perhaps, she thinks, she won't mind fighting someone after all.

19.

Patricia doesn't really think of herself as a day drinker, but within four hours of having both of the girls in her custody, she's already on her second glass of rosé. No matter how she begged, cajoled, or demanded, Homer refused to bring her the girls' things, even though his job is basically to sit there doing nothing, so she finally had to go fetch everything, hoping desperately that no one important would see her heaving garbage bags into her backseat. So embarrassing. Chelsea must've loved the thought of her mother wrestling with what looks like trash instead of packing the girls' things into luggage like a reasonable person.

Now she's trying to relax in the reclining chair under the patio fan and the girls are in their bathing suits—far too skimpy; they'll need new ones immediately—and splashing in the pool. It's perfectly safe, since they get their shots tomorrow. Sure, there might be a few mosquitoes around that have escaped the sprays, but Dr. Baird explained that the vaccine is therapeutic, so it cures those who are infected while inoculating everyone else.

Brooklyn is an attractive child but terribly wild, and Ella is a lost cause, somehow both meek and ornery, not that Patricia isn't going to try to get her up to snuff. At the very least, the older one is a decent babysitter for her younger sister, taking some of the pressure off Patricia to *Nana, look at this* and *Nana, watch me.*

Exhausting.

She's already made several calls. Dr. Baird will be by tomorrow morning, her regular girl at Dillard's is setting aside a full wardrobe in each girl's size for Patricia to peruse behind locked doors, and the warm coats they'll need for Iceland are on order. Once she explains the situation to Randall, he'll handle whatever paperwork they'll need to take the girls overseas. Amazing how much can be accomplished if one has the right phone numbers, a warm but firm tone, and a black credit card.

The girls are making far too much noise, and Patricia is glad the Pattersons and Herberts have already vacated and therefore won't be sending snippy little texts about noise control and headaches and the importance of maintaining standards. The neighborhood is quiet and orderly, and the only families with young children have such large properties that no one has to hear all the squealing and shouting, thank goodness. As she glances around the yard, she makes a mental note to hire a lawn service to take care of things while they're out of the country. With Miguel, Rosa, and Oscar completely out of the picture, things will soon get out of hand. Being gone is no excuse, as everyone in their circle is always summering or wintering somewhere else, most of the time. If only Chelsea had accepted her first, very generous offer, she wouldn't have to worry about anything other than her daughter's black thumb and utter lack of a work ethic.

The door opens, and Randall steps out onto the patio in his suit, his armpits swamped with sweat. Patricia holds up her watch and tsks. He's rather early. She'd hoped to have the girls dressed and primped and cowed into cheerful silence by the time he arrived.

"What's all this now?" he asks, frowning at her.

Oh, how she hates that frown.

Patricia stands, smiling, and greets him with an air kiss on either slablike cheek.

"Wonderful news, darling. The girls will be accompanying us to

Iceland. Don't worry about the fuss—I have a call in to the au pair service the Kellermans use for their grandsons' visits."

The lovely thing about Randall is that as long as his needs are taken care of perfectly, he generally doesn't care what else is going on. He's like one of those houseplants that require exactly the right amount of light but otherwise don't really impact everyday life, like an orchid. The judge is quite explicit in his requirements, and Patricia treats her job as his handler as, well, a job. He's rich as Croesus—eight figures, when they'd married—and when the littlest thing gets on his nerves, he simply pivots and plans a trip with his friends to escape completely. Patricia can't see a single reason why having the girls along should be an impediment.

"Patricia, are you out of your got-damned mind?"

She winces slightly; his country-boy accent only comes out when he's truly angry.

"I simply thought—"

"Did you, though? Sugar, we discussed this. It was in the prenup. There will be no outsiders to the marriage brought into the house. No homeless daughters, no bankrupt sons-in-law. Neither my no-good brother nor any of my shiftless cousins." It comes out *cuzzins*, syrupy and full of hate. "I have no intention of supporting anyone else's children, which is why I chose not to have any of my own."

Patricia is well aware that's not true. He has at least two byblows—that she knows of—and although he doesn't technically support them, he does pay their extremely young mothers to keep their mouths shut and stay away.

"I thought it might be fun," she says with a breezy shrug.

"Your definition of fun is very different than mine, darlin'."

"Hi, Grandpa Randall!" Brooklyn calls, having finally noticed something other than the Fourth of July pool noodles Patricia fished out of the garage.

Randall gives the child the same sort of stare he saves for the squirrels that keep breaking into the attic and defecating everywhere. He raises one hand in a wave, but he doesn't smile or offer any attempt at pleasantry. Before now, he's always put in a little effort, smiling and pulling pigtails and offering sticks of gum still warm from his pocket.

Brooklyn, at least, doesn't respond to the snub and goes back to her game with her older sister, who's watching Randall with a worried frown. Too clever by half, that one.

In Patricia's experience, with a man like Randall, clever doesn't go nearly as far as pretty and sweet.

"Like I said, we'll just bring along an au pair and you won't hear a peep—"

"Mrs. Lane."

He never calls her that unless she's in trouble. Sugar, honey, sweetheart, but never, ever that stuffy, distant reminder that she's just an extension of him now, and she'd better watch her step if she wants to stay that way.

"Yes, Randall?"

He reaches out to grasp her upper arms—more of a pat than a grasp, really. They don't touch very often, and if she's honest, she hates the feel of his skin. It's always warm and slightly damp, like a frog's belly. He's a sweaty man, the judge.

"Sugar, I've been meaning to have a little talk with you for quite some time, and it looks like today's the day. You've forced my hand here. Considering the state of the world, I'm retiring."

She . . . had no idea.

He's never mentioned it.

Retiring?

Visions of the future they've often discussed flutter through her mind, trips to Hawaii and Bali, opulent resorts where she'll see him only at luxurious dinners and then wake up in adjoining rooms to toddle off to massages by the sea as he goes off to golf or pester the local girls. "Congratulations, darling! That's a big decision."

"And we're getting a divorce."

Patricia freezes. It's as if a glass has shattered, something very precious and fragile and expensive, and there is no safe place to walk anymore.

"A divorce?"

Randall sits down on the patio couch, wipes off his sweaty pate with his handkerchief.

"It's not you, honey, it's me. I'm getting too old for all of it—work, the law, the Elks. You. Takin' care of folks. Dr. Baird says I need to focus on my health. I need to take some time for myself and not worry about anything else."

Anything else but secretaries and golf, Patricia thinks but doesn't say, because underneath the placid matriarch perfectly made up with fifty-dollar lipstick there still lurks a scrawny, desperate, clutching waitress in Goodwill clothes who's willing to do anything to survive.

"But who'll take care of you? Keep you company? You said yourself that your arm is awfully empty without me on it." She sits down beside him and pats his leg, but he gently moves her hand away.

"That's just it, sugar. If I'm not workin' and runnin' for office and showin' up to all those boring-as-hell charity events, I don't need anyone on my arm. If I give up work, I don't have to act so respectable all the damn time. And this." He gestures at her granddaughters, splashing in the pool. "It's the last straw. I don't want to ever come home and hear all this caterwauling. Water everywhere. Children are a goddamn pestilence." He grimaces and shakes his head. "I've worked myself to the bone for too long for . . . this."

He makes to stand, but Patricia holds up a hand, her brain struggling to settle on the right thing to say to change his mind, or at least stall him.

"But divorce, Randall? Honestly, I can just pack them right back home." She doesn't want to—oh, but she would hate to crawl back to Chelsea of all people! But she needs Randall more than she needs her pride. Or, to be more accurate, she needs everything that comes with Randall. The house, the money, the social standing.

He was never the marriage's attraction, himself.

But without him, she's back to being Patty, a pitiable thing with no resources, no home, no kingdom to rule.

Randall takes her outstretched hand between his own and rubs it like he used to do with Rosa when she burned dinner or broke a vase. On the surface it's comforting, but being pinned down like that, even for a moment, is a warning to any weaker creature, the cat's paw landing on the back of the unwary mouse, its claws not yet out but threatening. Pressing down.

"Just between us, this is a better way to do it. Retiring means I'm livin' on interest, and let's be honest, honey. You been spendin' real big lately. So here's what I'll do. I'll be putting the house on the market, but you can live here until it sells."

He releases her hand and stands, cracking his back like he's standing up straight for the first time in a long while. He smiles up at the sun.

"Real considerate of you to break the prenup like this." His voice is almost a whisper and humming with—is that glee? The nerve of the bastard! "Bringin' home children. I was thinkin' about hiring some pool boy to say you'd been cheatin', but this is so much easier."

Patricia is impressed in spite of herself. She knew he was intelligent enough, but she never suspected he might still be clever. He's certainly never hidden his indiscretions well, but then again, the prenup was all about *her* causing problems in the marriage. He's the one whose money needed protecting. She's toed the line perfectly, never dreamed he was just looking for an excuse, a gotcha. To think: Keeping her granddaughters for a while is what collapsed the house of cards she built so carefully. All along she thought he was the dupe, but apparently . . . he always knew it was her.

With nothing left to lose, Patricia lets her real feelings surface, tears springing to her eyes as if on command. "Randall, after all this, you're abandoning me? Leaving me with nothing? When you have millions upon millions?" Her voice breaks, her bottom lip quivering.

He catches her chin in his fat fingers. "Don't snivel, sugar. Don't tell me you didn't know what this was. We both needed something for a time. We both got it. And now it's past its prime, and so are you." He turns her face this way and that. "You were forty-five when I met you, but you looked thirty. Young enough to show well and mature enough to be respectable. And now you're just another stuffy old bird, expecting flowers and a tennis bracelet every got-damned day." He lets go. "We had a good run, didn't we?"

"But I did everything you ever asked."

She feels a fool, standing there, limp and empty, voice wobbling.

He nods. "You did. And then you got old and boring and expensive. Consider the vaccination my appreciation for past service."

As he opens the door, Patricia watches the back of him, letting the revulsion she's ignored for so long fully sink in. "And what about Iceland?" she asks.

He looks back at her and shakes his head sadly. "Honey, I never even bought you a ticket."

20.

Chelsea is singing "Life Is a Highway" at the top of her lungs with Jeanie, and it feels like she's sixteen again. The minivan windows are down as Jeanie crawls up I-4, and Chelsea has her feet up on the dashboard. She's wearing an old pair of cutoffs and flip-flops and has a sweating McFlurry in the cup holder at her elbow. Her hair is up in a bun, she's wearing sunscreen but not makeup, and pretty much everything about this moment would infuriate David.

Not to mention that while she took everything at home that he might need, she left behind her wedding rings.

Oh yes. David will be very, very upset.

And it feels good, if a little petty.

I-4 from Tampa through Orlando is normally stop-and-go, but these days, thanks to the Violence, it's free sailing. Not that Jeanie is taking advantage of that fact. She goes exactly the speed limit with the cruise control engaged, both hands on the wheel even as she sings. That tracks with everything Chelsea knows about her: Before the Violence, her entire personality hinged on the responsibility of being a school PE teacher, and she's going to follow the rules even if no one's looking. That's why she insisted on driving—she could tell Chelsea was upset. And of course, with all Chelsea's worldly belongings in the back, they couldn't take Jeanie's Mini Cooper.

According to the map on Jeanie's phone, they'll reach their destination in half an hour, now that they're on the other side of Orlando and past the theme parks, which are shut down, because kids getting attacked by their favorite princesses would be a PR nightmare. The address is a fairground, but no fairs have taken place since the pandemic began. Not because the government has made rigid rules about gatherings—that would of course infringe on personal freedoms—but because, as it turns out, being brutally beaten to death in front of your kids is a bit more threatening than getting sick ten days later, so events canceled themselves due to low ticket sales.

The song ends, and they trail off happily. Chelsea zips a hand outside and makes waves in the air. Everything feels like a new treat—everything David hated. Windows open, shoes on the dashboard, eating in the car, big sunglasses, which he always said made her look stupid. If the world was slightly different, she would try to convince Jeanie to stop at Disney World and spend a day without kids or husband, riding rides and eating whatever she wanted to without having to give a single shit about anyone else's needs or feelings. It's the most indulgent thing she can imagine, eating a Dole Whip on Jungle Cruise without someone being petulant or whiny.

"Guess you didn't see that post on Facebook," Jeanie says after taking a sip from her ever-present Yeti cup full of ice water.

Chelsea pulls her hand back inside. "Huh?"

"The post going around Facebook. About the girl who had her feet on the dashboard and she got in an accident and her femur basically ended up in her hoo-ha?"

Although her instinct after half a lifetime with David is to pull her feet off the dashboard, a tiny rebellion blooms in Chelsea's chest and she leaves her feet where they are. "I guess I didn't see that."

"Yeah, there was an X-ray and it showed her bones all messed up—like, in the wrong place. And another girl, the airbag threw her foot into her face and broke her skull or something. And her foot."

"Okay."

Jeanie drives on, and Chelsea watches her smile slip into a flat line as she keeps glancing over.

"It's just not safe," Jeanie continues. "That's what I'd tell my kids at school, and it's what I'm telling you now. I can't make you do anything, but I like to think you'd make the safe choice."

"I don't think that's my biggest problem right now," Chelsea says lightly.

"It will be if we're in an accident."

Chelsea looks over at Jeanie, who's frowning. "There aren't any other cars. What could we possibly hit?"

"It's not about what we're going to hit, it's about not doing stupid shit and annoying the driver."

"It's my car!" Chelsea splutters. "My feet! My hoo-ha! I swear to God, I did not leave David just to get told what to do with my god-damn body again!"

"Chel, you're being a real Debbie Downer, you know that?"

If she moves her feet, she feels like she's giving in to another David. Jeanie may not want to be like David, but for an adult to pressure another adult into doing something, to call her names? Well, that's not the freedom she went to so much trouble to find. But if she doesn't take her feet down, she's an idiot who makes bad choices, and she's an idiot who has to admit she's making bad choices.

Instead, she drops her flip-flops on the floorboard and sticks both feet out the window.

It feels pretty good.

"That's not safe, either," Jeanie starts.

Chelsea pulls her feet inside the car and turns to tell Jeanie to mind her own fucking business when everything goes black.

"What the fuck? Jesus, what the fuck?"

Chelsea squints against the sun and shields her eyes. There's a man standing there, just outside her window, white and in his sixties with a gray beard and wearing a red hat and a Hawaiian shirt. Weren't her feet just on the dashboard? And wasn't Jeanie driving? Why are they stopped in a field?

She looks to Jeanie, but . . .

Jesus, what the fuck is right.

Chelsea struggles out of her seatbelt and throws the door open, knocking the old man over, then jumps out and scrambles away to vomit in the waist-high grass.

Jeanie is . . .

Jeanie is dead.

Very dead.

Her head is a pulpy mush as she slumps against the driver's-side door of Chelsea's minivan, which is parked fifty feet off the road's shoulder, caught on an old barbed-wire fence in an overgrown pasture.

No, it's not parked. It's still running.

"What happened?" the old man asks as he staggers over. He leans into the van to put it in park before following Chelsea to where she's doubled over in the grass, staring down at most of a McFlurry splattered over a fresh cow patty. A bit away, a cluster of black cows stare back. "You-all swerved like crazy and tore off into the field."

Chelsea goes to wipe the vomit off her chin and notices that her hands are covered in blood. She quickly stuffs them in her pockets.

"I don't know. I don't remember."

It's true, but Chelsea knows full well it's more than that.

It happened again.

The Violence.

She lost time, and now Jeanie is dead, and she's lucky she didn't die, too, lucky that her minivan swerved off the highway and fetched up harmlessly against the fence instead of zooming into traffic or over a barrier. She touches her chest, and it's tender where the seatbelt was. Jeanie must've tried to stop the van. The airbags didn't deploy. The crash could've been a lot worse.

And things could still get worse.

Since everyone with the Violence is required by law to present themselves at an intake center for quarantine and testing, Chelsea knows that she's in big trouble, especially since the old man is staring at her in that angry, crafty way that suggests he's put all the puzzle pieces together and knows what's up and would love nothing more than a chance to take the law into his own hands.

"You infected?" he asks.

"No. Of course not."

"Then let's see your hands."

He's between her and the minivan now, his big, overdone truck purring loudly on the shoulder off to the side. Chelsea does the math. She does not show him her hands.

"No."

"What do you mean, no?"

"I mean I'm an adult and you're just some creeper who followed me into a field, and you need to get out of my way."

He squares off, gray sneakers planted, eyes alight. "Look here, missy. If you killed that woman, you need to do the right thing."

Chelsea stares at him.

First in surprise and then with blooming rage.

She has always done the right thing.

The thing she was told to do.

What was best for her, her mother, her husband, her daughters.

Maybe a few weeks ago, she would've hung her head and let the old man drive her to the nearest police station, sitting in the bed of his truck for his own safety. She can imagine how smugly he would bind her wrists with something from his truck, the speech he would give her about how he was only doing the right thing, which was of course whatever he'd personally decided was right.

He takes a step toward her, and her body reacts with a jolt of adrenaline and a single animal call:

Escape!

Escape!

Escape!

He takes another step toward her, hands up like she's a stray dog he's going to grab. Chelsea reaches for the cow patty and grabs a big handful of vomit and shit and lobs it right at his face. He starts dancing around, trying to scrape it off, and she bolts directly for his truck.

It's unlocked and running, so she throws herself into the front seat, slams the door, and screeches onto the highway.

Her foot can barely reach the pedals, so she's scooted up on the edge of the leather seat like a little kid, no seatbelt, pedal to the ground, motor howling like a wolf on a full moon. She doesn't look back to see what the old man is doing. By the time he gets himself under control, gets what's left of Jeanie out of the front seat of the minivan, and starts driving, she'll already be long gone. The exits here are far apart, but that doesn't mean as much when there's no one on the road and you're doing 110.

Chelsea knows this feeling well—pure terror. The only difference is that this time she's allowed to run when before, it's never felt like an option. Her heart is thundering, her feet are numb, her breath comes in the pants of an animal. Her mind screams that same word over and over:

Escape.

Escape.

Escape.

She has to get away. Can't be caught again.

She doesn't know what happens in the government's quarantine facilities, but she's certain it's not good, especially for those who actually have the Violence. And if she's captured, if the police take her, she knows David will find her. She'd have no choice but to sit there, waiting to be cornered by the predator who wanted her punished long before she'd done anything to actually deserve it.

She takes the third exit and parks outside a drugstore. She's still shaking, her teeth stuck together. She realizes that she doesn't have her phone, her clothes, any of her belongings, except the slender wallet in her back pocket, which is too small to fit more than a little cash. They're all in Jeanie's car—no, oh shit, her minivan. All her things. Everything so essential from her life—her old life—is gone now. It's back with the old man and Jeanie's body and all of David's tech, the things she was trying so hard to keep away from him.

The things that can now be used to identify her.

Shit.

She thinks about turning around, doing a hundred again but with her seatbelt on, and . . . Jesus, what's she going to do, threaten to hurt an old man who started out just wanting to help? No. Obviously not. But without what's in that car, she has no resources.

Or does she?

She wipes her filthy hands off on the jacket she finds on the passenger seat, then opens the glove box, checks the center console, reaches under the driver's seat. She finds three hundred dollars, more quarters than anyone needs in this day and age, and a stubby, evil-looking black gun in a Velcro holster. In the spare area behind the seats, there's a tackle box full of lures, weights, line, and, yes, zip ties, plus a knife. There's also a microfiber cloth and a bottle of Armor All, and as much as she hates doing it, she sprays her hands and cleans them off as best she can, knowing that anyone who sees all that blood will call the cops for sure. She also finds the truck's manual and oil change records, but that's not nearly as useful. And there, clipped to the dashboard, the old man's phone.

Chelsea goes inside the store and uses his money to buy baby wipes, a bottle of Gatorade, and some candy to make her body stop freaking out, and then searches the phone's map app for the nearest fairground. It's fifteen minutes away. She sticks the phone in a cup holder and starts driving.

She won't let herself think of Jeanie now. Sweet, earnest Jeanie, who was just trying to find a job and help a friend.

If anyone knows what the Violence can do, it's Jeanie.

They were so careful not to ask too many questions about the disease they share. This whole drive, not one word. But Chelsea knows two important things about Jeanie. One is that she is utterly devoted to her wheelchair-bound mother, for whom she remodeled the downstairs master bedroom of her house. The other is that she hasn't mentioned her mother a single time.

In a better world, she would go back and do the right thing for Jeanie.

In a better world, neither she nor Jeanie would be here in the first place.

But this is a new world, and the Violence has made her a different kind of person, and she's not going to let an accidental murder stop her from getting her girls back.

The only way out is through.

She scoots the seat up and drives it like she stole it.

Because she did.

21.

Ella isn't sure how it's possible, but Nana is being even more of a witch than usual. Whatever Grandpa Randall said to her really messed her up. When Brooklyn asked her to watch the dive she'd been practicing, Nana literally said, "No. I have more important things to do. No one wants to watch children play."

Who does that? Who says that to a little kid? Brooklyn almost cried, but Ella was able to distract her by showing her how to do a mermaid flip.

They're out of the pool now. Nana told her to find something for Brooklyn to watch on the patio TV while they dry off, but Brooklyn is starving, and Ella just knows that if she goes inside and asks for food, Nana is going to be terrible to her.

Nana has always been terrible to her—at least since she's been old enough to have opinions. She didn't have many warm, fuzzy moments with her grandmother after the age of seven, but she definitely remembers when Nana told her she was too "husky" for ballet and that time when she skinned her knee and Nana called her a hopeless whiner.

"Do you think Nana has any cookies?" Brooklyn asks, and Ella is annoyed at both her sister and her grandmother for making her be in the middle.

"I'll find out," she says, handing Brooklyn the remote control.

The moment she steps inside, Nana looks up from the kitchen island with murder in her eyes. She's leaning over her expensive laptop, and she snaps it shut and stands.

"I believe you were given an order," she says.

"Brooklyn is hungry."

"It's not mealtime. In this house, we eat only at mealtimes." Nana raises an eyebrow and looks Ella up and down.

Ella's temper flares, but she breathes through her nose. Losing your shit with Nana doesn't work. You have to go for logic. "It's not for me. She's little. She needs a snack."

They briefly have a staring contest, and Ella does not look away. For herself she might, but not for Brooklyn. She adds, "She's going to cry if her blood sugar goes down."

"Is she a whiner, too?"

"She's five."

Nana sighs and waves a hand at the pantry. "A light snack. That's all."

Ella opens the pantry and finds a strange array of foods. There are no Goldfish, no Oreos, no gummy snacks. She takes a box of water crackers and hopes they're just normal crackers.

"Thanks."

Nana's fingernails tap on the counter, one-two-three-four. "You're welcome."

She might as well have said, *Are we done?*

Ella takes the crackers to Brooklyn, who definitely whines about them. They're too dry, they don't taste like anything, she can't swallow, she's thirsty. When Brookie is acting like she's choking, Ella doesn't have a choice. She goes back inside, and Nana is gone, thank goodness. She brings a plastic glass of orange juice out, and Brookie mindlessly consumes her snack and watches a show on Nick Jr. while Ella scrolls through Instagram. Even though her feed is trimmed to calming art and funny memes, she tortures herself by checking out her friends' profiles. Olivia is on a whale-watching cruise in Alaska, and Sophie is visiting relatives in Canada, and Ella's heart constricts at how nice that must be. Maybe their parents suck, but at least they're somewhere else, somewhere not here. At least they're *with* their shitty parents. Her phone buzzes with a new email from Hayden, but she's not in the mood to read it.

"When is Mommy coming back?" Brookie asks during a commercial.

Ella isn't sure what to say. Brooklyn is the kind of kid who needs to know what's going to happen when, and nothing about this situation is something that can be penciled in on the calendar.

"Whenever she can. She has to go do some work first."

At least Brooklyn doesn't ask when Daddy is coming back. Ella can't blame her for that. She doesn't want her father to come back, and she knows Brooklyn is starting to think of him like some kind of god or monster, something big and uncertain and magical—in the bad way. Something to be charmed or feared as necessary.

"And Nana is going to take us to Ice World?"

"Iceland. Supposedly."

"I've never been on an airplane."

"I have. You'll like it. They have a rolling cart with cookies and sodas, and you're above the clouds where the sky is always blue."

Brooklyn sips her juice and kicks her feet. "I want to go to Ice World now. Are Anna and Elsa there?"

The show comes back on before Ella has to stumble over an answer, and Brooklyn returns to being mesmerized. Ella is bored out of her mind, so she might as well read whatever Hayden's written.

Hey, it begins, because that's how they all begin. Like they could be for anyone and just so happened to land in Ella's inbox.

It's more rambling crap about how terrible his life in the facility is, how much work he has to do, and how hard it is to care for little kids. You know, like the work Ella has to do all the time, and like most people have to do. If he's trying to make her pity him or even like him, he is definitely doing the opposite.

Only at the end does he say something interesting: He got tested, and he doesn't have the Violence.

No shit, Ella thinks. Of course he doesn't have it.

She never thought he did.

If school ever starts up again, he'll probably tell everyone that he did have it but got the vaccine. Everyone at school hates him now, or at least the good people do, and the bad people had to shut up or get shunned along with him. The video has gone viral, which means people all around the world hate him, too. And since videos of actual people with the Violence are all over YouTube, anyone with eyes can see that he's just straight up being an asshole, not actually storming. She wants to block him, but at the same time . . . as much as she hates these emails, she likes knowing where he is. What he's thinking. It's like checking the social media feed of someone you hate, rage-scrolling secretly late at night so you always know what your enemy is up to.

The moment he hit her, Hayden became her enemy.

And she will spend the rest of her life not letting him get anywhere near her.

Her mouth goes dry as she realizes that this must be how her mom feels about her dad. Like there's an enemy out there, and you want to be far away from them while knowing exactly where they are, tied to them, tethered by fear and this odd new awareness. With her dad, he's just always been there, this dark presence that she's learned to work around. But with Hayden, she doesn't have those schedules and rituals, doesn't know the right words. She has no idea what he'll do when he gets out of quarantine.

"What's wrong?"

She looks up from her phone, and Brookie is staring at her, worried.

"Nothing, bud."

"You look like you're going to cry."

Does she?

She does. Is. Shit.

Ella scrubs at her eyes. "Allergies, I guess. I didn't bring my Flonase."

Brooklyn wrinkles her nose. "Is that the icky flower spray?"

"Yep."

"I'd rather be sick."

But Ella knows that as time goes on, she's going to get stuffy and puffy and get a headache without her meds, so she needs to go through her stuff and find that bottle. It was on the list, so Mom must've brought it.

"Stay here and don't move, okay?"

Brooklyn's eyes don't leave the screen. "Okay."

Ella goes back inside and tiptoes down the hall and up the soft white carpet on the stairs. Nana's house demands silence, especially when Grandpa Randall is around. She heads to the guest room where she and Brooklyn will sleep on matching twin beds, noting that she'll have to quietly scoot Brookie's bed against the wall or she'll fall out. Her allergy spray is in her old duffel bag with her other bathroom things, and she immediately feels better as the scent of ancient flowers shoots up her nose.

As she's heading back out, she hears rustling and cursing coming from down the hall. The deep carpet muffles her bare feet as she sneaks down to see what could possibly make Nana sound that . . . not Nana-ish.

"Stupid goddamn asshole!" Nana murmurs. Ella peeks in the room—this door is usually shut and off limits—and sees Nana spinning the wheel of a wall safe, the dreamy landscape painting that usually covers it swung open like a door.

She knew Grandpa Randall and Nana were loaded, but a wall safe? That's next level.

She can't stop herself from watching. She wants to see what someone like Nana, who always has the latest iPhone in rose gold and is strung with real diamonds, needs to keep in a heavy-duty safe.

After a few minutes of fumbling and cussing with a scratchy southern accent Ella has never heard before, Nana gets the safe open. She pulls boxes out, some velvet, some leather, some bright teal blue, opening each one, muttering about it, closing it, and placing it on the low dresser under the safe. Ella sees rings, earrings, necklaces, and bracelets, all glittering and real. Nana seems relieved to find them, which is pretty weird. They're her things in her safe, so why would she care?

"There you are," she says to a ring with a red stone the size of a grape, sliding it briefly onto her finger and holding it up to the light. "You goddamn beauty."

When all the boxes are out, she slides a heavy bag with a zipper out of the safe, unzips it, and pulls out a stack of bills. Ella can't see what they are from where she's hiding, but they are definitely not ones or fives.

"Excellent," Nana murmurs.

Lastly, she pulls out a gun, small and elegant and a pretty bluish silver. She holds it between two fingers like it's a roach carcass she found in her shower. "You never know," she says to herself, and Ella almost makes the mistake of laughing because Nana sounds like some dame from an old gangster movie.

Nana reaches into the safe again, feeling around, and then huffs that very specific sigh she uses for when something has disappointed her. There's a big weekender bag open on the bed—not one of her Birkins or even a Coach, but something older and beat-up. Nana puts the bag of money on the bottom, then layers all the boxes on top of it with a sort of reverence. The gun goes on top of it all before she closes the safe, spins the dial, and closes the painting so the room goes back to looking like a perfectly normal guest bedroom that no one ever sleeps in because Nana hates guests.

Before Nana turns around, Ella darts down the hall, light on her feet, to hide in her room. She kneels by the garbage bags, heart thundering in her ears, hoping Nana didn't hear her. The last thing she needs right now is a lecture on being nosy or walking like an elephant or pretty much anything that Nana thinks Ella needs to know about her own flaws.

But Nana is walking with the same softness, the same care. She quietly shuts the door and tiptoes down the hall barefoot.

"That you, Patricia?" Grandpa Randall calls from his study, that sacred, manly, forbidden room with wood walls and bookshelves and a desk the size of a dead rhinoceros.

Nana tosses her bag into Ella's room, swinging it around the corner toward where Ella hides behind the garbage bags. Nana must not've looked in here first, because she's not the sort of person to toss her things like that.

"Yes, Randall?" Nana calls using her regular voice again, cold and formal.

A creak and groan suggest Grandpa Randall has stood up from his fancy office chair, and Ella can hear his footsteps as he walks into the hall. He moves like he's never had to be quiet, like he's never been forced to hide or scamper or run.

"You didn't leave those fool granddaughters of yours in the pool unsupervised, did you? I can't tell you how many lawsuits I've seen about drowned children."

Ella can imagine Nana rolling her eyes. "Of course not. They're drying off on the patio before I let them back inside."

As if they're dogs.

Ella looks down. There's a wet spot where her jean shorts are settled on the white carpet.

Oops.

"I'll be taking my essentials tonight, and I'll send Diane around soon to collect most of my things. Don't let those children into my study."

"Of course not, Randall."

Nana has always been cold, but Ella has never heard her voice quite this frosty.

"And I canceled your cards. And the appointment with Baird. And all that business with the shopping today. Honestly, woman, do you even look at receipts?"

Even without seeing them, Ella can hear Nana's posture change, can feel the anger rising. "Oh, I look at receipts. I look at the receipts for your trips, the massages that aren't therapeutic, and the special room service and the bottles of champagne. I look at the checks that go out every month to Jenna and Candice for their fat babies. I see the receipts from the florist that delivered two identical bouquets, one to me and one to God knows who. I see them all, Randall, and I'm certain your bottom line is higher than mine."

Grandpa Randall chuckles, and he sounds like the Big Boss in a videogame. "Well, when you're the one paying the bills, you get to set that limit, Patricia. And you throwing it in my face doesn't change anything. I told you: You knew what this was. And you know damn well it's over." He snorts juicily. "Just have to be right all the time, don't you? A man can't admire that." The floor creaks as he walks, and Ella sees his shadow in the hall. "I'll be at the hotel. And you can expect the papers next week."

He waddles down the hallway, and Ella shrinks down behind the garbage bags, knowing that what she's just seen is the sort of thing that will make Nana hate her forever. Nana, who is perfect, who knows everything, who is always in charge.

Nana whose gross old husband is apparently dumping her.

Now Ella realizes what they were arguing about on the patio. Now she understands why Nana was clearing out the safe.

Because she just lost all her resources.

She could almost laugh if she wasn't painfully aware that she and Brooklyn now depend entirely on Nana. Mom is gone, Dad is gone, and now all the money that made Mom dump her and Brookie with Nana in the first place is gone.

"Stupid garbage piece of shit—"

Nana spots Ella as she reaches for her bag. Her eyes narrow, their lack of wrinkles almost making her look like some freaky robot person.

"Gloating, are we?" she asks, sticking out her chin.

Ella goggles with surprise. "What? No, ma'am. I didn't hear anything—I mean, I wasn't—"

"Don't lie to me. You heard it. Probably understood most of it, too. And I'm guessing that your mother has poisoned you against me to the point that you're glad to see me knocked down a peg."

Ella shakes her head, desperate to get out of this situation but, again, utterly trapped. "No, Nana. I'm sorry. Grandpa Randall—"

"Randall. Just Randall. Let's not pretend he's your family anymore, shall we?"

"Yes, Nana."

"Now stand up and stop spreading that vile puddle on my carpet."

Ella stands, aware that her jean shorts are dripping, her hair is a wet mess, and she's still wearing her suit under her clothes. Funny how being around Nana makes her feel like an awkward, stupid little kid.

Almost like Nana does that on purpose. To everybody. It's definitely how she talked to Rosa and Miguel, when they were here.

"You shouldn't eavesdrop."

"I came upstairs to get my medication. I swear I wasn't trying—"

Nana massages her temples. "It doesn't matter. You know now. You would've known tomorrow, anyway. So here we are."

"Okay?"

"Stop doing that thing your generation does where you end every sentence on a question. It makes you seem weak and stupid."

"Yes, ma'am."

For a moment, they're silent, just standing there. Nana in her immaculate clothes, posed before her nondescript bag full of cash and diamonds, and Ella in her dripping cutoffs and faded tank, legs and feet bare, feeling self-conscious.

"Can you cook?"

That is not what Ella thought she was going to ask.

"What?"

"It's a simple question. Can you cook?"

"A little? I mean, yes, ma'am, a little."

"Then go downstairs and make dinner for us. I don't know what Rosa has in the pantry, but I'm sure you can find something."

Ella stares at her. "Is that it?"

Nana jerks her chin at the door. "Yes, that's it. Do as you're told." She seems different now, sharp and tough, as if under her tanned skin and cool exterior and soft pastels she's been made of twisted wire all along. She inexplicably reminds Ella of beef jerky.

Ella scampers around her, wondering where her grandmother is going to hide these things that probably belong to Grandpa—no, just Randall. If he wanted her to have them, he would've told her to take them. And if she thought he wanted her to have them, she wouldn't have bothered to sneak around trying to get them. Or waiting until Ella left to squirrel them away.

Ella hurries downstairs and checks on Brooklyn on the patio. Her little sister is still fully focused on the TV, which is good. Just a few feet away, the bright-blue water of the pool waits, too deep for the five-year-old to touch the bottom even in the most shallow places. Ella freezes in a strange new panic, as if an egg has broken over her head. She only now realizes that leaving a five-year-old by a pool by herself for ten minutes is probably the biggest mistake of her life, and she makes herself promise she won't expose Brookie to this kind of danger ever again. At least she can still see her little sister from every spot in the huge kitchen so she won't have to risk making Nana even angrier.

She bumbles around the pantry red-faced with shame over her mistake and decides to make macaroni and cheese from the noodles and wheel of hard orange cheese she finds in the kitchen. It's so weird, how Nana has no idea what's even in here. The cheese is much fancier than cheddar, but Brooklyn won't know the difference. It's her favorite food, and this is penance for leaving her unsupervised by a thousand gallons of death.

As she waits for the water to boil, Ella does a more thorough inventory. The pantry has some staples, but not a ton. No flour or sugar, lots of crackers and fancy cookies and tins of disgusting things like capers and anchovies. The only loaf of bread is brown and seedy and expensive. The fridge is mainly full of salad ingredients and raw vegetables and the things someone might put on a cheese plate if other old, boring people stopped by. The freezer is completely empty, aside from various contraptions that make ice cubes in unusual shapes.

Ella frowns.

If Randall cut off her grandmother's card, does that mean that the money in the heavy, zippered bag is all she has? And if so, how is she going to take care of two girls? And pay for all the bills that keep this castle running? The food here won't last more than a week at most, and Brooklyn will complain as soon as she's offered anything green that isn't covered in sour sugar.

Oh God.

If there's no money . . . there are no vaccines.

They're pretty much screwed.

Ella stirs the cheese into milk, staring as it melts. She begins to formulate a plan.

22.

The big truck's tires crunch over dirt and gravel as Chelsea turns in to the empty fairgrounds. These places are made for thousands of people to come together and ride brightly colored rides or cheer for cowboys or judge quilts and sheep, maybe even pull up a table and sell some antiques or iguanas. Without those people, exposed to the light of day, it's just a big, barren space, ugly and used-up and dried-out, baking in the Florida sun.

Out in the field beyond a crooked fence topped with barbed wire are two tour buses, the kind they use for bands or seniors descending en masse at Medieval Times, as well as tractor trailers. They're parked in a loose sort of circle with several RVs, set up with extended awnings and lawn chairs and large barbecue grills, one of which is puffing smoke. People are moving around over there, but the day is bright and it's far away. Something about the scene feels private.

A handwritten sign by the gate says VFR RECRUITMENT and points to the nearest of the cavernous metal buildings. Chelsea steps down from the truck in a puff of dust, feeling the grit seep between her toes. She was supposed to wear "clothes that allow movement," and technically hers do, but flip-flops are never an advantage at a job interview, and there's no way she could run in them. She wishes she had options, but all her clothes are back in her minivan with Jeanie's corpse.

Her lips tremble at the thought, at the image that flashes in her head, her last glimpse of what she did to her only friend.

She can't think about that now. What's done is done. It wasn't her fault. They both knew the risk when they got in the car together. It could've easily gone the other way, could've been Jeanie standing here, willing herself to stop shaking and not walk into the interview covered in snot as well as blood.

At least she has her wallet in her back pocket, plus the old man's phone. His name is George, and his phone is unlocked, and all of his texts are to other guys his age with names like Ed and Rick and Dan, mostly about fishing, lunch plans, and libtards. No wonder they didn't get along in their brief interaction.

She can't do much for her appearance just now. She did the best she could with the baby wipes, and she smells less like car cleaner. There's no way she's going to use the greasy black comb she found in the center console, and the red splatters on her shirt are undeniably blood, but she has literally nowhere else to go, so she just locks the truck, pockets the keys and the phone, and follows the sign. There are other cars parked in the lot, most older than the truck and her mini-van, both, but she doesn't see any actual people. Jeanie said it was an open call that lasted all day today and tomorrow, so at least she isn't late. At least she hasn't missed it. Whatever this is, it feels like her lifeline, like the only thing that could save her.

The building's glass front wall shows about a dozen people waiting inside, but Chelsea stops and slides into the shade under an overhang before joining them. She opens the phone and clicks the green CALL button and stares at the keypad. Ella's phone got stolen last year, and she got a new one with a new number, and this is the very first time Chelsea has been forced to realize that she has no idea what her daughter's number is. She knows the area code and seems to think it has a bunch of sevens and fours, but that's it. She stares so long that the phone goes dark, and she flicks it on again.

She has to remember this.

It's the only connection she has with her girls.

She doesn't know her mother's number, either, but that's one she's never even considered memorizing. It's just how life works these days, choosing a contact and hitting CALL. Or, in most cases, texting, because calling now feels strange and awkward.

"Goddammit," she murmurs.

She starts pressing numbers, but they don't look right. There are thousands of variations, and she's not going to find the right one randomly while standing outside a big metal shed at an abandoned fairground while covered in someone else's blood. An intrusive and unwelcome thought crosses her mind: *I'm a terrible mother.* But it's localized to not knowing her daughter's number. She's not ready yet to list all of her errors, every wrong turn and bit of bad luck that led her to here.

She tried, dammit.

She tried so hard it hurts.

And it still wasn't enough.

Her shame and guilt turn to rage as if she's flicked a switch.

Rage is so much easier.

All of this is David's fault, not hers.

The shame and the guilt—they don't belong to her. She's a victim. She's doing the best she can.

But it's insidious. Everything David has ever said to her about her own inadequacies lives under her skin. She's stupid, she's bad with numbers, she's not a decent cook, she's selfish, she's slow, she didn't teach the girls how to behave, she's not a good mother.

Over time, they built up until she just assumed they were true.

But what if . . . he's been wrong all along?

Tires crunch on gravel, and she whirls, brain screeching back into panic mode because that is what victims do, that is what prey animals do, that is what people who black out and wake up holding their friend's dented Yeti cup covered in chunks of brain do.

They react. They spin and prepare to fight for their lives.

But it's not David in a Mad Max car, roaring toward her with a flamethrower. It's not George in her minivan, ready to perform a citizen's arrest. It's just a beat-up SUV with a beachy-looking guy in his twenties who gets out, walks to the building in his own flip-flops, gives her an up-nod, and goes inside as if it's the most normal thing in the entire world. She gives the phone one last, hateful stare, shoves it in her pocket, and follows.

Inside, the air is frigid. A Black woman in her forties with her hair under a colorful turban sits at a folding table with a pile of papers and a jar of cheap pens. She smiles at Chelsea with a mischievous look in her eyes, and Chelsea smiles back.

"You trying out?" she asks.

"Yes, ma'am," Chelsea says.

In the quiet way that things come to mind after a major trauma like killing your last friend, Chelsea is vaguely aware that it might be weird to call someone just a little older than she is ma'am, but everything feels pretty unreal right now and the woman doesn't seem to take offense.

"Just fill this out. Sorry we don't have any clipboards. You know how it is."

Well, yes. With everyone staying home and avoiding crowds, plenty of stores have had to close, and since the mail carriers use open trucks and mosquitoes are everywhere, they got hit especially hard by the Violence in the South, which has slowed down the delivery of the next-day packages everyone is so accustomed to. While life goes on in cooler climes, Florida is struggling to stay afloat with the effects of the pandemic. Missing clipboards are the least of Chelsea's problems.

She takes an application, or whatever it is, and a pen and goes to sit by the sunny windows. The room is painfully chilly and sparse in the way of underfunded local governments. A crappy TV blares the news in the corner, and most of the people sitting in plastic chairs stare at either the TV or their phones. These people—they have a desperate look about them, one Chelsea can relate to. Like Jeanie promised, they are all ages, all sizes. Chelsea was expecting buff guys, but most of the hopefuls are just the sort of folks she would see at the store.

She sits cross-legged on the ground and uses her chair as a backing for the paper. It's the strangest application she's ever seen, not that she's had a job since she was a teen, before David, and even then she only had to fill out one.

Name, birthday, address, phone, all that is normal. So are the spaces for past jobs and the skills they encompassed.

But then it asks for three emergency contacts and allergies and clothing sizes. It demands height and weight and information on health problems and past surgeries.

And then there's a section for circling her skills. Gymnastics, sports, running, wrestling, martial arts, cheerleading, theater, singing, stunts, circus skills, clowning, barbering, makeup application, camerawork, PR, food service, commercial driving, forklift operation. The longer and stranger the list gets, the more Chelsea realizes that she has none of the skills they require.

At a loss, she circles theater, cheerleading, and singing. She did all three in high school, and she has a decent voice, even if she hasn't sung in public in twenty years. She swallows hard, the memory hitting her like a wave crashing as her eyes go unfocused, gazing out at the empty brown field in the hot sun.

It happened the night of the high school talent show. She was a senior, and she and her best friend, Whitney, had been planning their act for weeks—"The Point of No Return" from *Phantom of the Opera*. Whitney was Christine, wearing a big, poofy gown she'd found at the thrift store and altered to look less 1980s party and more 1800s. Chelsea was the Phantom, her thrift store tux a little ill fitting but mostly covered by a vampire cape they'd dug out of Whitney's brother's closet. She had a half mask and was in the dressing room, penciling in stubble. She'd been doing theater all through high school and loved nothing more than the energy of the dressing room, the hot lights and giggles and frenzy, everyone running around half dressed and fizzing, their eyes outlined in black. As she leaned in, carefully stippling her jaw with a Dollar Store eyeliner, David appeared behind her in the mirror, his hand behind his back.

He'd been so hot then, his hair gelled and his skin tan from summers lifeguarding. Every time she saw him, she swooned. They'd only been on a couple of dates, but she spent most of her time thinking about him, hoping he'd ask her out again, praying that when they talked by his car in the lot after school, he would lean in and kiss her for the first time. He looked amazing, dressed up in a white button-down and khakis, and he was smiling, right up until he recognized her.

"What are you doing?" he asked, clearly confused—and not in a good way.

She capped the eyeliner and turned around, smiling brightly. "Makeup. You're not supposed to be back here! It's supposed to be a surprise."

David squinted and cocked his head, taking in her face. She wore thick pancake, black eyeliner and mascara—the usual theater getup, even if half her face would be hidden by the mask. His lip curled in disgust, and her stomach clutched tight.

"I'm the Phantom of the Opera. See?" She took her wig from the Styrofoam form and draped it over her pinned-back hair, then added the mask for full effect. She'd done a lot of work putting it all together, and she knew it looked great. But his reaction didn't change.

All that energy and frenzy she'd felt began to wilt, and everyone else in the room faded into background as the boy she was crushing on super hard looked at her like she was an absolute idiot—a hideous, absolute idiot.

"You look like a dude."

"That's the whole idea."

She looked up at him, hopeful, wanting him to understand what all this meant to her, how she felt when the song's notes soared up and up as the Phantom pulled Christine into his sick world. They'd chosen the song for max drama, and there were even gobo lights that would make it look like they were in an underwater cavern, with light-blue ripples dancing on the black wall behind them.

David pulled flowers out from behind his back—tulips already going limp—but instead of dramatically offering them to her, which should've happened after the show, anyway, he placed them on the table behind her. He gently removed the mask and her wig, but he didn't put it on the form, he just flopped it down on top of the flowers. Her skin zinged at his touch, her knees weak.

"I thought you were going to be the girl. I was hoping to see you in a sexy dress." He clasped her jaw in both hands like he was going to kiss her, running his thumb over her chin, smearing the stubble dots she'd so carefully drawn. "It's just weird, right? You in a tux?"

"There's a historical precedent for gender swapping in theater. All the parts of women in Shakespeare's plays went to men." She looked up at him, hating how he was staring at her like she was a gross bug. "Wait. Aren't you in the talent show, too? Where's your costume? I've never seen you in the greenroom."

He pulled away, smirking, and pulled something out of his back pocket. It was a gold wire circlet of fake leaves.

"I'm reciting from *Julius Caesar*. I'll put on my toga beforehand, and my laurels. But no makeup or anything." He looked around the room at all the theater and dance kids getting ready, at the splashy costumes and sequins and rouged cheeks. "It's crazy back here."

"Yeah, but it's fun."

It was actually kind of weird that he hadn't been in the greenroom. He wasn't in drama or chorus, and he was a late entry to the talent show—his Academic Bowl captain had suggested it would look good on college applications, he'd told her.

"Are you not putting on makeup? It's hard to see features from the audience without it. I could help you—"

He scowled. "Uh, no thanks. Not my thing, historical precedent or not." He glanced back at the door. "I was going to ask if you wanted to come hang with us in the lobby, but . . ." He looked her up and down, frowning. Her heart sank. He couldn't show her off like this, was what he meant.

Whitney ran up right then looking amazing in her gown, her hair in huge curls. David stared at her like Chelsea didn't exist. "Are you ready? What happened to your beard? We need to fix that."

But Chelsea was watching David, and his interest in her seemed to be fading like the flowers he'd brought as he looked Whitney up and down. She'd had a crush on him for so long. He was so smart, so funny, so good looking, the kind of golden boy who was popular because he was involved in everything, knew everyone. And she was losing him. For whatever reason, seeing her in costume had killed that spark in his eyes, and he was now looking at Whitney like maybe he'd picked the wrong girl.

"See you in the lobby, after?" Chelsea asked, a hand on his arm.

He looked up, flinched away when he saw her face again. "Yeah, maybe." But he didn't smile, and he didn't say anything else as he walked away.

"So that's going well?" Whitney asked once he'd left the room.

"It was." Chelsea turned back to the mirror. Her eyes were turning red and her stubble was a smear of brown. She didn't care about that; she just wanted to fix things with David, wanted him to light up when he saw her and give her compliments and do that sweet, old-fashioned thing where he offered her his arm and made her feel safe and cared for. She'd never felt this way about another boy, and she liked that he was waiting to kiss her, that he cared about doing things right.

So what if he didn't care about theater? If he didn't really get something as special and incredible as *Phantom of the Opera*? People could have different interests. As long as he loved her, she would be free to do her own thing, just as he could do his. It's not like she was over the moon about Academic Bowl and basketball.

"Chelsea?"

Whitney held up a baby wipe, but Chelsea felt frantic, trapped, like she was being held back. She tossed her wig aside and picked up the limp bouquet of tulips.

"I'm sorry," she said, unable to meet Whitney's eyes. "I feel sick. Think I'm going to throw up. Gotta go."

She grabbed the baby wipe and her backpack and ran for the door. In the lobby, she darted into the bathroom and cleaned off all the stubble and most of the pancake until only her eyes were left, the heavy liner and mascara making her blue irises pop. She took out her tight bun and all the pins holding back her hair, fluffing it and running a little water through it until the honeyed waves came back. She sloughed off the vampire cape and hung it on the hook on the door and put on her regular clothes from her backpack, hip-hugger jeans and a tight-fitting tee. And then she went out into the lobby to find David, clutching his tulips to her chest and praying that she hadn't lost him.

No, there he was, talking to his Academic Bowl buddies. She touched his elbow, and when he turned and saw her, he lit up. "Now, that's more like it," he said, sliding an arm around her waist and tucking her protectively and possessively against him, right in front of his friends. "You guys know Chelsea, right?"

She and Whitney were supposed to go on any second, but she waited outside with David. She didn't want to know if Whitney was going to muscle through without her or maybe sing one of Christine's solos instead, didn't want to watch Whitney onstage and know she'd betrayed her best friend and missed out on something she'd been waiting months for, nor did she want to watch the stage stay black a little too long as the crew figured out how to skip ahead to the next act because Whitney had given up. She hid during intermission and only slipped into a seat in the back when David was going on.

There he was in his regular clothes with a white bedsheet belted over it and the little gold tiara on his head. With no makeup, his face was washed-out white. He raised his hand stiffly and recited the lines perfectly, but his heart wasn't in it. It was almost like he thought he was in on a joke, and Chelsea wondered if this is what he'd felt like when he saw her in her Phantom makeup, like it just didn't make any sense. But she wasn't about to let him know that she was disappointed in his performance, didn't want to make him feel self-conscious or weird. When he was done, she clapped, and afterward, she gave him one of her tulips, and he leaned in and pecked her lightly on the lips, and she knew she had made the right decision.

Whitney found out, of course—theater kids talk. And she chewed Chelsea out in B hall and called her every name in the book, including coward and slut, although Chelsea didn't know which one hurt worse because neither felt true. Deep down, Chelsea knew she deserved it, that she'd been a shitty friend and that Whitney deserved better. But she had David, so it didn't sting as much. That night after the talent show, instead of going to the cast party, he drove her home and pressed her against his car with a hand on either side and kissed her until her lips stung, his stubble scraping her jaw nearly raw.

Looking back to that night, she should've known then what he was.

Should've seen how he belittled her interests, was disgusted by the things she loved, ignored her friend except as a sexual object, welcomed her sacrifice as if it were his due.

But she didn't see any of that at the time. She only knew that when he looked at her, something inside her longed to feel his arm tighten around her waist, pulling her close, making her feel small and safe. She didn't know she was cozying up to a monster.

Hurray for hindsight.

Since then, she's tried to find Whitney via every route the internet has offered. Friendster and then Myspace and then LiveJournal and then Facebook, but Whitney has never turned up—that, or she has Chelsea blocked everywhere she goes. A few times a year, whenever she thinks about it, Chelsea writes up an ad for the Tampa Craigslist Missed Connections, pouring her heart out to the Whitney she used to know, offering her sincerest apologies. She's gotten plenty of garbage in response, but she's never found Whitney, and this feeling lives like a splinter in her heart.

"You done with that?" The woman in the turban is standing over her, hand out for the application. It looks pretty pathetic. Only two of the three job spots are filled, the first with her high school job at the movie theater and the second, embarrassingly, with homemaker, a job of the past eighteen years.

"I guess so." Chelsea stands to hand the application over, and the woman takes it and saunters back to her desk.

Chelsea sits down in her chair and looks around the room, dreading the fact that there's no way on earth anyone would offer a job to someone with her qualifications—and her disease. Most of the people are staring at their phones, infinitely scrolling in their own little worlds, but the surfer guy who passed her on his way in meets her eyes, and his jaw drops open.

"Holy shit," he murmurs.

Chelsea looks behind her, out the window, terrified she's going to see George in his red hat, followed by the police, or maybe even David with his baseball bat, but there's no one there.

"It's her," the guy says, pointing at the TV.

The brunette beside him stares at the TV, then at Chelsea. "Holy shit is right."

"What?" Chelsea says, her stomach dropping. "Are you talking about me?"

But no one answers. They're all focused on the TV.

On one side is an old photo from Chelsea's phone, a selfie of her smiling at the beach. The words underneath, in all caps, say WANTED BY POLICE.

On the other side is George, standing by her minivan on the side of the highway.

"I barely escaped with my life," he says angrily. "I guess that's what happens when you stop to help someone these days. She attacked me and stole my truck."

Now a reporter dominates the screen. "Police are looking for Florida woman Chelsea Martin—"

Holy shit, all the way.

23.

Ella is unsurprised when Nana doesn't offer to tuck her grand-daughters in. She doesn't read them stories or hug them good night. A soft alarm goes off on her phone at nine, and she walks in from her room as if she'd forgotten they exist.

"Bedtime," she says, flapping a hand at them. "I expect you both showered and dressed at breakfast."

And then she goes back to her room and shuts the door. She's still fully dressed, her glasses low on her nose. Brooklyn looks at Ella, and Ella turns off the TV and says, "Come on, Brookie. It's already way past sleepytime."

Ella's heard a few stories of what it was like for Mom, growing up. How Nana had to work from dawn until dark just to keep a roof over their heads, and how they moved a lot and often had to live in trailers or one-room apartments. How Mom spent most of her time with neighbors and in daycares and got food through free meals at school or leftovers from Nana's work, packed in greasy Styrofoam. When Nana got pregnant, she was a junior in high school, and she didn't even get to earn her GED. Her widowed mother kicked her out, and the rest of the family was so judgmental that Nana cut them off before they could cut her off.

Mom said Nana had never been the huggy type, which is why Mom always made an effort to hug them so much. One time, after Dad was mean and Mom drank too much wine, she told Ella that she was pretty sure Nana had always hated her, but she didn't know if that was because she had the audacity to be born an inconvenience or because she was who she was. Ella knew for herself that what Nana liked best in a child was compliance, and apparently neither she nor her mom had lived up to her standards.

Her only tolerable memories of Nana were from when she was really little, maybe Brooklyn's age. They didn't see their grandmother often, but when they did Nana played a game where she held out both of her fists and said, "Pick the right one, and you get a surprise!" Ella would point at a fist, and Nana would open it and there would be candy there. Sometimes, she picked the wrong fist, but then Nana would let her try again. She liked that version of Nana and remembered the comfortable house where she'd lived with Grandpa Terry, a sweet old man who told her the names of the flowers in his garden and let her hammer nails into pieces of wood because he was a builder and said girls could be builders, too. Ella was sad when Grandpa Terry died, although Nana gave her a dirty look when she cried too hard at his funeral.

Then Ella was seven, and it came time for Nana to marry Grandpa Randall. Nana presented Ella with a big white box wrapped in a beautiful satin ribbon, and Ella thought it was about the size and shape of an Xbox and got very, very excited, as Daddy had told her she was too young for such an expensive toy and Nana liked to make Daddy mad. But when she opened the box, she found a huge, puffy dress. Nana helped her put it on and asked her to be a flower girl at the wedding as if this was the best surprise ever. The dress was pretty, but it went too high up her neck and choked her, and it pinched under her armpits and was scratchy. Nana beamed and clapped and told her she looked beautiful in it, but Ella told Nana she didn't care. The dress hurt. She wouldn't wear it.

Nana and Mom got in an argument over that dress. They were loud and mean, making big gestures with their arms, and they wouldn't listen to Ella at all. So Ella took the beautiful dress and cut it in half with scissors so they couldn't make her wear it again.

That was the last day Nana was kind to Ella, the last day she gave her that special smile. The next time Ella came over, Nana offered her both fists, but neither fist contained candy. "Sweets are only for the sweet," she'd said. They didn't play that game again. Since then, Nana was distant at best, cruel at worst. At Ella's next birthday, she "forgot" to bring a gift, and when Ella's eyes pricked with tears of embarrassment, Nana called her a complainer and selfish, and Ella ran out of the room crying in front of all her friends.

Ella is still that same defiant girl, the one who cut the itchy dress in half, but she's learned that there are better ways to play the game. Living with Dad taught her how to follow directions and stay out of the way while secretly seething with disdain. Open rebellion makes people angry. It earns punishment and grudges. It means that someone is always watching, expecting a problem. She now focuses on learning the rules and obeying them exactly to avoid pain, and most of the time it works. She can think whatever she wants to think as long as she flies under the radar and meets expectations. It's hard, sometimes, hiding behind a fake smile, but it keeps her from being hurt. It's not like any of these people *need* to see who she is—or really want to.

At least Nana hasn't turned on Brooklyn yet. She's such a sweet, innocent little kid; she probably would've worn Nana's dress not just because it was pretty, but because she knew it would make Nana happy, even if it itched. When she looks at her little sister, Ella wants to wrap her arms around her and protect her forever. She's often imagined her love like a turtle shell, like she's grown hard so she can stand between Brooklyn and the world, and especially between her and Dad. When Mom told Ella she was pregnant, she'd been worried that Ella would be jealous or angry, but Ella had immediately felt a fierce love for her baby sister that's continued all along, even when tiny Brookie cried too much or current Brookie gets annoying. With Mom out of the picture, it's up to her to make sure that Nana doesn't smother that sweet smile, crush that precious spark.

Ella digs through their things and hands Brookie her toothbrush and toothpaste. Together they go into the spare bathroom Nana has assigned to them, and as Ella brushes, her little sister mimics her exactly, white foam dripping onto the marble counter. This bathroom is

Brookie's favorite, done up in an elegant sort of jungle theme, the yellow wallpaper covered in palm trees and tiny, clever-looking monkeys. When they're done, Ella cleans off the counter and lays their brushes on a neatly folded washcloth. She doesn't like Nana, but much like dealing with Dad she knows the rules to follow, and the first rule is Don't Leave a Mess, especially now that Rosa's gone and can't follow behind them with a rag and a wink.

As Brooklyn puts on her My Little Pony pajamas, Ella pushes one of the twin beds up against the wall and borrows the throw pillows from a nearby velvet chair to build a ledge along the open side of the bed. Brooklyn has terrible nightmares and thrashes like an octopus. Her dreams are mostly about a monster that lurks in the garage or behind closed doors.

Ella knows that the monster is their dad, but Brooklyn is only starting to understand.

"Do we have to get shots tomorrow?" Brooklyn asks. "I know what *vaccinations* means."

"Maybe."

"Why maybe?"

"Because things are weird right now."

Ella is certain they won't get shots that cost thirty thousand dollars anytime soon, but knowing her current luck, she'll promise her little sister no shots and a doctor in a white coat will show up with a huge needle and prove her wrong.

She gets Brooklyn into bed and plugs in her tablet for her. Earlier today she found Nana's modem and nipped up the Wi-Fi code, so now Brooklyn can curl up watching one of her shows, the only way to calm her to sleep. Mom has so many rules about screen time, but they're stupid. Screens aren't going to hurt Brookie more than, oh, say . . . Dad. Or Nana. Screens are a constant. They can be counted on. These shows are Brookie's friends now that she can't go to kindergarten with real kids after Brayden G. got the Violence and gave Maddie L. a concussion with a wooden block. Screens don't go to quarantine jail, or stomp the dog to death, or abandon their kids to live with an evil grandmother.

Shit. Only adults could invent screens and make TV shows and then tell kids that they can only enjoy them when it's convenient for adults. No one has lectured about screen time since Covid landed years ago because without screens, everyone would go insane having to parent their own kids all day.

Lying on her back on the twin bed, staring at the ceiling fan, Ella herself is nowhere close to sleep. The mattress is very tall and way too hard, as if Nana went to a store and asked for the world's most expensive brick. The house is weirdly quiet aside from the incessant hourly tolling of the grandfather clock, the carpet dampening every other sound. Randall is gone, and Nana's bedroom is downstairs, and it would be spooky if this wasn't the least hauntable place on earth, this sprawling McMansion that manages to be both very overdone and deeply, aggressively average. Ella hates this place and wishes she were back home, where things felt . . . if not safe, then at least reliably annoying. Most of all, she misses her car and the freedom she once had to roam.

She misses time spent reading on a bench or scrolling through her phone while babysitting kids who pretty much sit themselves. She misses knowing Mom would be there to take care of Brooklyn in the afternoons. She misses drama practice and going out for milkshakes afterward, even if it was starting to get awkward with Hayden. She misses the packed bag she's always kept in the trunk of her old Honda, knowing that one day Dad would really cross the line and she might have an excuse to sweep Brooklyn up and leave.

To where? She had no idea.

She has almost two hundred dollars in her savings account, and she knows full well that it wouldn't support the two of them for more than a month. It's not like she can babysit anymore, much less get a real job. At least she's smart, and she knows she can graduate with online schooling—if she can get her laptop, which Mom apparently forgot. Just one more year of high school, which now seems like an impossibly tall mountain to climb. Nana didn't graduate high school, and Mom did but didn't go to college, and Ella is determined to do both.

And yeah, she knows full well that it was a stupid, childish dream—her being the hero, marching out the door with Brooklyn and driving away in the night, windows open so she can hear her drunk dad yelling for her to stop. She realizes now that in this silly fantasy, she always left her mom behind with Dad, a final fuck you for choosing him over the safety of her daughters. Now, away from him, having seen the depths of her mother's pain, Ella floods with shame for ever thinking that her freedom could taste sweet if she knew Mom was still with Dad and probably being punished even more.

She used to think Mom chose to stay, and that it was a bad choice. That she deserved being stuck there with someone who treated her like shit but expected her to feel grateful.

Now Ella is living that same nightmare.

She always wanted to escape with Brooklyn and start over somewhere safe, away from Dad's abuse and Mom's weakness.

And they are away, but it's the same damn thing.

Helpless people in thrall to another asshole with power.

She scrolls through Instagram, hoping it'll quiet that line of thinking and bore her to sleep. This is her constant. Pretty pictures, don't read the comments. She follows lots of graffiti and tattoo artists, guerrilla knitters, photographers who sneak into locked-up buildings, makeup artists who do 3-D effects, dressmakers defying gravity, cosplayers defying reality, people decorating cakes that look like crystalline vaginas. Anyone making art that pushes the edges of what's acceptable. Once the Violence happened, they started up a new hashtag to counter all the ugliness in the news: #unviolent. People just post beautiful surprises they find in their day, ladybugs and painted rocks and skateboarding dogs and old, wrinkled women with red lipstick and tattoos. That's her favorite thing to look at—just people rebelliously searching for a glimmer of hope in a dark time.

It finally works. She falls asleep and dreams of an empty Kmart full of tiny beds splattered with blood.

The next morning, she and Brooklyn arrive downstairs smelling like Nana's guest room conditioner and dressed in wrinkled but nice enough outfits. It reminds her of a scene from *The Sound of Music*, especially when Nana raises an eyebrow in disappointment. What did she expect—matching sailor suits?

"Breakfast is on the counter," Nana says from the sunroom, where she goes back to sipping black coffee and reading a newspaper at the table.

On the counter, Ella finds two boxes of adult diet cereal that both look equally terrible. They might as well be Cardboard Flakes and Gravel Nuggets.

"Where's the good cereal?" Brooklyn asks.

"Don't worry. I'll make it better," Ella promises her quietly before Nana calls her little sister a complainer.

She takes the flakes and adds sugar and sliced bananas, plus Nana's watery 1 percent milk mixed with a swirl of half-and-half. As they weren't invited to join their grandmother, they sit at the counter side by side and crunch. Ella hopes neither of them breaks a tooth, since Nana surely can't afford dental visits. Once they're done, she rinses out the dishes and puts them in the empty dishwasher.

"Nana, are we getting shots today?" Brooklyn asks.

Ella feels a tiny ping of panic as her sister walks over to the sunroom table and invades her grandmother's space. Nana stares down at her. If she were a cat, her ears would be flattened.

"No. There were no open appointments. Perhaps another day."

"Good. I don't like shots. Do we get to go try on clothes?"

Ella flinches. She told Brooklyn not to do this—ask questions, make demands. But she's a little kid, not a robot, and it's too late now.

Nana folds her newspaper, carefully sets it down, and glares down her nose at Brooklyn.

"We do not."

"Why?"

Brooklyn's favorite word. Ella isn't sure how to intervene. She wants to keep Brookie on Nana's good side, but she also wants to see how Nana is going to react. What will she tell them? When will she admit how screwed they are? She has studiously avoided looking at Ella this morning, as if she's trying to forget last night ever happened.

"We can't go shopping because Randall said no."

Ella has to stop herself from snorting. That's a very Nana answer—putting the blame on someone else who isn't there to defend themselves.

"Oh. That makes me sad. I like pretty clothes."

A normal grandmother would lean forward and start a conversation about clothes. *Oh? Me, too! What do you like? When I was little I loved dresses.*

But Nana just shrugs. "Yes, well, disappointment is part of life."

She picks up her paper and goes back to reading, but Brooklyn just stands there. It's funny, though. Watching Nana sit in a sunbeam at her expensive metal-and-glass table reminds Ella of what her mother looked like, sitting at their own breakfast table. Nana and Mom look so much alike, and they both have really pretty kitchens, but they both seem utterly miserable to be there, so what's the point?

"Are we still going to Ice World?" Brooklyn asks.

Ah, shit.

Ella definitely should've stepped in.

Nana stands up suddenly, glaring down at Brooklyn like some sort of giant monster getting ready to step on a slug.

"We are not. Perhaps if you'd behaved better and had not been so troublesome, we could go, but now we can't."

Brooklyn's eyes get big and wet like the characters on one of her cartoons, and the corners of her lips pull down, and then she's crying, completely heartbroken. Nana steps around her like she's a pile of cat barf and walks away, disappearing into her bedroom. The moment the door clicks behind her, Ella runs to her little sister and sweeps her up into a hug.

"Is it really my fault?" Brookie asks between sobs. "Was I bad?"

"No. It's not your fault. You're not bad. You're wonderful. She's just a stinky, farty old stick-in-the-mud."

Brooklyn gulps a laugh between sobs, her face red and pressing hot tears against Ella's neck. "But Nana said—"

"You don't listen to Nana. She's like Daddy. Sometimes they say things that aren't true. I don't think they even know they're being mean, but they are. It's never your fault."

Ella has a brief flashback of her mom saying something similar to her when she was very young, but once she was older, they both knew it was at least partially Ella's fault.

"Who wants to go to Iceland, anyway? I don't like ice. I like the swimming pool."

Brookie hiccups as she powers down from crying. "I like swimming. I thought Nana would buy me a new dress."

"She bought me a dress once, and it was so itchy I cut it in half with scissors."

With a gasp, Brooklyn draws back to look at Ella very seriously. "Oh, that is so bad, Ella! You shouldn't do that. It's not very nice."

Ella rocks her a little and chuckles sadly. "Yeah, it was pretty bad. I'm not saying you should cut stuff up when you're mad. I'm just saying that Nana has bad taste in dresses for little girls."

"Can I watch my tablet now?"

Ella pulls her in for another hug, feeling snot drag across her neck as she releases her little sister to stand. "Of course, bud. Just use your headphones so you don't wake up the sleeping bear."

"What bear?"

"Nana Bear." Ella curls her fingers into claws and snarls quietly. "Grr! Time for shots!"

Brooklyn giggles and says, "No!" and runs off for her tablet.

Ella watches her, wondering what she would've been like at that age if she'd had someone to protect her as ferociously as she protects Brooklyn. If she hadn't had to grow up so quickly so the adults in her life wouldn't notice her and hurt her.

Her phone buzzes, and she groans as she pulls it out. Every time her phone buzzes now it's either an email from Hayden or a message from someone at school trying to stir up some more drama. She's texted her mom ten times with no answer, but she's losing hope that her mom will text back. Maybe Mom thinks that if she answers, if she hears how rough it is for her girls, she'll come running back. And Mom is determined not to run back.

It's a text, and the exact one she's been waiting for.

I'm home. Where are you?

But it's not from her mom.

It's from her dad.

24.

The moment slows and stretches out forever as everyone in the room stares at Chelsea. She can't help but think that this must be what Frankenstein felt like when he saw the torches on the horizon. She takes a step back, and then another, backing completely out of her flip-flops. The door should be just behind her. If she runs, she can probably beat them to the old man's truck. Her hand slips into her pocket for the key fob.

"Wait," the woman in the turban says, hands out in a soothing gesture. "Let's all calm down. Everybody have a seat, and we'll sort this out."

That is . . . not what Chelsea expected to hear at a job interview after being outed as a murderer on the local TV news.

"Calm down?" the surfer guy says, doing that thing where a guy sticks out his chest and steps forward in a way he could swear on a Bible wasn't threatening but definitely is. "Shouldn't we, like, tie her up and call the cops?"

But the woman in the turban is not cowed. She stands tall and sturdy and walks right up to him, unafraid. Chelsea knows she should turn and run but freezing is built into her DNA, and there's something fascinating about this interaction.

"I'm asking you to calm down if you want this job. If not, there's the door. She'll let you leave." She tilts her head toward the door, eyebrows up. Chelsea is still barefoot, tight as a bowstring, and if she turned and bolted, she could be out the door, but the woman adds, "You should have a seat, too. You go out that door, I can't help you."

That last bit dangles there, implying that if Chelsea stays, she'll get help.

God, it would be so nice to have help right now.

Her muscles twitch, and then she's collapsing back in her chair, her flip-flops splayed where she left them in the center of the room. The surfer guy sits, too. The woman in the turban puts her hands on her hips and stares at each person as they return to their seats. Chelsea recognizes that look on their faces—helpless resignation. They need this job as much as she does.

"I'm going through that other door." The woman points at the metal door that leads deeper into the building, where Chelsea can only suppose the actual interviews are being held. "You all can leave now if you want to, if you're scared, because you're almost certain to come into contact with infected people here. Self-control and good interpersonal skills are necessary for anyone who works with us, so if you don't have either, do us a favor and check on out. And I don't want to see a single phone in use until we've sorted this out."

She glances back at them one more time like a stern but dedicated kindergarten teacher before disappearing through the metal door, leaving it cracked. Chelsea stares at her feet, her throat dry, feeling that same smallness she felt around David.

"Is it true?" the brunette asks. She's got little sprays of stars tattooed around the corners of her eyes and looping snakes along the sides of her neck.

When Chelsea doesn't answer, the surfer guy waves his arm and snaps his fingers. "Hey, lady. We deserve to know. Is it true?"

Chelsea looks up, a gaping hole of emotions, and is about to answer when the metal door flies open and the biggest guy she has ever seen bursts out like the Kool-Aid Man. He must be six-foot-seven and three hundred pounds, and he has to duck just to get through the door.

"Hot shit! It's Florida Woman!" he crows with a southern accent.

The closer he gets, the smaller and filthier and more bare Chelsea feels. He's got a man bun and sunglasses and leather cuff bracelets and one of those breezy infinity scarves that only movie stars can get away with, but muscles bulge out of his black T-shirt and his sweatpants look painted on and expensive. He's familiar somehow, but Chelsea doesn't know why. She is desperately aware on an animal level that if she tried to run or fight, he could easily tie her into a pretzel and throw her over the building.

"I told you," the woman in the turban says, smirking.

"Five points to Arlene," the man says, accenting it with finger guns. He looms over Chelsea, but cheerfully, like an overenthusiastic St. Bernard, and she fights the urge to shrink away. When he sticks out his hand, she flinches. "I'm Harlan Payne. You might know me as Rampage." He grins, showing teeth so white that they're almost blue. "Three-time winner of the Majestic Meltdown in the World Wrestling Conglomerate." His smile goes crooked, showing a gold tooth. "When it existed."

Chelsea automatically sticks her hand out, and it's engulfed by both of his, warm and dry and mostly callus, far gentler than she'd expected.

"What's your name again, Florida Woman?"

No point in not telling him; it's already on her application—and splashed across the news.

"Chelsea Martin."

"Well, I'd like to talk to you about an exciting opportunity, Ms. Martin. If you'll join us?" He releases her hand and gives a little bow, directing her to the metal door. She stands, feeling shaky and as if she's living in someone else's dream, as nothing that's happened today makes any sense.

"Mr. Payne, sir?"

It's the surfer guy who wanted to zip-tie her and call the police, and he's blushing and stammering. "I'm a big fan." He holds out his leg to show a capital R shaped like a howling wolf on his calf. "I used to love watching you and Rayna—"

"I'm gonna stop you right there," Harlan snarls. "And let you walk away with your dignity and both your arms attached."

The surfer guy's mouth opens and closes like a fish, but then Harlan's hands clench into fists with a creak like old leather and the guy hurries for the door.

"He knows who I am," Chelsea murmurs quietly so that only Harlan can hear it; right now, she feels like he's the only adult in a room full of children. "He's going to tell them—"

"Hey, kid."

The surfer guy turns back to Harlan, eyes alight. "Yes, sir?"

"You tell anybody you met Florida Woman here, and I will personally hunt you down and tear you apart and feed you to my pet hyena. We got his vitals, Arlene?"

Arlene is by her desk and she holds up an application, her eyebrows up.

"We do, boss."

"Well, then."

Surfer guy nods in agreement, so red he looks like he's gonna puke, and bolts.

Chelsea relaxes, just a little. She has never believed anyone's threats as much as she believes that Harlan will do exactly what he says he will do. She's fairly certain he has that pet hyena somewhere, too. And yet . . . she feels safer now.

"Thank you," she tells him.

He puts a huge hand on her shoulder. "Don't let little shits like that scare you. The world is full of 'em. They wiped the floor with me until I had my growth spurt and hit the gym." His voice is softer than it was before, and even though everyone in the room is staring at them, it somehow feels as if they're all alone in the world. And it's not like she's attracted to him—he's just got this way about him. She met a dog whisperer once, and it's like that, but for people. And something about that terrifies her.

"You want her application, boss?" Arlene asks, holding it up.

Harlan takes it with a grin. "You know it. Come on back."

He holds open the door, and Chelsea slides her feet into her flip-flops and follows him back. She's suddenly aware of her ratty shorts, the rusty dots flecking her shirt, the black blood caked under her fingernails that she couldn't scrub out in the drugstore bathroom. But she got this far, goddammit, so she holds her head up and walks through the metal door.

The meeting room beyond is achingly boring, the kind of place the city government built using the architect and construction company with the lowest bid. The walls are a dirty tan, the carpet is dark green, and there's an odor that suggests that farm animals spend a few hours nearby each year. There's a long, definitely-not-wood conference table down the middle with a ragtag bunch of chairs around it. Two of these seats are filled, and Harlan sits at the head of the table, facing her, a stack of papers and a pen in front of him. He takes off his sunglasses, showing a glimpse of bright-blue eyes lined in black, and slips on a pair of reading glasses. When he puts his head down, she can see tiny glints of silver peeking out from the bleached blond in his hair.

"You can sit," he says, looking up briefly over his glasses like an ogre accountant.

Chelsea sits, and as he reads through her pathetic application, she fields the stares of the other two people, smiling blandly and knowing that if they're in here with Harlan, they're somehow important.

On Harlan's right is a short man so packed with muscle that he reminds Chelsea of the springs on a trampoline. He has warm brown skin, dark eyes, and ink-black hair shaved down. He looks like the guys David used to watch on MMA, and he eyes her critically as if looking for flaws—of which she has many, for anyone looking at her outsides just now. To Harlan's left is an older woman with steel-gray hair streaked with purple in a braid over her shoulder. She is svelte and shredded but graceful with a tough look about her, like a ballet instructor who got bored and turned to rock climbing and marathons. She's wearing a stylishly droopy altered sweatshirt emblazoned with a black logo, VFR. Underneath that, it reads, WE FIGHT BECAUSE WE HAVE TO.

A weird trill goes up Chelsea's spine. She can't tell if it's excitement or fear or disgust, or maybe all of the above.

When Jeanie pitched her this idea, it was like the kids from *Stand by Me* going to see a dead body. It probably wasn't real, and if it was, they probably wouldn't find it, and if they did, it probably would be very disappointing. But here she is, talking to a famous professional wrestler about joining the Violence Fighting Ring, which is real enough to have a logo, merchandise, and two tricked-out tour buses parked out front.

Harlan looks up from her application, but he doesn't look disappointed by it. "Chris, Sienna, this is Chelsea Martin. I'm pulling rank on this one. If you want a job, you're hired," he says.

That is not what Chelsea was expecting.

"Just like that? You don't even know me. Don't you want to ask me what my biggest flaw is?"

Everyone at the table laughs.

"Your biggest flaw is that you have the Violence," the woman—Sienna—says, but not unkindly. Chelsea clenches her jaw. She won't let herself think about how the little speckles of blood on her shirt stick to her skin.

"Or else you wouldn't be here," Harlan agrees. "You'd be living your sweet, Nerfy life at home with your husband and your two-point-five kids and your picket fence and your purebred dog."

Chelsea winces at the uncanny reality of that description, but they don't seem to notice.

"But something went wrong," he continues with practiced showmanship. "Judging by the pale stripe of skin on your left ring finger and the way you flinched when I approached you, I'm guessing it involved running like hell from that old life." He grins and throws his arms wide. "And now you're here. If you found us, I take it you know what we're doing?"

"A little. The Violence Fighting Ring. So we fight?"

"You *pretend* to fight. You *act*. Put on a show. Bread and circuses. Big costumes, dramatic rivalries, spitting into that microphone about how you're gonna get the belt. Chris here will teach you the ropes of pro wrestling and Sienna will cover wardrobe and feed. Arlene out there will help with acting. We're doing what the WWC used to do and can no longer do. We're doing it underground. We'll travel, put on shows, and leave town before they can shut us down. Now, I think you'd do real good on the mat, if you remember any of this high school acting." He flicks her application. "But if not, we can find a place for you." He leans in, looking serious. "You say you're a homemaker, and

I respect the hell out of that. My mom stayed home and raised three boys, and there was no harder job. So you might end up in the kitchens or bleaching the mats or writing for the website, if being in the spotlight doesn't suit. The pay won't come until we go live, but then you'll be paid according to our profits. Until then, we take care of everything you need. That work for you?"

Chelsea's head is nodding before her mouth can catch up. "I can do that. But what about the real Violence? All those people, packed together in the stands . . ."

She trails off as the image of Jeanie's dented Yeti cup flashes in her mind, and Harlan nods in an understanding way. "Seems real dumb, doesn't it? But people are dumb, and they're getting restless. Two pandemics in five years is making them desperate for something new. We reckon most of our revenue will come from online subscriptions, and for anyone who needs a thrill enough to come out and see us in person, we'll have ironclad hold-harmless agreements and plenty of security in place."

"That sounds reasonable, I guess."

After all, it can't be any more dangerous than working at a grocery store or hotel, and she'd rather have Harlan and Chris and Sienna keeping her safe than the junior manager of a shoe store.

"And you're okay to travel? We won't put down roots or carry much with us, but you'll have a bed and food and doctoring. And if you storm up, we'll keep you from hurting anybody, and that's a promise. The goal is to get everybody vaccinated as soon as we can afford it."

Vaccination. These days, that's the magic word. Chelsea will do anything to be safe again, to know she can hug her girls without worrying about killing them. She doesn't even hesitate.

"Sounds good."

He stands and walks over to her, hand out, grinning his thousand-watt grin. "Then welcome to the VFR, Ms. Martin."

But Chelsea doesn't stand and take his hand. She cocks her head and glances at the other two people. Chris is watching her with a smirk; Sienna looks preternaturally calm and like she's seen everything there is to be seen and can no longer be surprised.

"Why?"

Harlan drops his hand like he's never heard the word before. "What do you mean, why?"

"Why would you take me on? You already know I killed someone today, on the way here. They're looking for me."

Harlan raises an eyebrow at her, then looks at the other two people, and they all burst out laughing. Big, full belly laughs with a not unfamiliar hint of madness. Chelsea feels off-kilter, like she's the only one at the bar who isn't drunk, but somehow this response seems appropriate to an admission of murder. The world is crazy now, and thus crazy is a reasonable reaction.

"Ms. Martin, we've all killed people. All of us. That's what the Violence does. You black out, and you wake up covered in blood, and whoever had the bad luck to be standing next to you is dead. Blaming you for that would be like blaming someone with epilepsy for having a seizure. It's scary and dark and grim and tragic, but . . ." He holds out his hands as if he's hugging the world.

"None of us can change that. So we're using it to our advantage. If you join on and can work the mat, people will pay good money to watch Florida Woman going apeshit, hitting people with chairs and bottles of Costco ketchup. They know who you are, and for us, that's a good thing. You'll help legitimize what we're doing. So if that's your only problem, we should be good now?" He holds out his hand again, eyebrows up, and she gets the sense that if she doesn't shake now, he will oh so politely march her right out the door and wish her well.

She reaches out and takes his hand.

25.

The next morning starts early when Brooklyn falls out of bed at dawn and starts crying. Being her sole caretaker makes the day stretch out long and boring, and Ella feels like a dog straining at a leash. Nana clearly doesn't like her granddaughters and doesn't seem to want to be anywhere near them, but she's not dealing well with the fact that she's stuck with them. She ignores or pooh-poohs all of Ella's suggestions for entertaining Brooklyn—scavenger hunts and pillow forts and cookie baking—and becomes increasingly cold to Brooklyn as the poor kid starts to go stir-crazy in the afternoon. Like, yes, the pool is fun for an hour or two, but of course a little kid is going to get bored and hungry and complain about being pruney and sunburned. They can't stay out there all day just to make life more convenient for Nana.

So that's uncomfortable, but even worse, she gets a flurry of texts from a new number that she soon realizes are from her dad. She blocked his old number, so it must've taken him a while to get a new phone to bother her with.

Ella, where are you?

Tell me right now.

Where did your mother take you?

Tell her the police have her license plate number.

And then, later, more troubling, *Tell Mom she's all over the news. They have all the evidence they need. Tell her to turn herself in, and it won't go as badly.*

"It's very rude to use a screen at the table," Nana snaps, and Ella puts her phone away.

She understands by now that anything she tells Nana can and will be used against her. And if Nana's disgust and exhaustion with them continue, she might think that unloading them on their father would bring welcome relief. Ella knows that if she tells Nana that Dad is an abusive drunk, she'll just be called a liar.

No wonder Mom hates Nana so much.

It was bad enough when they saw her four times a year, but living with her is like living under a magnifying glass, being watched every moment by someone looking for a fault or a crack big enough to stick their fingers in and pry wide open. Ella has been told that her posture is bad, her haircut and color doesn't suit her face, she uses the wrong skin cream, she doesn't dress for her figure, she's an inattentive sister, she has bad manners, and she's in general a whiner, a complainer, and a sourpuss.

Nana's pep talks are not good.

And poor Brooklyn has been told that she's rude, pudgy, dirty, annoying, loud, sticky, whiny, badly behaved. It's like Nana's never met a little kid before. Or maybe, Ella thinks, Mom had to learn the rules just like she did, so Nana hasn't spent much time with a kid who hasn't yet been forced to make herself smaller to accommodate a cruel adult's random whims.

The worst thing is that Nana won't let her leave the house, and there are things back home that Ella needs, things her mom forgot, things worth dodging Dad for. Her car is in the driveway, and it contains her school bag full of the notes and laptop she needs to do summer reading work, plus her purse, money, and ID. It also includes her birth control pills, which she's on not because she's sexually active, but because her cycle is really rough and the pills help with the cramping, heavy bleeding, and horrible mood swings. If she misses any more pills, she's going to have to ask Nana to buy her pads, and—no. Just, no.

She has to get her stuff. Now.

She acts like a perfect angel all afternoon, doing exactly what Nana asks with no attitude and dedicating her time to keeping Brooklyn busy and quiet. She cooks dinner, boxed couscous with canned vegetables, which Nana approves of but Brooklyn hates. She gets her sister to bed early without a fuss, and then she softly knocks on Nana's bedroom door.

"Yes?" comes the annoyed call within.

She opens the door and finds Nana sitting up in bed in silk pajamas. With a scowl, Nana rips off her reading glasses and sets her book aside. "Well?"

"Nana, would it be possible for me to please borrow your car?" she asks.

Nana's eyes bug out. "Are you joking? Of course not. Out of the question."

Just like Nana not to ask why she might need a car. So Ella tries another tactic.

"Then could you drive me by my house? I need to pick up something."

Nana snorts and puts her glasses back on. "Absolutely not. You have everything you need here. Or we can simply order—" She stops, her eyes sliding sideways. "You are not lacking. Now go to bed, please."

"It's medication."

"And your mother didn't include that with your things?"

Now it's Ella's turn to look away. Her mom's still hurt and angry that she went alone to Planned Parenthood for the pills. They don't talk about these things.

"She forgot."

Nana shakes her head in a gesture that in most people conveys sadness and actual pity but here just suggests that Ella is an idiot who should learn better.

"You don't appear to be dying. Bed, please. Now."

"Yes, ma'am."

Ella closes the door softly behind her and walks to the kitchen counter. It's nine, and Nana hasn't set the security system yet.

This is Ella's only real chance.

She hurries upstairs for her keys, shoes, black jeans, a black hoodie. The Florida summer nights are already well into sweltering, but it's more important to avoid being seen—or bitten by mosquitoes. Nana's neighborhood runs mosquito trucks day and night, and Ella rubs Brooklyn and herself with a repellent towelette every time they go swimming, but she's going to need all the protection she can get. She tucks her phone in her back pocket and slips out the side door, as far from Nana's room as possible.

Over on the side of the house, there's a tiny gap between the fence and the garage, and she sucks in her stomach and slides through. She keeps to the shadows as she hurries down the perfectly clean sidewalks. No one is out, not walking and not on the road. Birds twitter and bats sing and frogs scream about frog sex and bigger things rustle in the bushes, but Ella isn't too scared. This part of Florida doesn't have bears, and there are no wolves or big predators, and Nana's neighborhood probably had all the wildlife shipped away or groomed into poodle cuts, anyway. Soon she reaches the little hut by the gates, where she unlatches the pedestrian door and steps outside. There's a shape in the hut, but it's huddled in front of the TV. They mainly worry about people coming in here in cars—not going out on foot. There's not even a sidewalk beyond the gate.

Nana's house is a little under four miles away from Ella's house, and there are sidewalks and crosswalks most of the way there. Before the Violence hit, there were tons of people on this route walking and biking and pushing little carts for their groceries. This part of the suburbs isn't supposed to be walkable, with everything stretched so far out, but people have to get where they're going somehow. Ella has never traveled between their houses on foot, but she knows the way.

It's easy, at first. No cars pass. The night is hot but balmy, with a breeze that smells like the ocean, even if they're a few miles away from the bay. She sweats inside her heavy hoodie but is grateful to blend in with the darkness. It doesn't occur to her until she's waiting for a walk signal at a big intersection that there are bigger threats out there than the Violence, that there are still kidnappers and pedophiles and rapists and flat-out creeps walking the streets. She presses the button again and again, hoping the light will hurry up and change but unwilling to risk being caught jaywalking past the state-mandated curfew.

Finally it changes, and she hurries across. An awful smell hits her face, diving down her nose and mouth and making her retch. She scouts around for a dead possum or raccoon, then sees the lump under the eaves of Big Fred's Floors. In the darkness, with the shadows, she can't see the plaid shirt and busted-in head, but she can see the stark splatter of blood on the yellow wall. From here, it looks black, not red.

Something deep inside her whispers, *That's a corpse.*

The only dead person she's seen before now was Grandpa Terry, and he was clean and powdery and nicely dressed and contained in an expensive, velvet-lined coffin with classical music softly playing and little butter mints placed nearby. This corpse is a wild thing, uncontained, untouched, uncared for, and it scares the shit out of her, as if it could infect her. It's been here for at least two days, and . . . that's not how corpses should be treated. But there's nothing she can do about it. That's just another part of the Violence—this odd helplessness.

She jogs along the sidewalk to get away from it and ends up in front of Red Lotus Massage. Everyone says it's a human trafficking place where gross guys go to get happy endings, and it doesn't feel any safer than Big Fred's. A shoe skids over gravel under the shop awning, and a rough voice says, "You lost?"

Ella runs.

She is, to say the least, not a good runner. That month of Personal Fitness where the coach made them run a mile three times a week was probably the worst month of her life. But she runs until she can't breathe, and then she pauses under a streetlight to catch her breath. She's in front of a big red barn now, a folksy shop on the corner where they used to sell fresh produce and raw cow's milk and expensive honey, where food trucks used to pull up, bringing Latin music and strings of Christmas lights. One time she and Mom and Brooklyn ate corn off sticks at those picnic tables, but now all those homey touches are gone. Like most small businesses, it struggled through Covid and gave up when the Violence hit and hasn't yet come back, if it ever will.

A lone security light shines down on a row of dead tomato plants out front, their wire cages hovering like little ghosts.

Jesus. Everything is creepy, when you're alone at night.

Ella starts walking again, picking up her pace. She's back on a residential street, but because it's Florida, most of the houses are in fenced neighborhoods. Dogs run out to bark at her through gaps in hedges, and a big truck honks as it screeches by, nearly giving her a heart attack. She's never walked like this, walked because she had to. Her family relies on cars for everything—except for taking the golf cart to that red barn for fruit and corn and Jarritos. Walking feels exposed and unsafe. Walking makes her feel small and slow.

And it also makes her feel wildly, strangely alive.

She can smell everything: swimming pools, dogs, a rogue skunk or badly hidden weed, roses, the difference between pine trees and orange trees and oaks. The air is hot in places and cool and wet in others as she passes by lakes and ponds. Music rides the breeze as she hurries past open windows, and somewhere, unfortunately for their neighbors, a terrible band practices in a garage, making her wince. She stops thinking of herself as an invader, an outsider, and starts thinking of herself as another animal roaming the world. It helps, reframing her role here as part of something instead of as an interloper.

And then she's finally at her neighborhood. They don't have a guy in the little hut all day, but they do have keypads at the gates for cars and pedestrians. She punches in the number, which has been the same for five years, even though it's supposed to change quarterly, and breathes a huge sigh of relief when the door swings open.

She's safe now. She's home.

Except . . . well, home was never that safe.

Still, it's a nice feeling, even if it lies—that sense of belonging.

As she nears her house, Ella pulls up her hood and ducks from shadow to shadow. There are no lights on, and the garage door is closed. Dad's car is no longer in the driveway. Ella's Honda Civic is in the grass to the side of the basketball hoop, untouched. She takes out her key fob before remembering that it makes a cheerful beep when it unlocks. That is definitely not what she wants, so she pulls the rarely used metal key out of its fob.

In the patch of azaleas off the driveway, she pauses, sending out her senses. Yes, Dad is most likely drunk in his man cave or asleep in his bed, but it's unlikely yet also possible that he's sitting in the hot tub out back with a cigar or staying up late to watch the news. She doesn't smell the nasty funk of cigar smoke that her mom was somehow always supposed to magically get out of the laundry, nor does she hear a single noise. This must be what a mouse feels like—small and vulnerable and hunted, tasting the air and squinting at lights and listening so hard that it feels like she can sense her own ear hairs quivering, knowing all the while that the predator is nearby and might be watching. Her heart bumps up to a jagged staccato, and her arms and legs tingle and fizz with energy.

It's now or never.

Ella springs for her car, light on the balls of her feet, and fumbles with the awkward metal key, trying to slot it into place in the pitch darkness. She can't see a thing, so she whips out her phone and uses a flash of light to locate the keyhole and twist the key. She winces as the door squeaks open, throws herself into the seat, and locks the doors.

It feels safe, now. Her dad would have to bust open the window to get to her.

Amid that relief, there's a brief burst of reality: There's also a chance her dad actually *would* bust open the window to get to her. To hurt her.

No time for weird, useless thoughts like that. Ella pushes the starter button and sighs in gratitude as the car turns on, glad she filled up the gas tank before the shit hit the fan. She takes a moment to reach over and touch her purse where it sits on the floorboard, feeling for her wallet and the thick plastic box that has enough pills to last her for almost three months. She even has her Switch now, although not the power cord. Her backpack and laptop should still be in the trunk, and she doesn't have to check to know her bug-out bag is still there, too. Her dad doesn't have a key to her car—she stole it from the spare drawer months ago without him knowing.

These are the things she needs to feel okay, and a surge of triumph makes her grin. She hasn't grinned in weeks.

Now all she has to do is drive back to Nana's and she'll have her car, her pills, and everything in her wallet, which also means she can order stuff online, if she needs to. Nana won't be happy, but what is Nana going to do—have her car towed back here? There's a spare spot in the four-car garage, anyway, with Randall gone for good.

She puts it in reverse to back down the driveway, leaving the lights off so her dad won't see the flash of headlights through a window. So slowly the car rolls backward, the engine barely humming as she watches for the mailbox in the rearview mirror, wishing she had a newer car with a backup camera.

"Ella!"

She jerks her head over, and there's her dad, on the front porch in his boxers and an undershirt, a beer bottle dangling from his fingers by the light of the open door. He must've heard her, even though she knows she was careful. He looks thin and sick, and their eyes meet, and then she slams her foot on the gas. The car roars backward, and her tire bumps over something as she overcompensates on the turn into the road. When she glances at her dad as she puts the car into drive, he's running after her, barefoot, his face a familiar mass of rage, and he rears back and chucks the beer bottle at her car as hard as he can. She floors it, and the car peels away, fishtailing, side mirror banging into the mailbox. The bottle erupts against the car with a loud pop but doesn't break any windows, at least.

Ella knows her neighborhood, knows all the tight curves, and she doesn't look in the rearview mirror to see if her dad is following on foot. She takes the short streets as fast as she can and runs the stop signs until she's idling in front of the gates, waiting for them to open.

On the best of days, these gates take forever.

On the worst of days, when she's late for school or a babysitting job or, say, now, they inch open so slowly that she can hear her teeth grinding together. The whole time, she's glancing nervously in the rearview mirror, glancing at her phone in the cup holder, glancing back to the slowly unfurling gates. The second she thinks she can make it out, she's inching forward, nudging them open the final foot. It's not like she's going to get in more trouble for scratching up a ten-year-old car, and besides, her dad was the one who threw the bottle.

As she pulls to a stop at the main road, her phone buzzes in the cup holder.

Cons back Rich now or I deport the car as stolen

He's clearly had more than just one beer.

Had so much beer, in fact, that he's not even going to try to follow her. Because he can't.

Good.

She turns onto the road and even though she'd love to do sixty back to Nana's, she drives exactly the speed limit. The police don't have much time these days for traffic stops, but with everything so quiet, driving too fast would definitely look suspicious. Every red light takes a century. Her phone doesn't buzz again. She imagines her father calling up Uncle Chad and Uncle Chad's mean little pig eyes narrowing as he radios his friends about a stolen car. It would be nice if Dad's text was a bluff, but Drunk Dad isn't smart enough to bluff. She constantly checks her rearview mirror for red and blue lights.

Ella can't believe it, but she makes it back to Nana's neighborhood without any problems. It took her over an hour to walk home, but it's less than ten minutes to drive the same route. When she pulls up to the guardhouse, some guy that isn't Homer shines a flashlight in her eyes.

"Name?"

"Ella Martin. I'm Patricia Lane's granddaughter."

The man—older, bald, decked out with belt holsters like he lives at the army supply store—flips through a clipboard full of papers.

"You're not on here."

Ella looks around her car, wishing she had the kind of grandmother who took selfies or sent birthday cards, any kind of evidence that she has a connection to the woman on the other side of the gate.

"My mom is Chelsea Martin, my dad is David Martin. Are they on there?"

He flips through the papers and stares at her, hard, like she's an enemy. "They've been removed."

Ella feels desperation rise, acid in her throat. "My grandmother is Patricia Lane, and my grandfather is Randall Lane, the judge. They live at Twenty-Three Oh Five Chatsfield Drive. The usual guard is named Homer."

The man puts the clipboard in the hut and hooks his other thumb around his belt by his gun holster. "None of that means a thing if your name is crossed out. Why don't you try giving your grandmother a call, see if she's expecting you?"

Ella scrolls through her contacts, but of course she doesn't have her grandmother's number. Nana has never wanted to talk to her, and why would she ever need to talk to Nana?

"It's a new phone," she lies. "Can you call her?"

The man shakes his head as if disappointed in the youth of today. He goes back into his guardhouse and picks up a phone, his eyes glued to Ella as he dials. For a long moment, nothing happens. He doesn't speak. Then he hangs up the phone and walks back.

"No answer. Why don't you try coming back in the morning?"

Tears prick at the corners of Ella's eyes, and although normally she would find that inconvenient and embarrassing, now she's grasping at straws. Let him see how scared and upset she is. Let him look in the eyes of a crying kid who wants to see her grandmother and still not let her through.

"Please. My parents are in quarantine and I'm living with my grand-mother and my baby sister is in there and she needs me and I just ran out to get my medicine and I really, really need to get back. Please."

The man sighs and rubs his head as if he had his pity gland re-moved and she makes the scar itch. He stands on the curb, just out of striking distance, the holstered gun and his crotch at her eye level.

"Look, kid. That's a sad story. It is. Lots of sad stories going around these days. But my job is to keep out people who don't belong." He crosses his arms and takes in her face, her body, her car. "And you don't belong. I see a kid in a beat-up car wearing a black hoodie who's got a sob story, I see someone trying to lie their way into a much nicer neighborhood than they can afford, I assume they're about to do a B and E."

"A . . . what?"

"Burglary."

He tucks his fat thumbs through his belt loops, one by the gun and one by a knife, and rocks back on his heels like this is the best thing that's ever happened to him, having some little smack of power over a terrified girl.

"So if you really think your grandma is in there, you get in touch with her and tell her to put you on the list, or else you stay out there where you belong."

Ella is full-on crying now, her throat a raw ache. She has to get through. She has to. Brooklyn is in there, and Brooklyn needs her. She's all that Brooklyn has left. The thought of her little sister falling out of bed and waking up alone in the dark after a nightmare, calling for her big sister and getting no answer—it makes her hands go to fists and her whole body glow red hot with impotent fury.

"Let me in," she growls.

The guy sneers as if her answer proves his point.

She doesn't belong in there.

"Or else what?" He snorts. "Get the hell out of here, kid."

When he saunters back to his hut, he picks up his phone and holds a threatening finger to it. Who's he going to call—the police?

It doesn't matter.

He's not letting her in.

She uses the turnaround, slowly, tires crunching over the expensive stone. With her car facing the intersection, she doesn't know where to go.

She'll come talk to Homer in the morning. He'll let her through. He knows her.

Until then, she has to find somewhere safe to spend the night.

But there is nowhere safe. Not anymore.

26.

Patricia has a prescription to help her sleep, so she barely has time to worry before she falls insensate. This house is a fortress—she's made sure of that. She had every name but hers struck from the list to get into the neighborhood, which means neither Chelsea nor David can get in without her say-so, and neither can Randall or his squirrelly secretary. He hasn't contacted her at all, even though he said he would send Diane over. For now, this place and its contents are hers, and she'll protect it with every resource at her service. That's how she spent the first forty years of her life, and it comes back as easily as riding a bicycle. Her sleep is deep and dreamless.

Until she jerks awake in the dark, unsure of where she is or what's happening. There was some sort of loud noise.

"Nana? Nana!"

Patricia Lane is not a woman who likes to be woken up. She prefers to set the terms of her days, and even if everything else is out of control, there is no reason on God's green earth that a small child should be standing outside her locked door, knocking and screeching like a dying cat.

She stretches and stands, resenting every ping and pop that reminds her that her body is no longer youthful and spry. With exaggerated care, she walks to the door, her room barely lit by the sunlight limning her heavy-duty curtains. She unlocks the door, and there is Brooklyn, her face tearstained and her eyes frantic. Patricia raises her eyebrows.

"Brooklyn, this is not ladylike behavior."

"But Nana!" Brooklyn's lower lip trembles, and she lurches forward and latches her arms around Patricia's hips like a lamprey, the child's face buried uncomfortably in the crotch of her silk pajamas. "Ella is gone. I had a nightmare, and I woke up, and she wasn't there, and she's not anywhere!" This last sentence ends in a wail that goes on and on. Good Lord. Does the child not breathe? Has no one ever taught her to . . . not cry?

Chelsea was a brat, but she was never this *needy*. Patricia has always believed that children thrive with clear rules and consequences, and that too much hugging and coddling will just make them weak and soft. She always kept Chelsea at arm's length for this reason and wasn't afraid to lash her with words or a wooden spoon if she didn't immediately toe the line. For all her faults, Chelsea understood how to take care of herself at this age, and it's clear she didn't pass that gift on to her youngest daughter.

Patricia pats the child's head as if she were a dog and gently pries her away until Brooklyn is standing on her own in a too-small night-gown with garish horses on it.

"Have you checked the restrooms, or outside?"

Brooklyn looks at her like she's speaking another language. "No?"

"Well, I think you should do all of your research before resorting to waking people up before dawn."

"It's after seven."

Patricia shakes her head. "Don't talk back."

"I wasn't talking back! I was telling you what time it is."

Patricia pauses, makes eye contact. "You're still talking back."

Brooklyn's mouth is open, her hands in fists. She looks angry and confused, and Patricia wonders what Chelsea was so busy doing when she should've been teaching her child how to respect adults. Not working, obviously. Not cleaning.

Just being a disappointment.

Which is why Brooklyn has not accurately assessed the situation and wisely chosen silence.

"I'm not talking back. I'm not! I'm telling you that Ella is gone and she shouldn't be gone and you have to find her!"

Brooklyn is red and angry now, and she bursts back into tears and runs away, saving Patricia from explaining that she was indeed still talking back, and really just digging herself deeper into that hole. With the child's probing eyes off her, she takes a deep breath and goes through her normal morning routine, trying to reestablish her calm. She opens the curtains, takes her pills, stands on the scale to make sure nothing untoward has happened in her never-ending battle against her failing metabolism. All is well, and after fluffing her hair and tying on a robe, she tours the house, looking for any sign of her older granddaughter's whereabouts.

Patricia is sharp-eyed, especially when it comes to things in her home being out of place, but she can't find anything out of the ordinary. All of Ella's things are where she left them, and she doesn't appear to have taken anything. She's nowhere in the house, nor outside by the pool or in the pool house, which is locked now. Patricia's jewelry and money are still in their hiding place under the bed in an old bag. A thorough search suggests nothing was taken, and Patricia takes a moment to transfer the bag to her own closet, hidden by her floor-length furs. Her car and keys are still here, thank goodness, and the security system didn't go off last night.

Which means the girl must've left before Patricia set the alarm.

But where did she go, and why? She seems to love her sister, yet she left no note? And there are no messages on Patricia's phone—ah, but she doesn't have Ella's number, which means Ella might not have hers. It's doubtful that Chelsea would use her as an emergency contact. She has Chelsea's number, just in case, so she sends her a quick text: *Is Ella with you?*

Chelsea doesn't answer.

Perhaps they've run away together, leaving the youngest and most troublesome child behind? Surely not. Chelsea isn't a great mother, but she's certainly not that cold-blooded.

But David, perhaps, is.

She texts him the same message.

Is Ella with you?

He texts back immediately: *No. Is she with you?*

And when she doesn't answer: ***WHERE ARE THEY?***

Patricia raises an eye at the phone and blocks his number.

He's certainly the last port she would turn to in a storm.

She's had suspicions, of course. Has noticed, over the years, how Chelsea has changed, become more withdrawn and sullen. Has seen her daughter flinch when her husband reaches past her for a glass in the kitchen cabinet. But she was never certain about exactly what was happening, never saw any bruises, and her relationship with her daughter is not the kind where they ask personal questions. She has never liked David, and she is not about to trust him now.

Brooklyn finally reappears, sad and pink and soaked with tears, rubbing her eyes. "Nana, can I have breakfast?"

Patricia points to the cabinets. "There's cereal."

Brooklyn looks at her as if she's been asked to do trigonometry. "Can I have some?"

"*May* I have some."

"May I have some?"

"Go ahead."

Still with that stupid, squirming confusion.

"I don't know how."

Patricia's lips purse in distaste. "You don't know how to pour yourself a bowl of cereal?"

"No."

"But you're five."

"Mommy and Ella make it for me." A long pause. Softer, "I'm little."

It's like they don't even speak the same language.

"Your mother could make cereal when she was five."

"Can you show me?"

Well, at least that's an attempt at trying.

Patricia sighs, realizing her day is going to be full of big sighs, especially if they can't find Ella soon. She pulls down a box of flakes and a bowl, and Brooklyn points out that she's too short to reach either item on her own, which Patricia concedes is true. She takes them to the table and shows Brooklyn how to pour the right amount of cereal. When the child goes to pour the milk, a little spills, and Brooklyn stares at her, waiting to see how she'll react. Patricia's instinct is to say something acerbic and cutting, but instead, she gives a tight smile.

"No crying over spilled milk. Just get a napkin and wipe it up."

Brooklyn does, and when Patricia smiles at her, she smiles back. They're getting somewhere.

Except the child then demands a cut-up banana and a spoonful of sugar in her cereal, and honestly, her granddaughter is just terribly spoiled.

When Brooklyn has finally gotten everything she demands, Patricia goes to get her own grapefruit ready for breakfast, but her phone rings.

"Thank God," she murmurs, hoping it's Ella, or someone with some good news. It's a local number she doesn't recognize, and she picks it up.

"Hello?"

"Hi, is this Mrs. Lane?"

Not anymore, she thinks, but that's not yet public knowledge.

"It is."

"This is Carrie Green at the club. We have a delivery for you here?"

Patricia's heart lifts. She was expecting several items to be dropped off for the auction, which was originally postponed for the pandemic and will now be held exclusively for club members who can prove they've been vaccinated. But . . .

"This isn't the club number. And I don't know you."

Carrie chuckles. "Yes, now that everyone is getting vaccinated, the lines are busy today with lunch reservations, and I'm new. I'm using one of the cells. I apologize if I startled you. It's for the auction."

Patricia smiles in spite of herself. "No problem. I'll be by shortly. Do you have room for two at lunch?"

"Let me check." A brief pause. "We do! Right at noon. Will the judge be joining you?"

"No. My younger granddaughter."

"Wonderful. We'll be sure to have some crayons ready. We're looking forward to seeing you."

Finally, something to do.

Yes, Randall has left her. But she can get in front of it, spin the tale in her favor. He'll be in Iceland soon, paying for whatever ice-blondes he wants. It's unlikely he's been by the club since he left. Chances are, no one there will be any the wiser. And if she can find something suitable for Brooklyn to wear, the child will show nicely. She's very attractive when she's properly styled.

It grows tiresome, Brooklyn asking where her sister is, and Patricia finally, sternly says, "There's no point in asking me again. I don't know any more than you. We can look for her on our way to lunch."

And then Brooklyn gets so excited about doing anything except sitting at home that she's quite pliant. Patricia soon has her bathed, her hair blown dry and shiny, a pretty dress buttoned up the back and sweet little white sandals on her feet, if a bit too small. Patricia spends extra time on her own hair and makeup and tosses on some extra jewelry. Brooklyn asks for a car seat when they get in Patricia's sedan, but a five-year-old can ride with a seatbelt, as far as Patricia is concerned. It was good enough for Chelsea, after all, and she came to no harm.

They wave Patricia through at the club gate, and her heart thrills to be here again, in the place where she holds all the power. The lot is emptier than usual, with most of her cohort gone north or, like Randall, to Europe. She's kept up with the auction committee, of course, but the world has noticeably slowed down. They have two months still before the rescheduled event, and she'll have to find Ella to watch Brooklyn so she can dive back into her duties with verve now that everyone's getting vaccinated. Maybe she'll even set her sights on her next husband.

Yes, she can turn all this around. She has to start planning her next move.

"This place is fancy," Brooklyn whispers, and Patricia has to remind her that children only speak when spoken to.

At the front desk, she releases Brooklyn's preternaturally sticky hand and says, "I believe you have a package for me?"

The girl behind the counter ducks down and pokes around but

comes up empty-handed. "I'm sorry, Mrs. Lane, but we don't have anything. Who did you talk to?"

"Ms. Green."

The girl cocks her head.

"Carrie Green," Patricia adds.

"We don't have a Carrie Green."

Patricia's fingers twitch.

"Carrie Green doesn't work here?"

"No. Could it have been someone else? We have a Carolyn Goss, but she's a groundskeeper."

A terrible, sinking feeling makes Patricia's chest tight. She holds up her phone. "This is her number."

The woman shakes her head, only now beginning to look apologetic. "We only call our members through official means, Mrs. Lane."

"Then I suppose she also neglected to make the lunch reservation I requested?"

The woman flips open the book and runs a finger down the page. "No, ma'am."

"I see."

Which is how rich, powerful people say, *Oh shit.*

"If you'll excuse me?"

Patricia grabs Brooklyn's hand and drags her out the door and toward the sedan.

"Ouch! Nana, that hurts!"

"Then move faster," she snaps. "We need to hurry."

"I thought we were going out to lunch. Like a tea party, you said."

Patricia opens the door and struggles to snap the seatbelt over the squirming child.

"Another day, perhaps."

Because she understands that whoever called her wanted her to come here, which means they wanted her out of the house.

She drives just above the speed limit on the way back, wary for policemen and preparing to lie about Brooklyn needing to urinate, should they stop her. Without the judge's presence and protection, she's just as susceptible to tickets as anyone else, and she hates how that makes her feel like she's already doing something wrong.

When she stops at the guardhouse, waiting for the gates to open, Homer steps out and waves. "Mrs. Lane, do you have a granddaughter, maybe seventeen? Drives an older Honda Civic?"

She stares at him coldly for a moment before her eyes bounce back to the gate, waiting for it to open. She has no idea what kind of car Ella drives, but that doesn't signify.

"I do."

"She came by twice, once last night with Greg and once with me this morning. But she wasn't on the list, so . . ."

"Add her to the list. Her name is Ella Martin. Call me immediately if she returns."

And then she's all but peeling past the gates and toward her house.

On the outside, everything looks totally normal. Maybe she's just being paranoid?

The car screeches to a halt in the garage, and she jumps out and slams the door.

"Nana!" Brooklyn screams.

Cursing softly, she turns back to help the child out of the car, even though a five-year-old should be able to extricate herself from a seatbelt. Laura Ingalls Wilder was babysitting an infant and cooking with open fire at that age, for crying out loud.

Only once the door to the house is open and she sees that the security system has been disarmed does it occur to her that she—an older woman pulling a young child by the hand—is entering what might be a dangerous situation. She whips out her phone and dials 9-1-1, preparing to hit the CALL button. With the judge no longer on her side, she's not willing to risk the call unless there's really an emergency.

"Hello?" she calls into the hallway.

"Is it Ella?" Brooklyn chirps, trying to move past her into the house.

Patricia jerks her back by her arm, gently shoving her into the garage as the child squeaks a protest.

"Stay here. If you hear anything unusual, run."

"What do you mean?"

Patricia doesn't have time to explain everything. She holds up a finger to her lips, grabs a mallet from the garage tool bench Miguel once used to fix the lawnmower, slips off her mules, and tiptoes into her own home. It's silent inside, no whispers or scent of smoke or footsteps on the stairs, nothing that would scare her, just the sturdy march of Randall's grandfather clock ticking, ticking, ticking.

"Hello?" she calls again, unsure what the protocol for this sort of thing is or what she would do if anyone responded.

To her knowledge, only she, Rosa, Miguel, and Randall know the security code, and while they were in Utah, Randall admitted that he'd forgotten it; he never uses it, anyway. Someone has always been home. There's no reason anyone else would know it. She didn't even tell her granddaughters—purposefully kept it from them, in fact. Could this perhaps be an inside job by the security company?

Room by room, Patricia moves through her home, a sense of unease rippling up the back of her neck. Something is very wrong, and she isn't sure what. Nothing obvious has been taken—not her laptop, sitting conspicuously on the sunroom table, not any of the flatscreen TVs. She doesn't hear a single sound, and the house feels empty and hollow.

Whoever was here—and someone was definitely here, she can feel it in her bones—was after something very specific. Maybe it was just Randall, stopping by to collect his things and maneuvering her out of the house so he wouldn't have to deal with her?

He did say he would send Diane.

She hurries upstairs, but Randall's office appears untouched, as does the closet in the bedroom he keeps for himself. Of course, most of his things were already packed for Iceland. What else could he possibly want?

Everything in the house that's worth anything—

"Shit," Patricia murmurs under her breath.

She runs down the hall, heart thumping so hard she can feel it in her ears. She storms past Brooklyn's room, barely noting the clothes strewn everywhere, tossed out of their bags. In the spare room, the painting hangs open, the empty safe exposed to the world.

And in her own closet, the old bag she's hidden under her furs is gone.

27.

After shaking hands with everyone, Chelsea is sent out to the RVs to get some dinner. It should feel weird but it doesn't, walking through the waiting room as people stare at her, whispering. She holds her head high—because she got the job, didn't she?—and thanks Arlene before heading out across the baked earth toward the shade of the awnings.

There are five people sprawled out on lawn chairs and picnic blankets in the shade around the RVs and tour buses as a tall, skinny teen girl, maybe sixteen with an undercut and galaxy hair, babysits the hot dogs and hamburgers on the grill, a phone in her hand. Chelsea is surprised to see that no one looks like a professional wrestler. There's one tall guy, but he's thin as a breadstick; one young, muscled guy of average height with a shaved head and blackwork tattoo sleeves; a fit silver fox in his sixties who looks like he belongs on TV; a sad but beautiful Hawaiian woman in her thirties; and a pretty but fake-looking brunette in her twenties with painted-on eyebrows who probably calls herself an influencer. Chelsea immediately feels bad for assuming the worst of her.

"You're Chelsea?" the teen at the grill asks.

"Yep."

"I'm Sienna's daughter, Indigo. You want a dog or a burger?"

"A burger would be great."

Indigo nods and points to a cooler by the RV. "Cool. We have plenty. Just grab a drink and chill. Should be ready in five."

Chelsea heads to the cooler and digs out a water. It's cold enough to make her teeth hurt and drips condensation down her arm. She's aware that everyone else is watching her, and she hasn't felt this judged since the first Mommy and Me class she went to with a new-born Ella. She'd thought it would be all about woman power and sisterhood and mommy wisdom but it was more about losing the baby weight and buying the hottest artisan booties. This isn't an artisan booty crowd, but whatever they're looking for in her, they don't seem to find it. Then again, she's in old cutoffs, flip-flops, and a blood-spattered T-shirt. She wouldn't talk to herself, either.

All the chairs are taken, so she sits on the blanket in the shade with her back against the RV, next to the sad-looking woman. Out of the six strangers, she feels like she might have the most in common with a sad woman in her thirties because she is also a sad woman in her thirties.

"Weird interview, right?" she says to the woman, because she has to say something because if she doesn't say anything, she has to remember that she killed her only friend a few hours ago, even if the day feels like it's lasted a year.

The woman perks up a bit and turns to her. "Right? I've never felt so inadequate about my CV. I'm Amy." Amy holds out her hand to shake, although it's awkward since Chelsea is on the floor beside her. "How'd you get in?" She motions to the whole group, all of whom are not-so-subtly listening in. "That's the question of the day. Most jobs, they need definitive skills, but here, it's a crapshoot. They took me on because I'm an accountant with marketing experience who looks 'exotic.'" Amy makes finger quotes and rolls her eyes.

"Why'd they take y'all?" Chelsea asks, turning to the group to give herself time to answer the question without scaring them all off. If this is a job where they all live together, she wants to be on the best possible terms from the start, and she knows that if she lies, she'll just get caught.

They're all listening, of course, because it's a small group of people in a big, empty field.

The silver fox speaks first. "I've done some commercials and modeling. I'm Steve." He gives a little wave.

"I think it's just because I'm unusually tall," the unusually tall guy says, frowning. "And I brought my own leather duster. I'm Matt."

The punk and the Instagram girl stare at each other uneasily like a badger and a fox facing off, and he finally nods for her to go first. She fiddles with her navel ring, and Chelsea is very glad that Ella never got into the crop top and high-waisted pants trend. "Ugh. Fine. I guess they took me because I'm hot and flexible and don't mind showing skin and I have a million followers on Instagram. I'm London. And that's my real name, not, like, something I made up. My parents are ex-pats."

They all look at the punk guy. His violent exterior—muscles, tattoos, shaved head—is at odds with his meditative, quiet manner. "I'm TJ. I do jiu-jitsu. And the tattoos, I guess."

"And you do art," Indigo says from the barbecue. When they all look at her, she says, "He's famous on TikTok. Like, graffiti and stuff." He smiles and gives a small nod.

London snorts and flops in her chair like she's unimpressed.

TJ raises an eyebrow at the display and looks to Chelsea. "What about you?"

They're in a loose sort of circle, nursing their sweating drinks, and for a moment Chelsea wonders if this is what an AA meeting feels like. She knows there's no point in lying, since she's apparently all over the news, so she might as well get it out of the way.

"I'm Chelsea. I think they took me on because I'm on the news right now. My friend and I were driving here, and I stormed on I-4. Woke up and . . ." She stares down at the red splatters on her T-shirt. "So, that. And I guess I did some drama and singing in high school."

Matt honks a laugh and rocks back in his folding chair; he reminds her of an awkward goth pterodactyl. "Yeah! I saw that. Like, you threw manure at some old guy and stole his truck. Classic."

Chelsea looks down, feels her face flush. It's not something in which she can take any sort of pride. "So they say."

"Hey, sorry about your friend." Amy touches her arm briefly, and Chelsea wants to double over and cry. She's been touched more today than she has in weeks, thanks to her self-quarantine and barricade, and she misses her girls like a punch to the gut.

"Thanks." It comes out a half sob, and Chelsea has to look away and drink some water.

Steve goes to a different cooler and pulls out a mini-bottle of pink wine. "Sounds like you've had a hell of a day."

Chelsea takes the bottle with a smile of thanks, screws off the top, and learns firsthand how awkward it is to sip wine from a tiny bottle. It goes down in a flash, sweet as soda, and warmth unspools in her stomach. She's tried to limit her drinking for the last year, after David went after Ella, but God, she's missed this feeling, responsibility and anxiety sloughing away like a heavy coat on a hot day.

"Yeah, I'll have one of those, too." Amy heads to the cooler and comes back with three of the mini-bottles, handing another one to Chelsea. "It's only like half a glass, right?"

London was already drinking a can of alcoholic seltzer, Steve has an elegant, monogrammed hip flask, and Matt's brow draws down as he does the math. He strides over to the cooler and comes back with three little bottles of red wine, and Chelsea is pretty sure this guy wishes he was a vampire.

"No drink for you?" London asks TJ.

He holds up his fist to show a big, black X on the back of his hand. "Nah. That shit's poison."

London snorts. "Anything can be poison if you misuse it. I know a girl who OD'd on Tums."

"Then she was an idiot."

"She was depressed, you asshole!"

"Hey, c'mon." The teen girl at the grill takes a few uncertain steps toward them, the burger spatula in one hand. "It's all cool."

"It's not fuckin' cool," London grumbles, slumping back in her chair and gulping her seltzer, silver rings flashing on all her fingers. "She almost died. They had to pump out her stomach."

"But she did it to herself," TJ counters, sitting forward in his chair with the air of an exhausted college professor who's given this speech too many times. "It's a series of bad choices. No one wakes up one day and randomly picks up the Tums. If you're having problems, you should do the deep work on fixing your psyche. Meditate, do yoga, see a therapist, see a doctor, get meds, reach out. Don't take a bottle of chewable calcium. That's the coward's response."

"So what, you're a fuckin' doctor now? A psychologist? You think people can just get fixed by doing some downward dog?" London throws her shoulders back against the chair, tossing her hair and snarling. "Jesus, what an asshole."

Chelsea can feel it building—the goading, the denial, the insults, the body language, the tension brewing between two strangers in lawn chairs. It's like watching a tornado coming, knowing she can't stop it. But she has to try.

"I think we can all agree that there's nothing funny about depression or being sick," she says in what she recognizes as the same voice she uses when she's breaking up a quarrel between her daughters. "But getting in a fight here, now that we all have jobs, isn't going to help anybody." Movement draws her eye away from the danger zone between London and TJ, and she gives a tiny smile as she notes Indigo texting on her phone, hoping she's letting the people in charge know that there's some weird, useless argument happening out here. Sure, tension is high, but . . .

"I've met so many assholes like you," London continues, her voice rising. "Like, you'd think with the economy trashed and dead bodies everywhere, you could be, I don't know, nice. Like, give the benefit of a doubt. But no, Mr. Don't Drink here knows everything. You think you're so great?"

"Says the girl who doctors her bikini pics to sell diet pills on her thinspo Insta," TJ mutters. "Yes, I know who you are, and you're obviously just here for the attention."

London explodes from her chair, knocking it backward, seltzer can crushed in her hand. "Don't you insult my feed, you little turd! You don't know me! You can't talk about me that way!"

TJ stands, arms crossed, giving her a look meant to express his disdain—and his lack of fear.

"You don't get it, do you? People can say whatever they want. People can judge you. You can do whatever you want, but then people can think and say whatever they want about that. You can't control other people." He raises one eyebrow like he thinks he's the Rock.

London stops, close enough to slap him. Steve and Matt leap to their feet, looking like they want to stop the fight but unsure who to help. Amy and Chelsea stand, too, and Indigo has forgotten the sizzling meat on the grill and is straining anxiously toward the interview building, phone against her ear.

"I'm not scared of you," London snarls with all the bravado of a Chihuahua pissing itself in front of a Doberman.

"You *should* be scared of me," TJ explains with aggressive, Zen-like calm. "I've got more body mass than you and I'm a brown belt in jiu-jitsu. I could literally kill you. And what are you going to do to me?"

London shoves him, and he takes a step back but doesn't show any emotional response, doesn't even uncross his arms. It's weirdly fascinating to Chelsea, watching a grown man goaded by a woman, who doesn't seem the least bit interested in hitting her or choking her, who may say cruel things—cruel, but true—but doesn't seem to want to cause harm. London is out of control, and TJ might be an asshole, but he's giving off the aura of a yogi.

And it's only making London angrier. She owns some sense of safety, of untouchability, that Chelsea has never known. It's a privilege to act this way and know you won't be attacked.

"I've killed people, too, you dick!" London growls. "I beat a guy's head in with a wine bottle at a club and went right back to dancing, so don't you act like I'm nothing!"

"I'm not acting like you're nothing," he responds calmly. "I'm being honest because that's my right as a human being and because I believe in truth and authenticity above all things. If I wanted to act like you were nothing, I wouldn't be talking to you."

With a grunt, London shoves him again, her hands pressing against his crossed arms, her perfect ombre nails spread like cat claws. He steps back and shakes his head sadly at her.

"Why are you doing this? I'm not your enemy."

"You keep saying that, but you also called my friend dumb and you think I'm dumb for drinking and you insulted my feed and you're just an asshole!" She shoves him again, and his arms uncross.

He doesn't hurt her, though, doesn't make a move toward her. His hands hang at his sides, easy, and he takes a deep breath and cocks his head at her.

"You're the one acting like an asshole."

London's hands go to fists, and she's about to punch him or slap him or something when a loud voice booms, "Stop right there!"

Everyone, even London, turns to focus on the figures walking briskly across the fairgrounds. It's Harlan, Chris, Sienna, Arlene, and the tattooed brunette from the waiting room. Harlan leads them, striding across the field like an action hero, long hair and scarf blowing behind him as if he's led by his own personal fan. London relaxes, the fight gone out of her as she focuses on the approaching group. TJ's posture doesn't change. Harlan steps forward, close enough that he could grab both of their heads in his gorilla hands and slam them together, if he wanted to.

"First rule of the VFR is we don't fight for real. You want a job, you shake hands and sit back down."

TJ immediately holds out his hand to shake. London stares at it resentfully and looks back to Harlan without shaking.

"But we're allowed to insult each other and get away with it?"

Harlan shrugs. "I can't make people be good. I can just set limits for what behavior's allowed on my property. If you want this job, if you want to get paid, you've got to get along, just like any other job. Did he hurt you?"

"He said—"

"I didn't ask what he *said*. Did he physically hurt you?"

"No."

London's got to be in her twenties, but she sounds like she's five, sullen and resentful and anxious for everyone to know it.

"And did you hurt him?"

"No."

Harlan looks to TJ.

"She shoved me. It didn't hurt."

With a sigh, Harlan squats to pick up London's dropped seltzer can, which sits crumpled in a little puddle. He stands and gives her the saddest look, a look of disappointment and pity. "I guess you're out."

"But I—"

"If you shoved him, you leave."

London's face wrinkles up like a bulldog. She clearly doesn't hear the word *no* a lot and doesn't like it. She looks like she wants to talk back to Harlan—not apologize and beg for her job and make good with TJ, but argue and get up in the huge man's face. Harlan is even less intimidated than TJ was as he stares sadly down at her.

"Go on now, honey. It's over."

But London bares her teeth, going full Veruca Salt. She fiddles with one of her rings and holds her hand up to her face, and Chelsea is about to ask Amy what the girl is doing when London's eyes go completely blank and she lunges at the grill, grabbing the wood and metal spatula and swinging for Harlan.

Chelsea goes cold down to her toes.

This is it.

This is the Violence.

She's experienced it at least twice, but she's never seen it like this before.

Never watched it happen, not in real life.

It's just like on the YouTube videos but more real, more terrifying.

London, the girl, is gone.

Her body is a weapon, and its only aim is to kill Harlan Payne.

She swings at his face with the spatula, slicing sideways like it's a knife.

She doesn't make a noise, doesn't growl or grunt or scream.

She simply attacks.

Harlan gets his hands up in time to fend off the first blow, but the spatula slices into his forearm with the thick thunk of metal on bone and sends blood flicking against the side of the RV. Harlan dances back, uncertain, clearly not wanting to hurt the much smaller girl. His face wasn't made for confusion.

But then an odd thing happens.

TJ leaps on top of London from the back, throwing her to the ground with his full weight. She's flat on her belly, the blood-spattered spatula still in her hand, and he's pressing down on her, legs over her legs and arms over her arms, one hand wrapped around the wrist that holds the weapon. She's bucking underneath him, every line of her body filled with tense potential and this strange, silent rage, taut and furious as an animal pouncing.

And then an odder thing happens.

Matt throws himself on top of TJ. And then Steve throws himself on top of Matt. And then Chris and Sienna add to the dogpile while Harlan backs up, panting, staring at the deep cut on his arm.

Chelsea doesn't know what to do, but she has to do something, so she scurries over on hands and knees to pry the spatula out of London's hand. The girl doesn't register her, doesn't even see her; London only has eyes for Harlan, and her pinprick black pupils in the field of green iris are trained on him, unblinking. One of her eyebrows is tragically smudged. She looks like the love child of a zombie and a broken doll.

"Pile on," Sienna calls. "We need everyone. The more weight and pressure, the better."

Amy leans onto Sienna, and the teen girl creeps forward and reaches for London's grasping hand, catching it in both of hers.

"Get her other hand," the girl says to Chelsea, and Chelsea tosses the blood-covered spatula far away and takes London's hand, noting the open poison ring flecked with black dots of pepper.

"What is happening?" she asks no one in particular.

Harlan squats down beside the knot of people, one hand over his wound.

"This is how you stop it," he says, gently. "Restrain them like this for long enough, and they go back to normal. But it takes a lot of weight, a lot of heat, a lot of tightness. There's power in groups. You didn't know?"

Chelsea shakes her head.

Harlan snorts softly. "Yeah, they're not putting it on the news. Can't sell a thirty-thousand-dollar vaccine if there's a cheaper alternative, can they? Not that this'll help you when you're alone with someone else." Their eyes meet, and Chelsea feels . . . seen. Harlan's gaze goes soft and inward, and Chelsea wonders who he was alone with, who was beside him, dead, when he woke up from the Violence.

Judging by the grief written across his movie-star features, it was someone important.

He stands back up and walks to the RV. "I need a bandage," he says apologetically.

And he does—blood is running down his arm, and Chelsea can see meat and a thin line of bright yellow fat.

"I'll sew that up for you once we're done," Sienna calls. "Don't you mess with it!"

Somewhere in the pile, Chris chuckles. "Thank God we have a medic on staff, right?"

There's another chuckle, and Steve murmurs, "Jesus, you're bony. It's like lying on a box spring."

"Well, your damn beard tickles, so don't think it's any fun lower in the pile," Matt shoots back, but in a friendly way.

"Every single one of you must go on a diet," TJ says, muffled, from way down on the bottom.

And then they're all laughing the mad, giddy laugh of people who live in a world this insane. The pile is shuddering, people shifting this way and that and then steadying themselves.

"I did not sign up to play Twister," Amy calls amid the frenzy, and Chelsea starts laughing, too.

Is this all it takes, to stop the madness? What amounts to a heavy, full-body hug?

"What the fuck?"

Everyone shifts aside as London struggles to get out from under them, cussing and shouting. "Get off me! Freak! What the fuck? What are you people doing? I am going to sue you to the fucking moon."

Everyone slides off, easing back to standing or sitting in the chairs. Clothes are askew, hair is mussed, faces are red. Finally TJ is revealed, and he takes a deep breath and sits back on his knees as London flips over and sits. She looks utterly disgusted.

"What the fuck?" she says again.

Sienna grabs her hand and holds up the poison ring.

"You peppered up, that's what. Now get out of here, you little shit. You could've killed someone."

London's face goes from surprise to cunning to disappointment as she works through what happened. "So I didn't kill him?"

Harlan stands in the door to the RV holding a wad of bright-red paper towels. In their short acquaintance, Chelsea has seen him look amused, pleasant, charismatic, professional, sympathetic, and haunted.

But now he looks furious, and it's terrifying. There is nothing scarier to her than an angry man. She shrinks back, heart thumping like a rabbit's leg as Harlan steps down to the ground like he's walking into a wrestling ring, staring murder at the crumpled girl on the ground.

"No, you didn't. Get out. While you still can."

London stands, her face stricken, and looks from person to person as if hunting for empathy. There is none.

"I am so going to sue your ass."

Harlan sighs and looms. "Yeah, well, get in line."

When he takes a step toward her, London scrambles up and runs for the parking lot.

The mask of rage falls off the biggest man Chelsea has ever seen, leaving him smaller, diminished, woeful. Harlan goes to the cooler and gets a beer and slings himself into a lawn chair, which creaks in protest as blood drips down his arm.

"Welcome to the VFR, everybody," he says, popping the tab.

28.

Once she's back on the main road, Ella drives like a zombie, her mind overloaded and her whole body numb. Where do you go when you have nowhere to go? Where can you sleep in your car without being carjacked or, at the very least, questioned by the police? Before the Violence, there were twenty-four-hour stores and restaurants. She could go sit in a Waffle House and drink a Coke for a few hours or slip her car into a shady spot at the park. Now there's a curfew, and people aren't supposed to be out all night. You're not supposed to be out driving unless you've got a good reason. And *I have nowhere else to go because my life is falling apart* is not considered a good reason. Most people's lives are falling apart, just now.

Without really meaning to, she's back at her neighborhood. She passes it by the first time, then turns around in someone's driveway and goes back. There are several houses for sale where she might not be noticed, but right now she's thinking about Mrs. Reilly. Ella used to do a lot of babysitting and petsitting around the neighborhood, and she watched Mrs. Reilly's cats when the elderly woman went on trips to New York and then when she was in the hospital after a heart attack. After Mrs. Reilly died, her daughter was supposed to pick up the cats, but then the Violence hit, and the house has probaby been empty since then, at least according to the unkempt yard and broken shutters. Ella still knows the code to open the garage, and if nothing has changed, she can park inside and spend the night there. Mrs. Reilly's daughter lives in Georgia, so it's unlikely that she's done anything to the house since picking up the cats.

And luckily, Mrs. Reilly lived on the opposite side of the neighborhood.

Ella pulls into the driveway, noting the high weeds and the pile of sodden cardboard boxes on the porch. She leaves the car running and jogs up to the garage door, tapping in the code, her heart in her throat, expecting at any moment to get yelled at by someone, anyone, for doing everything wrong. But the door just beeps and crawls open, revealing Mrs. Reilly's Miata on one side and a familiar pile of cat food boxes on the other; Mister Mistofelees only eats a certain kind of fish, and Mrs. Reilly always kept stocked up.

Ella shoves all the cat food aside and pulls into the empty spot. Even if the house door is locked, she can sleep in her car in the garage and know that no one will tap on the window and give her a heart attack. But she was right—things are exactly as she left them the last time she fed Mr. M and Griz. The door is unlocked.

"Hello?" she shouts into the house. "Mrs. Reilly?"

Because if someone else is here, someone who belongs here, she can always pretend she was checking up on an elderly neighbor, even if that neighbor has actually been dead for a while.

No one answers, and she pushes the button to close the garage door and fetches her bags from the car. With her backpack, purse, and bug-out bag dangling from her arms, she heads into the house.

First of all, it's hot, and it fucking reeks. Ella's nose wrinkles against the mingled odors of cat piss and poop and rotten food. The hum of appliances tells her that the electricity is still on, at least, and the first place she goes is right to the temperature control. It's still set on heat—of course, because Mrs. Reilly died in the winter. She switches it to air-conditioning and sets that to seventy degrees.

After closing all the curtains and blinds, she turns on a couple of lights—nothing too bright. It looks exactly as it did the last time she was here, when she fed and watered the cats before Mrs. Reilly's funeral, giving them extra so they'd be okay until her daughter Toni came by. She only knew Mrs. Reilly was dead because the old lady had begged her nurse to let the catsitter know to keep feeding her precious babies. It was kind of creepy, but apparently on her deathbed, what she cared about the most was her cats. In any case, Ella never got paid, and she never spoke to the daughter, and she just assumed adults would take care of everything.

Judging by the smell, no one took care of anything. The house hasn't been cleaned or sold—a bowl of fruit sits rotten and black and melted on the counter, and Ella isn't brave enough to open the fridge. Lucky for her Mrs. Reilly was the kind of older lady who was tech-savvy, which means she must've set up all her bills to be paid automatically online, which is why the AC is humming and the toilets are flushing.

For a moment, Ella wonders if maybe Mrs. Reilly's daughter never came after all . . . then she finds the cats. They're in the kitchen. Mr. M is crusted to the floor by the food bowls, the meat stripped off his bones and chunks of long, gray fur everywhere. Griz is uneaten but just as dead, spread flat by the hole she was trying to claw in the back door just a few feet away. Ella's stomach comes up and she runs for the sink, barely making it before she pukes up some bile.

They were nice cats. She wishes they'd made it to Georgia.

Holding her breath as well as she can, she gets garbage bags from under the sink and uses an old pair of tongs to peel up the cats—*oh God, these cats used to crawl in her lap, and Mr. M would chirp when he heard a can open*—and puts them in the bag and carries the bag out to the garbage can in the backyard. Opening the top, she finds a hot, seething mass of maggots that just makes her heave some more. She tosses in the bag and stumbles inside, where she takes down a spotless glass and runs water from the tap, swishing it in her mouth before gulping it down. It's hot and tastes of minerals and metal.

Jesus, this place.

It should be heaven. Safety! Air! Water!

Instead, it's a new kind of torture.

For the next hour, Ella gives up on any kind of relief or comfort and cleans out all the nasty shit that's making the house unbearable. She holds her breath in big gulps as she cleans out all the rot in the fridge.

She scrapes up what was under the cats. She struggles with the heavy, overloaded litter boxes and chucks them into the outside trash. She tosses out the fruit basket full of wet black glop and maggots. She dry-heaves again and again but doesn't let herself have any more water because she knows she'll just puke it up.

This pain will be worth it, she tells herself.

If she can just get it clean enough to let her gorge settle, she can microwave one of Mrs. Reilly's Lean Cuisines and pop a diet soda and curl up and watch TV and pretend for five minutes that life is normal and safe and that there aren't dead things everywhere that have been left behind. This house is a time capsule—everything here is exactly like it was before the Violence, before that first lady beat someone to death with a bottle of salad dressing. There's even pepper in the cabinet—now a class 3 substance, according to what she heard on the radio while driving around. She shoots her mother a quick text about it but, again, receives no response.

Finally it's all done. The stink is still there, but it's more like a foot-note, and she opens the screened windows and turns on all the ceiling fans and lights the candles Mrs. Reilly thought would cover up the reek of the weed she smoked for her back pain. Ella remembers the day she found it, thinking it was catnip at first but then recognizing the smell. She doesn't do that sort of thing—not before, when it was rebellious, and not now when it could get her killed for being too slow and stupid—but she's glad for the strongly scented candles.

She eats a shallow pan of fake macaroni and drinks a Diet Sprite—delicious, indulgent, the taste strange on her tongue—and watches a cooking show in which jolly, kind British people cheer one another on as they make desserts. Every time her mind tries to settle on a topic like Brooklyn or Mom or Dad or the sound Mr. M made when she pried him off the tiles, she refocuses on the cooking show, on the pastel meringues and macarons and puddings. It almost works.

It's past midnight now, and even though she feels like a live wire, her eyes have that dry, pinched feeling of sleepiness. She blows out the candles and closes the windows and turns out the lights before heading up to the guest bedroom she remembers from her catsitting. The double bed is neatly made up with a quintessentially Florida quilt, white with blue seashells, so new it still has creases from the bag. Ella plugs in her phone on the bedside table and drags in her bags from downstairs and does one more round of the familiar but unfamiliar house, double-checking that all the doors and windows are locked.

This is a difficult world with little safety, but for now, finally, she's found a place that feels safe. She pulls out her laptop, stares at the screen blankly, and closes the browser. She's too tired to catch up on whatever she's missed since she and Brooklyn became Nana's prisoners. All she wants to do is keep watching that cooking show on her phone.

She falls asleep while they're making gingerbread houses.

The next morning, when her eyes open, she's momentarily lost. Where is she? What is this bright, pretty room, as bare and welcoming as a beach condo?

Then she sees the cat tree in the corner and remembers.

For a moment, lying there in the fresh bed that smells like detergent, she expects Mr. M and Griz to come running and hop on the bed, meowing and chirping. If they had ghosts, that's what they would do, crowding around her with the brush of spectral fur. She dreamed about them, that they were tiger-sized and hunting her to eat her. But now that she's awake, she's just sad.

Downstairs, she finds frozen waffles in the freezer and scratches an itchy spot on her neck as she waits for them to pop up in the toaster. The maple syrup is still good, and there are cans of fruit cocktail, so it's not the worst breakfast. Poor Brooklyn is probably still chewing through Nana's diet cereals. As Ella eats freezer-burned waffles off Mrs. Reilly's flowered plates she scrolls through the news, determined to find out what her dad was talking about in his text.

When she types her mom's name into the search bar, she can't believe what she sees.

Her mom killed Jeanie.

With a Yeti cup.

On I-4.

Ella snorts, then snorts again, and then she's straight up laughing so hard that her eyes water.

This is utterly insane.

The situation, and the fact that she can't stop laughing about it.

It's awful.

It's horrendous.

Jeanie was really nice, and she used to help Ella with basketball when she was shooting hoops in the driveway and bake them Hershey's Kiss cookies at Christmas.

But the thought of her mom . . . doing all that.

She tries to imagine it and can't.

Her mom is soft. Wilting. Curved in. Hunched over. She is a repository of abuse.

Aside from the time Ella watched her stomp the dog to death.

The Violence—God, it's terrifying and strange and impossible.

Ella doesn't know which is harder to believe, that her mom beat Jeanie to death in a moving car or that she reached into a cow patty and threw it at some old guy before stealing his truck.

And that wasn't even the biggest news story that day.

The only thing for which Florida Woman and Florida Man can be counted on is that a new Florida Man or Woman will supplant them within hours by doing something outrageous, stupid, or dangerous.

She texts her mom: *Are you okay? I saw the news. Dad is home. He keeps texting me.*

And then she adds: *Don't go home. Please.*

She scrolls back through all the texts she's sent her mom, but they're all unread. Now she thinks she knows why. Her mom's phone was probably in her minivan with Jeanie when her mom ran away.

So there's no point in texting her at all.

And yet . . . there's something comforting about it, too.

I'm scared, she types.

There's no response to that, either.

Please help me.

As if by magic, the doorbell rings.

For the tiniest, briefest, stupidest moment, her heart lifts. Have her prayers been answered?

But then reality descends. No one should be here. No one should ring this doorbell.

This is not a good sign.

Ella scrambles to the knife block by the fridge and selects the biggest blade that's not a butcher knife. It feels solid in her hand and reminds her of the one she kept under her pillow back home. She sneaks to the side window and peeks out without rustling the curtains. Her brain goes to Threat Level Red when she realizes it's a police officer.

"Come on out, Ella. I know you're in there."

Uncle Chad.

How . . . could he know?

He has to be here because Dad asked him to come.

But he never came to Nana's to find her. Maybe he couldn't. Maybe Dad didn't know she was there. And if he did, the guard said no one was on the list. Maybe police can't just go through those gates anymore. Or maybe when Ella took her car, Dad really got mad.

Wait. *Her car.*

Dad must have her car . . . bugged? Tagged? Whatever.

As long as the car was home, Dad had no idea where she was.

And now he knows exactly where she is.

Which means she can't take her car. Maybe she can run out the back?

But no. Mrs. Reilly has a very high plastic fence to keep dogs and kids out of her backyard. There's only one door, and it opens up to the side of the house . . . where Chad is.

"Ella, it's Uncle Chad. I need you to open the door, or I'm going to have to bust it down and come in there with my gun up. You don't want that, right? I sure don't."

"Yeah, right," Ella mutters under her breath.

Uncle Chad is an asshole. He calls his wife "the ol' ball and chain!" He sometimes wears shirts that say things like COOL STORY, BABE, NOW MAKE ME A SANDWICH. Much like that guard last night, she's pretty sure Uncle Chad sees women as the enemy, and that he's got a boner for threatening them with his gun.

No way she's opening the door.

She runs to the guest room for her bag, throws her laptop in it, and grabs her keys.

But no. Those are useless. She needs Mrs. Reilly's keys. And she needs the Miata to work and have gas in it.

"Ella, honey, I'm gonna count to three, and then things are gonna get scary. I don't want 'em to, but that's my job. Don't make me do something we'll both regret."

Shit.

But she can't get out of the garage with his car parked right there.

She pockets Mrs. Reilly's BEACH LIFE key chain, puts down her bag, and walks to the door like she's going to the electric chair. She slept in her clothes, and her hair is a mess, and there are still some speckles of bile on her shirt from throwing up.

Good. Let her be as pathetic as possible. She's got to find a way out of this, because the only two places Uncle Chad can take her are to the police station or to her dad, and both choices suck.

"One."

"I'm coming."

A pause. "Good, Ella. I'm gonna need you to open the door now. I've got my gun out, but I'm not going to shoot you."

There's an implicit *probably* in there, and they both know it.

Ella puts the knife down on a side table.

"Okay, Uncle Chad. I'm opening the door now. Please don't hurt me."

She undoes the chain and twists the lock and opens the door, and even though he warned her, she's not prepared to see a man she's known all her life pointing an evil black gun right at her chest.

The moment he sees her, his eyes flick to her empty hands, and only then does he lower the gun. He doesn't put it back in his holster, though—just lowers it and holds it with one hand instead of two.

"Okay, good girl. Thank you. Now we can talk."

Yeah, because nothing makes a girl want to talk like an angry man holding a gun.

"Okay," she says, because he's staring at her like she's supposed to say something.

"Let's have our little chat inside."

Fear trills up her spine. She doesn't want to be trapped in that house, alone with this man, every curtain shut to outside eyes. But she can't say that, so she just nods and steps aside. Chad walks in and does that little FBI gun dance from the movies as he checks every corner, face twisted in a scowl as he aims. When he spots the knife on the side table, he glares at Ella like she's betrayed him.

"I was here all night by myself," she says. "I was scared."

He throws it across the room and jerks his chin at the couch. "Sit down."

She does, hands fidgeting in her lap.

"Ella, honey, what are you doing here? Why aren't you home?"

And she thinks about lying but it just takes too much energy and anyway, who cares? There's no way out of this. No way Uncle Chad is going to let her stay here, safe and left alone.

"I'm not home because my dad chokes me unconscious, and he beat my mom up, and that was before he was really angry," she says, her voice flat.

Uncle Chad's face screws up. "Now honey, that's just not true. I've known your dad almost my whole life, and he's a good guy."

She shakes her head. Of course he would deny it. "Not to me."

He plows on like this doesn't matter a bit, and to him, it probably doesn't. "Well, the thing is, you're a minor. By law, I have to return you to your parents' house. So we're going to get in my car, and I'll escort you there right now. Your dad's waiting. He's real worried about you."

That is not what he's worried about, but Ella knows arguing with a guy like Uncle Chad is stupid. He'll tell her she's lying, she's wrong, that she's remembering things incorrectly, that there are other points of view. He'll tell her to be a good girl, to submit to her father, to follow the law.

He'll deliver her right back into the hands of a man who will hurt her, all because he's never witnessed it with his own eyes. And even if he did see it, he would tell himself Dad was only playing around, or she needed to be taught a lesson.

"Why didn't my dad come?" she asks.

For the briefest second, Uncle Chad looks surprised and stupid, like she caught him. But then he covers that up with his Policeman Scowl. "He didn't know if it was you or if someone maybe stole your car. So he sent a professional. He's waiting at home for you right now, worried sick."

They stare at each other for a long moment, Uncle Chad looking smug and like he thinks he's pulling one past her, and Ella hating everything about him and the situation.

"What if I don't want to go home?" she finally says.

He looks confused by this thought, and it occurs to her that this whole time, he hasn't asked if Brooklyn is here with her. Dad only seems to care about keeping tabs on the women who take care of him. The women who defy him. A little kid like Brooklyn is just . . . well, not worth the trouble. Yet.

"You have to go home. Like I said, that's the law." He holds up a pair of handcuffs. "Trust me, you don't want these." And then he smirks. "Although you might when you're a little older."

Ella is about to tell him how gross that is coming from her "uncle" when she goes unconscious.

29.

Patricia is sobbing into her hands on the floor of her closet when a tiny voice says, "Nana, you're crying."

Once she knew the house was safe, she unbuttoned the fancy dress and sent Brooklyn upstairs to change to buy herself some time and save herself from whined complaints about itchy crinolines. It didn't take her granddaughter very long to follow those orders, and now Patricia has been caught in a vulnerable position, which she hates. She takes a shuddering breath and rubs her fingertips gently over her eyes from the inside corners to the edges in that way that makes her mascara smear less.

"Yes, I know."

"What's wrong?"

With a big sniffle, Patricia changes gears and stands before Brooklyn can touch her face with those sticky hands. "Someone stole something very important from me."

"Jessie stole my favorite princess dress at school last year. I was so mad I wanted to pull her hair."

A wild half sob escapes, and Patricia shakes her head.

"This was something much more than a dress." She looks around her enormous closet, calculating how much she could get for her Birkins, Louboutins, and furs . . . if those were the sort of things anyone was buying right now or that she knew how to sell. She hasn't set foot in a pawnshop in thirty years but she knows damn well she won't get enough to pay for a week's worth of groceries, just now. "Go on now, back to the kitchen. This closet is off limits."

"It's bigger than my room!"

Patricia allows herself a small smirk. "It is. When I was a little girl, I used to dream of a closet like this, a big one with windows and a mirror tall and wide enough to show me twirling in my own princess dress."

Brooklyn runs over to the mirror in question and attempts a twirl. She's dressed herself in a hot-pink skort, a bright-yellow tank top, and green rain boots with frog faces, but the smile she gives herself suggests she's very pleased with her work. Patricia has asked the child to leave, but she pauses when she sees Brooklyn's utter enchantment with the mirror. God, was she ever so young?

She must've been, but she doesn't remember.

The 1970s were a different time. Children had to grow up faster. At five, she was staying home alone and roaming the neighborhood without a second thought. She could vacuum and sweep and make macaroni and scoop cold, slimy Vienna sausages out of their can without cutting her fingers and light a cigarette for her mama. There were no comfortable clothes like the ones Brooklyn wears, bright colors and cheerful, glittery designs of smiling unicorns and pretty cursive saying GIRL POWER and BELIEVE IN YOURSELF. Things were heavy, scratchy, meant to last. There were no tablets, no colorful shows on demand about being sweet to your friends. Just an unreliable black-and-white TV with rabbit ears, and if you were lucky, you might catch *Sesame Street* or *Mister Rogers*.

These days, this time . . . it's just so *soft*. So sweet and quiet. No wonder children are helpless and living at home until their thirties. No wonder they can't get jobs. They're told that everything is okay, that everything will be fine, that they need to focus on self-care. Ha! They need to focus on being functional humans.

Brooklyn swings her little skirt back and forth, does a clumsy curtsy, sings softly to herself, mesmerized.

Patricia narrows her eyes. It's up to her to teach this fragile, silly child all the things Chelsea failed to impart. Thanks to the Violence, they no longer live in a soft time. As much as Patricia hates to consider it, her own days of softness and luxuriance are over. She has to go back to being sharp, grasping, cunning.

She won't be Patty again—she'll die before she stoops that low—but she can't just sit here, pretending everything is going to be fine.

Her life won't be fine until she makes it fine.

She stands behind Brooklyn in the mirror.

"Imagine a string on top of your head, pulling straight." Patricia reaches over her own head, grasps the imaginary string, and pulls up, her posture naturally elongating. Her chin is up, shoulders back, belly tucked. "This is how a lady stands. Graceful but strong. You try."

Brooklyn reaches overhead, her forehead wrinkled. She reaches up like she's tugging on a lamp chain, but nothing changes.

"It didn't work."

Patricia chuckles. She reaches down and adjusts the child's posture. "That's because you're the one who has to do the work. Feel that? Like you're a foot taller."

"I am?"

"It certainly looks that way when you stand up straight and don't slouch."

Brooklyn's face rumples up as she tries to hold her posture—and her breath.

"You have to breathe, too. And smile. It may not be easy, but you must always make it *look* easy."

"Why?"

Patricia bends over, her face beside Brooklyn's in the mirror. They have a similar smile, she notes with some triumph, glad that her genes have trumped the men who've helped bring the child about.

"Because that's how you become strong," she whispers. "Confidence is key."

"I thought it was about being nice. That's what they say on *My Little Pony*. That friendship is magic."

Patricia chucks her chin. "Power is magic, darling. Don't ever forget it. Now come along. Nana has some work to do downstairs, and as I told you, this closet is forbidden unless I am with you."

Brooklyn follows her out of the closet and casts a look of exquisite longing as the door closes.

"Why? Do you have guns in there?"

Honestly, the things in this child's head!

"Of course not. That's ridiculous. I have coats that cost as much as a car."

"Why?"

Patricia's brief moment of connection with her granddaughter is lost as she realizes that Brooklyn will badger her to death with the word *why* if she allows it.

"Because I said so. No one owes you the answers to everything. Now come."

Once they're downstairs, Patricia fixes Brooklyn a peanut butter sandwich and a tin of peaches and sits in her sunroom, her phone in hand. The question isn't so much who will help her as who can she trick into thinking she's helping them . . . while they are helping her. She scrolls through her contacts, nixing this name and that. Some because they're already out of the country and unreachable, some because of a silly old grudge, some because just talking to them gives her a headache.

She finally lands on the O'Malleys, whose house backs up to theirs. They maintain an appropriately tall wooden fence between the properties, and the O'Malleys were supposed to pay for half the cost of fixing it after a falling branch toppled a tree, damaging a section of the wood. Patricia clicks call and gathers her confidence and calm around her like an ermine-lined cape.

"Hello?"

"Barbara, darling, it's Patricia Lane from the neighborhood."

"Yes, of course." There's a babble of voices behind Barbara, and she sounds flustered, or at least otherwise engaged. "How are you, dear?"

"As well as can be expected. The auction is ramping up. So many donations coming in."

A fussy little exhale. "Ah, yes. I did forget to send over a basket, didn't I? Please forgive me. It's been such a time."

"And I thought we might discuss the fence, while we're chatting."

Patricia knows that as long as she stays serene and regal and wears her sly, smug smile, she'll always have a hand up on Barbara, who's distracted at best and flighty at worst. She needs firm managing, Barbara does.

"The fence. And an auction basket. If you can send me an email, I can handle that when we land in Ontario. Don and I are laid over in New York. The lounge is so crowded you'd think it was Thanksgiving. Honestly."

Damn.

They're not even home.

They probably didn't bring a checkbook.

"That sounds ghastly."

"Oh, it is. But once we're settled in, things should calm down. We have tickets to—" Don's voice babbles in the background. "Oh, that's our group. Look, Patricia, while I have you, could you be a dear and check the front porch? I'm expecting some important packages, but it was too late to reroute them, and we'll be here through the end of the summer, and we're having trouble finding a house sitter. The key is under the mat, and the code is one one one one—for the garage and the security system. Just leave the packages in the mudroom." Before Patricia can accept this task, Barbara squawks and hurriedly adds, "Thank you, darling! You're a lifesaver!" And hangs up.

Patricia growls. She wanted money that she's owed, and instead, she was given a job to do. Not even a job. A neighborly kindness. She won't be paid. It's just drudgery.

And they don't have a gate in the fence between their properties, so she'll have to walk all the way around the block. No one is walking these days. Even behind the neighborhood's stone walls and six-foot iron fences, even through constant, roaming clouds of mosquito poison, the Violence can still get in. A mail carrier, a delivery person, a rogue pool boy. A quiet little old man like Miguel. But this task—she has to do it. Now is not the time to ignore someone who owes her several thousand dollars. She'll have to leave Brooklyn here at the house and take the golf cart. And then schlep packages into someone else's mudroom as if she were someone else's maid.

An idea begins to form. A desperate, gritty, clawing thing, more Patty than Patricia.

She has the key. She has the code. She has a reason to be in the O'Malley house.

And the O'Malleys will be gone for months.

"Brooklyn, darling."

No answer. She finds the child with her giant headphones over her tiny ears, firmly engaged with her silly tablet. No wonder it was so pleasantly quiet. She gets Brooklyn's attention and, when the headphones are off, says, "I need you to sit right here and do exactly what you're doing. Nana needs to just pop over to the neighbor's house."

Brooklyn's eyes fly wide. "I'm not allowed to stay home alone. I'm too little."

"Nonsense. I stayed home alone at five and so did your mother. And I'll be so close! Just one house over. It won't take even half an hour." When Brooklyn chews her lip nervously, she adds, "I could leave you with some of Grandpa Randall's candy so you'll have something to do."

Any worry disappears. "I like candy!" Brooklyn squeaks.

"Good girl."

Patricia goes upstairs to the closed door of Randall's office and stops. This room has always been forbidden, and honestly, Patricia never cared enough to snoop. Even when she glanced in here earlier, she didn't step a single toe inside. But nothing is forbidden anymore, is it? She turns the knob, feeling a pleasant trill of boldness.

It's always dark within. Randall had this room paneled in wood with built-in bookcases and a heavy, custom desk, almost like he's trying to replicate his office at the courthouse. Patricia knows that he keeps sweets and snacks squirreled away up here somewhere. Heaven knows she doesn't buy all the garbage that he compulsively gulps when he's feeling stressed.

She starts with his desk, pulling out the most obvious drawer first and finding a rat's nest of candy. Half-eaten bags of jelly beans, mostly the black ones left. Big candy bars with squares snapped off, their wrappers carefully folded and neatly clipped. Necco wafers, of all things. She wishes she'd brought a bag, but she can always take one thing and come back later if she needs to bribe the child further. She opts for an unopened bag of jelly beans, supposing that Brooklyn, like Randall, probably isn't a fan of licorice.

The childlike glee she feels when closing that drawer with a bag of treasure in hand is addictive. She methodically goes through every nook and cranny of the grand desk, uncovering three hundred dollars in cash under the blotter, a ruby pendant that's far too garish and small and obviously not meant for her, and a tasteful diamond anniversary ring that probably is, considering it fits her ring finger and their anniversary is next month.

Would've been next month?

She takes both pieces of jewelry and all the money.

Everything else is either cheap snacks or more of Randall's paperwork. For all that he's fastidious in his person, he's an utter slob in the office, which is why always having a coterie of secretaries and aides is a great cover for his proclivities. Patricia almost wonders that she didn't find a little black book, but then she remembers that Randall's phone is always in his pocket and has a complex password. He would never leave something so precious behind.

Not like he left her behind.

Before closing the door, she breathes in deep, noting the odors of Randall's cologne, his unfortunate body odor, a faint tinge of scotch, old books, new leather, and the clingy ghosts of his cigars that were never allowed inside. She will miss what Randall provided, the safety and comfort and legitimacy, but she won't miss his actual presence.

She wonders if he feels the same about her.

He must, or he wouldn't have taken this step. He arranged this theft, she's certain. He's the only one who knows her habits—and the security codes, even if he said he'd forgotten them. She knew the judge could hold a professional grudge, but she never thought he would stoop this low, be this needlessly cruel.

Back downstairs, she presents Brooklyn with the bag of jelly beans, to which the child responds, solemn and impressed, "The whole bag?"

Patricia smiles her Nana smile, indulgent and magical. "The whole bag. I'll be right back." She collects her phone and keys and a rather large tote and checks herself in the hall mirror, then backtracks. "And

remember: No cooking, going in the pool, or doing anything dangerous."

But the child is already plugged back into her tablet, happily divid-
ing her sugar hoard into rainbow order. No point in distracting her.
Time to go.

As it turns out, without Rosa and Miguel around, the golf cart bat-
tery is dead. Annoyed but undeterred, Patricia locks the front door
behind her and heads for the sidewalk for the first time in months. It's
bright and hot outside, trademark Florida summer, and there's not a
soul in sight. No cars, no golf carts, no posh women walking posh
dogs. The birds sing a mad riot, and the bugs are already howling. As
Patricia marches up the clean but empty sidewalk, she swats a mosquito away, grateful that she's already been vaccinated and will never
experience Chelsea's dilemma. The little fool. Patricia told her marrying David would be a mistake. His family wasn't wealthy at all, and she
detected something sinister under his Golden Boy charm, but did
Chelsea listen? Of course not. Hopefully she's learned her lesson.

At the corner, a car passes, and Patricia smiles blandly and waves at
Marion Montrose, a gaudy widow in her flashy red Corvette. Of
course Marion would stay here instead of heading up north; she probably considers the quarantine oodles of fun.

Patricia thinks she's in the clear, but then Marion circles back
around, Fleetwood Mac blaring from her sports car. The tinted window rolls down, and Marion lifts up her cat's-eye glasses.

"Patricia! I thought you and the judge were headed off to Iceland."
Her eyes spark with the thought of scandal, and Patricia longs to slap
that smug smile off her face.

"Alas, plans change. I'm surprised you haven't jetted off to somewhere exciting yourself."

Marion waves at the gorgeous day outside. "And leave this little
slice of paradise? Although I've half a mind to drive down to Key
West, if I can find a cute beach house. The islands are deliciously
empty these days, I hear."

"C'est la vie."

"Too true. By the by, now that everyone's vaccinated, we're doing a

ladies' Bunco night at Cynthia's house this Thursday at seven, if you'd
like to join. Just bring a bottle of wine or some charcuterie."

There's no way in hell Patricia would join; Marion and her cronies
are the C-level players in the neighborhood dynamic, whereas Patricia is in the top rung. But part of her status is that she never lets on
that she's too good to rub elbows and throw dice.

"That sounds delightful. I'll see if I can squeeze it in. The auction
is heating up, you know."

Marion smirks. "Ah, yes. Your auction. I'm surprised there are
enough people left at the club to hold it."

"We need open hearts and wallets more than ever," Patricia reminds her. "We have this clever little setup this year where everyone
can bid electronically. Email me if you'd like a link. I know you enjoy
signed guitars, and we have one from Aerosmith."

Marion's eyes flash; she's not good at hiding anything.

"That does sound juicy. I'll let you know. Ta."

And with that, she floors it, screeching away as if she could ever
impress someone like Patricia, someone who obviously finds loud
noises, gas fumes, and black streaks on the neighborhood streets dis-
tasteful.

"Grotesque," she mutters to herself.

It's one of her favorite words, and she remembers perfectly the moment she discovered it while taking a break at the diner. Her last customers had left a battered copy of *Reader's Digest* in the booth along
with a huge tip, and young Patty slid the book and the bills into her
apron to enjoy later. Sitting in an alley on an overturned bucket, she
sipped black coffee and flipped through the book, landing on a section
called "Word Power." It offered a selection of fifty-cent words that
looked impressive and elegant, and she realized that this, perhaps,
was the first step in becoming a classy lady like the ones who'd left the
book behind.

Grotesque, alcove, julep, damask, lapis lazuli, umbrage, pique.

Before then, Patricia hadn't known words like that existed. They
tasted rich and complex in her mouth, and she set herself a goal of
using one big word a day. Sometimes it went badly, like when she told

a friendly customer that he was very lugubrious and he called the manager over because he thought it was an insult. But sometimes it was exceptionally rewarding, like the time she correctly identified a man's malachite tie pin and he tipped her an extra fiver because he said he liked smart girls.

In hindsight, that book—and that word—were the first steps on her journey from Patty to Patricia, from a scrawny single mother barely scraping by to a wealthy, powerful woman whose closet is bigger than most of her previous apartments.

She hates to admit it, but perhaps Randall was a mistake. She never hoped to find a love match—her own mother had fallen for too many terrible men, and Patricia herself had fallen for one and didn't want to be that captive and beholden again, so she'd locked up her heart like a poorly behaved dog. Things were good with Terry because he looked at her like the sun shone out of her eyes and never suspected her own feelings were far more tepid. But she sees now that the arrangement with Randall faltered because he wasn't in thrall to her, because there were too few feelings instead of too many. For her next husband, she'll have to be more careful. She'll have to make him fall in love with her.

But enough about that. She has to survive this hurdle, first.

Randall has left her with nothing but a house with an expiration date, and she has two mouths to feed—three, if Ella has the good sense to come back—so she has to soldier on, as she always has. She's at the O'Malley house now, and, yes, there are the packages Barbara's expecting. Patricia uses the code—1111? Honestly?—and the garage door rumbles up, revealing Barbara's Infiniti, a six-seater golf cart, and that awful tricycle motorcycle thing they use for bopping up and down the coast. Patricia drags in the packages, closes the garage door, and opens the house up.

Her first thought is that Barbara leans awfully hard into lavender as a decorating choice and a signature scent, and her second is that the O'Malleys are exactly her kind of idiot. Their pantry shelves are full to bursting, and their fridge is freshly stocked as if they just woke up today and decided to move to Canada on a whim without any preparation. Seeing such bounty, it's like Patricia's brain switches channels and she's no longer an elegant woman eating for antioxidants and weight management but a starving woman with a baby who knows to an ounce which cheap foods will give her the most bang for the buck. She's only brought the one tote bag, so she doesn't feel bad at all as she pulls a few garbage bags out from under the kitchen sink and stuffs them full of soft things that can't break. Chips and puffs and the sorts of snacky things Brooklyn will like—because the O'Malleys have noisy grandchildren who show up every week like locusts. Of course she wouldn't try to walk through the neighborhood carrying garbage bags—so gauche and attention-grabbing—so she opens the patio doors, navigates around the trampoline and custom tree house, and tosses them over their shared fence into her own yard.

She finds reusable shopping bags under a different counter and begins carefully adding pasta boxes, rice, beans, cans. There's actual fruit in the crisper, so she takes all that; Brooklyn may crave jelly beans, but she needs real food. Cheese, salami, nuts, a gigantic frozen lasagna—it all gets tucked into her handbag or tote or the O'Malleys' bags. It's going to be heavy going, carrying them all home, but it would be too obvious, driving someone else's golf cart, and the fence is too high to toss a frozen twelve-person lasagna overhead. It was hard enough getting the garbage bags of fluffy things slung over.

Standing in the center of the kitchen, hands on her hips, smug as a cat in cream, Patricia glances at the clock. It's been half an hour. Surely Brooklyn is still fine, happily giving herself diabetes and ADD as she watches her show. If Ella were still where she should be, Patricia would feel so much better about being away from the house. She'll have to teach Brooklyn how to use a phone, as she's certain Chelsea has taught her daughter how to use such a device for literally any purpose other than making a phone call. She probably doesn't even know what to do with a landline.

Sighing in annoyance, she hefts her bags and hurries back home. Fortunately, she doesn't pass any more busybodies. Not a single car. No one on the street. She concocts a story about taking donations for the local food pantry to help others in this time of need, which would keep any of her neighbors from knowing she's just committed a crime and which might possibly result in further donations that she can definitely find a use for. That story becomes her truth, and her posture straightens. Now she would welcome another visit from nosy Marion, although no opportunities present themselves. She sees the curtains twitch at the Robinsons', but Sandra doesn't immediately text her, so it was probably whatever elderly relative is currently convalescing in their front room.

Back home, finally, her heart calms down, and she wonders if she will notice one day the first symptoms of a heart attack, considering her chest feels tight every moment of her life. This past week has pushed her further than she would prefer.

"Brooklyn, darling, do you like clementines?" she calls as she enters the kitchen.

As usual, there is no answer. Those dratted headphones!

But when she goes to the couch, the headphones and tablet and a pile of black and green jelly beans are there without their mistress.

"Brooklyn?" she calls.

For the longest time, there is no answer, and her heart jacks right back up again like a good little soldier. But then there is a sound, one she wasn't expecting.

The sound of glass, breaking, as something rams into it, over and over again.

30.

The interviews go on all day the next day, and Chelsea is put to work with the other new hires getting their training gym set up. At first, she's pretty annoyed, because she didn't sign on to carry dusty boxes and heavy mats. But then she sees everyone else just pitching in cheerfully and realizes . . . it's a job. She hasn't had a job in almost twenty years, and it's not exactly a booming time for the hiring market, and she'd rather do manual labor and get paid than sit around thinking about Jeanie. Indigo turns on some thumping EDM and puts her phone on a chair, and it starts to feel like a college moving party.

They're unloading a giant semi truck's guts into the back part of the interview building, which is an agricultural-type hall. Just a huge, metal room with a concrete floor and big double doors at regular intervals. She can imagine it on fair day, pies and quilts and pigs waiting to be judged. But now it's empty and echoing, and they're putting together a wrestling ring and laying down tons of mats and what feels like hundreds of weights. She smirks when ladders and chairs and folding tables appear. They really are going full smackdown.

As the day progresses, more new people arrive until there are a total of twenty, ten men and ten women. By the time they're done working and interviewing, everybody is more than ready for dinner. The people Chelsea met yesterday—Amy, Matt, Steve, TJ, and the tattooed girl, Joy—now feel like an in-group, and the new people look as lost as Chelsea felt when she first showed up. They're as surprising as everyone else. An immense white man with a long beard and a tattooed bald head, an older Latinx woman who has to be a bodybuilder and fitness model, a gorgeous Pamela Anderson look-alike, a hot Black man with long locs, a stylish redhead with geek glasses in a *Star Wars* shirt, a lumbersexual, among others. Nobody starts a fight or acts weird. Once you've been in a dogpile with people, they just feel more like family.

They have another round of hot dogs and hamburgers for dinner, but the chip variety packs are running out, taking them down to just Cool Ranch Doritos, and the cooler full of liquor is noticeably less full. Sienna warns them not to drink too much. Training starts tomorrow.

"If you're hungover or dehydrated, you're going to feel it. And you're going to puke your guts up, possibly on whoever you're training with. Which won't be fun for anyone," Sienna says, hands on her hips. She and Indigo are vegetarian, and they have some tofu dogs that no one else seems to want.

At night, they sleep in bunks on the two tour buses Chelsea saw on her way in. Each of the two buses has twelve bunks on it, stacked three up from floor to ceiling, each with its own privacy curtain. It's not the newest bus in the world—each bunk has its own phone, for example—but it's clean and the sheets are fresh and she's not worried about David, as she's chosen a bunk all the way in the back and anyone who wanted to hurt her would have to go through a locked door and ten other people to get to her. Sienna and Indigo stay in their own RV, but Arlene bunks in the coach, almost like an innkeeper. Chelsea likes her. She's fun most of the time and stern when she has to be.

Last night, Chelsea slept like a log. She noticed that, after her first bout with the Violence—the sleep afterward is deep, dreamless, and heavy. She normally wakes up every night at least once to pee, but last night, she was out the moment she got comfortable in her bunk and didn't twitch until Arlene's phone alarm went off at eight. Hard to believe that just yesterday she left her house with Jeanie driving her minivan, and then . . .

Well, now she's here.

And she's going to do her very best, go back to being the perfect student so that she can keep this job until she's vaccinated and has enough money to bring her family back together.

Well, her family without David.

Her, Ella, and Brooklyn. That's what she's fighting for.

Tonight, she doesn't sleep as well, but it's not terrible. She's never lived like this, surrounded by so many other women, shoved into a bunk the size of a coffin. If she sits up too fast, she'll bonk her head. And if she forgets how high up she is and goes to pee, she'll break her ankle. Everyone is trying to be quiet, but the space is not large. The hum of the air conditioner and the generator driving it helps, but no machine can disguise the squeak of a fart or the sharp bark of a cough, a sound that's still startling even after everyone got the Covid vaccine and multiple boosters. Of everything she's left behind or lost, right now, Chelsea just wishes for some earbuds so she could go to sleep watching something comforting, which she knows several of the others are doing. One asshole is actually watching some sort of documentary on full volume, and Chelsea is furious for a moment before just accepting that she finally has something to listen to.

The next morning, Arlene's phone alarm goes off, and the women rumble awake. The fairgrounds have showers . . . of a sort. Basically, Harlan somehow jury-rigged showers into the horse stalls behind the hall, and that's all they've got. Women on one side, men on another, separated by a firm wood wall that's had any conspicuous knots filled in. The water is cold, but there's shampoo and conditioner and body wash and razors and a big stack of cheap towels.

As if sensing the crowd's discontent, Sienna says, "Don't worry. It won't always be like this. Once we're under way and touring, we'll have better facilities."

"Easy for her to say," Amy murmurs to Chelsea as they wait their turn. "She has a real shower in her RV."

Once everyone's clean, and it does feel wonderful to be free of all the dirt and sweat from moving yesterday, they head to a little kitchen in the agricultural hall and have a much better meal than Chelsea was expecting. The eggs are soft, the bacon is crisp, the bananas aren't brown, and the coffee is . . . brown. Chelsea misses real creamer as she pours in the powdered stuff, but it could be a lot worse. In a different world, after what happened the other day, she might be in jail.

Again, Sienna warns them not to overindulge.

"You need fuel, but you don't want to train with too much on your stomach."

"More puke problems?" Joy asks.

Sienna nods knowingly. "Trust me: It's going to happen. Just make sure it's not you."

After breakfast, they clean everything they prepared yesterday, sweeping and spraying and polishing. Chelsea gets stuck wiping down every mat and rope and prop with harsh industrial cleaner. At least they give her long yellow gloves. Once she realizes what's coming next, she's glad they had an hour to let breakfast settle, even if it was spent cleaning.

Training, it turns out, is no joke.

Chris takes control, explaining that they need a mix of cardio and weights. They start with stretches, then sprints. Despite the exercises she did in her room back home, Chelsea is so out of shape that she's embarrassed, but she's not alone. At least Chris isn't the type of guy to yell at them like an army drill sergeant. He's honest but encouraging, and everyone has to finish their laps, even if they do it walking and clutching their sides.

After a water break, Chris divides the room into three different stations and he, Sienna, and Arlene each take up a post. Harlan is noticeably absent, Chelsea realizes.

Her first station is with Chris doing weight training, and . . . she hates it. She feels like her arms are floppy noodles. She hasn't done anything like this since high school, and even then, her heart wasn't in it. No one in her group seems to know what they're doing—they were probably divided up like this on purpose. Chris is patient but firm as he shows them the exercises they'll be expected to do every weekday, demonstrating and perfecting their form over and over until they get it. He's markedly relieved when the alarm goes off and it's time to switch stations.

Next, they go to Sienna, and Chelsea is grateful to not be doing anything physical at all. Sienna has a notebook and leads each person behind a screen one by one to take measurements. Chelsea isn't sure what the screen is for until she's taken behind it and realizes that that tape measure is going *everywhere.*

"This is worse than a TSA patdown," she murmurs as Sienna nearly unfurls her measuring tape in her birth canal.

"Tight costumes," Sienna says before nodding and writing more numbers in her little notebook. "Because you're going to get thrown around, and everything needs to stay in place. If I'm gentle and respectful, your costume doesn't fit, and then we have to fix it or sew it again. I'm not the sort of person who likes to do things twice." She steps back and smiles, warm and real, woman-to-woman. "And you're not allowed to lose weight, either."

Chelsea chuckles and exhales, no longer sucking in her belly. "See, no one's ever said that to me before."

Sienna puts a hand on her shoulder. "We need you strong, not skinny. Muscles and curves are all good here. Never make yourself smaller to suit someone who wants to feel big."

She turns away to write in her book, and Chelsea has one of those rare moments of complete clarity in life. It reminds her of looking at one of those Magic Eye posters and crossing her eyes just right and suddenly *seeing* what's really there.

David wanted her small for a reason.

He wanted her thin and weak. He didn't like it when she wore heels. He liked to loom over her.

And she's felt small, just like that, for years and years.

She remembers back to their time in student housing at David's college, that tiny one-bedroom cinder-block box where the windows didn't open and the heat gathered while she cooked until the hair curled up the nape of her neck. They had this little stool for reaching the top cabinets and he would make her sit on it while he talked at her, and her knees would scrunch up to her chin. He was so annoyed when she got too pregnant to fit on it, and when they moved out, she made sure it got placed poorly in the U-Haul truck and snapped a leg.

Even then, he wanted her small and scrunched up so he could stand that much taller.

"Chelsea?"

She blinks.

She lost time.

Oh God, did she . . .

No. She didn't storm. Sienna is smiling at her.

"You're all done. Just chill out until Arlene calls you."

Chelsea gives a wobbling smile and thanks her and heads back out to the stack of exercise mats the rest of her group is relaxing on. The big guy's name is John. Amy and Matt are also in her group, along with three other new people, none of whom stand out in her mind. Matt heads back to get measured, and Amy hands Chelsea a granola bar.

"So that was intrusive," Amy starts.

"Right? I mean, what are we wearing—bikinis?"

"Leotards, probably. Something like that."

"But do they assign it or what?"

Amy shrugs. "No idea. But we're in it now. I'll wear a giant purple dinosaur suit if it'll get me vaccinated and earn more money than running myself ragged delivering takeout."

As Amy crunches her bar, her eyes go far away, and this, too, is familiar. Chelsea did it with Sienna a few moments ago, and . . . well, almost all of them do it, sometimes. Get lost in a thought from the past. Shell-shocked, like they've come back from a war and can't help but fall back into it now and then. No one asks anything so common and tawdry as, *So what are you thinking about?* because they know from personal experience that they don't want to know the answer. It's strange to suffer from a trauma in which the main event is forever hidden from memory while its aftereffects continue to cause horror and pain. Every time someone takes a sip of water out of a Yeti cup, Chelsea has a quick flash of Jeanie driving the minivan, and she has to force herself to focus and not fall into the memory. It's like stepping back from the edge of a cliff.

They get called over to Arlene last, and Chelsea has heard all sorts of odd noises coming from what she thinks of as the interview room. The door has been closed all day, so whatever's happening in there must be intense. It's cooler, at least, the air conditioner grinding and the plastic chair cold against the backs of her legs. She's still wearing her clothes from yesterday, and she hasn't yet figured out how to ask to borrow something less filthy and bloody. They sit around the conference table with Arlene, who has a notebook, a smile, and a new, brightly patterned green turban.

"We're here to develop your characters," Arlene says, meeting each person's eyes with a warm smile. Chelsea wonders if she was once a therapist or social worker. She's got that way about her—kind, warm, wise, but like she could shutter down and kick physical, mental, and emotional ass if she had to. "And I'm going to tell you the bad news first: We're leaning heavily into tropes and clichés. Entertaining the public is a cheap stunt, and we connect with what's primal in them and what they want to see, whether they know it or not. Nobody here is going to be Superman. Or Batman." Matt deflates a little. "You're all going to be more like their kookiest evil villains. But you're not alone. We're all in it together."

Feet shuffle, and everyone looks around as if their characters are going to jump out from behind every closed door.

"Amy, let's start with you. Did you have some kind of character in mind?"

Amy's fingers tap on the tops of her thighs, and Chelsea gets the idea she wouldn't choose to go first.

"Well, I'm hapa, so I'm guessing something traditionally Asian and pretty racist?"

Arlene nods. "Sure, but it doesn't have to be based on your actual racial makeup. You're looking to play on what the more ignorant side of America would expect you to be, but something that you could connect with and inhabit. You could even twist it so you're taking back your power."

Amy shakes her head. "I'm not down with that bing-bong Chinese shit I used to get in elementary school or the geisha girl thing. I'm Hawaiian on my mother's side, but most ignorant assholes just ask me where I'm from."

"Go with that. Hawaiian. What could you do?"

Amy meets Chelsea's eyes, a little desperate. Chelsea gets the idea she's not the most creative woman; she was an accountant and has thus far seemed very logical and straightforward. Chelsea gives a little shrug and makes wavy motions with her hands.

"I could do something Hawaiian," Amy says, nodding along like Chelsea has thrown her a life preserver. "Like, wear a grass skirt and a coconut bra? Hula Lulu? Honestly, it's the dumbest thing I can think of."

Arlene grins. "Hula Lulu. That's fantastic. It just rolls off the tongue. Your trademark moves could have to do with lava and tiki and surfing. Good job."

Amy sits back, relieved, but still uncomfortable. "But isn't it . . . I mean . . . isn't this just giving racists what they want?"

Arlene raises an eyebrow. "I don't think I've mentioned this, but I'll be on the mats with you as well. I'll be Shaka Zuri. Merging Black Panther with bright kente cloth. So believe me, I get that you can both accept it and do your best to inhabit it while being uncomfortable with it. It's okay to have challenging feelings right now. And we'll do more workshopping tomorrow and as we train, so don't worry. You'll have support every step of the way."

And then Arlene turns to Chelsea. "Now. Chelsea. I saw you give Amy a little tip there. Got any ideas for yourself?"

Chelsea realizes that not only hasn't she given it any serious thought, but perhaps she's been actively avoiding it. Who is she? Or worse, what stereotype does she fill?

"I could be some kind of homemaker," she thinks out loud. "Or maybe Karen who always wants to speak with a manager?"

Arlene's smile is apologetic. "Good thought, but we've already got someone doing that, and she even has the hairstyle to do it. Remember Liz, who joined us yesterday?"

Of course. The lady with the Karen haircut. She was so bland that Chelsea totally forgot about her.

"Okay, so a homemaker. A stay-at-home mom. A crunchy mom? An MLM boss bitch? I could have a rolling pin from baking or . . . throw essential oils in people's eyes and tie them up with leggings."

There are a few rumbles of laughter from around the circle of chairs—not mean, just an acknowledgment of how true it is. Not that Chelsea will ever admit she fell for an MLM herself.

Arlene gives her the sort of look Hannibal gave his patients right before they made a breakthrough.

"We have an idea for you, but I was hoping you'd come upon it yourself. This sort of thing . . . it works best with your input. What are you best known for?"

Chelsea looks down at her hands. She's not known for anything. She has no accomplishments. She's not a particularly good baker or one of those moms who's heavily involved in the PTA. She's never had a thing for painting or writing or sewing or gardening. Looking back, she's not even sure what she did to fill all that time.

Worry, mostly.

But known for?

Nothing.

She's a cardboard cutout of a woman.

She looks to Amy as Amy looked to her, and Amy smiles encouragingly at her like a mom working with a little kid who can't quite remember her colors but is soooo close.

"Florida Woman," Amy says quietly.

Chelsea wants to shrink down into herself.

Florida Woman.

It's been an online joke for decades, thanks to Florida's freedom of information laws. Florida Man rides tiger down the road naked on meth, Florida Woman beats clown to death in a Burger King.

And yes, Chelsea is now a member of the Florida Woman club, at least as of yesterday. She hasn't checked her phone today, because it's not really her phone—it's George's phone, and he disconnected service. Her phone is still in her minivan. Or, most likely, in an evidence bag.

She wonders briefly if all those other Florida Women had any idea what they were doing while they were doing it, if meth or crack or whatever is as consuming as the Violence. What Chelsea did, that's not her. She has never wanted to hurt anyone except David. Jeanie was her friend. It doesn't seem right to turn her into a Florida Woman story if she had no choice about what she did.

But that's out of her hands.

She already *is* Florida Woman.

The question now is: Can she embrace Florida Woman?

Can she embody that crazy-haired wildness, the madness, the . . . what, beating people with selfie sticks?

If it'll help her get her girls back from her mom, hell yeah she can.

"Okay. Florida Woman. But I'm not riding into the ring topless on an alligator."

That gets everyone laughing again, and Arlene nods. "No nudity. We're clear on that. Harlan is thinking your costume should be a play on what you were wearing yesterday, as it was described in the news." She holds up a hand. "Which may or may not be true, so go with me a moment. Cutoff shorts, a tank top covered in blood, cowboy boots."

Chelsea points down. "I was wearing these flip-flops."

"Which is obviously the most Florida choice of all, but you can't fight in 'em."

"All due respect, ma'am, but I've seen folks get the everlovin' shit slapped out of 'em with flip-flops," one of the new people says.

Arlene tilts her head in concession. "Well, you can't jump around a wrestling ring in flip-flops. We need closed-toe shoes for safety reasons here."

Chelsea looks down at herself. She's still wearing the outfit Arlene just described. She needs to ask if anyone has any spare clothes, or if they can make a Goodwill run or something, but she's too proud. She's never been a person who could ask for help. Living with her mother taught her that only weaklings asked for help, and that only suckers helped them. You take care of your business, you do your work, you mind your own beeswax. Yes, now Patricia is a pampered white cat, sleek and sated, who no longer hunts, but she was once a panther, and for at least the first five years of Chelsea's life her mother was her hero, her idol, her everything. That's what's left of the Patty that once was: You take care of your business. Period.

But Chelsea has nothing, and she needs help, and asking her to do this right now, to dig deep and create a character as if this is some acting class in the college she never went to instead of a tawdry replay of the worst moment of her life that she'll somehow never remember . . . it's a lot to take in. Her eyes are prickling.

"Chelsea, are you okay?" Arlene is leaning forward, watching Chelsea, focused and intent and cautious.

"I just . . ." Chelsea trails off with an embarrassing sob. She can't cry here. She can't even wipe off her nose. But she can't cry in the trailer, either. There's always someone around, and the little berths don't even hide the rustle of covers, much less choking sobs.

"Does it make you uncomfortable, the Florida Woman thing?" Arlene presses.

"Of course it does," she snaps. "It's embarrassing."

"Why?"

Chelsea looks at Arlene like she's an idiot, but Arlene looks at Chelsea like a fisherman at a prime spot who knows the bites are coming.

"Because Florida Woman is typically stupid and on drugs."

"What else?"

Chelsea snorts. "Stupid and on drugs is bad enough."

"We also think of Florida Woman as ugly and poor. The kind of woman who hurts children and animals, who has no empathy or self-control. That can hit you pretty hard, if you let it."

Chelsea's next breath is a gasping sob, and with nowhere else to hide, she doubles over, face flat on the table and hands over her head. The tears come like a hurricane, unstoppable, as it breaks over her.

She feels like all of those things. She is the kind of woman who has hurt an animal and a friend.

She doesn't know how to feel worse about either death that she caused, and something about the way the Violence strikes prevents her from really connecting with it. She knows she should feel more guilty about it, that she deserves punishment and hate, and yet . . . she wasn't really there when it happened. It wasn't her. She was left with only the aftermath. It's like she doesn't have empathy but knows that she should, knows that something vital and human and real is just . . . missing. And the Violence removes all self-control. And she certainly doesn't feel pretty right now, in yesterday's filthy clothes and dirty underwear, still speckled with blood, after showering in a horse barn with cheap shampoo.

She would feel worse about the crying if Amy wasn't crying, too.

She can hear the sobs next to her, heaving gasps of breath, and between her own loud gulps for air, she sees that no one in the circle is unaffected. Even Matt has red eyes and keeps dashing away tears against his shoulder.

"I'm all those things now," Chelsea says, low and moaning. "Everything but the drugs is true."

"But it's not your fault," Arlene says, her voice steady and honest and strong. "You are a victim. You are suffering from a disease. You're still human, and you're not alone in these feelings. None of this is your fault."

"I should've . . . I should've . . ."

"What, not gotten bit by a mosquito . . . in Florida?" The way Arlene says it makes it sound so obvious. "Not get a disease that took the world's best scientists weeks to figure out the contagion point? Would you tell someone with malaria that they should've done something else?"

"I . . ."

"No. No, you wouldn't. Because you would extend empathy to that person. We're all doing the best we can. These are strange times and strange circumstances. But we are survivors."

Chelsea lifts her head a little, called to Arlene's voice, to Arlene's burning eyes, crystal brown and so earnest.

She should run for office. Chelsea would vote for her.

"We are survivors of a new epidemic, and we have each other. The old world might be over, but we're making our own way. Our own family, our own jobs. If you're here, it's because you had nowhere else to go, which means we all have nowhere else to go, which means we can only move forward. Together."

Arlene stands up and walks to Chelsea, pulls her to standing, and hugs her, and Chelsea wants to tell her not to, knows that she must reek, that she's trembling and soaked in snot and tears and yesterday's blood, but being hugged by Arlene is a revelation. Arlene means this hug. It's fully frontal, tight, solid, sturdy. It's like the hugs on sitcoms that make everything okay, when the music hits a tender crescendo. It's the kind of hug that Covid denied everyone for over a year, that feels all the more precious now. Then Arlene waves Amy over, and

Amy joins them, still sobbing, and then everyone else, and then it's like yesterday's dogpile but completely different.

Seven people, crying together.

Seven people, arms wound around one another.

Seven strangers who met yesterday but are now more intimately connected than most people on the planet.

They are victims. They are infected. They are survivors.

"Okay, so I'm Florida Woman. Please tell me I get to hit someone with a rolled-up newspaper," Chelsea finally says, unsure how long a hug can go on before it gets weird.

"All the newspapers are dead," Matt says, looming over them all.

"Then I'll throw a toy alligator."

"That works," Arlene croons like a lullaby. "That works."

31.

Ella blinks, and she's standing in Mrs. Reilly's living room. She's just had a thought, but now she's forgotten it. Her eyes are burning like she's been crying. Ah, well. Time to get back to . . . what was she doing? Lunch.

Then she notices the body on the floor.

It's Uncle Chad.

Everything comes back.

Or most things.

Not *the* thing, the big thing, the vital linking scene between a freezer meal and the bloody pulp of a police officer oozing onto Mrs. Reilly's carpet.

It's like coming out of anesthesia. It's not real yet. It hasn't sunk in.

Someone else did this, surely.

She looks down at her hands. Her knuckles are bruised and swollen and red. Some of her fingernails are torn, skin and blood layered underneath them.

She did this, but she can't remember it.

She can remember . . . wanting to do it, but in the normal way of any trapped animal.

So this is the Violence.

This is how it works.

She was here, and then she was gone, and now she's back.

She has to put things together.

First she locks the door. That's important. Her dad is waiting at home to hear from Uncle Chad, and she doesn't want him to get curious and let himself in, which is just the sort of thing he would do. There's blood all over the inside of the door now, but that's something to worry about later.

Next she looks at . . .

The . . .

What happened. What she did. What's left of Uncle Chad.

He's on his back on the floor. His head is a pulpy mess of bone and pink brains and blood. His face is mostly gone. Beside him there's a crystal candy dish broken in two, blood painting the glassy surface. She must've . . .

Old butterscotch candies litter the dark blue carpet like winking stars.

There's a disturbing distance to how she sees this man she's known and feared all her life, like viewing a gory Goya painting at the museum and knowing that it was planned and posed, that the painter stared and stared. She's mesmerized by tiny details, by the flap of an ear and the way the blood is different colors depending on the surface it's landed on.

She can't tell if she's numb from the trauma of what she's done or whatever the Violence does, or if maybe she's still stuck in flight, fight, or freeze.

It doesn't matter.

She doesn't have much time.

She strips and stuffs her clothes into yet another garbage bag and hurries to the shower and turns the water on high and scalds off all the blood and scrubs and scrubs and scrubs. Then she gets dressed in an older, ill-fitting outfit from her bug-out bag and realizes that all her real clothes are locked behind the gates of Nana's neighborhood. Shit. She has to leave here, but she can't go home, and she can't wear these clothes forever. It feels horribly gross on a lot of levels, but she raids Mrs. Reilly's closets for the clothes that she doesn't seriously hate. Everything smells like laundry detergent and is absolutely not her style—long, swishy watercolor skirts and loose tank tops meant to go with short-sleeved cardigans and long necklaces of glass beads. Mrs. Reilly was one of those ladies who wanted to be an artsy witch.

With murmured apologies to the ghosts of the cats, she stuffs a garbage bag full of their mistress's long skirts and tunics and even some hideous clogs and sandals, knowing that she has to live life like a videogame now, taking whatever she can while she can. She collects all of her own things, too, and takes them downstairs to Mrs. Reilly's little white Miata, which is horribly small for her purposes but the only real option. It has gas, at least, and has been meticulously kept. The long-neglected engine turns over with barely a splutter.

She keeps glancing back at Uncle Chad while she scurries about her business like a mouse preparing for winter. Knowing Mrs. Reilly is gone, knowing her daughter Toni is either dead, in quarantine, or not interested in her mother's things, she loots the house. She takes all the food she can eat on the road that won't need refrigeration. She stuffs the car's trunk with soft drinks and bottled water. She takes a blanket and a pillow from the guest bedroom and finds a flashlight and a first-aid kit in Mrs. Reilly's hurricane box. She takes that big, sharp knife Uncle Chad threw across the room. And even though she hates herself, she combs through the old lady's drawers and lifts every mattress, gratified and grossed out when she finds five hundred dollars in cash carefully folded in an underwear drawer, hidden amid high-waisted pink polyester panties.

Finally, the only thing left to do is the thing she's been dreading. She heads back inside from the garage and holds her breath and plucks Uncle Chad's keys from the carabiner on his belt. She washes the blood off her hands and peeks out the front door, scanning the street for any movement, any twitch of a curtain. When she's satisfied that no one is watching, she moves the police car to the other side of the driveway, backs the Miata onto the street, and pulls the police car into the garage and shuts the door.

That's when the real terror kicks in.

Not when she found a police officer dead, not when she washed his blood out from under her fingernails, not when she passed by his body five times as she ransacked an old lady's underwear drawer.

It's the moment she knows that someone out there might be calling the cops, reporting the strange occurrence of a teen girl driving a cop car.

Because the cops won't come out for Violence killings anymore. They did in the first few weeks, back when she called 9-1-1 on her dad, but they always arrived too late to help anyone. Now they know there's no point, and that whoever is being attacked will be dead by the time they arrive, anyway. So no, they don't care about things like that. But they do care about their own, and if they call Uncle Chad and don't get a response and then hear something about his squad car being moved around by a kid, they're going to come here with a lot more than a gross joke about handcuffs and a speech about being good.

Back inside, she takes one last look around, trying to think of anything else she might need. The last two things she grabs are acetaminophen for her growing headache and the mermaid-shaped shaker of pepper from Mrs. Reilly's kitchen table. She's almost out the door when she doubles back and considers taking Uncle Chad's gun, knife, and, yes, now-illegal pepper spray.

She's about to be alone in the world again, and she'll need all the help she can get . . . but she can't bring herself to steal from a cop.

She locks the front door behind her as she runs to the Miata and drives out of the neighborhood with jaw-grinding slowness, checking her rearview mirror constantly for any sign of her dad. Just because he can't see Mrs. Reilly's house from theirs doesn't mean he wouldn't park down the street to monitor Uncle Chad's progress. Dad would probably love to watch her marched out in handcuffs.

But she doesn't see him, thank goodness.

He's left the dirty work to someone else.

He never did know what to say to her, drunk or sober. Not once she started to look like a woman and ask questions and push back.

She makes it safely out of the neighborhood without anything horrible happening, which is a goddamn miracle. She realizes she's been holding her breath for at least a minute, just like she used to do as a little girl running from her room to the bathroom at night in the dark, praying a monster wouldn't leap out of the linen closet and eat her.

Back on the road, she feels like she's restarting a videogame level. Last night she was right here, on this road, trying to find someplace that might feel safe and feeling utterly alone and at sea.

Here she is again, same thing—but now she knows she's got the Violence.

Probably from the mosquitoes she let in when she opened the windows to air out the house. Or, if it takes longer for the disease to develop, from sitting outside by the pool at Nana's with Brooklyn.

It's strange—she doesn't feel any different.

At all.

Physically, that is. No fever, no achiness, just the headache, which is pretty normal without her allergy medicine and which will soon be driven away by the acetaminophen. She'll have to stop at a pharmacy and spend ten precious dollars on allergy spray if she doesn't want to feel like her head is full of wet cotton until next December. It's weird that she could have the virus that's currently sweeping the warmer parts of the world, destroying local economies and spreading trauma and fear with random murders, and yet she feels . . . exactly the same.

She stops at her least favorite red light and glances at Big Fred's Floors. There's a dog licking the spot where the body was, some kind of pit bull mix.

And she's deep enough in that all she can think is that she wishes the poor dog had a real meal, as she can see his ribs from here. She's glad someone finally took the body away—Big Fred must not've had any loved ones, or maybe his loved ones were too scared to go looking for him. The way things are now, people just disappear. They hide so they won't hurt anyone, they hide so no one will know they've hurt someone, they hide because anyone could kill anyone at any moment. There are no funerals. She even received a spam email about how easy and cheap it is to start a crematory business on credit.

She shivers.

It's just hit her that she killed someone and left a body to rot in an empty house, and that whoever opens that door next will find something much more horrifying than a bowl of melted bananas.

The light turned green at some point when she was staring at Big Fred's mess, and she turns onto the main road and realizes she has nowhere to go. Home? Nope. Dad's there. Nana's house? Nope. Not only because she's not on the list, but because now that she has the Violence, she can't be near Brooklyn. She doesn't have any super-close friends, and she knows Olivia and Sophie are hundreds of miles away. Hayden keeps texting her, but she hasn't read the texts, and he's the last person on earth she would follow behind a locking door. She almost wishes her Martin grandparents were still alive, but Grandma Becky thought her son was the most perfect man on the planet and would've just called Dad on her, anyway.

She needs to find Mom and get Brooklyn back, but she has no fucking clue how to do it.

A drugstore appears up ahead, and she turns in to the lot, grateful that this, at least, is something she can do. She can get a cold drink and a new bottle of allergy meds and know, for at least a few moments, that she's accomplishing some small task. *Thank you, Mrs. Reilly, for your humble stash of cash.*

At the door, she's greeted by a gawky guy in his late teens wearing a navy-blue shirt that says SECURITY. He's got a gun on his hip and something else—a Taser, maybe?—in hand. He smiles awkwardly and nods, then clasps his hands in front like he's in the FBI. That's a fun new thing in the age of the Violence—minimum-wage jobs that give you a gun and an excuse to shoot anyone who looks like they're vaguely threatening. She hurries inside, hoping he won't try to start a conversation that might lead to him getting mad at her for rejecting his advances.

Before she shops, she hits the restroom, realizing that she's been about to pee herself all this time. If she's going to live out of her car, she's going to need toilet paper, but does she bury it or what? Or should she use the restroom at McDonald's? She can't do that five times a day. But she doesn't want to get dehydrated. Even the most basic things have suddenly become insurmountable.

If only Dad hadn't found her. She could've camped out at Mrs. Reilly's until she found her mom.

But wait.

Mrs. Reilly wasn't her only petsitting client. Her phone contacts are full of families in the area with kids or cats that she's watched. She just has to figure out which houses are empty.

Buzzing with hope, Ella buys the drugstore-brand nasal spray and a giant bottle of water and heads back out to her car, zipping past the security boy before he can make some terrible joke about how she would be prettier if she smiled, or how glad he is that she's not wearing a Covid mask, or how maybe he needs to pat her down, or whatever. She locks the car doors and scrolls through her phone until she gets to a likely option.

Just checking in. ☺ *Do you need someone to feed your cats?*

She sends the texts to the Canons and the Zelinskys, both of whom live in her neighborhood but far enough away from her own house that her dad would have no reason to know they exist.

No, we're home, thanks! the Canons text back with a smiley face.

The Zelinskys don't text anything at all.

She sends the same message to Mr. Reese and Mrs. Hunt.

Took cat with me, thanks, Mr. Reese texts back.

And nothing from Mrs. Hunt.

What happens next won't be comfortable. Ella is an introvert. She keeps to herself. She doesn't want trouble. She remembers how much she hated selling Girl Scout cookies door-to-door when she was tiny, even hated having to stand in front of Publix and ask shoppers to buy cookies that—let's face it—pretty much sell themselves. But she's going to do it anyway, because a little bit of embarrassment is better than living on the street in a Miata during a pandemic. She thinks about what she'll say as she drives.

The dog that was licking the spot where Big Fred was is gone, but there are tons of vultures there, black and hopping around excitedly. Ella misses the dog.

Back in her neighborhood, she has that hunched-down feeling of being hunted, but she chose the families to text carefully, knowing she wouldn't want to drive down Mrs. Reilly's street. Luckily, it's a huge, sprawling neighborhood with multiple entrances, so big that most families don't know more than a couple of their neighbors. Halloween is like a huge block party where strangers wave but don't know one another's names or faces. Right now, that's a great thing.

At the Zelinsky house, there's a car outside, which might mean they're home or could mean nothing. She continues on to Mrs. Hunt's house, which is definitely not her favorite. Mrs. Hunt is nice but . . . kind of a crazy cat lady. And a bit of a hoarder.

Ella parks right behind where Mrs. Hunt typically keeps her car in the garage, knowing that if she's gone, that's the only place her car will fit, thanks to piles and piles of stockpiled paper goods and Amazon boxes. She glances around as she heads for the front door, glad, again, not to see anyone walking around or watching her.

She knocks a cheerful sort of knock and waits, but no one answers. She tries the doorbell and hears the thunder of dozens of cat paws thumping toward the door. Horrific visions fill her mind of abandoned cats eating Mrs. Hunt and growing fat, but then the door opens just a few inches, and Mrs. Hunt peeks out, her eyes wide and red and haunted. The scent of fouled litter and cat piss mixed with human body odor and baby powder rolls out.

"What? What?" Mrs. Hunt asks, her voice shaking.

All of Ella's embarrassment flees as she realizes Mrs. Hunt is so messed up that Ella is the one in charge.

"Mrs. Hunt, are you okay?" she asks.

Mrs. Hunt glances around as various cats meow and try to squeeze out the door around the legs of her filthy sweatpants.

"Otis is dead," Mrs. Hunt says. "I don't know what happened to him, but he's dead. It was awful. I just found him lying there, crushed to bits. And then Leo. And then Keanu. All crushed and torn up. I don't understand."

Ella understands.

"Have you been watching the news or . . . um . . . talking to people?" she asks.

"No. Of course not. Conspiracies. Lies. The lizard people in Washington put trackers in the Covid vaccines so they could turn us on and off like the Terminator."

Ella would like to help, but she's a seventeen-year-old girl, and this is just way, way too big for her. She starts backing away.

"Okay. Well, I was just checking on you. Bye!"

"You're the Martin girl. You fed my babies when I went to San Antonio."

Ella stops by her car's open door. "Yes, ma'am."

"You knew Otis."

"He was a good cat."

Mrs. Hunt nods like this is the news she's been waiting to hear. "He was, wasn't he? Gone too soon. I'll call you if I go to San Antonio again. If I can find my phone."

The door shuts, and Ella lets out a shuddering breath. It would be great if there was something she could do, but . . . there's just not. Mrs. Hunt is a grown woman, and if she chooses to spend the rest of her life locked in her house with her cats, slowly going crazy, sick with the Violence, that's her business. What's Ella going to do—offer her therapy? Clean up all six overflowing litter boxes? At least Mrs. Hunt is fully stocked on food for herself and her cats, judging by the stacks and stacks of bags and boxes she's always seen in the garage.

She pulls away, glad to be far from the mad terror of Mrs. Hunt and her house. Pulling into a cul-de-sac, she flicks through her contacts, trying to figure out who might be the next best target.

But wait.

Mr. Reese said he took his cat with him. Which means he left his house.

Which means it might be empty.

It certainly looks promising when she arrives, the grass knee-high and a pile of moldering newspapers on the front doorstep. Old Mr. Reese is very particular about his mail and papers—Ella was always supposed to bring them inside whenever he was out of town and keep them in order by date. With a lift of hope, Ella pulls into the driveway behind where Mr. Reese usually parks his truck in the garage. She gets out and heads for the front door. When she knocks, no one answers, and Leroy the cat doesn't come paw at the door like he usually does. She walks along his porch to peek through the break in the blinds that Leroy made in the front window, noting that the house looks extremely empty. These are all good signs.

Hoping that she's not about to get the cops called and that Mr.

Reese didn't suddenly become paranoid, she punches in the code for the garage door, and it lifts up to reveal an empty parking spot. The hot reek of garbage smacks her in the nose, and she knows well enough now not to look in the garbage can—and she also knows Mr. Reese really is gone, because he's very sensitive to smells. Before pulling in, she hurries to the door and opens it, calling, "Mr. Reese? Leroy?"

There's no answer, and the house feels just as empty as it looks. The air is stale, the temperature set to what feels like bathwater. But Ella's been catsitting Leroy for three years, and she knows that the real proof will be the dust.

Mr. Reese hates dust. He pays her extra to run an electrostatic wand over everything before he gets home, and yet she finds a thick layer of gray on the bottom edge of the TV.

No way is he here.

No way has he been here for weeks.

And, she notes with the weirdest sort of gained experience, it doesn't smell like anyone or anything died in here, which is swiftly becoming a major bonus.

Ella hurriedly pulls the Miata into the garage and lowers the door, then does a brief circuit of the entire house before bringing her things in. Everything she sees confirms that Mr. Reese conscientiously cleaned house before leaving, taking his butterball of a tuxedo cat with him. The fridge is empty and spotless, there are vacuum marks on the carpets, and Leroy's litter box is empty and scrubbed clean, his food and water dishes gone.

She breathes a sigh of relief.

Finally, finally, she can relax for a little while.

And as a bonus, there's no one here she can accidentally kill.

32.

"Brooklyn?" Patricia calls again as the sound continues. "Brooklyn!"

Thud, thud, thud.

Her heart clatters back up as she drops her bags and runs toward her bedroom. The sound is getting louder, and it's the most terrifying thing she's ever heard. It doesn't falter, doesn't slow, is almost robotic in its unnaturally steady rhythm.

Thud, thud, thud.

Her closet door is open, and she steps inside to find a chilling scene.

Brooklyn holds her big mirror in both hands, slamming her forehead into it again and again. The girl's beautiful golden hair is matted with blood, her long eyelashes painted red.

"Brooklyn, you stop that this instant!" Patricia shrieks, so scared that she's moved into anger. But Brooklyn can't hear her, doesn't respond.

She doesn't have to see her granddaughter's eyes to know what she'll find there: nothing. Just like with Miguel.

Brooklyn's fingers are so tiny as Patricia's much bigger hands pry each finger away from the mirror's ornate frame. Her skin is burning, feverish. Red-splatted shards of glass dangle and fall with each strike. The girl's soft little body is taut and hard as a china doll as her grandmother pulls her away from the mirror that so enraptured her just a few short hours ago.

It's destroyed now.

Unable to reach what's left of the shiny surface, Brooklyn arches her back and strains toward it, hands in claws, grasping for what Patricia well knows are shards of glass. But Brooklyn can't see that, apparently can't feel the pain of the gashes and bruises painting her forehead. As she wrestles her granddaughter away, Patricia lashes out with one foot and kicks the mirror over, hard. It slams backward into the wall, shattering utterly, and tumbles sideways, all the glass falling onto the once-pristine white carpet.

Brooklyn's body goes limp in Patricia's arms.

There's a soft intake of breath, a measuring gasp, and then a shuddering sob.

"Mommy! Mommy, it hurts! Oh, Mommy! The monster got me! Help!"

Patricia pulls Brooklyn against her chest, cradling her, trying so hard not to touch the red flower of her forehead.

"Shh, sweetheart. It's Nana. Nana's here. There is no monster. You're safe now."

Brooklyn writhes in her arms, turns to look at her in utter horror. "But where's Mommy? She can make it better. Mommy won't let the monster hurt me. Neither will Ella."

Patricia snuggles in closer, stroking the girl's back, which is now sweaty and cool as the fever breaks. "Mommy and Ella are gone right now, but Nana is here," she croons. "Nana can keep you safe. Nana will make the monsters afraid."

She can feel her granddaughter considering this, can sense the moment she must accept reality. Brooklyn softens, snuggles down, sighs. It's telling, how long it takes the poor child to realize that Nana is all she has. It feels like Brooklyn . . . just gives up.

"Did I fall out of bed?" Brooklyn asks, reaching one hand up to touch her forehead.

Patricia recognizes an out when she sees one. "Well, that's my fault for having such high beds. Let's go get you cleaned up, shall we? You're definitely going to need more jelly beans."

Brooklyn stands up, leaving a perfect red handprint on the carpet that she doesn't even notice. Standing up is a bit of an ordeal for Patricia right now. Her legs are bloodless and wobbling, and she's still in shock from what she saw. The mirror—hideous, awful thing—is on the ground now, and it looks like a crime scene on one of those dark FBI shows on TV, a jagged, gory mess in the middle of her pristine white closet. She is not sorry to close the door just now.

In the kitchen, she installs Brooklyn at the table with her tablet and remaining jelly beans and goes to the pantry for the first-aid kit. The resilience of children is amazing—Brooklyn just shoves her sticky hair out of her face and goes back to her show while Patricia cleans her off with wet paper towels. There are flinches, winces, an occasional gasp or whimper or angry, "Ow, Nana!" Once she can actually see the wound, Patricia is beyond grateful to find that it's not actually that bad. She was worried stitches would be required, but from what she can tell, there are just a few cuts. It's a miracle, really. It reminds her of the time Chelsea fell off the monkey bars at a fast-food playground and busted her chin in the pine bark nuggets below. Lots of blood, lots of tears, but then it was solved with a bandage and the application of a strategic strawberry milkshake. Brooklyn desperately needs a shower, but otherwise, she seems just fine.

"Nana, what can we eat? I'm hungry!" she says as if she doesn't look like something from the final scene of *Carrie*.

Glad for something to do that doesn't involve blood, Patricia goes to paw through the bags she dropped when Brooklyn attacked her. There's nothing good here. Ah, yes. She threw all the snacky things a child would enjoy over the fence.

"If you'll run outside, you might find something nice in those bags," she says, pointing to the sacks splayed out in her knee-high grass, their cheerful colors promising sugar and salt. "But do bring in all the bags and their contents, please, not just your chosen snack."

Brooklyn stares outside, and when she sees the bags, she lights up like the Fourth of July.

God, has July already passed? It must've.

How could anyone celebrate something like that these days, glee-fully running the grill and shooting off fireworks when mosquitoes live outside and random people are attacking strangers?

It's funny how strangely time runs during a pandemic. When Covid hit, they lived here in luxury, ordering everything online and giving in to every indulgence. She even sent over Easter dresses for the girls, knowing full well they weren't going to come over for their usual brunch but unwilling to deny herself the joy of the selection process. This year, she missed Easter entirely. They were in California. The hotel maid left beautiful chocolate eggs on the bedside table. She didn't think about Chelsea and her girls for days on end.

Perhaps she is not the best grandmother.

It doesn't matter now. The child, at least, is happy at her task.

Brooklyn lopes outside—and why not? She's already got the Vio-lence; she can't get sicker—and runs in with the bags bumping along behind her.

"Can I have the puffs, Nana?" she asks, holding up an orange bag of God only knows what.

The rest of the day is a bit of a blur. Patricia puts up all the grocer-ies, lugs the broken mirror out into the garage, cleans up the shards, and hunts through Rosa's cleaning supplies for something to spray on all the bloodstains. In a stroke of genius, she encourages Brooklyn to go for a swim, which should wash away all the blood without any sort of disagreement over bath time. When Brooklyn asks her to swim, too, she barely puts up a fight before she's pulling on an old maillot and wading in. Sure, it'll wreck her hair, but who's going to see it? Brooklyn can't touch the bottom of the pool on her own, and Patricia isn't willing to have another cardiac event today.

That night, full of Kraft Macaroni and Cheese for the first time in decades, Patricia realizes that she is bone-tired. Panic, action, swim-ming, cooking, keeping up with Brooklyn in general—for all her claims of being busy in the past, she was actually very busy today, and it feels decidedly different.

"Let's go to bed now, dear," she says gently.

Brooklyn frowns from the couch, where she's sprawled with her tablet, already half asleep. "But I'm so tired. I want to sleep here. It's comfy."

Patricia's instinct is to sharply remind the child that she shouldn't have her feet on the couch in the first place, and that children take themselves to bed when bedtime is declared. But something about the constellation of bandages on that tender little forehead weakens her. She leans down and remembers to lift with her legs as she pulls Brooklyn against her shoulder—God, the weight of a sleeping child, so heavy and soft and warm and tender and stubborn—and carries her down the hall.

"Let's just get you upstairs to your cozy bed."

"No," Brooklyn moans, writhing in her arms. "Please. I don't want to fall out of bed again, and Ella isn't here, and it's scary waking up alone. I don't want to sleep there."

Patricia looks at the tall staircase, so grand and beautiful with its curling, shining banister and snow-white carpet. She doesn't want to go up the stairs, much less carry or drag Brooklyn up there. And in that room—well, there's no way to keep the child in there. The door opens inward, locks from the inside.

Brooklyn can no longer be seen as innocent and devoid of threat.

But there is one place she could stay.

"Brooklyn, how would you like to sleep near me?"

"Oh yes, Nana!" the child agrees, nodding eagerly. She squirms down from Patricia's arms and scampers toward the master bedroom. "Your bed is the biggest bed in the world!"

"Not my bed, dear. What if we made you a cozy nest in my closet? Then you'd be right near me, and it even has a door to the bathroom."

There's a moment of silence, and Patricia wonders if Brooklyn has any memory of what happened this afternoon, if she'll shrink from that room for the rest of her life and see blood every time she looks at a mirror.

But Brooklyn's face scrunches up adorably while she thinks about it until finally she says, "Okay, but I get a lot of blankets."

"As many as you need. Bring them all from upstairs, if you like."

Brooklyn gallops upstairs, and Patricia returns to the closet to make sure all evidence of today's incident has been hidden. The mirror is

gone, the shards discarded, the floor sprayed and blotted and vacu-
umed. There are some faint stains, so Patricia takes down her least
favorite fur coat and carefully arranges it to hide the orangey splotches.

Some time later—because time is indeed going strangely—she
leans down into a huge and untidy pile of blankets and pillows, most
quite expensive and the sort of gleaming, creamy white that doesn't go
well with small children who favor food coated in powdered cheese.
Brooklyn clasps her neck in a hug and kisses her cheek wetly and asks
for a nightlight. Patricia fetches her own nightlight from beside the
bed and plugs it in before edging out of the closet.

"Wait. Nana, where did your fancy mirror go?"

Patricia pauses in the door and smiles.

"It was too big and clunky. I moved it so you would have more room
for your nest. We can bring in a new one tomorrow, should you need
to twirl some more." With a blown kiss, she closes the door and slides
a chair under the closet doorknob.

This is the only way to be sure.

33.

Chelsea thought training for the Violence Fighting Ring would be like a movie montage, but really it's more like giving birth—long, grueling, sweaty, and painful. And that's just the first full day. She didn't know her body could push this hard, that her muscles could tremble and strain and not collapse. She didn't know she could eat so much without feeling guilty. She didn't know she could . . . do something. She's so accustomed to busy nothings, to always feeling like she was behind even though she didn't have a job. Life without David is a miracle.

They're on break now after their grueling morning workout, drinking Gatorade mixed up weakly in a big orange canister to replenish their electrolytes. The weight training and cardio were brutal, and the wrestling practice was deeply uncomfortable. As an only child with a non-hugging single mother and no family outside of her own home, Chelsea has never really gotten the hang of non-sexual physical intimacy with strangers. Grabbing and fake-slapping and slamming these women around, having moments where their bodies are entwined or clasped or, her least favorite, crotch-to-face during a move, is just something she's going to have to get used to. And she will, because she needs that vaccine.

"Ladies, with me," Arlene says, and Chris follows it up with, "Guys, over here." Everyone stoppers their new VFR water bottles, wipes their mouths, and moves to follow their teachers. Sienna and Indigo are out in their RV, sewing costumes. Harlan is probably in his own RV. Chelsea hasn't seen him today, but she's surprised he's not here supervising like an owner watching his prized horses run from far away, judging their progress. Arlene told the girls he's setting up their tour, fixing dates and places and marking them on a map and building the website. It's odd to think that her entire future rests in his giant hands.

Arlene pulls the women over to a set of mats and tells them to sit in a circle. Chelsea goes on alert; this seems like it's going to be touchy-feely, and she's still on edge after her big Florida Woman outburst. She wasn't the only person brought to tears when choosing a name and character, and she's pretty sure now that Arlene worked in a rehab center or psych ward, running circle time there, too. She seems to have a gift for walking the fine line between truth and comfort.

Arlene stands as Chris leads the men out the door, and Chelsea breathes a small sigh of relief. The boys will be running outside in the ninety-degree weather, which sounds like her definition of hell. At least the women get air-conditioning. And privacy.

"Poor boys," Amy says, sitting to Chelsea's right.

Chelsea nods her agreement, but she's not so sure the women will have an easier time of it.

Instead of sitting with them on the mat, Arlene paces around the outside of their circle, her thumb on her chin as she thinks.

"We're going to play Duck Duck Goose, but when I tap you, I'll give you an emotion or adjective, and I want you to embody it. Don't get up and run, though—I know you're still tired from cardio." A chuckle goes up around the circle. "Just put everything into the emotion. Okay?"

Everyone nods. This is a new game, but it seems straightforward enough.

Arlene walks around the circle and touches Joy on the shoulder.

"Arrogance."

This one comes naturally to Joy. She rolls her eyes and sneers, snorting as she crosses her arms and turns away.

"Good." Arlene walks around the circle and taps Amy on the shoulder. "Pain. You just got slammed."

Amy throws herself into the circle, rolling around and clutching at her arm like an invisible giant snapped it in two. Tears spring to her eyes, and she struggles to get up and fails. Amy is good at this; although she doesn't speak of her past—no one does—she did admit to doing some improv as part of her business training.

"Good." Arlene stops behind Chelsea and taps her shoulder. "Rage."

Chelsea bares her teeth and roars, following it up with gnashed teeth and growling, but Arlene doesn't move on.

"I don't believe it, Chelsea. It feels more like you're imitating a dog than channeling a hidden well of rage."

Chelsea puts her mouth back in place and looks up. "I'm not really an angry person."

Arlene steps through the circle and stands in front of Chelsea, arms crossed as she looks down, annoyed. "I don't think that's true. I see your face when we run out of coffee in the morning or Chris assigns extra laps because someone was lagging behind. Maybe you don't express your anger, but it's in there."

Chelsea looks away. "I mean, that's like saying you want me to show you my liver. We both know it's in there, but there's no convenient way to make it visible."

Arlene squats down and looks her in the eye. "Clever simile, but I think it's more like you holding a marble in your mouth and telling me there's no marble. You've just spent so much time pinning your lips and pretending there's no marble that you've forgotten how to spit it out."

Her eyes bore into Chelsea's, and it's all Chelsea can do not to look away. Because looking away would mean that Arlene is right, and Arlene is not right.

"I can see it in there," Arlene muses with the tiniest quirk of her lips. "I can see that ol' furious marble rolling around in there."

She stands again, looming.

"There."

Chelsea looks up. "What do you mean?"

"When I stood over you. You flinched. You made yourself small." Arlene steps closer, somehow putting more weight and menace into her stance. "You're still doing it."

"Yes, well, you're looming over me. What am I supposed to do?" Chelsea snaps.

"What you always wanted to do. Talk back. Feel something besides helpless. The more I loom, the smaller you make yourself, like you're trying to disappear." Standing directly over her, Arlene puts her hands on her hips. "Chelsea, who are you scared of?"

"C'mon, Arlene," Joy says, squirming a little. "You're freaking her out."

"Chelsea can fight her own battles. So what is it, Chelsea? What do you want to do?"

Arlene is so close overhead, leaning down now, that Chelsea can smell her perfume, and Arlene nudges her with a foot, and there's nowhere else to go, she's trapped, she can't get away, this is her boss, she can't hit Arlene, she doesn't want to hit Arlene, but God, you can only push someone so far—

Arlene nudges her shoulder with a knee, and Chelsea scrambles back, her blood singing, her head hot, her hands sizzling, her body telling her to shrink and freeze and to stand and fight, all at the same time, her muscles tense and quivering, an animal caught between a wall and a box.

"Chelsea!" Arlene barks, loud and harsh. "Are you gonna let me push you around like this?"

"No!" Chelsea shouts, scrambling to her feet, hands in fists and shaking. "No! You're not my mother! You're not my husband! You can't make me do anything!"

"Let it all out, Chelsea. Scream!"

And Chelsea does. She fucking roars, all those years of rage bottled up and now unleashed on the world, an explosion that rattles her, inside and out.

The silence, after, is deafening. No one moves. Chelsea's throat is sore, stripped.

Arlene goes quiet, the tension gone from her body. "What does it feel like in your arms, Chelsea?"

Chelsea looks down, surprised by the question. Her arms are up, palms open, defensive, like she's pushing someone away.

Like she's pushing David away.

"Tense. I want to push. I want to push so hard."

"Go on and do it, then. Push him away."

"He's not here."

"He doesn't have to be. Push the air."

Chelsea does, and it feels strange, but now it feels there's a warm ball of sunshine in her stomach, like it's okay.

"What do you feel now?"

"My arms stopped shaking. They feel lighter. Buzzing."

"What else do you feel?"

"Just . . . light. Like when you tense up a muscle and release it. But everywhere."

Her hands are by her sides now, and her cheeks feel warm. She looks to Arlene, questioning, amazed at how she feels twice as big as she did before but light as a feather.

"Was it your husband, Chelsea? Is he the one who hurt you?"

Chelsea nods. It's all coming back. It never left. "He pushed and pushed and pushed." She's panting now, memories flapping past like her mind is flipping through a photo album, layers and layers of the same old thing. "Put me in a corner, sat me on a stool, cornered me against the counter. Bigger and more dangerous. His fingertips would bruise my chest when he'd poke me to make a point. I'd say the wrong thing, and his arm around my throat, choking . . ."

She trails off, one hand to her neck. Everyone in the circle is staring up at her, silent. Arlene is a few feet away, looking alert and open and smiling kindly, her eyes alight like Chelsea is a kid riding a bicycle without training wheels for the first time.

"Go on."

"He . . . he would never let me talk back. Or fight back."

"He made you small."

"He . . . wanted me small. Smaller and smaller every year."

"He silenced you."

"He hated everything I said. Didn't want to talk about feelings unless he was drunk, and then it was only *his* feelings." Chelsea's throat hurts in a different way, like the words are clawing their way out; she's never spoken about this before. It's like she's been under some sort of magic spell and talking about it now is painful. Her mouth is dry, her eyes wet and burning. "I couldn't tell anyone."

Arlene nods knowingly, as do several women in the circle. "That's a common tactic of abusers. They gaslight you, convince you you're remembering it wrong or that if you told someone else they wouldn't believe you. They want you to think you're crazy, irrational, helpless. They want you cut off from your support, to have no one to tell. They want you silent."

Chelsea nods; God, it makes her feel stupid, that she let it happen. Here on the outside, it's ridiculous, it's obvious, it's clumsy. But on the inside—

"It happened for so long. I forgot what normal was."

Arlene steps forward, hands up, careful, watching Chelsea like she's a skittish cat that might run or lash out.

"It's okay. It's not your fault."

Chelsea hangs her head. "It was my fault. I let it happen."

Arlene shakes her head, eyes smiling and yet sad, and Chelsea wonders if maybe something similar happened to her, too. "It's not your fault. It's something that happened to you, not something you let happen. That's like saying you let a boulder fall on you. You didn't ask for it. If abusers telegraphed their playbook, there would be no victims." She puts her hands on Chelsea's arms and squeezes gently, and Chelsea feels a rush of warmth. "You aren't small. You don't have to make yourself small. You are allowed to have feelings. You are allowed to experience rage. You are allowed to take up space. You are allowed to be irrational and loud and ugly. You don't have to make yourself less. Not ever again. You don't have to play by those rules anymore."

An odd, gulping laugh escapes, and Chelsea rides it out. "Just like that?"

"Just like that."

"It's not that easy."

"No, it's not easy. It's hard work. Building yourself back up from nothing is always hard work. But it's worthwhile. And you have support." Arlene smiles at the other people in the circle.

Amy stands up and walks over to put a hand on Chelsea's back. Joy stands, and the other women stand, and they all put a hand on her somewhere. Chelsea wonders, for a moment, if this is what it feels like to have a big family, to be connected to other people who come from the same place, whose hearts know the same jagged landscape. It feels good—but it also feels awkward. She's not used to everything being about her.

"Are we doing trust falls next?" Chelsea asks jokingly.

"More like trust body slams," Arlene offers to get a laugh. "Now back to our game. Let's try something a little less complex. If y'all will sit back down?" They all do, including Chelsea, who has a feeling she won't be called on again today, like a kid who already turned in their big project and is now off the hook. Amy shoots her a friendly smile and a nod, but Chelsea isn't sure if it's just supportive or if the quiet woman has a similar history.

Next the bodybuilder, Maryellen, has to act insane. And then Leah has to act devastated. Amy has to act disgusted. Paz has to act elated. No one gets rage again. Chelsea gets skipped. Things happen, and she's there, but she's also inside her head. It feels like walking around a house after you've moved, after all your belongings are out and you're just cleaning up the remaining mess. There's a brightness, a cleanness, a welcome emptiness. Whatever Arlene did—therapy, whatever—it helped. It worked. She feels more relaxed, more free, less tense. It's a miracle, it really is.

For a moment, she forgets that David is still out there.

And then she remembers.

With her phone gone, there's no way to get in touch with anyone— not Ella, not her mom, and not David. She has no idea if he's out of quarantine, although last night she read on her phone—well, Amy's phone—that Florida wasn't doing much to clear out their holding centers, probably because they're acting as private prisons and there's a lot of money in keeping them running. Then again, Huntley said Brian was working on it, which means David is probably out, because Brian tends to get what he wants.

It's a comfort, at least, that her mother's home is currently the safest place possible for her girls—even David wouldn't be able to get into the Fort Knox of Patricia's neighborhood. And there's really no safer place for Chelsea herself than here. She doesn't have her van or phone, there's no way to track her, and she'd love to see David try to hurt her while she's under the care of Mr. Harlan Payne. He'd split David in half like a log.

The rest of the day passes, and Sienna takes Chelsea and the other folks who came here with nothing to the nearest Target. Armed guards prowl the aisles as people shop, and Chelsea is given two hundred dollars against her first paycheck to get what she needs to function. Considering the heat and what's expected of her, she goes for the sale racks and buys three-dollar tank tops, T-shirts with stupid sayings that no one wants, ugly leggings, shorts, cheap white socks. She finds undies and hideous bras on clearance. And she's grateful to find sneakers in her size for seven dollars. Once she adds toiletries and moisturizer with SPF, she's pretty much maxed out. She looks longingly at phone cards, but it would take at the very least eighty dollars to make George's phone work. It's kind of scary, how two hundred dollars doesn't go particularly far when you're starting with nothing. Considering she's been borrowing Sienna's old sneakers and washing her undies in the tour bus sink every night and hanging them to dry from the ceiling of her bunk, she can't complain.

That night, it's raining, hard, and they eat in the interview room, barbecue that's better than it should be with big, industrial aluminum vats of green beans and mashed potatoes. As they eat, Arlene tells them that Sienna and Indigo make up the menus, Harlan okays them, and then Indigo cooks all day long or helms the grills at night, for which she's paid like an adult. Chelsea almost wishes that were her job, but then she realizes that she'd actually rather train and get stronger than get herself locked into another kitchen, taking care of people.

It's . . . God, it's a new kind of joy, not taking care of anyone. She went straight from living with her mother to taking care of David to taking care of David and the girls, in that order. There hasn't been a single time in her life when she wasn't technically a child or caring for someone else. It's nice, not having to cook or do dishes, and her old kitchen table in its sunbeam seems like something that belonged to another person in another world. To think: Just a few months ago, her biggest worry was a letter from the bank. Now she has no money whatsoever, only what Harlan chooses to pay her. The next time he does, her first purchase will be a sim card and plan for George's phone, as she misses having control over her connection to the world—and there's so much she needs to know.

She doesn't miss checking the flatlined Dream Vitality sales numbers, and she doesn't miss the beauty pageant of Facebook, but she does miss being able to look up that movie she forgot or whether the price of the Violence vaccine has gone down at all. The vaccine was created by some grad student and snapped up by a private company, and that means supply and demand are in full effect. The government is working on their own vaccines but say it will take several more months of testing. The CDC has firmly stated that the privately owned vaccine hasn't met their requirements, but that hasn't stopped anyone who can afford it from getting it, and data suggests those who have it are suffering no ill effects—and no cases of the Violence. It's a therapeutic vaccine, meaning it cures those already infected and prevents further infection, and like most of America, Chelsea isn't holding her breath on a free government shot. After the president fumbled the initial Covid response and vaccine so badly, no one trusts him this time around. If the pandemic had started before he was reelected, there's no way he'd still be in charge.

Chelsea knows all this from scrolling through Amy's phone to check the news and search for the names of her family members to see if anything bad has happened to them. And she checks her own name for updates in her news story, but nothing new ever pops up. Keeping track of current events just now would be a full-time job, considering the huge differences in the quality of life in hot places compared with cold places. In frigid climes, life is totally normal, and everyone benefits from the huge uptick in long-term tourists grateful to be alive. Hotels are packed and business is booming, everyone fiddling in their puffer coats as the southern areas burn.

But in the South, and especially in the poor countries around the equator, life has become brutal and unruly. The governments, unable to protect or help anyone, basically gave up. Charities popped up to help the unfortunate, their coffers drained by the unrepentant. Any aid money disappears before it can do any good. Just like with Covid, the essential workers who have no choice but to go to work must go to work, wondering all day long whether their next customer might be the one who kills them before the heavily armed security guard can pull his weapon. Online ordering is through the roof, and delivery driving is considered the best and safest job available, meaning the competition for gigs is fierce.

Yes, Chelsea is very glad to be where she is, right now. It could be a lot worse.

She also noticed today that George's pickup truck disappeared. She suspects that Harlan arranged to have it found somewhere far away, but he certainly doesn't share his plans with his employees.

Back in the tour bus, they all take their turn in the tiny bathroom, brushing teeth and getting ready for bed. Chelsea is grateful for the little jar of Cetaphil; her face feels cleaner and softer than it has in weeks. The rain pelts down hard on the bus roof as she snuggles into her bunk, and she smiles, thinking she might actually sleep well tonight, considering the tough workout this morning followed by emotional catharsis. At the front of the bus, Arlene sets up her phone to play classical music, both to signal bedtime and help cover up the sounds of bodies rustling around. It's unusually soothing, the same soft lullabies Chelsea used to play when her girls were babies.

She's just drifting off when the curtains on her bunk brush aside.

"You awake?" Amy asks, leaning in.

"Sure." Because Chelsea is a mom, and it doesn't matter that she was falling asleep; it only matters that she's awake now.

"Can I—I mean . . ." Amy trails off. "Can we talk?"

Chelsea scoots back toward the wall. The bunk isn't very big, even smaller than a twin bed, but both of them will fit, if awkwardly. Chelsea wishes she knew what was going on; Amy is so serious and private that she can't imagine what it'll be like, sharing this intimate space with her. Arlene's therapy this morning may have helped Chelsea, but it didn't magically give her the ability to say no when someone needs her help, even when she'd like to roll over and go back to sleep in privacy.

The curtains part, and Amy slithers in. Her pajamas are almost comical—those old-timey man pajamas that button up the front. Her glasses are off, her hair back in a silk bandanna. That's all Chelsea can see before the curtain falls back into place and they're in darkness again. For a moment—just a moment—Chelsea panics. Does Amy want to kiss her, something like that? Because she's so close Chelsea can smell the minty mouthwash on her breath. But then Amy shudders with an intake of breath bordering on a sob, and Chelsea goes very still.

"You okay?" she asks.

Amy clears her throat softly, and her voice is a husky whisper, barely loud enough for Chelsea to hear. Surely everyone else is listening in now, although Amy is trying to keep it private.

"So that was pretty heavy, today," she whispers.

Chelsea is wary. She'd hoped she wouldn't have to talk about it again.

"Yeah."

Amy pauses, considering.

"It sounds like you had a hard time, back home. I was just wondering if you—" She clears her throat again. "Are your kids okay?"

Chelsea blinks in the darkness. "My kids? I hope so. I mean, there's no way to know, but they're with my rich mom, and she's a narcissistic asshole, but she lives behind a guardhouse with huge walls. So yeah, I hope so. Why?"

She can barely see Amy, just a shape and the gleam of light on her eyes, but she senses her deflate. "I was just . . . I just wondered if you . . . never mind." The bed rustles as she rolls to leave.

Chelsea puts a hand out. It lands on Amy's shoulder, and she stills. "Hey, you know my darkest secrets now," Chelsea muses, keeping her voice low. "I'm a human punching bag. Can't get any lower than that. So you can tell me what's on your mind, if you want." After a moment of silence, she adds, "It feels better, having it out in the world like that. I feel better now."

Amy resettles, sniffles, clears her throat, sighs. Chelsea's hand doesn't move, but Amy seems to soften a little, to relax. Chelsea isn't the sort of person to just reach out and touch another person, but it's more natural, in the near-dark. It's easier, knowing this woman has watched the most painful, embarrassing splinter removal of her life and still wants to be friends. It's a tender sort of exchange, a scary one, but Chelsea would rather ride it out now than ignore Amy's obvious need and know her new friend is in pain.

"I'm not infected. I have—" Amy clears her throat again. "I had a son. Joshua. He was four. We lived just outside of Miami. He was at home with the nanny while I was at work. Big, important account. Deadlines. All that." She goes quiet, and Chelsea rubs her arm a little, like she would for Brooklyn after a bad dream. "I came home late that night, and . . . the nanny . . . she was nice. An older lady. Great references. She loved Josh. But she had the Violence, and . . ."

Her voice breaks, and her sobs are silent but take up all the room in the little bunk. Chelsea squeezes her shoulder gently, holding the connection, tears silently spilling out onto her cheeks.

"It was early, in the spring. We didn't really know yet, what it was. Didn't know it was mosquitoes. Didn't know Miami was going to be a hotbed. It was so early, before it was even in the news much. I came home and she had—he was—I can't—" A sigh. "I was in shock. My husband came home from work and found me there, holding him. Pieces of him. The nanny had run off. She was gone. My hands were shaking too hard to try calling her. Now we all know that when it hits you, you don't know what you're doing, it doesn't matter how good of a person you are or how much you care about the person you're with. You just . . . do what you do. But then, we called the police, there was a manhunt. They caught her, put her behind bars. We wanted the electric chair. My husband . . . we didn't do so well without Josh. We fought over whether he should've ever been alone with someone besides his parents. John said I should've been home. That if I'd been home . . ." She takes a shuddering breath. "It was a quick, messy divorce. He took everything. I still don't understand how."

She breaks down into sobs, and Chelsea can feel echoes of heartbreak in her own chest. She reaches for Amy and pulls her into a hug. It's awkward, as they're both on their sides in a tiny bunk, and they can't see anything, but this is how people deal with the Violence. They hug, they press, they wait patiently to ride it out. Amy cries against her shoulder as if she's been holding this torrent in all along with that same gut-deep rage that Chelsea roared earlier when Arlene prodded her.

They both contain these deep wells of pain, these dammed-up rivers that need to run.

"It's not your fault," Chelsea whispers. "You couldn't have known. It was just bad luck. He shouldn't have said that to you."

"It was a dick move," Joy growls from the bunk overhead. "Fuck that guy."

"Who could know?" Maryellen adds. "If he was at work, too, it was equally his fault. Fuckin' patriarchy."

Hearing their voices, Amy ducks her head into Chelsea's shoulder, and Chelsea can feel a hot flush of embarrassment surge up her body.

"I stomped the dog to death," she says to the darkness behind Amy. "And then I beat my only friend to death with her water bottle trying to get here. She had it, too."

"I killed my neighbor with a shovel," someone else says from the darkness.

"I was taking care of my mom. She was in hospice. Afterward, I was almost relieved," says someone else. "And I hate myself for thinking that."

"It was my boss," someone else says. "That pedophile deserved it."

"I was a teacher," someone else says, voice breaking. "One of my kids. I fucking loved my kids."

One by one, the voices ring out in the darkness.

Everyone has killed someone.

Everyone but Amy, but Amy feels as if she did.

Neighbors, friends, baristas. Amy is the only one who lost a kid. And maybe she didn't do it with her own hands, but that just means she was there for every moment of it, didn't even have the mercy of lost memories.

Chelsea wants to ask Amy why she would come here, why she would put herself in such proximity to the very thing that killed her son.

But she thinks she knows.

Because, like her, Amy has nothing, and she needs that vaccine because it's only a matter of time before she'll get infected and hurt someone herself.

And if Amy were to die by the Violence here, then that would make things even.

Holding Amy like this, her shoulder soaked with tears, Chelsea is almost grateful.

At least she still has her girls to go home to.

At least her girls are safe.

34.

Ella's food isn't going to last long. Mr. Reese's house isn't like Mrs. Reilly's. Mrs. Reilly had electricity, a freezer full of Lean Cuisines, running water, air-conditioning. Mr. Reese's house is much cleaner, much better smelling, but hot and humid and empty. There is no electricity, which means her phone is on power-saving mode. She has to change bathrooms multiple times as the tanks run out of water to flush. She drinks hot, fizzing sodas and eats the individually packaged snacks she brought with her.

The most important thing right now is finding her mom, and she needs Wi-Fi to do that. She sets her phone alarm for four in the morning and wakes up, hot and sweating on top of the covers, in Mr. Reese's guest bed. The heat is so unbearable that getting up isn't that much of a pain. Outside, the air is a little bit cooler, but not by much. She should've left a window open, but now mosquitoes feel like little grenades, even if she's already got the disease. It's not raining, but the low-lying clouds and feeling of heavy expectation suggest it will soon.

With her charged laptop in her bag with Mrs. Reilly's knife, she hurries out Mr. Reese's side door and scurries a few streets over to the neighborhood playground, keeping to the shadows. It's the last place her dad would look for her, but she knows for a fact that she can pick up her home Wi-Fi signal from here.

The playground is deserted, cordoned off with yellow caution tape. Ella doesn't know if that's because someone got hurt here or because the neighborhood is trying to keep the HOA from being sued in case some kid gets killed on their property by someone with the Violence. The equipment is a bit run-down and has seen some changes since she was a little kid, but this playground still holds good memories.

Mom used to bring her here, when she was tiny, back before Brooklyn was born. Before things got bad. She has odd, fractured, dreamlike memories of swinging in that swing with buds on the trees, coming down that slide after a rainstorm and soaking her jeans. The neighborhood used to do an Easter egg hunt here every year, and Ella loved the feeling of being held back until someone counted down from ten, then the glorious feeling of being released to run free, careening in a crowd of kids, certain this year she'd find the big prize egg they always hid for one lucky kid to find and cash in at the local chocolatier. She never found the egg, but there was never a shortage of candy, either.

Now it's dark, lit only by a few streetlights strategically placed so that if any teenagers come here to get in trouble, their hijinks will be highly visible to the nearest Concerned Carol with a phone set to record. Ella hasn't seen a single light on inside a house on her way here. Half the homes are completely dark, but many of them have their outside lights on. Even during a strange pandemic, four in the morning is forgotten time. She sits at one of the picnic tables, checking it first for gum and bird shit, and opens up her laptop.

There's her family Wi-Fi, uncreatively named with a string of letters and numbers. She signs in and starts by searching for Chad Huntley to see what the papers had to say about that. The story is barely a blip, these days—brave hometown officer killed in the line of duty, protecting citizens from the Violence. Unknown assailant.

Ella releases a huge breath she didn't know she was holding.

They don't know it's her.

Or they know and aren't making it public.

Maybe Uncle Chad wasn't bringing her in officially but as a favor to her dad. Maybe he wasn't even supposed to be there, and it was embarrassing to randomly track his phone or car or whatever to a dead old woman's house. Maybe the labs are so backed up that no one is testing for DNA. Maybe they're to the point where it doesn't matter. Since you can't prosecute someone for violence committed while storming, what's the point in wasting a bunch of taxpayer dollars on it? It's a crazy time for crime. But for Ella, this is a good thing.

At least in this regard, she has one less thing to worry about.

She next hits up Facebook. There are a zillion messages and posts from people at her school and people she randomly met once, but she ignores them. She sends a long, rambling private message to her mom and then looks up Nana, whose profile image is a professional Glamour Shot, and shoots her a friend request and a private message checking in on Brooklyn. Ella isn't sure why she hasn't tried this route yet, but it's only just occurred to her that something as annoying and stupid as Facebook could still be a thing. It's so out of favor she doesn't have it on her phone, which is old and doesn't have room to spare.

While she's there on Facebook, she tries to think of anyone her mom might still be in contact with. Weirdly, sadly, only one person comes to mind, so she sends a private message to Mom's Dream Vitality manager, Ashleigh. She then spends twenty minutes scrolling through her own feed and her mom's feed, looking for any sort of helpful clue about where her mom might be, but it's just endless garbage and tons of fake news and statistics about the Violence. Everyone still has their STAY HOME, SAVE LIVES frame around their profile picture, recycled from Covid. Sad that the message still stands.

Looks like Nana wasn't lying—there is a vaccine, but only rich people can afford it until the government vaccine is ready, which might take months or up to a whole year, as the president again gutted the pandemic response team the moment he was back in power. The vaccine is the only cure, and it feels so out of reach right now that tears prick at Ella's eyes. Even if she could go back to her grandmother's house, she's not safe, not to be around Brooklyn. But her heart aches, just to talk to someone familiar, just to know that her mom and little sister are okay. That's all she needs—just to know.

Even though it's four in the morning, she keeps hoping for a response from Nana but gets nothing. She leaves her cell number, just in case, before opening a new tab. For several moments as the frogs and bugs sing and the mosquitoes buzz and land and leave itching welts that can't hurt her anymore, Ella thinks about how to find her mom. There's no way, and she knows it.

She types her mother's name into the search bar anyway.

She already knows what she's going to find, but it's comforting, seeing evidence that her mom still exists.

At least this time, there are more details.

The pic they're using is one she took using her mom's phone, back when Mom was still trying to sell her dumb oils online by looking pretty and carefree. Lifestyle photos, they were called. Ella would feed them through filters to add highlights and warmth and then her mom would put sappy inspirational quotes on top of them and slap them up on Instagram, like that was actually going to help her sell her woo-woo oils. But Ella was always happy to take the pictures, to help her mom look nice. It was one of the rare times it felt like she had her mom's full attention, when she felt necessary and useful.

She reads several articles before realizing that all the stories say the same thing that she's already read. Her mom and Jeanie were driving east on I-4 in the minivan. Her mom beat Jeanie to death with a Yeti bottle and the minivan ran off the highway and into a cow pasture. A man named George Blinn stopped to help, and when he approached, Chelsea Martin threw cow feces at him and stole his truck, leaving behind her wallet, phone, and several bags of belongings.

And that was the last anyone has seen of her mother, who is now . . . well, not a wanted criminal. A person of interest. Her concerned husband begs for any information. George Blinn has a reward out for his missing truck.

No reward offered by Dad to find Mom, of course.

As Ella now knows, they don't have enough money to pay someone for that sort of thing.

But Dad was looking for Ella, and she's pretty sure he's looking for Mom, too, which means if Mom is smart, she'll be staying off the radar.

There's nothing newer on her mom than that oft-repeated news story that feels like word salad. No mugshots. No updates. It's less of a news story, actually, and more just another dumb Florida Woman joke. If her mom hadn't thrown shit at some guy in a red hat and stolen his truck, it probably wouldn't have even made the news.

So now her mom is out there, somewhere, without her phone. Without anything. Ella doesn't even know her mom's email address.

Which leaves Ella wondering: How do you find someone who doesn't want to be found?

And the strangest idea comes to mind, scratching at her memory like Olaf at the back door.

Her mom tried to find her long-lost friend Whitney on that Missed Connections site, so maybe that's a place Ella could try to find her mom. It feels silly and stupid, but Ella is willing to try anything.

Feeling like a complete idiot, she heads over to Craigslist and, after a ton of thought, writes up an ad for Tampa's Missed Connections and posts it under two titles. One says *Smella looking for her favorite Swamp Momster,* which is an inside joke only her mother would understand, and the other one says *Chelsea Martin, please email your daughter.* She knows she'll probably get all sorts of garbage in the inbox, but she can't think of another way to maybe possibly reach her mom.

She also searches for her dad, but his name is so basic that there are dozens of David Martins just in their town. There's not even any mention of him being in quarantine. His online footprint is nonexistent. Luckily, so is her own.

Next up, she checks her email and finds yet another message from Hayden. He's out of quarantine now after getting tested—negative, of course, but scientists still aren't sure if maybe the body gains immunity over time, so it's possible that he had the Violence but now doesn't because his immune system is so great. He's very emphatic about that part. He's back home with his parents and doing summer e-school so he can still graduate on time.

She rolls her eyes. Yeah, as soon as she started squatting in people's homes and killing police officers, she stopped believing that calculus was valuable to her current life. Hayden wants to know what she's up to, why she's not answering his texts, when he can see her again. He wants to meet privately and apologize. He's had a lot of time to think about it, and he wants to make things right.

Ella considers what it would be like, taking him up on that offer. Inviting him to Mr. Reese's house, or meeting him at his house. Would his mom—who didn't really like her to begin with—be apologetic, as surely she's seen the footage of him hurting Ella? Or would she be cold and blame Ella for her son's months in quarantine? She can almost see it in her mind. They would go upstairs to the rec room, the walls white and boring, and sit on the creaky leather couch where he'd brought her to watch old movies that he thought were deep and cool but bored her to tears, and he'd calmly recite some bullshit speech he'd been composing for weeks that would amount to gaslighting and a pity party and probably yet another clumsy attempt to get in her pants.

She would listen to whatever he had to say.

In one version, she nods and tells him to go fuck himself.

In the other, she snorts pepper and attacks him and beats him to death with the glass jug full of pennies to the right of the TV and then calmly walks downstairs and out the back door, bypassing his mom and reminding everyone in his family what the Violence really is, which is very different from coddling and apologizing for a passive-aggressive shitbag kid.

Ella shakes her head.

She doesn't have time for any of it. She doesn't have the emotions to spare. Hayden was something that happened to an outdated version of her, and the version that's here now sees him as a waste of time then and even more so, now.

She closes the laptop, shoves it in her bag, and stands.

The night is cool, the clouds low and puffy, the still air promising rain.

It's beautiful, and for the first time in her life she's not afraid to be out alone at night. She has Mrs. Reilly's mermaid pepper shaker in her pocket, after all.

The only sounds are the wind in the summer leaves and the flapping yellow caution tape, the high strain of bugs, the desperate bleatings of summer frogs. There are no lights on around the playground, no one outside smoking a cigarette or walking a dog.

Tentative still, Ella walks to the swing set and sits on the cool black swing. She starts slow before kicking off and pumping her legs. It's a delicate thing, swinging in a child's swing as a seventeen-year-old with big hips and long legs, but she figures it out, splaying her feet as she swoops back and pumping forward aggressively on the upswing. She goes high enough to bump the wood set and rattle the chains, and the clouds momentarily part to reveal the moon, and it feels like she's swinging into the sky among a blanket of glittering stars like the Little Prince. When she was younger, she'd wait until just the right moment and then jump off, but she's all too aware right now that if she broke an ankle or wrist, she'd be fucked.

She lets the swing slow down gradually and then climbs up the ladder to the slide and zips down the cool green plastic, laughing at the way it jostles her shoulders. She wishes the playground still had the old metal merry-go-round so that she could spin on it until all the stars blended together, but they pulled it out of the ground years ago after Sophie flew off it and busted a tooth and ran around the playground spitting blood and screaming.

Time passes as she plays in a way she hasn't been able to for years. When she was twelve, Logan Johnson made fun of her for being at the playground, and after that, she didn't come here unless there was something rebellious about it, like sitting on top of the tables with Sophie at dusk and scratching curse words into the scarred wood with a ballpoint pen, but even then, some older guys showed up and offered them weed and tried to lure them into their skeevy van. After that, she didn't come here unless it was fully light outside. If there were adults here with little kids, she felt safer . . . but the adults always shot her dirty looks, like she didn't belong here at all.

Like she was the dangerous one instead of just a big, floppy kid who missed swing sets.

She used to bring Brooklyn here and push her on the swings and catch her on the slide and wish she could play, too, but there was just too much that could go wrong. Logan would see and call her a baby, some terrified new mom would complain to the HOA, creepy guys would approach her again, something. It's dangerous for teens to be seen having fun like that, like they actually care about something.

But behind the yellow caution tape, alone at five in the morning, Ella can swing all she wants.

For once, she really is the dangerous one.

As she dangles from the monkey bars, she has an odd realization: This could be her last time on this playground. She can't stay here much longer. Her old life, this neighborhood, this playground—they will soon be in the past.

She doesn't know where she's going next, but she knows it'll happen soon.

PART III

35.

Chelsea fights for space in front of a mirror lined with lightbulbs, coating her lashes in thick black mascara. A few weeks ago, she would've been disgusted by the thought of sharing her mascara, much less a communal tube, but she's already infected with the most dangerous pathogen around. It's hard to be scared of a little pink eye.

Amy squeezes in, and Chelsea rams the wand home and hands over the tube with a grin. She hasn't been backstage since the night she abandoned her *Phantom of the Opera* costume and her last best friend for David. It feels good now, just as good as she remembers. She feels free. Energy thrums through the room, grins spread from face to face, costumes shimmer in the lights. She feels . . . alive. Like she hasn't in years. Like she's been asleep, all this time.

She could've always had this, if she'd just been brave enough. If she hadn't been so naïve and fallen for a monster.

She could've been in local plays, could've helped with Ella's drama productions.

Could've felt the hot kiss of the lights, her stuttering heart as she stepped onstage.

But David took all that away. He didn't even have to ask, really. Just a few well-placed comments, a few disappointed frowns, and she dropped theater and chorus just to please him. She gave away something she loved for so little. She hates herself for that, but that version of Chelsea was so young and stupid, and she's gone now. David choked her to death.

This new version of Chelsea is something else entirely. Born of pain and tears and failure, she has nothing left to lose. When she screams her rage now, people feel it.

Tonight, they'll all feel it.

Because it's finally the big day: The VFR is officially launching. After all the training and practice, all the acting that was actually therapy, all the time learning to do their own hair and makeup and put on their costumes, all the publicity photos, their very first show is tonight.

It's amazing how quickly it all came together. How they learned the moves, practiced their theatrics, embodied their characters. Harlan came out to watch, finally. He always seems to wear the same perfectly fitted black V-neck, black wrestling shoes, and pants halfway between sweats and slacks, but his scarf is always different. Arlene calls it a shemagh. He's the first person she's ever met who wears a uniform, and Chelsea is also relatively certain that he blows his hair out every morning. Perhaps wrestling is no longer his calling, but Harlan Payne continues to act like a rock star. As they trained this week, he watched them from a chair by the door, scribbling into a notebook with Arlene by his side. It was fascinating . . . up until it was Chelsea's turn. In that moment she knew she was being graded, and harshly.

Everyone received notes, that first day. And the next day. And the next.

And then Arlene posted a program of the matches they'd be performing on opening night. Those who had taken their criticism to heart made the list. Those who blew off their notes or didn't give their all didn't feature and were listed as cleanup duty. Lisa cried, seeing her name on the bottom like that, but sharp looks exchanged around confirmed that this was the right choice. Harlan had seen who was really trying and who wasn't, and he'd drawn accurate conclusions.

That left Chelsea somewhere in the middle. The opening act was one bound to capture imaginations: Maryellen versus Matt. The tiny, steel-haired Valkyrie facing off with the tall, skeletal goth maybe a third of her age. Small woman, large man. Old and young. The Violence Fighting Ring is going to start with a bang and, hopefully, a shock. Maryellen is going to win.

That's another thing: Much like pro wrestling, they all know who will win each round. There's room for improvisation in each bout, but major moments are hammered down. Everyone knows their job and will perform it. No one will go rogue, and if they do, they'll end up back on the street without a job. And if they have any problems or questions, Chris or Arlene will be waiting by the ring, ready to handle any physical or emotional issues. Sienna is stationed in the greenroom, ready with makeup and hairspray, needle and thread and safety pins, to keep everyone looking fabulous.

"C'mon, everybody!" Arlene calls, and the room goes quiet. She glances at the laptop set up to show the ring. There's no sound, and it doesn't show the stands, so there's no way to know if they have a crowd or not. With one last attempt to separate her eyelashes, Chelsea abandons the mirror and with her compatriots forms a circle around Arlene. It's instinct now, and the energy is warm and excited. She feels like a horse about to run a race, all legs and nerves and the need to buck.

"I just want to say what a joy it's been, working with you," Arlene says, giving each person in the circle that knowing, genuine smile that always makes warmth bloom in Chelsea's chest like praise from a beloved teacher. "You're ready for this, and the crowd is ready for you. Oh, and Harlan—"

"You talkin' 'bout me?"

Harlan strides into the room in a well-fitting silver suit with a shimmering violet tie. He's wearing makeup and has his hair blown out and carefully pulled back to show the angles of his face. Charisma rolls off him like cologne, and every one of his fighters turns to follow him like a sunflower chasing the sun. It isn't lust, the way Chelsea is drawn to him, and it isn't just her—she's given this some thought, because she isn't accustomed to reacting to men like this. It's been years since she's had any feelings about men, she's realized, whether that's because David walled her off or she walled herself off. With Harlan, it's just who he is, like the Greek gods chose him and dipped him in some river that made him bigger, prettier, and more alive than anyone else.

It's not anything sexual, she just wants to be near him, and she isn't alone. Everyone here, men and women alike, is drawn to him, fascinated by him. Even Arlene seems to glow in his presence.

"I was just relaying your message," she says.

Harlan inclines his head in thanks. "Well, I figured I could do that myself."

Now he turns to meet each pair of eyes, and when it's Chelsea's turn, it's like he's pouring strength into her. Her mouth goes to a determined frown, her shoulders jerk back, and she's no longer tugging at the short hem of her jean shorts or plucking at the tight strap of her padded sports bra. She feels a foot taller and ready for anything, a lightning rod waiting to be struck. It's only the briefest moment, and then his eyes slide to Amy beside her, but Chelsea doesn't feel diminished by the loss of his gaze. It shines on in her like fire, leaving warmth in its wake.

This is why movie stars are movie stars, she thinks.

What he has is a gift.

Harlan finishes his circle and puts his hands behind his back. When he speaks, his accent is honeyed, southern, studied, strong, his voice projected and striking her right in the heart.

"I want y'all to know that I've dreamed of this moment for years. All the time I was getting beat up in the ring, I felt like there was something more out there, something that I was meant to do. When I killed my tendon and was out of the game for a year, I spent my time daydreaming and writing out business plans, and that included this one idea that wrestlers didn't all have to be big guys with long, greasy hair." He fondly touches the lush locks lying over his shoulder. "Heroes can be regular folks. Surprising combinations. Equality." He flaps a hand at them. "And now y'all are here, living that dream."

"Hell, yeah," someone mutters, and Harlan nods acknowledgment.

"It's been a hard year." His voice catches on the last word, and he looks away, blinking mascaraed lashes. "But we've risen together as phoenixes. So go out there tonight. Do your job. Have fun. We'll party, afterward. And tomorrow morning, you'll wake up superstars."

Chelsea's hands are clapping before she's even registered the action; everyone is clapping. Harlan gives his little salute and saunters off to their applause. She'd follow Harlan into battle; hell, maybe she is following him into some sort of conflict. No one has any way to know how tonight's going to go. There's been some discussion that what Harlan's doing here is illegal, that having an event this crowded is like asking for a lawsuit, and that the performers aren't legally employed. Chelsea's never filled out a tax form, never offered her Social Security number. Thus far, she's been paid in cash—that one time—and room and board and glad for it. No one has mentioned what happens if the police or feds show up. And they're not even in a theater or stadium, like real wrestling would be.

They're in an old warehouse out in the middle of nowhere.

Chelsea doesn't even know how Harlan gets the word out, how he's promoting what they're doing. When she borrows Amy's phone to search for the Violence Fighting Ring, all she sees are whispers, questions, assumptions. At the beginning, at least, it's going to involve a lot of secrecy.

She hasn't asked him. No one has.

They need these jobs more than they need the cold, hard truth.

They need . . . this.

Everything about it.

Somewhere to be, a purpose, the promise of hope, three square meals a day and a safe place to shower and sleep. They need one another. It reminds her of watching *Tiger King*, back during the first pandemic, when Covid had everyone getting used to staying home, noting that every one of the workers on the show was someone who had nowhere else to go. They were all drawn in by the big cats and stuck with no money, living in a trailer because they had nothing else in their life.

Maybe Harlan Payne is their tiger king, but at least their living situation is clean and no one's gotten injured yet, much less had an arm bitten clean off. They've only had one more Violence storm, and everybody just jumped on top of Steve like it was normal and flopped there, chatting amiably, until he came back to himself. Over the past few weeks, they've somehow become a family.

And in about an hour, Chelsea's job is to fight Steve in front of . . . well, whoever the hell showed up. Maybe a few people, maybe a hundred, maybe just a couple of strategically placed cameras. Their green-room is in the back of one of the tractor trailers she first saw when she drove up in George's truck for her interview. Turns out they were full of metal stands, plastic chairs, a thousand seats, a cushy wrestling ring, and nicer versions of all the props they've been training with. Rehearsing in that big warehouse made it real. The mats smelled so new when her cheek was pressed up against them. The ropes were so springy as she leapt from a corner. Now she has to do all that but make it look real.

Has to embody the Violence even though she can't remember how it feels.

"Maryellen, Matt. You're up."

Chris stands on the loading dock, calling up into the back of the semi. He's dressed in VFR-branded sweats and looks like a wrestler who quit to become a trainer, which is exactly what he is. When Chelsea first saw him, she thought he was going to be a hard-ass drill sergeant, but she's come to see him as the CrossFit leader she'd always dreamed of, gently encouraging yet sternly threatening as needed, turning her body into a weapon. Maryellen finishes powdering her gray hair to look whiter and grins at Matt, who looks like The Crow in his long black duster and heavy black eyeliner. They've got Maryellen dolled up like a grandma so no one can see her huge muscles—Mildred the Magnificent. Tonight she battles The Raven.

Maryellen is going to win because that's how Harlan planned it.

But Chelsea—and everyone else, including Matt—knows that she'd beat Matt in a real fight, too.

They walk off side by side, and Maryellen punches the air as everyone else whoops and shouts encouragement. After they disappear through a heavy metal door, it's anyone's guess what happens on the other side. Harlan will introduce them, their fight songs will play, and they'll . . . perform. It's not quite fighting; more like sparring with some acting thrown in. Chelsea watches on Arlene's laptop screen as they appear in the ring, seen from the overhead camera. Matt is in the ropes first, flapping around like an angel of death and shaking his fist along with the music's beat, then Maryellen appears, acting confused and clutching her purse and extremely unnecessary cane like she's not quite sure why she's there. It's a trip, the way Harlan has them all set up, some as villains and some as heroes and others, like Maryellen, almost as innocent bystanders.

Once Maryellen starts tugging at the ropes like she's trying to climb out, Matt sneaks up like he's going to rob her, and a cloud of glittering gray descends from the ceiling. It's gray chalk, but it's meant to look like pepper. They both inhale it and go still like robots booting up, and then the fight begins.

Because that's the biggest difference between the VFR and all the pro wrestling that's gone before: Whereas pro wrestlers are actors pretending to fight, Chelsea and her friends are normal people pretending to go insane and try to kill each other. That means that, just like when they're under the spell of the Violence, they don't make a noise. No threats, grunts, shouts, curses. Just vicious attacks, each one barely stopped by an opponent until somebody gets supposedly lucky. Harlan has the stage rigged with heavy, pounding music, lights, and fog. If an actor slips up, if something isn't believable, there's a chance the audience will miss it.

It helps, actually. The thumping metal and techno make it real, bring a physical sensation to the backdrop. Performing these moves in a silent building makes it almost embarrassing, makes them look like children going through badly learned dance moves. But there's something about the loud, angry music and the shifting lights that viscerally represents what it's like to watch the Violence happening.

From the outside, that is.

From the inside, time simply ceases to exist, and then you wake up.

It's like being anesthetized, really.

How many people in the audience know that? Chelsea wonders.

How many people know firsthand that the Violence doesn't feel like Fight Club—it feels like waking up after a colonoscopy?

Maryellen and Matt get through their match without any major mistakes, just a few stumbles that Matt fights with dramatic posing and Maryellen covers by pretending to be a fragile old woman—right up until she pins him and the refs have to pull her off. The music stops, the lights come back on, and they act like they've just woken up from a confusing dream. Matt gallantly helps Maryellen out of the ring as if she's infirm, subtly but noticeably stealing her purse in the process.

Chris is already at the door, calling out the next pair. Chelsea and Steve go third. She helps him with his eyeliner—he's got some weird thing about touching his own eyeballs—and then they stand by the door instead of watching the next match.

"You worried?" Steve asks her. He's the silver fox she met on her first day. They've got him dressed up like a very dapper businessman. There's no AC, and it's hot in the trailer, and he's got to be dying in the suit, but he looks cool and calm.

"I just wish I knew what was out there," she says, staring at the door, waiting for Matt and Maryellen to come back. They should be here by now, but they're not.

Steve shrugs. "Doesn't really matter, does it? The way I see things, Harlan Payne is our audience. If he's happy, who cares what some hypothetical audience thinks? He could film it and post it on YouTube and still make a million dollars, if he does it right. Which he probably will." He shakes his head. "It really is a genius idea."

Chelsea compulsively tugs at her tank top, the padding awkwardly giving her those boobs David always offered to pay for. "You think people won't be able to tell we're not really peppered up and storming?"

Steve grins. "I don't think they care. They're here for the madness, not the reality."

Chris appears in the doorway, looking annoyed.

"Joy got mad at TJ and yelled, and Harlan pulled it. You guys ready to go?"

Chelsea feels as if the breath has been knocked out of her. She's ready, and yet she wasn't quite ready? She wanted five more minutes to process things. She's not surprised at Joy and TJ, though; much like his first day with that Instagram girl, TJ always seems to get a rise out of people by simply being far too calm and reasonable for a buff guy. This is not a time for calm and reasonable, because frantic, irrational people hate something about that odd combination of strength, vulnerability, and lack of ego. Chelsea hasn't seen him much since that first day, but she hopes Joy won't get him kicked out. Everyone knows

Joy is the closest thing they have to a loose cannon, which is one reason why she works here.

"M'lady." Steve gives a bow that's meant to be both courtly and joking, and Chelsea gives him her Florida Woman face, and snarls, "M'bourgeoisie," as that's the contrast they're going for in this match. Steve is urbane and smooth and looks quite rich, while Chelsea looks like a cheap goddamn train wreck. Her hair is sprayed into a big rat's nest, her neon-pink lipstick is smeared, her tank top is ripped and reads FLORIDA WOMAN in red glitter, her shorts are short, and she's splattered all over with fake blood. The first time she saw it in the mirror, she flinched.

"It didn't look like this," she'd murmured to Sienna. "When I—"

"I know it didn't. I did that on purpose," Sienna responded, squeezing Chelsea's hand.

And that's why the VFR works, at least from the inside: because everyone here understands. Sienna's costumes are caricatures that lead them away from their lived reality. Arlene's work has been untangling their trauma, and Chris has worked their bodies to exhaustion, making them strong and ready to sleep and let their minds and bodies heal. These are people who need something to do, something to focus on besides the snakes in their heads and the horrors they've lived through, and the VFR gives them that.

"Ready, Chel?"

Steve and Chris wait for her inside the door. The lights are dark, and she can hear murmuring, but it's confounded by the bone-thumping beat of whatever music Harlan has blasting in the arena.

She nods and walks through the door.

The lights go on, the music starts playing, and . . . holy shit.

36.

Everything's been going so well, aside from the constant dread. Every day, Patricia expects to be thrown out of her own house or descended upon by thieves or—worse—the authorities, but the days pass as they always have, or perhaps a bit more slowly. Over the past few weeks, she and Brooklyn have developed an understanding. Brooklyn doesn't wake Patricia up until it's light outside, and she goes to bed when bidden. The child no longer asks when Mommy and Ella will return, which is a relief for them both.

They have a schedule now, with designated times for cleaning, swimming, reading, watching shows, and taking meals. Patricia has taught Brooklyn how to sweep, how to make pasta, how to cut an apple with the big knife, although the apples ran out weeks ago. The judge, for all his promised cruelty and secondhand thievery, has not yet turned off the utilities or phone or internet, and the O'Malley food has kept them alive. But it's running out, and Brooklyn is becoming more and more difficult as she finishes off her favorite snacks. Patricia had forgotten how children, like armies, march on their stomachs.

When there's nothing snacky left but rye crackers and rice cakes, she knows they're in trouble. The O'Malley house is tapped out, but there must be other families in the neighborhood who've flown the coop, leaving full pantries and freezers behind. There's something gauche about going through the HOA directory, though, and many of her neighbors don't know about the auction, so she won't have that convenient excuse. She needs some way to gather information without seeming interested.

It comes to her one long afternoon, when Brooklyn gets fussy about the puzzle they're working on together and tosses a piece across the room. "I want to play a game!" she pouts. "A real game. Like Chutes and Ladders or Sorry! Puzzles are stupid."

"Puzzles are not stupid," Patricia chides her, "You just . . ."

She trails off.

Games.

Dice.

Bunco.

And tomorrow is Thursday night. Perfect! Those bawds will have all the neighborhood gossip—who's here, who's not, whose yard is well below the HOA standard. She sends Marion a text message, asking who's hosting and if they prefer white or red, and she's in.

The next day, she goes out of her way to make sure Brooklyn is exhausted. They swim together for three hours instead of one, and by six, her granddaughter is fussy and rubbing her eyes. Patricia makes their last frozen pizza and lets Brooklyn eat as much as she wants. Soon she's scooping up a heavily sleeping child off the couch and tucking her into her cozy closet nest. After making sure the closet doors are secure, Patricia gets dressed, puts on a full face of makeup, and walks to Robin Steele's house, a bottle of Pinot from the judge's wine fridge under her arm.

It's annoying, actually, how much she enjoys Bunco with the girls. There are six of them and six bottles of wine and deviled eggs and charcuterie and a fresh fruit and cheese tray that Patricia would like to devour with both hands. They drink and laugh and toss dice, and even if she has nothing to contribute to the scuttlebutt, she takes it all in and says the right things and makes a mental note of possible targets. The Herberts next door are in Sweden, and Dr. Brown in the cul-de-sac was killed by a patient at the hospital and has no children. Both of their houses are empty, and she knows the Herberts' security code. She leaves with the rest of the fruit tray and a promise to come next week. She's actually looking forward to it. Without the judge around, without a reputation to uphold, she was almost . . . herself.

Whoever that is now.

Back home, she tiptoes into the kitchen and slides the fruit tray into the nearly empty fridge, smiling at how happy Brooklyn will be when she wakes up and sees the big chunks of melon and pineapple and the last remaining strawberry. Patricia will have to cut up the melon, of course—they've already had one minor choking scare, and she doesn't care to repeat it.

Barefoot, tipsy, happy, she arms the security system and does a little dance down the hallway on the way to her room. Marion insisted on playing some old Dolly Parton, and Patricia had forgotten how much she used to enjoy music, how they used to play it in the diner at night as they cleaned up, taking turns picking the songs on the jukebox. She doesn't sing, though—she doesn't want to risk waking Brooklyn. Aside from the occasional nightmare, the child sleeps like a log.

She opens the door to her room, and something is wrong, some slight disturbance in the air, some breath of a sound, some animal signal that makes her freeze. She fumbles for the light switch, and a shape lunges at her.

Patricia throws her hands in front of her face as if she's being attacked by a leaping pit bull, but she's made a mistake.

The shape is Brooklyn, and Brooklyn is five and can't jump that high.

Instead, she grabs for Patricia's leg and sinks her teeth into her thigh, in the meat right above her knee.

If the situation didn't feel real, the pain now does, and Patricia feels her entire body kick into fight or flight, something she hasn't truly felt in years. Her heart is clonking and pattering around, bolts of energy shoot down her limbs, and she smacks the child's face away from her leg on pure instinct, knocking Brooklyn to the ground. She immediately feels a hot wash of guilt, but the way Brooklyn looks up at her from the floor, mouth open, teeth red, drooling blood, removes some portion of shame.

There is nothing in Brooklyn's eyes, nothing.

Vast fields of blue with a tiny black pinprick pupil.

Her hand is raised but Patricia can't bring herself to strike her own granddaughter again. Two oppositional animal instincts thrum in her body and mind, two wolves fighting: Hurt the child, or hold the child?

In a heartbeat, Brooklyn is on her hands and knees, and she crawls like a spider to grab Patricia's leg, latching on to her like a koala, wrapping arms and legs around her lower leg before Patricia is sure how to react. She kicks feebly, and the child bites her again, this time right in the muscle of her calf.

"Brooklyn, no!" she shouts, even though she knows it won't do any good. This time, her granddaughter won't be knocked off so easily, and when Patricia tries to swat her away, Brooklyn clings, grinding her teeth together.

Patricia's heart—well, it's not ready for this. It feels like a hummingbird bashing against a wooden box. She's not eighteen anymore.

She kicks and kicks, twinges something in her back, but Brooklyn won't unstick, and then Patricia reaches down and sticks a thumb in the corner of her granddaughter's mouth, back where her molars haven't come in yet. She wedges a thumb into each side and grasps the tiny skull in both palms and pries the girl's mouth open with shaking fingers until the teeth unlatch from her leg, which is good but also terrible because now she can feel it, feel the torn muscle and the ache and the deep burn. Blood runs down her leg into her shoe, wet and slippery. Brooklyn snaps at the air, turning her head back and forth like a confused dog, and Patricia frowns and uses gentle but unrelenting force to move the girl's head back, thumbs still deep in her wet mouth. Brooklyn hasn't made a single sound, and it's unholy and unnerving.

Now that she's got the child's head firmly in her hands, Brooklyn unwinds from her leg and tries to scratch and kick her, as if she doesn't know how to reach up and tug at the hands that hold her, as if she's caught by some unseen force, wind or a storm, and can only fight aggressively forward. All offense, no defense, no intelligence. Time slows for a moment as Patricia holds the small skull, fragile as an egg, unsure how to move forward in a way that won't damage one of them permanently. Her leg burns in two places, a harsh reminder that this is no game, no childish rebellion that calls for a curt word or appropriate punishment.

Her granddaughter is currently a mindless beast.

There is no good solution here. No treat she can offer. No punishment she can inflict.

No carrot, no stick.

Brooklyn's hands scrabble madly like the monster from some old zombie flick Patricia saw when she was much, much younger and had the time for banalities. She's afraid that if she holds the child's head much longer, something bad will happen to the bones in her neck—after all, if Brooklyn turned her body too hard right now, it could snap her spinal cord.

Patricia is close to the wall, and she backs up toward it, gently pulling Brooklyn along with her—or allowing her to follow, more like, still holding her away from anything she could reach with hands or teeth. With her back against the wall, Patricia feels more certain. Something, at least, is still solid.

Carefully, her knees groaning, her wounds complaining, her heart stuttering, Patricia slides down the wall and sinks to sitting on the white carpet, rocking back on her butt, holding Brooklyn's head all the while. At this angle, she looks the child directly in her eyes and still finds nothing, nothing, nothing.

"Brooklyn?" she asks.

Nothing.

"Brooklyn Madilyn Martin!" she snaps in a voice that never fails to get attention.

Nothing.

Bared, bloody teeth, reaching hands, flailing fingers, each tiny and pink and perfect.

She remembers seeing Brooklyn in the hospital, counting fingers and toes as is every grandmother's right. She likes tiny babies—flawless and soft and sweet and unblemished by the world's ills and the failures and whims of imperfect parents. And further back, she remembers Ella's fingers, and further still, Chelsea's.

They'd been perfect. Every one.

Everything about Chelsea was perfect when she was born. Patricia wanted to spend all of her time holding her baby, had bristled when anyone else touched her or when she had to lay her down to sleep.

But Chelsea had become such a *contrary* thing as she got bigger.

Crying, defiant, pushing her own mother away. The tears, the snot, the rage, the first time that perfect Cupid's bow of a jolly pink baby lip screeched, "I hate you!" before Chelsea was even two years old. And her eyes, alternately judging and yearning. Wanting things Patricia couldn't provide and measuring what she could offer against some invisible, imaginary yardstick. Even now—

With a burst of energy, Brooklyn lunges forward; Patricia got lost, for a moment, and didn't hold tightly enough. She's in shock, perhaps. Everything seems to be happening very far away, as if to someone else. The bites on her leg pulse with each heartbeat but feel as if they're a mile away, something she's watching on a movie screen. She must hold on to the child tighter.

Much tighter.

Patricia takes a deep breath and lets go of Brooklyn's head.

When the thing that her granddaughter currently is lunges forward, Patricia grabs her, one hand behind her head and one on her back, gently, firmly, and tucks the child into her shoulder, Brooklyn's face pointed away from her own neck. She used to hold Chelsea like this when she would cry for absolutely no reason. Colic, she sometimes thinks, might've been the beginning of the gulf between them, all that frantic wailing despite Patricia doing everything that could possibly be asked of her. By the time Chelsea was Brooklyn's age, they never hugged like this. They were already too different, too distant. Chelsea flinched at her touch, which made her stop showing any interest in hugging her daughter.

But Brooklyn isn't crying. The way Patricia is holding the child's head against her shoulder, Brooklyn can't do anything but squirm against her. Her other hand pulls tight around Brooklyn's body, fingers digging in. Little legs automatically splay around her waist, squeezing tightly. Little arms curl around her, tiny fingers pressing into her ribs as if trying to reach for her heart and squeeze it. An odd thought floats up from somewhere like a balloon: If they survive this, get through this, she'll have to trim all of Brooklyn's finger- and toenails so that the next time this happens, it won't hurt so much. She'd thought that the mirror was bad, but this is so much worse.

The tension in Brooklyn's body is obscene, and Patricia's only response is to pull her closer, hold her more tightly. The utter silence in the house is despicable, and Patricia starts singing the song she sang Chelsea when she was all colicky: "You Are My Sunshine." She hasn't sung out loud in years; she knows her voice isn't ideal, and she doesn't publicly do anything that isn't perfect. Her room is big and echoey despite the plushness, and her voice comes at her from every side, mocking and uncertain. Still, she sings, maybe to soothe Brooklyn and maybe to soothe herself.

She feels everything and nothing, now; the ache in her throat, the heat in her wounds, the hot, sticky mess of her blood pooling underneath her, the chill where it's drying in her shoe. Brooklyn's body is burning hot against her, the child writhing every now and then like some sort of reptile, something that is mindless, muscles moving without conscious thought. Patricia holds her until her hands are numb. She holds her until she knows there will be dime-sized bruises all over her torso from those tiny, insistent fingers. She sings and sings and sings that same song as if it's a holy mantra, a psalm, a prayer. "You Are My Sunshine," over and over. Even makes up a few verses, just to break the monotony.

When you attacked me
When I walked in, dear
I was surprised to see your teeth
Now I will hold you
Until you stop, dear
And then I'll have relief.

Her voice gets creaky and rusty, and she's surprised to hear that she sounds like an old woman. Her fingers are numb, her legs are falling asleep. She wonders what will happen if she lets go, if her body just gives out and the child frees herself.

She can't let that happen.

The arteries in her neck are *right there.*

She clings tighter.

She forgets what she's singing.

She can't stop staring at the open closet door, wondering how on earth it came to this.

In another life, she would call to Rosa for help, but Rosa is gone.

"Nana?"

The voice is tiny, tremulous, right by her ear.

"Brooklyn?"

"Nana, you're crying again. And you're hurting me."

Patricia lets out a big breath and wiggles her fingers, unsure whether it's safe to let go. Brooklyn's body has relaxed, her fingers have released their death grip on her sides, and her head is moving in a manner that's more curious than feral, a child trying to see what's going on rather than an animal going for the jugular. Patricia's hands are numb, but she lets go, just enough to allow Brooklyn to pull back and look at her. The child's rump lands in Patricia's lap, and Brooklyn looks very seriously into Patricia's face. Her eyes are back to normal—Patricia's eyes, Chelsea's eyes, Ella's eyes, blue as the sky—and her brow is rumpled down.

"Nana, you cry a lot. You said big girls aren't supposed to cry."

Patricia swallows around the lump in her throat and reaches up to dash away her tears.

"Yes, well, it's a challenging time, isn't it. How do you feel?"

"I think I forgot something. It's nice to sit in your lap."

Brooklyn settles down like a chicken on a nest and smiles. If she can taste the blood on her teeth and lips, she doesn't mention it, and neither does Patricia. She can't remember the last time a child chose to sit in her lap—it must've been Chelsea, as a toddler, before she got so standoffish. Ella never really did; she was always a cold creature. Sitting here together would be nice if not for the incipient trauma and the ongoing issue of two wounds that would normally have Patricia calling for an ambulance.

Brooklyn turns her face and lays her head on Patricia's shoulder, and Patricia sits there for as long as she can, idly rubbing the child's back and feeling her thoughts race a mile a minute. Does she need stitches, and if so, how does she handle that with no money? Is she still on Randall's insurance, or did he have his young, busty secretary cut that off already? Does she still own a sewing kit, or is that just one more thing she left behind when she decided to never be self-sufficient again but to instead relax into the rest and comfort she's deserved for a long time?

Finally Brooklyn pops up out of her lap. "I need to potty. That's why I'm out of the closet, you know. Ella taught me how to open doors with a bobby pin. But I was so, so mad that you locked me in. Don't lock me in again, okay?"

And without a backward look, the child is gone, with no apparent memory of anything that happened, without even noticing the blood.

Patricia's head falls back against the wall, her neck numb and aching. She does a quick run-through of her body. Headache. Neckache. Backache. Bruises over her ribs and on her back where those tiny fingers plucked. Bruises on her hips from the child's legs wrapping insistently, straining to hold tight, heels digging in. One bite above her knee, on the inside meat of her thigh. A worse bite on her calf, in the muscle, where Brooklyn worked her teeth back and forth. When Patricia glances down at it, she can see a little flap of skin and meat hanging there like the butt end of a cheap steak. She shuts her eyes and looks away; she can't afford the sort of plastic surgeon who could make a wound like that disappear.

In Florida, in the South, elective surgeries have all been canceled to deal with the Violence. She'd have to fly somewhere up north, if she could find a slot.

She'd have to have money.

She doesn't.

Everything has changed.

There's a strange distance, just now.

Her body and mind seem entirely separate.

A thought flits by like a butterfly: Sometime soon body and mind will crash back together, and that won't be pleasant.

"Oh, well," she says, mimicking her mother's famous saying, the one that drove her utterly mad every time it was muttered until the day she came down pregnant when it wasn't said at all and she learned there was something too big, too terrible for *oh, well*.

This is why Patricia did her best to raise Chelsea to be independent. This is why she was so hard on her daughter, always pushing her to be strong and resilient and self-reliant. Because someday, everyone has to be.

Patricia laboriously climbs to standing, using the floor and then the wall. She steps out of her bloody shoe and is careful not to slip when she reaches the tile in the hallway. It's almost funny, the thought of slipping in her own blood and getting hurt even worse, that dreaded broken hip that always seemed like an older person's problem until her doctor told her she had the beginnings of osteoporosis.

She can't really look at the wound; ever since the Easter pageant dress, she's hated the sight of her own blood, would do anything to avoid seeing it. She learned how to flush a toilet while still sitting on it when she was just a girl. The moment she found out tampons existed, she spent what little money she could find on them.

When her periods stopped at eighteen, she thought God had answered her prayers.

He . . . had not.

And now here she is, limping through her own home, leaving indignant red splotches behind on the tile on her way to paw through her pantry for the first-aid kit. Again.

Back in her room, Brooklyn calls, "Nana, there's ketchup on the floor, but I didn't do it, I promise!"

"It's okay," she calls back, hating that she sounds out of breath. "Just go back to bed. Nana will fix everything."

"Yes, ma'am. Good night again! I love you!"

"Good night again. I love you, too." She says it every night because it must be said, but tonight she realizes that she means it.

When Brooklyn is safely in the closet, Patricia closes her bedroom door. With no way to lock it, she turns a heavy ottoman on its side and slides it across the doorway. She didn't lock Brooklyn in the closet, but at least this way, she'll hear a big noise if there's to be another attack.

She's glad Brooklyn won't see what's next, won't ask what happened.

If she told her granddaughter what she'd done . . .

Well, who could believe such a thing?

In the walk-in pantry, she turns on the lights and closes the door, grateful for the privacy. She finds the first-aid kit and cracks it open, wishing for the tough, harsh, stalwart tools of her youth, for the iodine and styptic and firm bandages rather than all of this individually packaged plastic stuff. At least it was enough for Brooklyn's forehead, which healed beautifully; she barely has a scar now. Oh, to have young skin again.

Patricia slips out of her remaining shoe and, after a look, calls the pair a loss and tosses it in the trash can where Rosa disposes of the dryer lint. It takes an effort to get her leg up on the utility sink, but she does it, cleaning out the calf wound with soap and water with her face half turned away. The one on her thigh just gets a pour of hydrogen peroxide. It's not as deep, and she'll clean it more thoroughly in the shower later.

But the one on her calf is a mess. Thank goodness for the odd, floaty distance she has right now. She doesn't view it as part of her body, but like a piece of bad meat, something inconvenient that she'd rather just see gone. She's not sure what to do, whether to push it all back in or . . .

God.

Cut it off.

Cut off the . . . dangling bits. She'll have to ask the internet about that.

For now, she braces herself and pours peroxide over it, wincing at the burn. She sprays it with antibacterial cleaner and wraps gauze around it with some sort of springy, bright-purple bandage that clings to itself. The one on her thigh just gets a big, flat Band-Aid. And that's as much as she can handle just now.

She remembers, too late, that Brooklyn is in her closet, where all of her clothes are. For the first time in years, Patricia must hunt through the dirty laundry and step into a worn pair of pajamas. She hates that the blood will most likely seep through and ruin them. Funny, how at some point her wardrobe rejected comfort for pretense and propriety. Most of her pajamas are beautiful, expensive silk sets, pants and collared tops that feel like butter, shimmering and elegant.

She told herself she didn't care what Randall thought, that she'd never wanted to attract him sexually, and yet she would've died before letting him see her in something that cost less than two hundred dollars, something that wasn't elegant and sumptuous and well-fitting in the right color palette for her complexion.

When the hell did that happen?

It was all sandcastles built on the shoreline by someone who'd forgotten that sand was just another kind of dirt.

Her next stop is in the kitchen for ibuprofen. Codeine would be vastly preferable, but she's got a child to care for.

A child who is also a ticking bomb.

With Brooklyn barricaded in her own bedroom, and two dozen stairs between her and the next available bed, Patricia drapes a towel over the living room couch and sinks into a sea of cushions that she's just now realizing look a lot more comfortable than they actually are. She's never spent any time sitting on this couch before. She pushes the cushions onto the floor, reaches for the remote control, and turns on the TV, marveling at the hundreds of buttons. Brooklyn always handles the remote, these days; Patricia has an older, simpler TV in her sunroom, but the couch isn't long enough for her to stretch out on.

Once she's found some harmless reruns of *The Golden Girls*, she pulls down the decorative blanket that's never been used before and carefully pats it around herself. Moving is an awful lot of work, after all, and it's her house, so she might as well arrange things for her own comfort. She closes her eyes for just a moment, sighing out all the pain, all the tension, all the . . . goodness, yes, fear, a thing she hasn't felt in a long time.

Fear, a thing she's arranged her life to avoid entirely.

Her wounds pulse with each heartbeat as she sinks into the darkness.

37.

The last month has been the longest month of Ella's life, mostly because she is starving to death. She can't remember the last time she was this hungry. There were days back at home when she would whine that she was starving because they were out of her favorite cereal and she didn't want to eat her second-favorite cereal, or because the only apples left in the crisper were slightly bruised.

That was nothing compared with this.

Her entire life has shrunken to the size of her stomach. She ate the last bag of Cool Ranch Doritos, even shaking the powder into her mouth directly from the bag, which is really saying something because she hates Cool Ranch Doritos. She's been rationing food for the last week and knows she's well under her caloric requirements, but she just never imagined that not eating could hurt so much. As much as she hates to do it, Ella has to go out and spend some of her precious money on food.

Unlike Mrs. Reilly, if Mr. Reese left a single penny in his house, she can't find it. And she's looked, because she has nothing else to do. With no electricity, she can't use her phone much without having to recharge it in the car. Pretty much everything she enjoyed doing in her normal life is unavailable—no videogames, no internet, no drama club, no music. If it wasn't for Mr. Reese's library of old paperbacks, she's pretty sure she'd be insane.

Well, more insane.

Ella has a sense that she needs to save the last few dollars she has, hoard it like dragon gold for . . . something. Going out to find her mom. Rescuing Brooklyn. Some imaginary emergency that's somehow, impossibly, worse than killing Uncle Chad and stealing a car. It's like when she's playing a videogame and won't use her potions even when she needs them because there might be a bigger boss coming up. Even now, it could still get worse.

As her stomach crunches and her headache builds, she realizes that . . . this has to be the time for potions.

She gathers all of her things, packs them tightly in the backpacks and bags she's borrowed from the places she's stayed, and stuffs them in the tiny trunk of Mrs. Reilly's Miata. She understands now that there is no real safety and that she might have to run at any moment. She felt that way back at home before the Violence happened, which is why she already had a bug-out bag. But it was more a fairy tale she told herself, back then.

One day I'll be free, and I'll be ready.

I can walk away from this.

He doesn't control me.

She used to tell herself all sorts of lies just to stay afloat. *Mr. Brannen would never actually touch me or threaten me—he's the vice principal, not some dangerous criminal. Hayden doesn't mean to be so dismissive—he really cares about me, he's just bad with emotions. When Uncle Chad whispered "jailbait" to Uncle Brian, it was just boys being boys, and they were drunk, anyway. Maybe Kaylin really did lead on the assistant basketball coach, maybe she was into it. I'm smart and tough. I would never let something like that happen to me. If someone tried to hurt me, I would just leave.*

That was back before she'd killed someone, back before she'd hidden in an impossible-to-find place and almost immediately been found.

She doesn't know if her dad has other cops looking for her; the only one she's ever met is Uncle Chad. *Was* Uncle Chad. She's heard her dad tell her mom that he has "friends on the force," but maybe that only worked when Chad was alive to spread the word. She doesn't know if they're looking for Mrs. Reilly's car tags or a white Miata. She would take Mr. Reese's truck, but it's gone, and she has no idea how to ride his pristine Harley-Davidson motorcycle, even if that was a safe thing to do and he'd left his keys behind.

She leaves the door to the garage unlocked, hoping that nothing terrible will happen and she can simply go to the store and return here to . . . What? Wait out the storm? Keep hiding in a hot, stuffy house with no running water and sneaking out at night to fill water bottles at the playground spigot? Ella doesn't know what to do with her life. It's like she's on hold. Her only action items are keep away from Dad, and find Mom. The first can be accomplished by lying low and doing nothing, and she still hasn't figured out the second one. Before now, she always believed you could just find whomever you were looking for, plug them into Google or Facebook and they'd pop right up. That was before she started looking for someone with a relatively common name who didn't want to be found—and who was already in trouble with the law.

Outside, the neighborhood is still quiet. Just like with Covid, the Florida governor hasn't forced any lockdowns, but people are smart enough to realize that you can't get randomly killed by a stranger if you don't go out where the random strangers are. Everyone knows by now that Violence storms can be caused by capsaicin or stress, but they can also arise for no reason whatsoever. Delivery drivers now have to get tested before they can wear those branded T-shirts. To someone who lived through Covid, just staying home is the all-too-familiar solution. The government vaccines are still months away, with seemingly no plan in sight. People only go out for two reasons: because they have no choice, or because they're idiots who don't understand data.

Ella is leaving Mr. Reese's house only because she's desperate. She's all too aware that she's the dangerous stranger everyone fears, the one who brings the threat wherever she goes. But it doesn't matter. She has to eat. She's not going to starve to death to avoid putting some hypothetical person in danger. She'll be quick. And she's not even going to go to a big, nice store where mothers used to push babies around in strollers, making silly faces and peeling bananas as if everything would always be safe. She's going to go to that same drugstore she went to last time. It's small, there's a guard, and her dad wouldn't go there.

He is, at least, a creature of habit.

The only store he'll go into is his favorite Publix, and then it's only really for beer.

Ella pulls up outside the drugstore and parks. There are only two other vehicles in the lot, an SUV and a big, janky RV that reminds her of the one from *Breaking Bad.* At least the skeevy guard isn't there this time. It's an older woman with cropped gray hair, her mouth showing permanent frown lines and her hands clasped in front like she thinks she's in the Secret Service and protecting someone important, not a gross old drugstore with bad lighting that's visited only by sick people and drunks, thanks to the attached liquor store. The guard is wearing reflective sunglasses and gives Ella a thorough look up and down and a small nod, as if she's passed some invisible test. It's funny how people still look at her and just see a harmless teenager who might shoplift a lip gloss if she's not watched. She's a predator in disguise, but millions of years of assumptions about teen girls still make people underestimate her.

The cold swish of air-conditioning flows over her, and she stops and closes her eyes to savor it for a few heartbeats. She's gotten so acclimated to the hot, still air of Mr. Reese's house that she realizes now that she forgot to turn on the car's AC, just rolled down the windows and let the heat soak in. Funny, how quickly a person grows accustomed to their situation, like an animal in a cage that stops trying to escape. She read once that baby elephants were taught they could never break the chain that tethered them to the ground, and therefore older elephants who could easily break the chain never tried. She's learning that life is full of people sitting sadly beside their fragile chains.

"Good morning, beautiful," the guy behind the counter says, and she smiles tightly and dives into an aisle before he can ask her some inane question or start the usual awkward, skeevy, complimentary small talk guys in their fifties have with girls a third of their age.

She quickly realizes she's in the perfume aisle and doesn't have a basket or cart but is too embarrassed to walk the gauntlet past the counter guy and hopes she'll find something along the way to carry her groceries. She finds the food aisle and winces at the prices; things cost double what they used to, thanks to cascading economic fallout from the first pandemic and now the Violence. In other parts of the country, the supply chain is back to normal and prices are reasonable again, but in Florida, they're still unnaturally high because shipping companies demand more to travel down here—that's what her economics teacher told them, right before she left school. People who get the Violence while driving tend to cause massive wrecks. Ella hated economics, and all she knows is that a box of drugstore-brand crackers should not cost five dollars, and she's going to have to carefully consider prices instead of just grabbing Cheetos like she would've back when her parents were footing most of the bill. Cheetos, she knows now, are basically puffed air and don't provide much bang for her buck.

Around the next aisle, where the canned foods are, she sees a basket on the ground and looks up and down to see if anyone has claimed it. The only thing in it is a case of beer, which is not something she can actually use, so she'll need to go put it back in the refrigerated section. Even in a pandemic, infected with a disease, Ella is not the kind of person who could just leave someone else's case of forgotten beer in the middle of the aisle.

She's reaching for the basket when someone says, "Sorry, that's mine."

Ella snatches her hand back and flushes and tries to remember how to word.

"Oh. Sorry. I just thought. I mean. Sorry?"

But the other girl doesn't look pissed. She looks exhausted. She's in her twenties, taller and thinner, Japanese with her hair up in a messy bun and smudged glasses. She's wearing a drooping dress, black with white flowers, and Keds with no socks. She looks like she just stepped out of a 1990s sitcom and hasn't slept in a week.

Ella stands back, puts her hands up. "Really. Sorry."

The other girl smiles and picks up the basket. She has the calm, earned confidence of an Instagram artist. A beret would work perfectly for her. But she seems sad, too, and so tired, like if Ella pushed her gently with a finger, she'd keel over like a felled tree.

"Are you okay?" Ella asks.

The girl cocks her head. "That's an awfully weird question to ask during the second massive societal trauma in five years."

Ella flushes. "Yeah. Sorry. You're right. Weird. And too personal. I . . . uh, haven't been around people in a while. Excuse me."

She turns and blunders past the counter guy to get a basket, then disappears back into the aisles before he can finish asking her if she needs any help. That was completely mortifying. She feels like some escaped forest child no longer fit for society. She didn't even brush her hair today, although if she's being honest, her hair looks good no matter what. She lands in the cracker aisle again, but at least there's no one here, so she grabs Saltines and cookies and bread and peanut butter and checks to see if jelly is shelf-stable, but it isn't.

Her thoughts flash back to Mrs. Reilly's house, the air-conditioning and cold fridge and plentiful ice. Then they flash to Uncle Chad, dead on the floor. The police knew he was dead, so they must've collected his body. But they probably didn't clean up, and they're probably checking back in. Or calling Mrs. Reilly's daughter. Something.

She wants to go back, but she can't. Someone else will come.

It's not safe.

She's tried the houses of other past clients, but nothing else is empty.

She puts the jelly back.

There's no way to make Mr. Reese's house any better, no way to get that refrigerator running, and she's not yet ready to just start randomly knocking on the doors of abandoned houses, hoping like hell no one will answer and spending that first night alone and awake waiting for someone to return and . . . what, get her in trouble? It's hilarious that that's still what worries her.

She feels like a little mouse, and every direction she runs, there's something scary. She's so sick of being scared.

She can't live off this kind of food forever. She already has these annoying ulcers in her mouth. Maybe she should buy some cheap kids' vitamins.

But for now, just the picture of Cheez-Its on the front of the box makes her drool. They're pricey, but she wants them so bad. She puts the box in her basket and peeks around the corner to see if the other girl is gone, which she is. Ella is reading a soup label, imagining the luscious chewiness of beef between her teeth and trying to picture what stew will taste like at room temperature because she has no way to warm it up, when she hears the girl's voice again.

"Hey, I didn't mean you were weird. I just meant . . . most people don't bother to ask how strangers are anymore. It's nice."

Ella looks up, and the other girl is in her aisle now, holding her basket in both hands in front of her knees, her head cocked curiously.

"Like, you don't have to freak out. We're all weird now, you know? It's just nice to have someone actually see you and inquire. So thanks for that."

Another person arrives and stands slightly behind the girl. Ella can't tell their gender or if they even conform to one, but they're tan and brunette, about her height, stocky, with a kind of rooster-y haircut and a loose, ragged sweater worn over a T-shirt, skinny jeans, and Docs.

"Hey," they say, their voice low and brusque and their eyes alight like a crow. "You infected?"

Ella stumbles back a step, her eyes darting around for escape.

That is not a question you're supposed to ask these days, much less answer.

"No, don't freak out," the first girl says like she's talking to a scared dog. "It doesn't mean what you think it means."

Ella looks down at the soup can in her hand. She's not done shopping. She needs this food. She doesn't have the energy or brainpower to go elsewhere. But these people are . . . scaring her? It's funny, because on the surface, they're not threatening at all. But asking that question causes her entire system, body and mind, to go into panic mode, which is not good. Malnutrition, sleeplessness, extra stress. She would hate to storm in here and hurt the nice girl—or get shot by the security guard.

"She looks hungry," the brusque one says, as if Ella really is a skinny, skittish stray dog

"She looks scared," the tired one corrects. "Are you scared? You asked me if I was okay, but are *you* okay?"

And the strangest thing happens. Ella bursts out crying.

She's not a crier. Living with her father has taught her that crying in front of other people will earn ridicule and abuse, possibly get her poked with a single index finger in the chest or shoulder hard enough to leave a bruise. But no one has spoken to her in weeks except for Uncle Chad. All the messages she's received by text and online are more people talking *at* her, fishing for info and gossip and ammunition because they're desperately bored, not people who are actually worried about her.

No one has asked about her feelings since before her mom got sick. Once Mom had the Violence, even she stopped asking. Nana never asked. Uncle Chad didn't.

No one.

And so the floodgates are down.

"I didn't make her do that," the brusque person says, but they step closer and look concerned.

The girl, though, she drops her basket and pulls Ella into a hug. She smells—well, not that great, actually. Like Florida summer BO and something funky, like beer and bleach and maybe patchouli. Surely Ella smells no better. But the way she holds Ella is unreserved, warm, yielding, completely giving and open. Ella hasn't been hugged like this since she was in preschool.

That only makes her cry harder.

She feels like she's forgotten how to be a person, like she's some ratlike animal, some *thing* that has to hide and skulk in the darkness, something that deserves the oppressive heat and dull air and hunger of Mr. Reese's house. The brave, easygoing girl who came out to play on the playground got shed like a pair of old shoes as this new version of Ella scurried back to her bolt-hole, which should feel safe but just makes her feel trapped.

Maybe being alone for weeks on end isn't good for a person.

Maybe she's been messed up since Covid, going through a pandemic and puberty at the same time, stuck at home with her family for a year, hiding in her room, pulling away from hugs because boobs were awkward and girls were supposed to start acting like women. Brookie is pretty much the only one she's hugged regularly since she was thirteen, and sometimes she wonders if it will ever feel natural and normal again, just touching people.

"Hey, it's okay," the girl says, rubbing her back. "Get it all out."

"Is there a problem?"

Ella doesn't have to look up to know it's the cashier.

"No. Do *you* have a problem?" the brusque person says, stepping between the hug and the cashier, sounding more masculine now and downright mean.

"I don't want any trouble," the man says, but almost like he kind of does? "I can call security."

"Why would you do that? Do crying women seem like a threat to you?"

"I, uh."

Ella chuckles against the girl's shoulder. Even if she's messed up, she can recognize the beauty of leaving an asshole with no rational response that doesn't further reveal his assholery.

"We're in the middle of a murder pandemic," the girl rubbing her back says over her head, sounding eminently rational and intelligent. "Literally every human being who's alive right now is living with un-processed trauma. Someone crying in public should not read to you as a problem. It's not only reasonable, but also helpful to society as a whole. When was the last time you cried?"

The guy snorts. "Make a purchase or I'll have you escorted out," he finally says, and by the way the girl sighs in relief, Ella can tell he's beat a hasty retreat rather than talk about anyone's feelings.

"Fuckin' patriarchal bullshit," the brusque person mutters.

Ella pulls away and wipes her face, not that it's going to do much to make her look functional. The girl is right—everybody is still trauma-tized from Covid, and now lots of them are being retraumatized in exciting new ways by the Violence.

"I'm okay," she says, not quite meeting the girl's eyes but wishing she was the kind of person who could easily do that. She realizes she's still holding the can of soup, which is just goddamn ridiculous. "Or, as okay as anyone is. Which is not okay at all but functional enough to not buy a can of stew with no way to heat it." She shoves the can back on the shelf, feeling like an idiot.

The girl cocks her head, concern written in her features. "Why can't you reheat soup?"

"No, fuck that," the other person says, glancing over their shoulder. "We can reheat soup for you. Just get what you need and let's get out of here before Mr. Concealed Carry decides we're too dangerous to leave to the professional mall security cop." They grab three cans of beef stew from the shelf and start off down the aisle and then turn back. "Wait. You over eighteen?"

Ella shakes her head, her danger sense tingling. Because why would that matter?

"Damn."

They stomp off.

The girl standing in front of her smiles reassuringly. "I'm Leanne. That's River. We're totally safe. A little weird, but not in a threatening way, even if River is pretty grouchy most of the time. If you saw the RV outside, that's ours. We have a little kitchen with a microwave for your soup. It's nicer inside than it looks. Are you homeless?"

"Uh. Kinda?"

Leanne nods knowingly. "Lot of that going around. We should be done in five, if you want to come with us. We can help you."

Ella's eyebrows draw down, and Leanne must realize how creepy that sounds, as she looks mortified. "Sorry. Let me try that again. I'm a grad student. River is a YouTube star. We have resources. We don't want anything from you. We're just . . . trying to help."

Help sounds great, but Ella knows by now that things that sound too good to be true usually are.

"As long as it's not a cult or drugs," she says shakily. "Or . . . a lot of other things. I would love some hot soup, but I'm not willing to do anything gross for it."

"Nothing gross is wanted. We've just both been in dire straits before. If you can't heat soup, find somebody with a microwave, right? I'll be in the pharmacy aisles. You can hang outside by the RV for us, if you finish first. Nothing weird. Seriously. God, even that sounds weird? Ugh! I swear, I'm so tired I keep forgetting how to be a person."

"I know that feeling."

Leanne is so natural and confused and mortified that Ella gets the idea she couldn't be creepy if she tried. Picking up her basket, she gives Ella a little wave and turns out of the aisle, muttering to herself. Ella catches the words, "I'm going to kill River for that."

Alone now, Ella carefully selects foods, trying to merge good nutritional value with foods that will fill her up, all while mentally calculating the total. With no way to make money, she knows that every dollar she spends is gone forever, and if she tracks all the way down to zero, she'll have no choice but to return home and deal with her dad, which is the scariest thing she can think of. She leans heavily into peanut butter, bread, and crackers, hoping that splurging on the real fruit snacks and trail mix and cheap kids' chewable vitamins will keep her from losing her teeth. And she has to grab baby wipes and dry shampoo, because staying clean has become a challenge.

When she goes to check out, the guy at the counter doesn't attempt awkward small talk; he just stares hatefully. There's no way for Ella to know if this is because everyone distrusts everyone these days, because she rejected him when he feigned friendliness, or because she had the audacity to cry in his general vicinity.

"You got a discount card?" he asks.

She shakes her head no.

"Give me your phone number, and I can give you one."

The look she gives him must show how grossed out she is by the thought of giving him her number, as he snorts in disgust and says, "For the system, not for me. Jesus. Just punch it into the machine and it'll text you your code."

Ella's finger is hovering over the machine. She's so hungry and emotional that her brain barely works, and she's pretty sure she'll save like ten bucks if she has that card. Still, she doesn't want to put her number into any machine, doesn't want any way to be tracked.

"Here's her card," River says, handing over a red plastic card, and the cashier has no choice but to scan it.

A wash of relief makes Ella blink as the total goes down by twelve dollars.

"Thanks," she says.

She hands the guy her cash, and he takes it like she's diseased and shoves her change into her hands, not even bothering to stack the bills nicely.

"No coins," he says, pointing to a ragged sign taped to the counter that probably dates back to the coin shortage of the first pandemic.

Ella takes her plastic bags and moves to the side, waiting as Leanne and River check out. They have much more stuff than she does, including candy and dark chocolate and, of all things, rubbing alcohol, hand sanitizer, gloves, several cans of beef stock, several cases of cheap beer, and a full box of that weird new mushroom coffee that keeps popping up on Ella's Instagram ads. Their total is significantly higher than hers, but River doesn't blink. The man scans their discount card again, they pay in cash, and then they're all holding plastic bags. Leanne leads the way, fumbling with a big ring of keys with all sorts of little charms and doodads on it.

"We can park here for a few hours, but we'll hit a Walmart parking lot for overnight," Leanne says, opening the door to the RV.

Inside, it smells just like she does, slightly chemical and slightly funky. Ella stares at the darkness within and then looks doubtfully to Leanne, a mouse assessing the relative safety of a new possibility and finding that the hole in the wall looks an awful lot like a cat's open mouth.

Leanne smiles ruefully. "It's not *Breaking Bad*. We're not freaky sex weirdos. Like I said, I'm a graduate student—in epidemiology. I'm friends with the girl who created the vaccine for the Violence. This is my lab. That's why the weird smell."

All this sounds way too convenient for Ella, who takes a step back. "That is in no way believable," she says. "Thanks for the discount card, but I think I'm just gonna go."

River steps behind her, bags dropped on the ground and hands up. "Don't. Please. Like Leanne said, we can help you. We have the vaccine. We can teach you how to administer it. You could help spread it. I swear we're legit. You can look me up online."

River slowly reaches for the phone in their back pocket, flicks through it, and holds up the screen, showing a YouTube video of Leanne, wearing a mask, goggles, and shower cap, holding up a petri dish in what looks to be an RV bedroom but covered in clear plastic. THE MOBILE CURE is splayed over the pic in bright-blue letters with little dancing hearts. The video has—Jesus. Millions and millions of likes.

Ella thinks back to some of the weird stuff they bought, medical gloves and rubbing alcohol. She thinks of that smell, chemical and musty. Of River asking if she was eighteen, asking if she had the disease. And then she remembers when she was twelve and started walking to the library after school, when her mom told her that kidnappers and murderers don't come to you as gross old men in panel vans, but disguised as something that will giggle and compliment and lure you despite your defenses.

An awkward, girl, an interesting person, the promise of warm soup and a little AC.

Is she really that easy? Is she really that dumb?

River's hand lands on her wrist. "Just listen, okay? We're for real. We need you."

"Help!" Ella yelps, eyes searching for the security guard at the door. But the door is far away, on the other side of the RV.

"No, shut up! This is serious!"

"Please, just chill, okay? You're making it worse—"

"Help!"

River's hand is heading to cover her mouth, and Ella's heart rate spikes at the thought of that touch. They've got her boxed in by the door of the RV. She's a wild, feral thing, hunting for a way out. She reaches into her pocket, pulls out a closed fist, and holds it up to her nose, breathing in.

Mrs. Reilly's pepper, now a controlled substance.

"Oh shit," River says.

And then the world falls away.

38.

For the first time in years, Patricia doesn't take a sleeping pill, and she does not sleep well. She wakes up after midnight and watches gardening shows until non-emotional, fully physical tears dribble down her cheeks because she wants so badly to fall back asleep. She turns off the TV, turns it back on, tosses and turns, rearranges the horrible cushions, swallows more ibuprofen with water from the tap. She paces and fiddles with her bandages and takes a long shower in an upstairs bathroom. Hot water coursing over her hurt places wakes her up all the way and she grits her teeth as she soaps the wound and feels the detached chunk of meat with pruney fingertips. Blood courses down her leg and swirls pink around the drain. There's no way around it—she'll have to call Dr. Baird tomorrow and make it clear that this is an emergency on her own behalf. Maybe Randall won't swallow the cost of two vaccinations for wayward children, but surely he doesn't want his not-yet-ex-wife to die of sepsis before she can sign the divorce papers.

It's two in the morning, but she feels like it's noon. The house is silent and dark as she limps back to the pantry and goes through the ritual of treating her wounds again and binding them back up even though she knows it's a job badly done, which she hates. She has a cup of herbal tea that only makes her feel more awake—*Sleepytime, my ass*—and pulls out her sleek little laptop, a gift from Randall after she lightly, breezily complained about a few too many harassing calls from one of his women. It reminds her of a seashell as it opens, a delicate rose gold. She's been so busy with Brooklyn that she's neglected it.

Her inbox is a shambles. Dozens of emails about the auction in the last two days alone. The earlier ones are delicately pressing and the most recent ones are indignant and stiff and frosty. She's been removed from the auction committee and, on Karen's recommendation, has been declared unacceptable for reelection to the board due to gross negligence.

"For failing to satisfy commitments," Patricia murmurs to herself. "You bitch."

She clicks the little boxes down the left of each email, click click click, and deletes them all.

"There. That's better."

There are other emails she's missed—mostly from Randall's secretary, Diane, first information regarding their Iceland plans, and then increasingly chilly ones that include documents for her to e-sign with her e-signature so that Randall can easily e-divorce her. She opens one, reads a few paragraphs, and deletes the email. If Randall wants to go through with this, if he's really the kind of person who wants to destroy her life in the middle of a pandemic, then he can damn well subpoena her and make her sign in person at one of his big conference tables with a policeman standing over them both once he's gone to the trouble of returning from his icy paradise. She's not going to make it easy on him, she's decided.

Because he's not made it easy on her.

If he'd like to offer her some money like he does his discarded mistresses, perhaps she'll go back to being pliant and not troublesome.

Email, she thinks, as she scrolls through, was a bad invention.

Requests, demands, sales that she missed—there's nothing here that benefits her current reality.

Opening a new tab, she's forced to stare at her destroyed manicure as she tries to figure out the correct combination of words to type into the search bar that will produce the information she desires.

The Violence cure.

Well, that gets a lot of garbage.

Funny how she didn't research a thing when she got the vaccine herself, but now that her granddaughter is infected and living in her closet, she wants all the information she can find.

Much to her surprise, very little of what she sees online is accurate. It's mostly conspiracy theories, although it turns out the one about the vaccine only being available to the wealthy is actually true.

How many paid professionals, she wonders, are awake right now, scrubbing the internet for any mention of the reality of this vaccine to keep the general populace from rioting? She knows there are people who fill that job position; Randall has paid them to remove his own unflattering information and images before elections. But to the rest of the world, the vaccine is a Loch Ness Monster, something they'd like to believe in but can't quite prove. Her scar is an open secret, now. Tomorrow, when Dr. Baird stops by to tend to her wounds, she'll play on his sympathy for little children, tell him about her granddaughter's difficult life, her abusive father, runaway sister, and violent, missing mother, and try to convince him to give Brooklyn the vaccine, too. Hell, she'll offer him every jewel she has left, her wedding rings and diamond studs and tennis bracelet. It's not the cache she had before she was robbed, but it's certainly enough to make up for one measly little vaccine rubbed into the child's arm—half a dose, if that. The man took an oath, for heaven's sake. He must have a heart.

She googles "David Martin," but there are so many hits that there's no way to sift through them all. Homer told her an angry man in a Lexus had been stopping by the neighborhood gates, so David must be out of quarantine or prison or whatever they call it, but he won't find his way to her house.

Then she googles "Chelsea Martin" and is so scandalized she gasps and turns her laptop away, as if Brooklyn could possibly be sneaking up behind her and able to read.

Patricia's daughter really does have the Violence, and when she finds pictures of the crime scene in an online gossip mag, she feels nauseated.

Chelsea has truly hit rock bottom, and even if she had all of her former wealth and power, there's very little Patricia could do to help her. She's quite certain the judge would need to distance himself from this crime, and—

Yes, of course.

No wonder the emails from his secretary got so snippy and demanding. As long as he's married to Patricia, this is a smear against *him,* isn't it? His daughter-in-law is an embarrassing murderess.

Patricia smiles, chuckles a little.

"That bell can't be unrung, can it, Judge?"

She has no idea where Chelsea is now, and neither does anyone else. Ella is likewise out of her reach, and good riddance to the bad rubbish that was Randall.

Brooklyn is all she has left, and they will find their way together.

Patricia falls asleep on her sunroom couch, laptop balanced on her lap as she googles "squatter's rights" and "property law." If Randall wants her out of this home, this place she decorated and refurbished to suit her like a hermit crab selecting a new shell, he can by God show up and pry her out himself. Legally, he doesn't have a leg to stand on. No wonder she's still here with all the utilities. Of course he knows the law. His threats were empty, but he's still an asshole.

She wakes up to sunlight and a loud thump that puts her right into panic mode.

"Nana! Where are you?" Brooklyn shouts as she crawls over the fallen ottoman that Patricia used to block the door.

Annoyed, still half asleep, fingertips prodding what must be Birkin-sized eye bags, Patricia stands up and limps down the hall.

"Nana, why was that thing there?" Brooklyn holds her arms up, and it takes a confused beat before Patricia realizes she wants a hug.

"The ottoman? Well . . . I thought we might play Obstacle Course today." She opens her arms, a little awkward, and the child throws herself into Patricia's middle. It's not awful, but her leg does hurt, and, well, she's just not accustomed to being touched quite so much. She pats Brooklyn's back and pulls away. "But first, would you like breakfast? I found some fresh fruit."

Brooklyn's eyes light up, the ottoman forgotten.

Once the child is installed at the counter with her tablet, Patricia notes the time and calls Dr. Baird.

"Patricia," he answers, curt but not unfriendly. "What a surprise."

"How are you, Doctor?" she replies. She learned long ago that calling a man by his earned title will get her farther than calling him by his first name as if they're equals.

"Busy. What can I do for you?"

She smiles and bats her eyelashes. Even if he's not right there with her, she knows it changes her voice. "I had a little accident yesterday, I'm afraid; something that needs stitches, and I'm really trying to avoid the hospital. Are you still taking house calls?"

He pauses with a soft, drawn-out, "Hmm." Not a good sign. "I am, but my girl had a call from the judge's office. Sounds like you're no longer on his plan. But there's a nice little urgent care just two miles down the road—"

"Dr. Baird, I hope you'll forgive me for interrupting you, but you know Randall's . . . secretaries . . . can't be trusted. I do believe they're rather forthright when they need certain antibiotics or . . . procedures . . . but in general, they do not look so fondly upon me."

They have a long history, Randall and the doc, and Patricia knows for a fact that certain frowned-upon procedures to get rid of unmarital surprises have lined the doctor's pockets over the years. Her eyebrows are raised as if she's waiting for a little boy to confess to having put a frog in her boot.

"I'm sure that's true, Patricia." He used to call her Mrs. Lane. "But I'm afraid Randall has me on retainer, and thus he calls the shots. I believe he's in Iceland now with . . . Donna, is it? Or Alexis? I handled the vaccine for her right before they left."

She hates his tone—smug and self-assured, greasy as a rat that knows he can't be caught or punished. If he were here in person, she'd slap him, but he's on the phone, impossibly far away.

"Well, then. Tell me, what is the going rate for an hour of your time?"

"More than you have currently. Good day, Patricia. And good luck."

And then the cocky bastard has the balls to hang up on her.

On her! After all she's contributed to his coffers over the years.

Apparently golf outings to the tropics are worth more than a Hippocratic oath.

"Well, fuck you, too," she snarls, throwing her phone at the pillows.

The knowing little smile, the aristocratically cocked eyebrow, the careful accent, the learned vocabulary, the sly social games all flee as she realizes there is no way to get what she wants out of the snide little shit.

She opens her laptop again and googles "human bite wound." Ten minutes and forty tawdry Halloween makeup tutorials later, she's in her pantry, bare leg hiked up on the sink, tools laid out on top of the dryer: sewing scissors and needle and thread, hydrogen peroxide and gauze. Bright sunlight shines in from the window, and Brooklyn is happily eating carefully sliced chunks of melon and watching her show. Patricia pulls back the bloodied gauze on her calf and nearly throws up from the sight. What she's read online indicates that once it's cleaned out and sterilized, she'll need to hold all the parts of the wound shut and sew it neatly, and she thinks she's ready, but the moment she gets the needle through the first flap of skin, she almost passes out.

She can't do this.

Even if she could, the possibility of getting an infection is high. She has no antibiotics.

"Goddammit," she murmurs, an old word she'd abandoned in her new life, and the worst thing she's ever felt is the thread pulling through her skin as she yanks it back out.

She wraps the wound in gauze and hobbles back into the kitchen. "Brooklyn, I'm going to go out for a brief errand. Can you sit quietly and watch your show?"

Brooklyn nods vigorously. "Oh yes! I did real good the last time you went away. It was easy!"

A shiver goes up Patricia's spine.

It was not easy for her—the aftermath. Not of the mirror, and not of last night.

But she can't think of another way out of this.

She has to go to urgent care. She can't take a child with the Violence to a public space, with witnesses. If Brooklyn attacked someone, they'd take her away, and Patricia would never get her back. Just a few weeks ago, she was desperate for someone else to take over care for the child, but somehow, now, the thought of Brooklyn in a government facility, alone, confused . . .

Patricia knows she is cold, but she's not that cold.

She nods to herself and gets dressed—khaki shorts she doesn't like all that much, short enough to allow the doctors access to both her wounds with no need for one of those shabby gowns. She grabs one of Randall's hundred-dollar bills. She has her keys and her wallet full of now-useless cards, and she reminds Brooklyn of all the things she should not do: eat, drink, go outside, touch the pool, open any doors, answer any phones, play with any knives or matches. She realizes for the first time that her home is a vast collection of dangerous items that could cause a small child irreparable harm. There aren't even covers over the electrical outlets. The cabinets are full of bleach and Drano and rat poison.

But she can't mention that to Brooklyn now, a mile-long list of warnings that might become ideas. When Chelsea was a child, they weren't even considerations.

As she sits in a four-car garage in last year's nicest Infiniti, ecru leather seat cool against her gauze-wrapped thigh, Patricia puts her forehead gently down against the steering wheel and cries. It's destroying her mascara, but she can't stop herself. She has never felt this helpless, not even when her mother kicked her out. Then, she left out of spite, fueled by her rage and the drive to prove herself capable. Only now does she leave out of desperation.

39.

The room is completely packed with sweaty, heaving bodies, with heartbeats, with a riotous thirst for blood. "VFR! VFR!" they chant. Hundreds, maybe thousands, of people are crammed into the warehouse, holding up signs, punching the air with their fists. Steve's fight song starts up, and he gives Chelsea an encouraging nod, squeezes her shoulder, and starts his walk down the aisle, serious and arrogant as a venture capitalist about to swipe someone's cab. He reaches the ring and looks up at it as if expecting an elevator to appear.

Harlan Payne's voice booms from every corner, pressing the air out of the room: "Straight from the New York Stock Exchange, please welcome power broker turned power choker, Mr. Steven Nissen, Esquire!"

Half the room erupts in cheers, half the room erupts in boos—and then the boos take over. And it's not really a room. It's a huge cube bound in industrial metal, pounding with noise and emotion. Chelsea can smell them, all those bodies crammed in, not enough air-conditioning, no filters, their rage and desire rising into the air.

Harlan was right—the people want this. They need this.

There is no place more dangerous in the world right now, but they *love* it.

The music stops, and there's a single beat of glorious silence before

Chelsea's fight song kicks in. It's "Toxic" by Britney Spears, but under-cut with something that sounds like Rob Zombie, crazy and screech-ing.

"That's you. Knock 'em dead," Chris says, cuffing her on the shoul-der.

She looks at the aisle she'll walk down. Through the door, twenty feet, and then people are packed on either side, holding up big post-ers that say simple things because this is the first night, and no one knows who to love and hate yet. VFR, I <3 THE VIOLENCE, KILL 'EM ALL, that sort of thing. They'll be close enough to touch her, and most of them are men, rough men with shaved heads and country boys with big hats and little kids with fauxhawks. She's practiced for weeks, but it turns out she's not scared of the fight or even the Violence anymore—she's just scared of walking so close to so many screaming strangers.

"Go, tiger." Chris gives her a gentle shove this time, and her feet tangle briefly and then she's walking like a wobbly little deer. A spot-light swings to shine on her, hot and blinding, and then she remem-bers.

She's not a wobbly fawn.

She's not meek little Chelsea Martin, so beaten down she doesn't even tell the cashier at Target when something's been scanned twice.

She's Florida Woman, and she's here to fuck shit up.

She stops, bares her teeth, spreads her legs in an unladylike god-dess squat, and roars at the ceiling, watching her own spit fountain up in the lights like little stars.

Florida Woman doesn't trip and totter. She staggers. She shakes her fist and growls in the faces of guys who get in her way. She can't touch anyone—Harlan drilled that part into them, that the audience is 100 percent off limits—but she can make faces and noises and hand gestures. She's supposed to be crazy, and she falls into the insanity like a comfortable old sweatshirt from the back of her closet. When she reaches the ring, she doesn't look up like Steve, confused about the next steps and expecting a red carpet. She grabs the ropes and climbs up, loose-limbed and vulgar, to straddle the top rope.

"Please welcome one of your own," Harlan booms from every-where at once. "You've read about her online, you've seen her on the news, you've passed by her in Walmart. She's methed up, sexed up, and ready to fight. It's . . . Florida Woman!"

Chelsea winds her leg through the ropes and stands, legs braced, screaming into the void. Thousands of voices scream back, and their might flows into her like twenty shots of vodka and Red Bull. She has never felt this strong, never felt this unbreakable, untouchable, powerful.

And then the lights go out and the voices cut out to a low, expectant rustling.

Even though she knew it was going to happen, it's disturbing, and Chelsea hurries to climb down to the ring. Swirling spotlights twirl around the crowd, leaving the ring in the dark. She can see Steve right where he should be, still fully suited up. One of the refs—a guy named Pauley who used to be a pro ref—climbs into the ring and nods to each of them. Chelsea checks her bra straps, fluffs her hair.

"When the bell rings, let's see what Mr. Shit Don't Stink thinks of Florida Woman," Harlan says, his voice somehow both commanding and almost seductive.

With a boom, the lights go on and a bell rings, and Pauley slashes an arm in the center of the ring and runs away, leaping through the ropes like they're angry bulls about to gore him. Steve looks around like he's confused and would like to talk to a manager, and Chelsea rubs her nose like she's been inhaling drugs and bares her teeth. Their eyes meet, and she can see the glimmer in his baby blues as he winks. Overhead, someone shakes out a handful of chalk, and it falls down like glittering rain. She mimes a big breath and shakes her head, knowing that Steve is doing the same.

If this was really the Violence, there would be no theatrical pause. But this is acting, and so Chelsea soaks in the drama of the moment . . . and then launches herself at Steve right as the music kicks in.

They have the blocking down to a science. The hard part is not laughing, because it feels like play, like kids involved in a fun game. She runs for him, and he clotheslines her, flat on her back. As she falls, she smacks the ring with her hand, hard, and the noise sounds like she's busted open her head. The crowd makes a worried, collective groan and leaps to its feet. For a moment, she lies there—until she feels Steve's wing tip nudge her ribs and senses his shadow looming over her.

That's when she grabs his tie and yanks him over in a dramatic toss that sends him tumbling almost out of the ring. He catches himself just in the nick of time, well-clad arm and leg dangling, and pulls himself back in as Chelsea violently leaps from her back to her feet in a move that relies on the springiness of the ring floor. Steve slithers back inside the ropes, and Chelsea tries to stomp his head, but he knows exactly when and how to roll away before she can crush his skull.

It's a masterly dance, practiced dozens of times under careful scrutiny, and they play their parts to perfection. Throws, slams, pins—that they always kick out of before Pauley can count to three from the edge of the ring. His job is to look too frightened to get back in the ring while keeping a close eye on them, and their job is to pretend they're so messed up and violent that he doesn't exist. Just like people truly in the throes of the Violence, they only have eyes for each other in the way that a hammer only exists to slam a nail.

To Chelsea, on one level, it's ridiculous. The Violence is nothing like this. But she can feel the crowd's response, their ups and downs, groans and cheers and boos and moans. Every time Steve does something to hurt her, half of the audience ripples with discomfort and half of it cries for blood. The same thing happens when she attacks Steve, but these two parts of the audience are distinctly different. At one point, when she's on her belly with Steve pulling her hair back, she looks directly into the eyes of a nearby woman, young in a white tank top and cutoffs, unintentionally wearing the same outfit, and sees trauma replaying there, a flat-eyed, slack-jawed look that's all too familiar. It'll feel good when she wins this match. For women who've experienced domestic violence, the VFR will give them plenty of chances to see women choking men out for a change.

They reach the last bit of choreography, the crescendo of the match. In the past five minutes, Steve has had his breakaway jacket ripped off him, his tie used to choke him. Chelsea hasn't had her clothes ripped, but she did get thrown from the ropes once, a terrifying and exhilarating sensation that left her pleased when the crowd winced on her behalf, even if it didn't hurt that much thanks to the bouncy ring floor.

Steve is there now, on his hands and knees, rocking back and forth after a slam, and Chelsea laboriously and exaggeratedly climbs the ropes in the corner of the ring until she's balanced on the post. The first time she tried this, her cowboy boots were too slick, and she fell back onto the mats, so they had to get out sandpaper and really add some grit. Now she's secure, powerful, and knows every atom of the post and how to stand. Down below, Steve wiggles into position, feigning pain, preparing for her to leap.

Mouth open in a silent scream, Chelsea pushes off like she's flying and slams down on Steve's back, pinning him down.

"Okay?" she whispers, her lips hidden by her hair.

"Okay," he answers. "But ready for some Gatorade."

Pauley's hand slams the ring three times, and Harlan Payne calls out, "Winner: Florida Woman!"

The crowd boos and hisses and screams and chants, and Pauley pries her up, and Chelsea stands and staggers for a moment as if she's just waking up. She shelters her eyes from the spotlights and looks around in confusion, then glares down at Steve as if in understanding. She nods like she's just starting to hear a great bass line thumping, plants a boot on Steve's back, and pumps a fist into the air. Her fight song starts playing again, and the crowd goes insane.

Whether they love her or hate her, they feel it in their bones.

But then she notices something in the crowd—people turned the wrong way, people talking worriedly and shouting. Where she saw the woman earlier, a body is thrashing, and then someone is screaming. The crowd catches on and turns in a big ripple to watch the new show. The woman in the crowd is lashing out, fighting—silently.

Chelsea can see it from here, even if no one else does.

She's got the Violence.

That woman—she must've taken a note from Chelsea's book and peppered up, even though Harlan assured them there would be TSA-level pat-downs at the door.

The man she's attacking is in a camo hat and black T-shirt, hands up as she tries to rip him apart, and the rest of the crowd is backing away from them, running for the doors, freaking out. The hired security guys stationed around the walls are struggling upstream to reach the fight, but they're just too far away to do any good while everyone else is stampeding against them.

Chelsea looks down at Steve. "Come on. We've got to dogpile her."

She doesn't wait to see if he nods or agrees, just slips through the ropes and runs for that spot in the crowd where bodies are clearing out. When she gets to the woman, she grabs her by the waist and yanks back with all her might, tossing the woman like she's been taught to do and launching her onto the floor, scattering chairs. Before the woman can get to her feet, Chelsea flips her over and pins her down. They weigh about the same, and if someone doesn't get on her back soon, she's going to be in the fight of her life.

As the woman bucks underneath her, it occurs to her that she's not sure which would be worse—getting wounded without money or insurance in today's world or losing her job because of the bad press from this woman's desperate choice. Harlan's number one rule is Don't Touch the Audience, and she's breaking it, bigtime.

But she has to. There's no other way.

"Come on!" she shouts, holding the woman down, searching frantically for the nearest face. "Help me hold her!"

The first person she sees is the man the woman was attacking, his face scratched up and his ear hanging by a string of skin. Judging by his open mouth, he's in shock, and he just shakes his head as he backs away, turns, and runs.

"Piece of shit coward!" Chelsea screams at his back.

But then something heavy lands on her back, the heaviest damn thing in the world, crushing her.

"Keep on it," Harlan Payne says near her ear. "We'll get 'er back down."

Another slam as someone else lands on Harlan, and then someone else. It's crushing the air out of Chelsea's lungs, making her ribs creak.

She goes still for a moment, remembering what TJ told her one day during practice: No matter where you are, no matter how little space you have, you can find one breath.

There, crushed, in the dark, smelling a strange woman's cheap shampoo mixed with the scent of blood and Harlan's expensive cologne, Chelsea finds the space she needs to draw a breath. And then another one. She never understood the calm of the storm until now, until the Violence came and made everything a storm.

She knows the woman isn't there, her brain not connected to her body, but she also knows how hard it must be to draw a breath with this much weight on her back.

"It's okay," Chelsea whispers. "You're not alone. It's going to be okay."

Despite the fact that she can feel Harlan breathing on her neck, hear someone else sigh over that, part of her feels like she and this woman are alone together in the world, just them pressed against the ground like Atlas holding up the sky.

"What? What is this? Help!"

The woman underneath her starts crying as soon as the words are out of her mouth, and Chelsea feels her body go slack and limp.

"We're good," she says in Harlan's general direction, and he repeats it.

The weight lifts off her, bit by bit, until air dances over her back. It's not cool air, but she's finally free. Instead of standing, Chelsea goes to hands and knees beside the woman, whose face is still masked by her long black hair.

"Hey, you okay?" Chelsea says, real low. "Do you know what happened?"

"Is he dead? Did I do it?"

The woman's voice is a horrified rasp, and Chelsea can't tell if she's more scared that she killed the man or that she didn't.

"You messed him up, but he was alive when he ran out of here like a goddamn coward," Chelsea whispers back.

"Goddamn." It comes out soft and vulnerable and sad.

"You don't have to go back to him," Chelsea says, glad her hair is likewise hiding her face.

"I—we got kids."

A big, warm hand lands on Chelsea's shoulder, and she looks up and sees Harlan Payne crouched over her. He nods as if to say, *Let me do this,* and Chelsea returns the nod and stands and backs away.

Harlan kneeling is as big as a grizzly bear, but even in his posh silver suit, he does it. So low that Chelsea can barely hear it, in a voice with a heavy southern accent, he says, "Good try, but that shitbird got away. You can stay with us if you want. We got work to do, food and beds, decent pay. And we don't mind if you've got the sickness."

The woman's body, still facedown on the floor, shudders with a big sob.

"We got kids," she repeats, as if she's begging.

"Honey, he's just gonna turn you in to the cops now and find somebody younger to raise those kids," Harlan says. "And you know it."

The woman is shaking now, her bloodstained nails digging into the cement floor, or trying to. Chelsea can see every line of anguish in her body, knows what this feels like. This woman's brain is going a mile a minute, trying to find some way through, trying to make everything okay, and every tally she makes comes up short.

There's no good answer.

Harlan is right—she should leave, join the VFR—but it takes a certain kind of person to walk away from a bad situation that's grown comfortable in its constancy.

The woman sits up, and Harlan puts out a hand to help her, but she ignores it and stands on her own, wobbly as the fawn Chelsea once felt like. She can't meet anyone's eyes, this broken woman, but she wraps her arms around herself and checks her pockets, finding keys and a duct tape wallet. Her eyes rove over the floors and land on a tiny plastic bag flecked with black, and Chelsea goes to get it, seals it, and holds it out.

"Thank you," the woman says, taking the pepper. "It'll be okay."

She walks away in her flip-flops, head hanging. Harlan, Pauley, Steve, Chris, and Arlene all watch her go.

"It's not going to be okay for her," Chelsea says.

Harlan's big bear paw lands on her shoulder.

"No, but she's the only one who gets to make that decision. We tried. That's the best we can do."

The lights go on, bathing the big hall in buzzing fluorescents. The stands are empty now. The crowd has bolted. The posters are on the ground, the chairs are tipped over, drinks are spilled in sticky puddles. All that excitement, all that energy ran right out the door.

Chelsea heaves a sigh and looks at Harlan.

"So are we fucked now?" she asks.

He rubs his stubble and stares at the door the woman walked out of.

"Maybe" is all he says.

40.

Patricia has never been to an urgent care center before. She had to take Chelsea to the emergency room once when she nearly sliced off her thumb cutting an apple, but that at least felt serious and like an actual emergency. The child was gushing blood like a waterfall. Her own wounds seem less troublesome now that they've stopped bleeding, but she's done enough online searches by this time to understand how serious her situation really is. In a different world, she would go to the ER, but it's half an hour away and has a three-hour wait time. Urgent care should be able to take care of her—and it might also be less picky about payment. Plus, it's only two miles away, and the posted wait time is seventeen minutes.

She'd imagined it would be like a regular doctor's office, pleasant and balmy with fake palm trees in the corners and tidy spinning racks full of magazines and ads for fancy vitamins and male catheters, the same ads she sees if she tries to watch TV in the middle of the day in Florida. But the reality is that someone in charge of the urgent care center understands that people have to come here no matter what, and therefore they long ago stopped trying to make it pleasant.

It's a sty.

First of all, it's in the corner of the parking lot of a long-abandoned

Kmart, and just a few parking spaces away is a place where people have decided they can dump their couches and old TVs. The concrete is cracked and broken, but that's common in Florida. The hypodermic needle she has to step over is less common and the first sign that this experience is going to be worse than imagined. Inside, the floor is a murky, unwashed gray, the chairs faded and cracked after too much time in the sun. The people sitting in the chairs look hollowed out and desperate, except for the larger gentleman coughing so heavily and wetly that Patricia would rather sit next to a junkie than catch whatever he has. Ever since Covid, coughing in public without a mask is considered a major faux pas, but this man must've missed that particular piece of information.

At the front counter, she writes her name on the clipboard and stands expectantly. An exhausted-looking Black woman in her thirties glares up from her phone. Her scrubs have a child's cartoon character on them, some square-shaped thing dancing across her bosom. "Have a seat. We'll call you."

Patricia puts on her Benevolent Rich Woman face. "It's a bit of an emergency."

The woman raises an eyebrow. "Yeah, that's why they call it urgent care. Have a seat. Please."

Patricia doesn't like the tone, but she sits. There's a TV high up, too high for anyone to attempt to lower the excruciating volume or change the very annoying channel. Two twin men who look like sex robots are convincing someone to buy a beach house that's way out of the stated price range. Everyone else in the room is riveted. Patricia is bored. She flicks through her phone, but everything she sees gets on her nerves. She considers picking up one of the few magazines on a corner table, but they're months out of date and look like they've been colonized by a skin disease.

"Ms. Lane?" the woman at the desk finally calls, eleven minutes later.

Patricia walks up there, smiling. "I'm Patricia Lane."

"Please fill this out. When you bring it up, I'll make a copy of your insurance card and collect your copay."

The clipboard is translucent plastic with visible smears of God only knows what. Patricia takes it and a pen with a ragged fabric flower taped to it and goes to sit down. She hasn't filled one of these out in years—not since she married Randall. She mainly sees Dr. Baird, and anytime she needs a referral, he gets her right in immediately with someone he trusts and has his secretary transfer all her records. Now Patricia has to try to remember her medical history and list all her prescriptions and dig out her insurance card, which probably won't even work. Ah, well. She'll cross that bridge when it gets in her way.

When she returns her clipboard, she hands over her insurance card, too. The woman rolls her chair over to a printer and Patricia waits there, unsure of what to do. She hates this sort of moment, when there isn't a script for what should occur. The woman pretends she doesn't exist as she makes copies, writes things down illegibly, and taps at her keyboard with irrationally long nails.

"Is this your only insurance?" the woman asks, squinting.

Patricia smiles. One of the first tricks she learned once she was out in the world on her own was that confidence and a smile could get a pretty woman through most things. "Of course."

"It's not pulling up, but the system has been up and down all day. I'm not sure what your copay is yet. We can do that after you see the doctor. You're up next."

"Thank you so much. I really do appreciate it."

At that, the woman smiles, as if she hasn't been thanked in years.

"It'll just be a few."

Patricia doesn't even wince at the terrible grammar. A few what? She just smiles and sits back down, scrolling through news sites and hoping for giant ice storms in Iceland.

"Ms. Lane?"

She stands and aims her smile at the young man in scrubs who can't be more than twenty. He's a beefy thing and awkward, and she knows exactly what to do with him. She swings her hips as she walks toward him, feeling the burn from her wounds but knowing better than anyone how to function through pain. He holds open the door for her, and she bows her head and scoots in, always turning toward him attentively. He weighs her—she's lost a pound, which is a pleasant surprise, despite the fact that she's well aware she hasn't been eating—and takes her blood pressure, which is just this side of high.

"White coat syndrome," she tells him, a little shyly.

"We see that a lot," he agrees. He walks her into a treatment room and changes the paper on the bench. She hops up, girlish, and wishes she could cross her ankles.

"So what brings you in today?"

"I had a little accident." He raises his bushy eyebrows, so she reaches down to her calf and unwinds the bandage, steeling herself for the moment of disgust and horror she feels each time that flap of skin and meat dangles freely. It's stopped bleeding, with a rough, black scab outlining the clear marks of teeth.

"Oh." He swallows. "Wow. Yeah, that's . . . something. That might be a little beyond our, uh, abilities."

She puts a hand on his arm, where a cartoon ghost thing is crudely tattooed. "You look thoroughly capable to me."

It's funny how quickly she can tap into this old part of herself—the part of her who used to judge a man who walked into the diner and figure out exactly how to treat him for the best tip. This young man— nurse or doctor, she's not sure—when she touched him, his breath sped up. Maybe he likes older women, or maybe women his age never give him the time of day. He's large and rough and looks like he doesn't own a mirror, but he has something she wants very much, and so she'll resurrect the coquettish part of Patty if it'll get her leg fixed and send her home with a bottle of antibiotics.

"I'll send in the doctor."

Patricia's smile doesn't waver, but she's a bit disappointed. This boy would be easy to deal with, and now she has no idea who'll be sent in to tend to her—possibly someone better at saying no. She gives him a coy little wave goodbye as he galumphs out the door. Barely a minute later, the door reopens, revealing the exact kind of person Patricia was hoping to avoid.

The doctor is her age but a battle-ax to Patricia's rapier. She's wide and stocky and pasty, with dull-brown hair cut like a helmet and muddy eyes behind thick glasses. Her small lips are set in a scowl, and she's wearing Crocs and a stained white coat.

"Ms. Lane," she says—not asks—as she peers at Patricia's chart.

"That's me."

"I'm Dr. Ellis. How did this happen?"

The doctor puts down her chart and squats down laboriously to inspect Patricia's wound. Patricia holds up her thin, tan, sculpted, perfectly hairless leg for her frowning scrutiny. She's given this answer a lot of consideration.

"I was bitten."

The doctor glares at her. "I'm not an idiot. I know it's a bite. From what?" She reaches out to touch the dangling bit, her eyes snapping up to Patricia's face to gauge her reaction to the sudden pain.

But even if Patricia looks like a country-club woman, her backbone is a trailer-park girl, and she doesn't flinch.

"Does it really matter? I'd just like to have it cleaned up, sewn up, and defended against infection."

This time, when Dr. Ellis touches the dangling bit, she isn't as careful. She presses into the wound, tugs a little, and Patricia pins her lips against cursing or vomiting. Yes, the nice young man would've been vastly preferable. This woman is testing her. Either she's a sadist, or she's become hardened to her purpose, or she hates thin, beautiful women. Patricia has met all of their types, over the years, and she won't let any of them see her sweat.

"I suppose that is my job, but it would really help me if I knew what I was defending you against. The bite marks look human. Child-sized." Dr. Ellis stares at her, a dare.

Patricia is too smart to rise to the bait.

That's the thing about when both people know it's a lie—someone still has to say it out loud, and the other one has to agree to it.

"How peculiar."

The doctor snorts. "Yes. So very peculiar. If that's all you're willing to tell me, I'll just assume it's not a rabid raccoon and do the best I can. I can give you a shot of local anesthesia, but we're not fully equipped like an emergency room."

"That sounds perfectly acceptable."

Dr. Ellis shakes her head and stands, slowly, grunting, her knees clicking. "I'll be back shortly with supplies and help. You understand this isn't going to be fun?"

Patricia smiles sweetly. "Getting it wasn't particularly fun, either."

Once the doctor has left the room, Patricia takes one last look at her wound and then remembers to pull the gauze off her thigh. She forgot that one—but it's also not the one she's worried about. She flicks through her phone and snoops around for a remote control to turn off the TV, another high-hanging parasite that blares a little too loud and shows commercials she'd rather turn off. She had forgotten how time runs strange in blank white treatment rooms, how dehumanizing they are. She's just a faceless body with a problem, and the doctors here don't know her, don't know her history, just want to get her taken care of and out of the room so they can roll down a new length of crunchy white paper.

It's monstrous, really, how modern medicine treats people.

Well, poor people.

It worked quite well when Dr. Baird drove right up to her house in his BMW and already had her full history on his laptop. Here, she feels like a number. Like cattle.

"Here we go." Dr. Ellis bustles back in with a plastic bin. The awkward young man is behind her carrying yet more supplies.

Patricia braces herself for small talk or admonishments, but Dr. Ellis goes into teaching mode, explaining everything she sees and does to the young man and telling him what to do and pointing out how he could do what he's doing more effectively. Patricia goes from feeling like cattle to feeling like a piece of meat. The anesthetic they inject into her calf dulls the pain, at least, but she can still feel pressure and tugging, and she has to look away when the needle and black thread come out.

"Ms. Lane?"

Patricia looks up. She was lost somewhere in her thoughts. "Hm?"

"I'm afraid we're going to need to excise some of this dead tissue." Dr. Ellis is pinching the dangly bit of meat between her blue-gloved fingers.

Patricia just stares at her,

"I just wanted you to be aware."

Patricia waves a hand. She'd suspected as much. "I'll leave it to you."

The sound of—scissors? Something like them?—makes her look to the television, where those devilish twins are again offering a fidgeting couple their dream home at a hefty sum. She's grateful for the volume now and focuses on the shiplap walls and tile floors. If she doesn't break eye contact with the show, she can't look down at her leg. If she's listening to the selling and whingeing, she can't hear the snip of her flesh being cut away and the needle popping through her skin. It's ridiculous that she ever thought she could do this herself with Rosa's old button needle and some cotton thread.

She was always going to lose that chunk, her pound of flesh.

Well, not a pound, but the metaphor stands.

She's going to be . . . what's the right word?

Disfigured, certainly.

She's going to be *less*.

That's the word that keeps coming to her the whole time she racks her brain for the right one.

Less.

Such a small word when she'd like a bigger, grander one. What's the point of developing an inimitable vocabulary if she can't even find the right word for this exact moment?

Part of her, gone forever, leaving an odd divot behind.

She's never had something cut out before. Still has her wisdom teeth and her gallbladder and her appendix. Never even had a surgery.

And now she's awake as the doctor drops a chunk of her body into a plastic container full of liquid with a healthy plop.

It's probably too small to even register on her scale.

"It has to be tested," Dr. Ellis warns her, as if she'd asked to keep it as some sort of morbid souvenir.

"Then I bid it good journey."

Patricia refocuses on the TV as they conclude their grim work. She can feel tugging down below, but the pain is mercifully gone. At some point, one of them asks about her thigh, and she waves at them and murmurs something, and then they're washing out that wound without the benefit of all the anesthetic. It doesn't really hurt, though— she's somewhere else, floating overhead beside the TV, her eyes locked on those beguiling twins with their diabolical deals.

"Ms. Lane?"

"Yes?"

She looks up, surprised to find that she's still lying back on the bench.

"We're all done." Dr. Ellis holds out a hand, and Patricia takes it, unsure why until the doctor pulls her up to sitting. She looks down and finds her leg wrapped in two places with yet more gauze.

"They'll give you instructions up front. You'll want to keep the bandages on for forty-eight hours. Then they can come off, but you don't want to get the stitches wet. Take your antibiotics. If you develop a fever or the wound gets red and painful, let us know. Do you have a regular doctor?"

"Yes—well, no. Not anymore." Just saying it fills her with the oddest flush of shame, as if they know that her doctor has dropped her as a patient rather than supposing that, like anyone else, she's left his practice for her own reasons.

"Good luck, Ms. Lane," Dr. Ellis says as she backs out the door.

The awkward young man is still with her, though. "How's it feel?"

"I don't feel much of anything, I'm afraid."

He smiles, showing uneven teeth. "That's probably for the best. It was an impressive wound."

"Impressive," she echoes. "Hm."

He holds out his hand to help her stand, and she tests her leg and finds it numb but functional.

"They'll have your prescription at the desk. Make sure you take it every twelve hours, and you'll want to keep up with the pain meds. They won't let us give you the good stuff." He frowns, like this is very bad news. "Sorry."

"I'm sure it will be fine."

She has an entire cabinet filled with the good stuff, thanks to Dr. Baird, and she can't take a single pill of it, not with Brooklyn around.

It makes her zone out, makes nothing matter. And now, something always matters.

He holds the door open for her as she limps out to the front desk.

"Your insurance was recently canceled, it looks like," the receptionist says, glaring as if Patricia has lied to her.

"That can't be right."

"It is. I called them myself."

They stare at each other, the receptionist annoyed and Patricia cool and untouchable. She will never break, not for this woman, and not for the next.

"So the non-insured price for your visit is one hundred and fifty dollars. We can take cash or credit."

Patricia knows she has only one hundred dollars in cash with her, although there's a little more at home. She didn't bring more for this very reason—they can't take it if she doesn't have it. She knows that Randall has canceled all her cards because she's tried multiple times to order groceries online for her and Brooklyn. And she knows that unless she pays right now, she can't have her antibiotics.

"I can give you a hundred in cash," she says pleasantly, holding out the crisp bill.

The receptionist shakes her head like she's dealing with an idiot. "One fifty. You can split it between cash and card, if you need to." She points to a pricing sheet on the wall, the laminated paper faded tan and crinkled up in the corners. "It's all posted right there."

"Well, I'm afraid this is all I have. You can take it or leave it."

The receptionist stands. "Ma'am, you have to pay. That's how it works. This isn't a garage sale." Her voice is raised, and another woman comes out from behind the prescription window, a bigger, older woman, crossing her arms over her broad chest, the enforcer.

Patricia raises her chin.

"How it works is I have this money, and I'm going to give it to you and walk out, and what you do with it after that is your own business." Patricia places the hundred-dollar bill on the counter, nods as if to the queen, and saunters out the door. She's halfway to her car before she hears the door fly open behind her. She doesn't look back.

"Lady, you have to pay! You can't just walk away!"

Patricia opens her door. "I can and am. You have my address. Bill me."

Feet pound on the pavement behind her, and she slides into the seat, her leg groaning from the two wounds that are in the process of roaring back to life in a red-hot wash of pain and curious tingling. Before she can close her door, the receptionist catches it and wrenches it back open.

"Get out now. We're calling the police."

Patricia turns to look at her, and it feels like layers and layers of sediment fall off her, like she's some vast creature rising from the seabed shedding years of sand and silt. Patty's sneer curves her mouth, Patty's rage fills her chest and runs down her arms and legs, and she pries the woman's hand off her door and slaps her right across the face.

"Don't you touch my car, you bitch!" she screeches with Patty's old southern accent.

The receptionist stumbles back clutching her face, staring at Patricia like she's gone insane.

She hasn't, though. She's just called up the part of her that's a survivor, that's a scrapper, that will fight tooth and nail to be free.

"Lady, what the hell?" the receptionist says.

Patricia shoves her back with a hand to the stomach and slams the car door, locking it. She pushes the button to start the car and is already throwing it into reverse. The receptionist should know by now that if she doesn't get out of the way, she's going to get run over.

All bets are off when Patty comes out.

"You can't leave!" the receptionist shouts as she squeals out of the space.

Patricia rolls down her window the barest bit.

"Watch me," she growls.

She peels out of the cracked little parking lot past the abandoned sofa cemetery. She looks back once and sees the receptionist standing in her parking space, one hand still on her cheek.

What are they going to do, call the police?

They won't come, anyway.

Not to the judge's house.

He may have abandoned her, but he still owns that property.

Just because he's taken everything from her doesn't mean she's nothing. Even when all is lost, there's some part of her that won't give up.

Turns out Patty was not destroyed.

She was just waiting, deep underneath, until she was needed.

41.

Ella blinks. She's facedown on the ground with something very heavy on her back. Rough, old brown carpet is pressed to her cheek. It smells like bleach and sour beer. She can't breathe.

"Help!"

As she says it, barely enough breath to groan out the word, the weight presses down, and she can't reinflate her lungs. She panics, flails, wants to scream but can't. She flashes back to the time her dad choked her unconscious, to the world going gray and red and fading away. She wants to reach for her throat to protect herself, to push away the tightening there, but can't. Her arms are pinned to her sides.

"Shh," a voice says, right by her ear. "It's okay. You're not alone. You're scared now, and that's normal. You were storming. We dog-piled you. We're going to get off now. We'll help you through it."

Ella recognizes that voice—the girl from the drugstore. Leanne. She sounds so calm and reasonable and kind. It makes Ella go a little limp, and as if that's exactly the key that was needed, most of the weight lifts from her back. There's some grunting, and she hears another familiar voice—River.

"Where's the antibac cream? She clawed me."

The world comes into focus. Ella is on the floor inside their RV, facedown on the carpet. Up ahead, there's a thick sheet of plastic taped over an open, narrow door. Through it, she sees an entire tiny room coated in the same plastic, taped down. It's like something out of a serial killer story, and her body tenses, her hands whipping forward to help her stand so she can get the hell out of here.

She was wrong about them.

So wrong.

"Steady there." Leanne is still—Jesus, on top of her? But she doesn't have her full weight on Ella anymore. River must've been on top of Leanne, and that was the lifted weight that offered enough room to breathe. So they were both on top of her, holding her down? They just dragged her into their murder van and tackled her?

It starts coming back. Ella inhaled pepper on purpose because she didn't know how to escape. They wanted something from her, and she was trapped between them and the RV door, and the security guard wasn't coming, and the only option she could see was letting the Violence decide who was going to live. So . . .

"How are you not dead?" she asks in a tiny voice. "Get off me."

Leanne doesn't budge, but at least Ella has enough room to breathe now.

"Not until I'm sure you're safe. See, there are certain facts about the Violence that aren't commonly known." Leanne's voice sounds like she's teaching in a classroom, not pinning a teenager to the floor with her body. "One of them is that if someone is storming and you hold them very tightly so that they can't hurt anyone and you compress their body, they'll stop storming within a few minutes. It's pretty fascinating, actually, how the body goes from attack to playing dead, shutting down—well, that's probably more science than you want. But people who are storming don't actually have to kill anyone to stop storming. The people around them just need to be brave enough to dogpile them until they come back around."

Ella's mind races with this knowledge. Everything she's ever read about the Violence—and she did a deep internet dive, once she knew she had it—suggests there is no way to stop someone from storming, that they're simply going to act out their disease until they've killed someone and only then come out of it. But now Leanne is on her back and River is over by a table, neither one of them dead.

"Did I kill the security guard, then?"

"You didn't kill anybody. Nice trick, though, keeping pepper in your pocket. Smart."

"It's easier to admire if you're not going to have scars for life," River calls grouchily. "This face is my moneymaker."

"Your voice and wit are your moneymakers, and anyway, you told me you love scars," Leanne says, teasing.

River snorts. "On other people."

Ella is having a hard time grasping this reality. She was scared, and she made the choice to kill someone rather than be kidnapped in this very RV, but now she's learning that not only has she not killed anyone, she's in the van anyway. It's a very meta moment, as if her emotions haven't caught up yet but reason is definitely present and trying to understand the situation. She wants to be scared, but her system doesn't have any more fear juice to squirt.

"I'm freaking out," she says but it sounds like a question.

"You're not, though. The amygdala gets hijacked during a Violence storm, and then it's all used up for a little while afterward and can't do much. You're drained. You're out of spoons."

"Out of hearts and hp," River adds.

"Sure, if you're into videogames and D&D. Point is, if you can promise me that you're not going to try to hurt anyone or pepper up again, I'll get off you. And we can get our groceries out of the parking lot before someone steals them and we can eat hot soup like reasonable people."

"I don't want to hurt anyone," Ella says.

Leanne sighs. "Yeah, no one does. But you were still willing to do it. We started off on the wrong foot here. We are not kidnappers, and this is not a murder van, and if you will just chill out and trust us and possibly help us, we will vaccinate you. If you want to be vaccinated. I can understand how the disease can be a boon if you're alone in today's world."

It's her use of the word *boon* that finally gets through to Ella.

This is not how kidnappers talk.

Kidnappers do not offer to vaccinate or not vaccinate you based on your consent.

"Tampa is a leading city for sex trafficking," Ella starts.

"Jesus, we're not sex traffickers," River says from somewhere overhead. "If we were, we would drive a much better vehicle and hide the plastic tarps and not possess a centrifuge."

"How about this?" Leanne says. "I'll give you my phone, and you can go sit in your car and read anything on it you want. Most of my email is with other grad students. We're spreading the vaccine as far as we can, all underground. You can see my Facebook, my mom begging me to go back to University of Miami, my Twitter where it's revealed I'm big into *Animal Crossing* and *The Witcher.* I'm a normal person who's trying to do some good here, and I feel like maybe you are, too."

"What about River?"

"No way they'll give you their phone, but you can see their whole YouTube from my phone."

"I live my life in public," River says. "The freaky stuff I'm into is very easy to find."

Ella exhales.

She's scared, and it's been a long time since she's trusted anyone. Her parents betrayed her early on. She lost her best friends when they chose each other and gossip over her, lost her teachers' goodwill when her grades went south because she wasn't sleeping because her father was terrorizing her nightly. And then she thought Hayden would finally be the confidant she could be honest with . . .

The fact that she trusted any of them makes her feel like an idiot.

But her gut tells her she can trust these two random strangers she met in a drugstore, and she's not sure why. Maybe it's Leanne's kindness, the genuine concern in her eyes, and the way her old dress hangs from her frame as if clothes are a secondary problem. Maybe it's River's odd honesty, the fact that they don't seem to need to hide anything at all, including bad moods. The fact that they don't seem to hold it against her that she tried to inhale pepper to hurt them—

Well, really, she was just trying to escape. When you've been chased and harassed and abused, you get to the point where you'd rather fight and die than have to run again.

Ella is just so tired. Her emotions have run her ragged, she hasn't slept well, she's been on alert for weeks, she's severely malnourished. She remembers enough from biology to know that she's an engine that's been running hot for far too long without any relief. Her hunger has come back full force, and she would do anything to feel full and safe for just a minute. So, sure, maybe she'll sit in her locked car, cram Cheez-Its in her mouth, and search Leanne's phone. And if she doesn't like what she sees, she'll drive away with it.

"Okay."

"Good. I'm going to get up now. Please don't make any sudden moves."

Ella's heart stutters. "Why—do you have a weapon?"

"No. I'm just super clumsy, and it's a small RV, and we try really hard to keep things clean because bacteria are tricky and the vaccine isn't going to spread itself." Leanne awkwardly scrambles off her back, and Ella draws a full breath and lifts up to hands and knees. She's in a narrow aisle, and Leanne has moved back to sit at a kitchen table with benches on either side. River is across from her, using their selfie camera to dab ointment on some nasty scratches down the side of their face. Ella has to use the table to stand, and Leanne solemnly slides her unlocked phone across the faux wood. It's got a glitter case and a little Sailor Moon charm, plus a cracked screen.

"Once you're in your car, we'll bring in our groceries." Leanne meets her eyes, and Ella gets a flash of vulnerability there, of the fact that Leanne is just as worried as she is. "Please don't steal our things. And if you decide to leave, it would be great if you could drop my phone before you do. Or place it on the concrete. The screen obviously can't take much more."

"Why are you trusting her?" River asks, all gruff.

Leanne looks from Ella to River and back again. "Honestly? Because she looks as broken down as I feel. Like a lost cat."

Ella would be insulted if it weren't so true. She feels like a lost cat—alone and skittish and hungry and scared. She silently takes the phone and touches the screen to keep it from locking. Outside, she grabs her bags and throws them in her backseat, fishing out the Cheez-Its.

Oh, the blessed Cheez-Its.

She's in such a hurry she rips the box and the bag bursts, spilling crackers. As she stuffs them in her mouth, her saliva going into overdrive, she scrolls through the cracked old phone.

Leanne wasn't lying, but Ella somehow knew she wasn't.

All her emails are from college accounts with subjects like PROPER BASE TEMPERATURE and BIFURCATED NEEDLES ARE NOT FUN TO STEP ON and GOT A NEW RECRUIT! Well, and sale emails from Etsy shops and a few emails from her mom begging her to go back to school before they drop her scholarships and internship. Her Twitter is bare and fandom-based. Her Instagram is mostly pictures of flowers and bees. And when she opens TikTok, there's River, holding up a petri dish triumphantly with the words THE CURE—BACK ON TOUR. EAT YOUR HEART OUT, ROBERT SMITH. Ella is pretty sure The Cure is an old band from the 1980s or something, but it's comforting to see that River has several million loyal followers and nothing creepy in their feed.

Every bit of evidence suggests that she can trust them. And what's more, she likes Leanne. She liked her from the moment they met in the cracker aisle. River is prickly, but that seems like a front. Ella looks back at her groceries, at the cans of soup River paid for but placed in Ella's bags.

She doesn't want to eat cold soup.

Taking all three of the cans, she heads back to the RV with Leanne's phone. Leanne is sitting at the table, and when she sees Ella she perks up, grinning.

"So will you listen?"

Ella holds up a can of soup and shakes it, eyebrows up.

"Fine." River takes the can, pops off the top, slops the soup into a plastic bowl, and puts it in the microwave. "You can sit."

"I'll stand."

"Damn. You're more skeptical than I am." Finally, River gives her the slightest grin and sits back down at the table.

The soup has a minute to go. Ella looks expectantly to Leanne.

"I can make the vaccine for the Violence right here in the RV. But I need blood with the active bacteria, which means we're really hoping you'll donate, even if you're technically underage. In return—or, more like, in a spirit of giving—we'll vaccinate you. That's what we're doing—spreading the cure. It's a therapeutic vaccine, which means it cures those already infected and prevents future infection. Unlike Covid, we got lucky this time."

Ella raises an eyebrow, and Leanne reconsiders.

"In regard to epidemiology, at least, it's a much easier beast to vanquish. My grad school friend discovered the vaccine, but her professor stole it and sold it to some cringey little pharma bro who's selling it for thirty thousand a pop, so now it's technically illegal for anyone else to use it. Every time it goes up anywhere online, it disappears, and labs get ransacked."

"But what about the government? According to the news, they have vaccines in the works . . ." Ella trails off because they're both looking at her like she's a little kid who just asked if Santa Claus can pay the electric bill.

Leanne sighs. "Yeah, well, the thing about this particular president is that he and his cronies are big into free enterprise, which means they can't legally use the existing vaccine, which means they're trying to create a new one out of nothing with a skeleton crew because he already fired everyone who isn't an idiot. You can't count on the government."

"Ever!" River adds, and Leanne smirks fondly.

"So that's why it has to happen the old-fashioned way. My friend taught me the process, and I can teach it to other people who have the education and equipment. There are dozens of grad students and doctors spreading it like this all over the world, constantly on the move. The hard part is getting people to believe us, because if we make it too public, they shut it down."

"But I've got a ton of fans who're on board," River says, leaning in, "so we're having good luck doing pop-up shops. We show up, vaccinate as many people as we can, and get the hell out. Stick around too long, and your equipment gets confiscated. We were at USF last night, and there were so many people lined up that we're now out of both vaccines and infected blood."

The microwave dinged several minutes ago. River fetches the soup and places it along with a spoon and a napkin on the counter before Ella. "Stir it, or you'll burn yourself," they warn.

And it's a good thing, too, because she totally would've burned herself. She stirs the soup, blows on it, and sips, grateful beyond measure for what feels like real food served at the correct temperature, even if it came from a can. After a few slurps settle comfortably on a bed of crackers in her griping stomach, she's ready to talk.

"So let me get this straight. You're going to take my blood, and then you're going to go back into your creepy plastic room and make a vaccine? And inject me with it?"

"Not inject. It's done more like smallpox, with a bifurcated needle. But yes, the rest of that is true, even if you continue to make everything sound ten times more weird and dangerous than it really is." Leanne glances back worriedly. "Is it the plastic that's freaking you out? I have to keep the samples as clean as possible."

Ella softens a little. Whether it's because the soup is warming up her belly or because Leanne seems like someone's grandmother who's embarrassed because she didn't dust above the doors, she isn't sure. Some tiny voice in the back of her head wonders if they've drugged her, but she watched River heat up the food, and . . . well, she really does want to trust them. They're nice. They took care of her. She tried to kill them—even messed up River's face—and they not only don't hold it against her but understand completely. And they know the answers to questions the internet couldn't give when Ella had grown accustomed to always finding the answers on the internet.

She remembers the day her mother found her birth control pills and freaked out about it, and Ella had to explain that she'd learned everything she needed to know online, had made her own appointment and known exactly how to talk to the doctor.

"But that's a mom's job!" her mom wailed, failing to hold back tears.

Ella, awash with guilt, hadn't known how to explain to her mom that everything she said when attempting to parent had so much baggage, so many emotions attached and stories from her own terrible childhood. Ella just wanted some things to be on her own terms. She wanted no-nonsense answers, not tears and speeches about becoming a woman and being irresponsible and lifelong mistakes and tales about growing up under Nana. The thing about raising kids who have to be the adult in the relationship is that you can't be surprised when they act like adults.

With the Violence, however, there's a startling lack of real information. Tons of fake news, memes and bot attacks, lists of the right yoga poses or essential oils to keep it away, organic fair trade mosquito nets, preachers and politicians shouting and pointing fingers. Hundreds of think pieces about the meaning of violence in today's society, the separation of body and mind, man's descent as an animal, Democrat versus Republican and the right to bear arms or beat people to death with your bare hands, and what it's like to shelter in place for a new reason when everyone was still barely recovered from the Covid exhaustion.

With Covid, there was a constant influx of information from around the world, but this time there aren't many statistics or reports or charts. No one really knows what the numbers are. The thing about the Violence is that it happens between two people and in the aftermath, one person is often dead and the other person confused and flooded with shame and grief and fear. The Violence is hard to capture on a camera, and when it is, the person who clicked RECORD doesn't usually live to post it.

If Leanne and River aren't lying, there's actually hope.

Not only can it be cured—apparently so easily that it can be done in a shitty old RV—but individual outbreaks can be stopped by regular people with no real equipment, just the strength to touch and contain someone brimming with intent to kill.

It's beautiful and terrifying, but isn't hope in a dark time always that way?

"Does it hurt?" Ella asks between big spoonfuls of soup. "The vaccine."

Leanne leans forward, alight like someone who's just spotted a butterfly. "Do you know anything about smallpox?"

"Something about cows, milkmaids, and scars? I read the *Outlander* books."

"Fair enough. For the vaccine, we basically make little cuts and rub in some junk. So it's not the quick poke of a shot. You have to sit there, and you'll have a scar. But that's actually kind of cool, because then you can prove you've been vaccinated. Roughly. It looks a lot like the smallpox scar. And you won't get a fancy card like the people who pay for the vaccine do."

"They have a card?"

Leanne looks down and shakes her head like a bull with no one to charge. "That's how rich people can prove they're safe. That asshole pharma bro owns the vaccine, all the patents, and if you buy it from him for market price—"

"Like it's a fucking lobster!" River breaks in.

"—then you get your own laminated card with your own special number on it. Like it's a fucking Birkin or something. Like the useless garbage collectibles your great-grandfather buys on late-night TV that come with a certificate of authenticity."

"My grandmother has that. The fancy vaccine." Ella pauses. Sips some soup. "And also a couple of Birkins."

River stares at her. "Your grandmother inoculated herself but not you?"

Ella looks down. How to explain her grandmother? It was easy before, but now that she knows about Grandpa Randall leaving . . . "It's complicated. Anyway, she has my little sister, and my mom got the Violence and left, and I really need to find them. My mom and my sister."

Leanne and River share a look that Ella doesn't quite understand, but it's not a creepy look.

"We'll get you vaccinated and give you enough for both of them," Leanne says.

"But—" River starts.

"We will." Leanne says it forcefully.

Ella scoops up the last of her soup and looks to the narrow fridge. "Do you have anything to drink?" she asks. "Because I'm pretty dehydrated, and my veins kind of suck. It'll be better if I'm full."

River opens the fridge and pulls out a bottled water. "Drink up, kid. I don't want you passing out."

"Hey."

Ella puts down the water and looks over at Leanne, who is leaning forward across the table.

"I'm really glad we ran into you," she says. Ella gets the idea she's one of those complete lunatics who just says the truth and talks about emotions all the time. She probably tells the people she loves that she loves them every day. "Everyone is acting so crazy that it's nice to meet someone who still treats you like a human being."

"I mean, I tried to engineer your murder . . ."

Leanne throws back her head and laughs at that. "Perfectly reasonable response. We're used to it. I just . . . I appreciate any moment I'm reminded there's good in the world, you know? I forget that there are still good people out there, sometimes."

"So what next?" Ella asks.

River grins, and it's a very maniacal grin.

"I cut you open," they say.

42.

Harlan had promised his employees a feast to celebrate their opening day. But after the way the first VFR show just went, no one is sure how to act. It was over before it really got started. They got through only two of the five scheduled matches. The crowd ran away before they could applaud. Everything feels so unfinished, so up in the air. Chelsea walks back to the greenroom with Steve and Chris, Harlan following behind them like the stolid sheepdog keeping his dazed flock together. Everyone looks up expectantly.

"What happened?" Sienna asks.

"Somebody in the crowd peppered up, took matters into her own hands. Not with our fighters," Harlan hurries to assure everyone as they all go on point when pepper is mentioned. "Far as I can tell, an abused woman was looking for a way out with her piece-of-shit husband." He looks off over their heads, his muscles flexing in his jacket. "Wish I had five minutes in the ring with that coward. Offered to bring her on board, but she went right back to 'im." He comes back to them, refocuses. "Anyway, we dogpiled her, he ran off, and the crowd followed."

"So the show's over?" Amy asks, in full costume and clearly disappointed.

Harlan gives her a gentle smile. "Only for the night. We've got some damage control to do online, but the way I see it, we can spin this in our favor. Any PR is good PR, right?"

"Supposedly," Sienna allows.

"So what do we do?" Amy was supposed to go on next, and Chelsea feels bad for her. She's all done up like adult Lilo from *Lilo & Stitch* with a grass skirt, lei, and flower crown, shifting from foot to foot with unused energy.

Harlan looks around the room, collecting everyone's attention. "We have our dinner, we go to bed, we watch what happens. We sold a shit ton of live feed subscriptions, so the main question is whether they cancel or not. You'll all get paid, either way. But for now, we pretend it went fine and get ready for our next venue. Everyone who went on tonight did great. I couldn't be more proud."

With a bow of his head, he hops down to the concrete beyond the loading dock and saunters off to his RV, parked a bit away. The rest of them just loll around like cattle until Arlene shows up and says, "Dinner's ready. Under the awning of Sienna's RV. Just follow your noses."

"But get undressed first!" Sienna calls. "Remember: Costumes get hung up on your labeled hangers, right-side out. Take off all your makeup or you'll get acne. If you fought tonight, wipe off any exposed skin with the tea tree wipes for the same reason."

Chelsea feels odd, dissociated and a little numb, as she joins the other women behind some sheets hung from the ceiling and squeezes out of her costume, careful not to let it touch the dusty metal floor of the semi. She hangs it up on the plastic hanger, noting that it says CHELSEA and not FLORIDA WOMAN, which makes her feel more like herself. She pulls her own clothes back on, a soft V-neck and jean shorts, and scrubs off her heavy stage makeup and sweat with three different wipes. It's unsettling, how pale she looks afterward, as if she's wiped off part of her real face. She tucks her hair back in a messy bun and heads for the food. No one is really talking; it feels like a funeral, except there's no script, no one to console. The VFR has begun to feel like a family, but right now, she feels lost. She got to fight, and it felt great, but then she broke the rules and got involved with an audience member, and . . . well, things did not go to plan.

The smell of the grill helps bring her back a little. She's on autopilot, choosing food and a drink, collecting plastic silverware, and finding a lawn chair to settle down in. She realizes only after she's seated that everyone subtly arranged themselves so that those who fought got to eat first, so it's her and Steve and Matt and Maryellen in the only four chairs, with TJ gallantly taking a spot on the floor and Joy nowhere to be seen. No one speaks. These four were robbed of a job well done, and four more people were robbed of the chance to do their jobs at all. Everyone else will still have to clean up and pack chairs after this, doing their part offstage. Chelsea doesn't envy them. Their work feels way too much like what she did back home, a bystander for the big event and the person who always had to clean up alone afterward.

Chelsea's burger tastes . . . gray. Just gray. She swallows it, feeling each chunk catch in her throat. She randomly chose a soda, and it just tastes like fizz. She can't stop thinking about that woman. About the desperation in her eyes, and then the absence of anything there. About the way she came back online, desperate for the news that she'd killed someone and disappointed to find she hadn't.

Most of all, Chelsea feels carved out by the resigned way that poor woman turned right back to her old life . . . it was like a punch to the gut. Nauseating. That broken creature went back to a man who'd done her so wrong she wanted him dead, fully understanding that he knew what she'd done and was going to punish her for failing. She was so scared of the unknown that she chose certain abuse.

It's an all-too-familiar feeling that she now finds repugnant.

As much as Chelsea loves her girls, as much as she misses them with every heartbeat and thinks of them every moment, she could never go back to living under David's particular brand of oppression. She couldn't fit herself back into that tiny box, cut off parts of herself like Cinderella's stepsisters chopping at their feet, all to contort into some prearranged shape to suit someone else. She may be broke right now, she may own three outfits and one pair of shoes and the cheapest underwear at Target, but no one can make her do a goddamn thing. And it feels fantastic.

What's more, it feels like a starting point.

Back in her old life, everything felt like a dead end.

That night, she falls asleep more quickly than anticipated. It was exhausting, her bout, and even if she loved those old, familiar, most welcome sparkles of performance magic, what came after was draining. The whole tour bus is quiet. No one knows what will happen next. The VFR could be totally done. They could be sent home tomorrow. Some of them have no home to return to. Chelsea doesn't even have a car. If they let her go, she'll have to . . .

God, what?

She has no idea.

Hope Amy will invite her along, maybe. Amy still has a car, locked behind the gates back at the fair lot.

If not, maybe Maryellen. She likes and trusts Steve and Matt but isn't yet ready to enter into any sort of relationship, even friendship, where a man has power over her, or even where his vote counts for more because he owns all the resources. She knows all too well that the cycle can't be broken that easily, that if she had nowhere to go and a man told her to jump, there's a chance she'd bow her head and ask how high.

The next morning is likewise somber. Arlene tries to inject some levity, playing the B-52s as they brush their teeth and hair and take turns for tepid two-minute showers in the little RV cubicle.

"Y'all are all acting like it's the end of the world," Arlene says, shaking her head. "We're just getting started. If you think it's over, you don't know Harlan Payne too well."

Of course they don't know him. He's a celebrity. He changed personalities five times in his career, from hero to villain to lunatic and back again. And as for his fighters, they're all losers and killers and weirdos, and they know it.

Harlan has money and friends and resources. They don't.

That's why nobody corrects Arlene.

They shuffle over to Sienna's RV in a loose line, no one really talking. The sky is gray, threatening rain, the air as thick as soup. The scent of sausage floats up, and as they arrived first, the girls dig in, scooping up eggs from Sienna's big pot and pulling bananas from a bunch and pouring coffee from a giant carafe that no one can live without.

"Sleep well?" Steve asks Chelsea when he arrives with the boys, looking smaller in his Nirvana T-shirt and jeans as compared with last night's costume. There's still mascara stuck in his lashes; someone needs to teach the guys how to use oil to remove eye makeup.

"Yeah, but then I woke up."

He laughs, and she smiles a little. That's another thing she's learning at the VFR—she still has a sense of humor, for all that it's been buried for decades. For the past few years, she and David never chatted or watched shows together or went on dates, unless it was for a work function, and it's nice to have banter in her life again.

"Have you guys seen this?" Amy says, rushing up, holding out her phone.

VFR BLOWS UP, the news headline says—on CNN.

And right there dominating the screen is a shot of Chelsea standing on Steve, her face a feral mask, all teeth and crazy hair and mad eyes.

She really does look like Florida Woman—batshit insane and dangerous. She doesn't even recognize herself.

"Oh my God." She wants to take the phone but isn't yet that kind of person. "What does the story say?"

Amy squeezes in between her and Steve and slowly scrolls through, although it's hard to read.

"Surprises abounded in the first Violence Fighting Ring event," she recites. "Horrible grammar, but whatever. Ahem. It's not quite illegal, but it's definitely underground, and it's brutal. We saw a granny beat up a goth, a stripper cuss out an MMA fighter, and the embodiment of Florida Woman kick a banker's ass. And we loved it." Amy looks up at Chelsea. "They loved it! Um . . ." She scrolls a little further. "The event was cut short when an audience member stormed with a legitimate case of the Violence and was neutralized by the VFR fighters and Harlan Payne himself. Tickets for tomorrow night's show in Jacksonville are sold out, but the event can be streamed with a subscription." Amy looks up. "So that's good, right? We're okay?"

"That's just what I was coming here to discuss." Harlan Payne has appeared among them in his uniform, his scarf bright red and black. He's grinning, showing all his teeth. "I know we were all worried. Hell, I'll admit I had a difficult night. But we're a hit! Every event on the schedule is sold out and subscriptions are through the roof. Even the reviews that didn't like it had to admit that it was compelling and, I quote, *gleefully fills the empty shoes left by the WWC.*"

It's another odd moment. Chelsea's heart lifts, but she's not sure she can trust it.

"So we still have jobs?" Amy asks. Chelsea is grateful to have an Amy around, someone willing to ask the questions everyone else worries are too pushy or too stupid.

Harlan barks a laugh. "Of course you still have jobs. And everybody gets a bonus this morning for making it happen." He pulls out a stack of cash—greasy, crumpled bills. Chelsea can imagine them passing hand-to-hand last night, ten dollars for parking and a sliding amount for seats inside, based on how close they were to the ring. Harlan peels off some bills and hands matching stacks to her and Steve. "You two done good. I spent the morning tuning up your websites." He winks at Chelsea and turns to distribute the rest of his gifts.

Chelsea inspects her bonus. It's only two hundred dollars, but it's hers, and there's no David in her life to snatch it away.

"Not bad," Steve says with a grin. "Wait. Did he just say websites?"

Chelsea longs for complete access to the internet. She used to think nothing of her phone and laptop and tablet, how she could look up anything she wanted, anytime she liked. She's going to use this money to get a new card and pay-as-you-go account on George's phone so she can have that power again. Right now, she'd settle for a calculator so she could run numbers on how much they must've taken in last night, although she suspects most of Harlan's financial triumph comes from subscription sales.

"Oh shit." Chelsea looks to Amy, who has her money tucked behind her phone, still scrolling, her breakfast forgotten and her jaw dropped.

"What?"

"Joy did an exposé. *Overnight.* She sold us out. On *Medium.* It clearly hasn't been fact-checked. She went on and on about how everything is fake and Harlan plays favorites, and . . ."

"And no one cares."

It's Arlene, smiling her knowing smile. "But I hope they paid Joy well, because she'll never get a dollar out of us now. And she's going to wish she'd kept her mouth shut."

The mood is still sort of off as Harlan finishes playing Santa Claus, but then Matt throws his head back and . . . howls. Like a wolf. And it would be really weird, but then Harlan joins in, and so do Arlene and Chris and Sienna and Indigo, and then everyone is howling at the dull-gray sky on a warm Florida day, clutching dirty wads of cash and maybe seeing a ray of hope for the first time in months.

After that, the dreary spell is broken, and they're laughing and chatting. Harlan goes over their schedule and tells them he'll be changing the roster for their next match. Their job today is to pack up the rest of the gear, stow it in the semi, and get on the road. Tomorrow they fight, and a week later, they're sold out at a fairground near Tallahassee.

"If things keep looking up, I'll hire a crew to pack in and out," Harlan says, flipping through his clipboard. "But until then, consider it part of your strength training."

It's a hard day, but Chelsea doesn't mind the work. She's starting to realize that despite doing a couple of free yoga classes online and reading books about how to meditate and be happier, she's pretty much been ignoring her body for years. Sure, she's washed it and dressed it and moved it around, and she feels pain and hates menstrual cramps, but most of the time it's like her head is a balloon floating a few feet above her body, this thing it's tethered to. As if because it felt like it belonged to David, she abandoned it. She hasn't done any kind of real physical work in years beyond dishes and laundry, and the exercise she did when she was barricaded in her bedroom was almost like self-punishment. But the VFR has brought new clarity, forced her to consider what it's like to inhabit her own particular body.

It's funny how her life is actually pretty uncomfortable now, but she enjoys it more.

That night, they get dinner on the road, Harlan's treat, and eat their fried chicken and biscuits scattered around the bus. It's nice, curling up in her bunk, fed and tired, as the motor purrs and the bus gently sways. She's never really been able to nap, but she almost does, dozing comfortably to the hum of voices and Arlene's softly playing classical music. When they finally stop, it's not too late, and everyone who's still awake totters off the bus to see their new digs. It's another fairground, another baked parking lot and dried brown fields, some ancient wooden stands off to one side suggesting a weekly flea market. Nothing special, but not much in Central Florida is. She asks to stop by a store to pick up the phone card and other necessities, but Arlene says she can't make that happen for a few days, which is annoying but part of life in a collective.

Their bus is parked in the usual square with the guys' bus and the RVs, forming a sort of courtyard. The night outside is utterly silent and empty aside from the backdrop of frogs and bugs buzzing and humming. The stars are out and bright, the moon a clear sliver. They left the clouds behind in Deland, apparently. Chelsea has spent most of her life in Tampa, and it's odd to learn that things just smell different in other places, even if they look pretty much the same and are only a few hours away. The cities where they've vacationed have never been the sort of places where she's stood outside in the middle of the night surrounded by nothing. Vast, empty silences don't do well for men like David, when they're forced to spend time with the people they hold under their thumbs.

Harlan shows up carrying a cooler the size of a hippo, which he sets down with the wet rattle of drinks and ice.

"Don't go too crazy," he warns them with his trademark grin. "Just a little crazy. You go on tomorrow whether you're hungover or not, and those spotlights ain't kind." He raises his own beer, salutes them, and drinks.

Matt's the first one in the cooler, and everyone else lines up. Chelsea and Amy hang back, but Steve brings them each two of the little wine bottles they like. Steve and Amy will fight tomorrow, while Chelsea is going up against TJ. He's going to win, but that's fine. No one can win faked matches all the time, and he's bigger, stronger, and far more lethal than her in every sense. Fighting Steve, she didn't feel like they were even fighting—it was more like improv, and it was viciously fun.

"Have you guys been following the VFR online?" Steve asks.

Chelsea feels like an idiot as she shakes her head. "No phone."

Steve grimaces. "Sorry. I forgot. Want to borrow mine? I cleared all the porn off the browser."

Her fake grimace matches his. "Do I need to sanitize it first, then?" But when he holds it out, she takes it—the newest iPhone. Of course.

"If you go to VFR.com, you can read your bio and click through to your fan club page."

Chelsea's head whips around. "My what?"

He takes the phone, pokes at it, and hands it back as Amy murmurs, "Holy crap. That's new."

There's an actual webpage devoted to Chelsea—www.Florida WomanPosse.com. She's not super fond of how close *posse* is to *pussy*, but no one asked her. There's one of the promo shots TJ took in front of a screen covered with the VFR logo—and it's not one of the pretty ones. She's screaming into the camera, red lips stretched out, blue eyes wide, hair all over the place, holding a two-by-four spiked with nails, very Harley Quinn. It's got her stats, her motto, her backstory—found trying to ride an alligator bare-ass naked through the Disney World gates with a shotgun strapped to her back. There's even a T-shirt with her on it, listed as sold out.

"Holy crap is right. What's yours?"

Leaning in, Steve backs up to the previous page and clicks on his own pic, which is far more urbane and cool. He straight-up looks like an asshole stockbroker. His webpage is www.ClubNissen.com, as his fans are less a posse and more of a country club. Chelsea briefly considers that her mom would adore Steve's wrestling persona, probably ask Chelsea why she didn't marry a guy like that.

"Harlan's been *busy*," Amy breathes.

"Indigo and TJ helped," Harlan says from where he's leaning up against the corner of the RV, smoking a cigar and drinking his beer. Well, his third beer, as there are two crushed cans on the ground at his feet.

Chelsea looks back at Steve's phone and gulps down the rest of her wine and gathers up her guts. She's got to admit that Harlan intimidates her, but she's pretty freaked out, and she's determined not to let things go like she used to or pretend there's nothing wrong when something is indeed very wrong. She's determined to never carry that burden again. She walks around the corner of the RV to where Harlan stands and looks up at him, her arms crossed. She has to look up, and up, and up. The RV's shadow casts him in shades of black, a bare bit of light hitting the wet of his eyes and throwing back the red end of his cigar.

"Harlan, I'm so grateful for . . ." She throws her hands around, tongue-tied. "All this. But I guess I didn't know that the VFR would be such a big deal. The webpage . . ."

He smiles, starlight on square white teeth. "Chelsea, honey, if I told you how many hits and subscriptions and orders we're getting right now, it would blow your mind. It's really happening." He looks up at the sky and blows three smoke rings. "It really is."

"But you took us on knowing that we all had . . . things in our lives . . ."

"That you were running away from," he finishes easily, more easily than she could.

"And now people will be wearing a shirt with my face on it."

Harlan stands up, looming without meaning to. When he was slouched over, he seemed human, but now he's something else entirely, so big he blots out the stars.

"They'll be wearing a shirt with Florida Woman's face on it. And you got to remember: You're not her. She's a construct, a mask. A pound of makeup, a hairdo, a costume, a bunch of glitter, an attitude. They used to put a full tub of petroleum jelly in my hair and shave my whole damn body and oil me up and put me in a little black Speedo and kneepads. I'm not Rampage. Anyone could be Rampage. I just wore his face for a while. You don't strike me as the kind of woman who could confuse the two."

Were words always this hard for her, or is it just that she finally has something to say that matters?

"I don't confuse the two at all. I know who I am." It might be a lie, but in this context, it's not. "I was running away. I came here. Maybe . . . I don't want to be found."

Harlan looks pained, and his eyes slide away. He regards the glowing end of his cigar. "It might be too late for that, then, if someone's lookin' real hard. And you did sign the paperwork and sit for the photo session. We have full rights to use your image, in any way we see fit. But here's the thing." He turns the full force of his gaze and his body to her, and he's the realest thing she's ever seen. "I employ you here. I'm your boss and your landlord and your agent, and I take responsibility for that. After last night, I'm hiring more security, and what's more, I will protect you with my life. Whether it's jumping on top of someone storming or throwing out someone who threatens you. I would never let anything happen to you."

His eyes fly wide like he's seeing something far away, and his whole face crumples up, showing wrinkles that were invisible before. He dashes away tears, and Chelsea puts a hand on his huge arm as she hears him mumble, "Not again." It's like comforting a bull—his muscles are massive, his skin warm. Maybe they shaved him down before, but now he must do it himself, because his arm is entirely smooth.

He puts his large hand over hers and bows his head, letting a few more tears drip down under cover of the shadows. He's dropped his cigar, and Chelsea stares at it, burning in the brown grass by his beer cans, wondering if she should stomp it out before it starts a fire.

"She was my everything, Chelsea," he says, so soft and quiet nobody else can hear it, ragged and raw. "She was perfect. I never had no quarrel. And then I blinked and opened my eyes, and—"

He doesn't have to go on. She knows now.

His wife, Rayna. She was a wrestler, too.

When that surfer kid brought her up on interview day, Harlan kicked him out.

Chelsea doesn't want to think too hard about what happened to Rayna. She can imagine what those big hands could do when the Violence takes over. She hopes she never has to see anything like it.

"It's okay," she says, equally low. "It's not your fault."

"I keep telling myself that, and yet I just can't quite believe it."

"I know how it feels. We all do. That's why we're here. That's why I'm here."

He blinks down at her, eyes shimmering and soft. "You are, aren't you?" he murmurs. His hand moves to cup her face, his lashes sweeping down, his head moving toward hers, his lips parting, and they're atoms away from brushing hers in a warm whisper of beer and smoke—

"No!" She jerks her head away and steps back. "I mean, Harlan, I—"

He steps back, too, eyes wide and horrified, ashamed. Then a curtain falls, his posture straightens, and the spell is broken. When he speaks again, his voice is formal, the round edges of his accent gone.

"I don't know what came over me. I'm so sorry. You'll have to excuse me."

Harlan grinds the cigar under his boot and stomps around the trailer and out of sight.

Chelsea stands there feeling . . . so many things. Too many to name.

Awkward. Guilty. Rude. Bad.

But also strong and good and brave?

Harlan Payne was going to kiss her, and she said no.

The biggest, strongest, most lethal man she's ever met, and she defied him. Kindly, but still.

This is very much going to complicate their working relationship.

"Fuck," she mutters to the starry Florida night.

43.

River grins maniacally, holding an X-Acto knife, and Ella cringes back against the padded booth.

"River, stop. That's just mean," Leanne says. She turns to Ella looking earnest. "But, um . . . are you a fainter?"

Ella is still frozen in place. "I don't know."

"Are you going to bolt?" River asks. "Or, like, kick me?" Antibac gel glistens over the red slashes Ella left on the side of their face.

"You get how this is scary, right? Literally everything about today?"

River stops and thinks—it's rare to see someone actually think about something.

"Okay. You're right. I guess it's like when the dentist puts out all the freaky tools and then doesn't tell you their functions." They put down the knife. "I'm going to make a tiny cut on the inside of your forearm, a place that will heal quickly and not hurt too much. Leanne will capture the blood on a petri dish, where we'll grow the culture to get more organisms. But what you'll see me do is clean a big patch of skin off with rubbing alcohol, make a tiny cut, let Leanne get a few smears, clean the cut, and apply a bandage. No big deal. I've lived through it a couple of times."

"Really?"

River's brow draws down. "Yeah. I was a pretty good source of

Violence-rich blood, but then I attacked Leanne one night and she barely stopped me, so . . . if you've ever wondered what Frankenstein's monster felt like, I can tell you. Anyway, now we have to take volunteers before we vaccinate them. If you'd like to watch a video of how it goes, I have one."

Ella nods, and River pulls out their phone and flicks through it before turning it around to show Ella a YouTube video from a few weeks ago. A college-aged guy in a *Star Wars* shirt and skinny jeans sits at this very table, and River goes through the exact series of actions they've just described. The guy doesn't look scared or worried, though. The whole time, he's staring at River like they're a movie star, babbling incoherently as the "NeverEnding Story" duet from *Stranger Things* plays. In the end, Leanne holds up a petri dish with the blood smeared over it, and River gives the guy a cookie.

"See? No big deal."

"Do I get a cookie?"

Finally, River laughs, a big, friendly laugh. "You can have *two* cookies."

Ella holds out her arm, still freaking out a little but aware that . . . well, shit. Why not do this? If they wanted to, they could hurt her, bind her, overpower her, bleed her dry. Just like with her dad, she's stuck in their power in this tiny space, but unlike her dad, they care about her feelings and consent and are worried about her emotions. They would be sad to let her walk away, but they would do it because they're both good people.

"I'm ready."

The process is swift and professional. The scent of the alcohol takes her back to childhood trips to the pediatrician, but it's gone quickly, and River cleverly blocks her from watching as the cut happens. She feels it, a sudden hot line, but then there are two swipes and River is cleaning up the wound and putting on a bandage covered in palm trees.

"See? Not so bad," River says.

"My cookies?"

Ella hates to admit it, but she's feeling a little woozy. At least she can't smell the blood. After what happened with Uncle Chad, she's pretty sure that hot, coppery, drenching reek is going to be a problem the next time she encounters it.

Leanne, already dressed in her clean suit, whistles as she backs into her plastic room with two petri dishes, and Ella sees bright lights go on and hears machinery whir to life. River places two Oreos on a napkin in front of her like she's back in kindergarten, and she chews happily, glad to feel her stomach settle back down.

"So what's she doing back there?"

River glances back to the plastic room. "That used to be the bedroom, you know? Big, comfortable bed. But now it's her lab, and we sleep on the single bunk beds." They refocus with a sigh. "As to what she's doing, it's a little over my head. Growing a pure culture, settling it with a centrifuge she nicked from her old lab's trash closet, washing it, inactivating it using my old sous vide machine—RIP, perfect steaks!—performing literal magic, and when all that's done, she checks it a dozen times with her microscope, rubs a clean needle in it, and gives you a tattoo."

River rolls up their sleeve to show a raised scar about the size of a thumbprint on their upper arm. It does look like Nana's smallpox scar, but it's got a little bit of color, tiny dots of blue. "We add the pigment like a signature. We can't give you a fancy numbered card, but we can make your scar special."

"And then I won't have the Violence anymore?"

River shakes their head. "Nope. You might feel a little weird for a few days as your body learns to fight it off. Lots of people get a little fever and just want to hang in bed, which is totally normal. But then you can never get it again. Leanne says it's unlikely to mutate. It's not like Covid or the flu, changing all the time. If we can spread it far enough, it'll just . . . go away. That's what's so frustrating. It's a relatively easy cure, but because of capitalism and bureaucracy and outright theft, what should be free for everyone is suddenly the main weapon in class warfare."

"What do you mean?"

River looks deadly serious and like they've given this a lot of thought. "Let's say you're super rich and you don't like brown people or poor people. And then let's say a pandemic strikes Florida, the

South, Central America, Africa. And you can suddenly put a lot of those people you don't like in jail for no reason—in jail, and therefore into for-profit prisons. Or you can let them kill each other in the privacy of their own homes. You can deport people you don't like, forcibly sterilize people you don't like."

"Wait, what?"

River shakes their head. "You probably haven't done a deep dive on the prison system, but it's not pretty. It's a tool of oppression. Anyway, they could've solved this already. The cure costs almost nothing. Every lab in the country has the necessary equipment. AP kids could make this shit in high school. But instead, they sell it to the highest bidder and wipe all mention of it from the web and the news." They look directly into Ella's eyes. "All on purpose, because it serves their interests."

"Shit."

It's all Ella knows to say. She barely feels like a person right now, after all she's been through, but her mind is reeling. It's like a puzzle slowly coming together, pieces falling into place to make a familiar picture that she'd rather not see.

What they're going through? Her mom, her, her sister—much like with Covid, it didn't have to be this way.

In a different country, in different hands, Olaf would be alive, and they would all be at home . . .

Well.

Home wasn't that great, anyway.

If she could just be with her mom and Brooklyn somewhere safe, with everyone healthy, maybe that would be a better place to be. Or at least a better place to start from.

In a year, she'll be in college—or that was the plan. Probably University of Florida, since it's close and she can get a scholarship. She's been dreaming of the dorms in the way most people dream of winning the lottery, something beautiful and far away and impossible. Just the thought of a quiet night with air-conditioning is like aloe from the fridge, poured on a sunburn. She's been so busy running, so busy staying alive that she hasn't thought about that dream in weeks.

"So she was a grad student?" Ella asks, tipping her head toward the

plastic room where flashes of Leanne zip here and there like a hummingbird as she works. It's funny, how the plastic was terrifying and
nightmarish when the room was empty, but now, with Leanne in there
working, it makes sense.

"She *is* a grad student. She's officially taking a semester off. If they
find out she yoinked some of their equipment—old shit from the
closet nobody wanted—she'll probably get booted. And if they find
out what she's doing with it, they'll boot her and send her to jail. But
yeah. She read *The Hot Zone* when she was a kid and fell in love with
the idea of solving Ebola. Then she focused on malaria. It still kills
half a million people each year, most of them children." River grins
wolfishly. "That's why she's down with the Violence. She's been studying mosquito-borne illness for years. She was born for this."

"How did you two meet?"

River gets up and paces. It's not odd, though—Ella figures River is
one of those people who never stops moving.

"There's an underground matching service for people who can
make and distribute the vaccine and people with the ability to house
them and their machinery and get them around. I've been living in
this RV for years, traveling around, doing my thing. I used to foster
kittens in here and rehome them, but when I got matched up to help
Leanne, I adopted out my last babies, had the thing professionally
cleaned to get rid of the kitty stink, and helped Leanne move in."
They hold up their phone lock screen to show them holding three
super-teeny tabby kittens. "That's how my YouTube following got so
big. People love baby kitties. They love fighters."

"Fighters?"

River grins. "Every abandoned kitten is a fighter. Even when their
eyes are glued closed and they're on the verge of death, they scream
and press their claws. This is just a different kind of fight." They scroll
through some photos, frowning. "I miss the little bastards. But this is
more important for now. Not often you get to save lives and give end-
stage capitalism the finger all at once."

Plastic creaks and flaps, and Leanne appears, shedding the last of
her PPE. "Just got to let it grow for a while."

"So what do we do now?" Ella asks.

Leanne picks up a remote control and turns on an old TV Ella hadn't noticed, set into a niche near the front seats.

"It's time for my stories," she says firmly.

"Every day at two," River moans. "You'd better be glad you're done storming or she would've left us both to fight it out on the ground."

"Damn right." Leanne leans back in a recliner that resembles a minivan seat, her feet up. She looks pretty ridiculous with the imprints of goggles, mask, and surgical cap embedded in her face, but her eyes are focused and fiery, and Ella would not touch that remote for anything just now.

Ella watches for a moment before turning to River, incredulous. "*General Hospital*?"

But River is likewise entranced. "No judgment. I used to watch it with my abuela. Now shut up."

With nothing else to do, Ella tries to get into the show, but there's so much backstory that it's like listening to someone else retell their crazy dreams. Leanne is rapt, and at one point River puts a pile of cookies in her lap and backs away, only to watch Leanne methodically chew the cookies one after the other, eyes locked on the screen as she occasionally murmurs things like, "oh no," and "not again," and "that bitch!" Only when a commercial break comes on does Leanne look down at the crumbs in her lap as if she has no idea why the napkin is there at all.

"More cookies," she says, and River has them ready for her.

But Ella is more interested in the screen. The commercials are louder than the show, and a news lady looks thoroughly scandalized as the words VIOLENCE FIGHTING RING: IS IT LEGAL? flash across the screen in bright red.

"Ugh," Leanne groans. "I hate these mini-news-breaks for old people!"

But the helmet-haired woman onscreen is unaware that she's the topic of someone's disgust.

"This is our News You Can Use feature. Full story to follow tonight at six." The woman clears her throat and stacks her papers before looking directly into the camera. "Last night, the first event of the newly created Violence Fighting Ring took place in a warehouse just outside of Orlando, watched by subscribers and a small live audience. The first match featured The Raven against Mildred the Magnificent, if you can believe it, in which a young man was beaten by an elderly woman. The second match was shut down when an irate young woman named Destiny berated The Killer Cuban instead of fighting. And the third match, in which Florida Woman trounced Steve the Stockbroker, ended in a case of real-life violence—with a capital V. An audience member became afflicted, and you won't believe what Florida Woman did next. More, tonight at six."

Now it's Ella's turn to gaze into the TV, unaware of anything else in the world. Her focus is narrowed to the face on the screen, a promo shot of Florida Woman from the Violence Fighting Ring.

"Dude, you okay?" River asks. "You look like you saw a ghost."

"That's my mom," Ella says. "My mom . . . is Florida Woman."

River barks a laugh as the show goes back to *General Hospital*. "You've got to be kidding. Your mom is a pro wrestler?"

"I don't . . . she isn't . . . I mean . . . that's . . . my mom. I haven't seen her in weeks."

Leanne turns off the TV right as her show comes back on. River looks at her like she's been replaced with an alien.

"Sorry, but this is better than a soap opera," Leanne says, looking just as excited as she did when heading back to the clean room with Ella's blood. "So how do we help you find her?"

44.

The drive home from urgent care is short, and Patricia is completely exhausted. Most of the time, she manages everything in
her life with exquisite care, treats herself like a racehorse—only the
best food and medicine, plenty of rest, rejecting anything that might
drag down her mood or status. But that fragile web she's woven is falling apart. Money held it all together. Turns out it's very easy to eat
organic salads 'and do Pilates and look ten years younger than you are
when you have everything you need and quite a bit of excess, but once
worries and responsibilities begin to pile up, the safety net dissolves
and the wrinkles return with a vengeance.

The sign for what used to be her favorite fast food beckons, and
without thinking, she pulls right into the drive-thru. With Patty behind the wheel, her standards are tossed out. A cheap, hot meal that
will placate Brooklyn? Worth every penny. She has no idea what particular foods the child enjoys, but at least they still have her old order.
She spends more than she'd like to from the spare twenty in her glove
box—how the prices have gone up!—but they won't need to eat again
today. She even buys two biscuits off the all-day menu for tomorrow
morning. Once the sins start coming, they tend to pile up—that's what
her mother always said. And even if she's learning that most of what
her mother said was a lie or very misguided, she believes this much.

The more that goes wrong, the more that goes wrong.

The more she compromises, the less any of those tenets can last.

She did something illegal today. They have all her information.

She might as well enjoy a nice meal before she has to start worrying about that.

She hurries home, the scent of hot fries and oil so tempting that she eats a fistful right out of the bag. Back when she worked at the diner, she'd bring home food every night, save her lunch to bring home for Chelsea, too. The taste of fries melting on her tongue takes her back to a life of few resources and fewer pleasures, where every day was a fight and it felt like she was constantly losing ground.

It feels like that again.

First Randall, then the money, and one day soon the house and possibly her freedom.

How low the mighty have fallen.

She barks a laugh as she pulls into the garage. The thing about having nothing is that you have nothing to lose and therefore you don't really give a shit about anything. She can't imagine what she might say if Karen called about the auction now—

No, wait. She can. It would be magnificent.

There would be exquisite usage of the word *fuck* and explicit descriptions of where Karen could shove her cellophane and ribbons. Good thing they already kicked her out.

This time when she enters the house, Patricia doesn't just bustle into the kitchen with her hands full of bags and her mind elsewhere. This time, she leaves the bags in the front seat of her car and opens the door cautiously, calling, "Brooklyn?"

"Hi, Nana!" Brooklyn runs over from the couch. "I was so, so good. What did you bring me?"

Just a few weeks ago, Patricia would've considered this rude and assumptive, even for a five-year-old. Now she's just grateful the kid is conscious and not trying to take another chunk out of her leg. And, to be fair, every time she's left, she's brought back something her granddaughter wanted.

"I went to McDonald's. Do you like—"

"A Happy Meal? That's my favorite!" Brooklyn screeches. This time when she runs at Patricia, it's to throw her arms around her waist and hug her, hard. "I haven't had a Happy Meal in a million years!"

Hyperbole, Patricia thinks.

She's just a kid, Patty snaps, vicious even as an interior voice. *Let her enjoy something, for chrissakes.*

Funny that Patty's voice would favor the child when Patty herself never liked children and wouldn't have defended Chelsea in the same manner. That's one thing both sides of her can agree on, at least: Brooklyn is to be protected at all costs.

She fetches the bags from the car, then sneaks off to her bathroom for a Percocet to dull the pain, as her anesthetic has completely worn off. They eat together at the kitchen table in a bright patch of sun. It's wonderful. Patricia has had meals that cost as much as an entire year's pay at the diner, including tips. She's had wine that's older than some countries and that costs more than her car. And it was lovely, certainly. But it can't really compete with warm, oily, salty food now that she's hit bottom, so depleted and reduced.

Brooklyn eats her nuggets and plays with the little plastic doodad that came in the box and jabbers on about her television show, and, too exhausted to protest, Patricia actually . . . listens. She realizes she's never listened to her own granddaughter before, just viewed her as an interruption, an abstract annoyance to be corrected and guided. She watches Brooklyn as she chatters, notes that the little girl is wearing a plastic tiara with a corner broken off and a velvet dance costume with a spangled skirt.

"Do you like to dance?" she asks.

Brooklyn stops mid-sentence and cocks her head like a little bird. "Yes, Nana! I told you—I was watching *Vampirina,* and she was doing ballet, and she got stage fright, so I wanted to dance, too, because I'm not scared of anything, so I went to get my costume."

Motes of dust—dust? In her house? Yes, fuck it, because there's no one else to do the dusting—just that thought tells her the Percocet is kicking in—dance in the sun as she stares at this tiny, glowing, golden being as if for the first time. She wishes she could count the child's fingers and toes like she did when she was first born, inhale that sweet baby scent and pause to appreciate the preciousness unfurling. She's barely seen Brooklyn, all these years, has somehow missed out on baby laughs and rolling over and first steps and first parade and the chance to sneak a spoonful of ice cream into an open baby bird mouth and watch her face explode in understanding of how sweet the world can be. She wasn't able to appreciate all that with Chelsea—she was too busy making the money to keep them from being homeless, told herself she was doing the more important work—and now she's somehow managed to let it pass by with both of her granddaughters.

What the hell was she so busy with all that time, anyway?

All the money in the world, no reason to work, and yet when anyone asked her how she was, she proudly answered, "Busy."

Like it was a badge of honor. Like it meant something.

"Do you know how to dance?" Brooklyn asks her.

Lord, that takes her back.

"No, but I wish I did," she answers with perfect honesty.

She asked her mother for ballet lessons when she was little, after seeing ballerinas in a library book on *The Nutcracker*, and Mama told her dance was the devil's way of getting into little girls' bodies. She hasn't thought about that in years. She's always had an excuse for Randall regarding why she refused to use their yearly subscription tickets to *The Nutcracker* at the local theater, but she's never really poked around too hard under that rock to figure out why she never wanted to go.

"Come on, I'll show you!"

Brooklyn seems to talk entirely in exclamation points, as if everything that's happening is the best thing that's ever happened. It's gotten on Patricia's nerves before, but now she sees it as a boon. How lovely it must be, to walk through life like that, constantly delighted by whatever is happening. Not that the child can't be persnickety— heaven help everyone around her if she gets bored or too hungry— but what else could anyone expect from a little thing like her? Her natural state is delight.

As Patricia stands and takes the hand Brooklyn holds out to her, not flinching at the grains of salt and light stickiness of ketchup, she tries to remember Chelsea at this age. It's hard—that year was tricky. She was too old for baby classes and slightly too young for kindergarten, which meant preschool was far too expensive and nobody wanted to watch her all day and answer all her questions. They went through several daycares, but even Patricia had to acknowledge that her daughter wasn't treated well in them; something about this age almost invites abuse, as the child's constant questions and need for attention tends to infuriate adults who don't have a reason to care. Chelsea was a serious child, as if she was always thinking of something. She was an old soul in a young body, mature and quiet and responsible for her age.

Or maybe . . . she was that way for a reason. Because she had to be.

Just like Patricia as a child.

Patricia shakes that troubling thought off as Brooklyn leads her to the couch and turns on her tablet, showing some bendy vampire cartoon girl dancing about with a ghost in a tutu.

"Like this!" Brooklyn clumsily imitates the dance the girls are doing on the screen. "Come on, Nana! You can do it!"

Patricia wants to explain what's just happened to her—the wound, the trip to urgent care, the pain, the stitches. She wants to explain that Nana is hurt and had to take medicine, but . . .

Well, it doesn't hurt so much, now. That's the beauty of "the good stuff," as the young man at the urgent care called it. Patricia didn't take the damn Percocet before because she felt as if she were holding up the world, as if her awareness and anxiety might be the glue that held together her rapidly fracturing life. If she allowed herself the merest slip, the merest weakening, she might lose her grip.

But now she realizes that she's been like a fist held so long that it was frozen, ossified, held so tight that she'd forgotten how much it hurt. Yes, her leg is in less pain now. But everything else hurts less, too. Including her head and her heart. Kind of magical, really.

"Dance, Nana! You can do it!"

And Brooklyn is dancing her heart out, swaying back and forth in mismatched socks and plastic sandals.

"Oh, why not?"

Patricia follows Brooklyn's lead, although her steps are a lot smaller and more tentative. It only hurts a little, and the doctors didn't tell her to go to bed, after all—moderate movement, they said, although she didn't bring home her paperwork. It's not real ballet, and she doesn't feel sober at all, but Patricia realizes that . . . she's happy. That she is making a memory, caught in a golden moment, dancing with her granddaughter, their arms up and swaying like branches in a tree.

Did she ever have a moment like this with Chelsea? Ever?

Or did she push her daughter away, constantly on the lookout for . . . what?

Peace? Quiet?

As she sways to the music, she gently probes her own mind, an unusual process she's studiously avoided her entire life.

What was she trying to get to, all those years ago, what was on the other side of those awkward moments with her own child? It's almost as if she didn't want to get close to Chelsea . . . or to anyone.

Looking back, she was like a porcupine, covered in spines to keep everyone at a distance. And on the other side of those spines, she hid a soft underbelly, a soft everything. She was protecting herself. Trying to keep from getting hurt.

That's why Patty was such a bitch.

Because then no one could hurt her.

She was sharp, she was snappy, she was as slick and hard as Teflon.

Ever since her mama kicked her out.

She sees it now—a long chain of damaged women.

Mama used to talk about how Big Mama treated her, tried to beat the fear of God into her with the belt buckle. Mama hated Big Mama, swore she'd never beat her daughter as badly but did enough damage with her words and switches. And then Mama kicked Patricia out, and Patricia hated her own mother. And then Patricia told herself she did the best she could as a mother, but it's fairly safe to say now that Chelsea hates her.

And Ella? Who knows who she hates? She's gone, run away at seventeen.

Even earlier than Patty and Chelsea left.

And then there's Brooklyn.

This sweet, pure little soul who still has a smile. Abandoned by her mother and sister, father long gone and probably as cruel as Patricia always assumed him to be. This child left alone with a grandmother she barely knows and infected with a horrible disease, trapped inside a house with someone who doesn't have the time of day for her, and still, here she is, dancing.

"You are a very special little girl, you know," Patricia says.

Brooklyn doesn't stop dancing. "I know!"

It's stunning—as in, it actually stuns her—to see a woman openly speak that way about herself, even a young one. In Patricia's experience, few women can honestly say they're special, and the ones that do claim it know they'll be universally hated for it. A woman is supposed to blush or look away, deflect the compliment or pay it back, not just own it.

She blinks, tears in her eyes, as she realizes that out of all of them, Brooklyn might make it to adulthood in one piece, not weighed down by the bullshit trauma they've been passing along hand-to-hand like a coveted recipe that always omits some important ingredient out of spite.

The song ends, and Brooklyn throws herself back on the couch as if she's just run a marathon.

"That was fun!"

"It was," Patricia agrees, meaning it. As soon as she stops dancing, she, too, is overcome by exhaustion. Despite the glories of narcotics, she can feel her wound pulsing against the new stitches. Perhaps it's time to stop dancing, after all.

"Will you paint my toenails?" Brooklyn asks her.

"Only if you paint mine," Patricia says without really thinking but pleased to have said it nonetheless.

In her bathroom, she directs Brooklyn to pull out her nail caddy. It's rather sparse, as she has a standing weekly appointment at the salon and this is just for emergencies and touch-ups. There are various shades of nude, petal pink, and a bright fuchsia she bought for their last trip to Hawaii, and of course that's what Brooklyn picks. With a dreamy sort of gentleness, she teaches Brooklyn the steps of a proper pedicure, although they're not going to soak their feet. Brooklyn listens and asks questions and giggles as Patricia paints her tiny little toenails and reminds her she has to hold still until they're dry. But when it's time to do Patricia's feet, she finds that she can't get them into position without causing herself immense pain.

"Nana, what happened?" Brooklyn asks, gesturing to the bandages that she's only just noticed.

"I got hurt," Patricia tells her. "But I'll be okay. Maybe you can paint my fingernails instead."

Brooklyn takes her hand and turns it this way and that. Patricia can only see the way her veins rebelliously wiggle over her bones these days, just another flaw that can't be fixed with the money she no longer has. "But your nails are so fancy already."

Patricia smiles and wiggles her fingers. She's wrong, of course; the French manicure is overgrown and badly chipped.

"I'm sure you'll make them quite fancy indeed."

After her nails are sloppily but exuberantly painted the terrible fuchsia, Brooklyn wants to watch some show about tiny, colorful horses. Patricia fixes herself a cup of tea while Brooklyn hunts through the TV's onscreen guide to find it. They settle in on the couch, and the child just naturally fits herself against Patricia's side, and Patricia just naturally puts an arm around her. This change in her—all these deep thoughts and kind instincts—she's not sure whether it's the shock, the exhaustion, the oxycodone, or the fact that when Patty broke out back at the urgent care, she left the door wide open for all sorts of thoughts and feelings that Patricia has kept bottled up for years. But she doesn't mind it. Which, again, is probably thanks to the oxycodone.

It's just so pleasant not to hurt for a little while. It makes her . . . nicer.

Even though everything is wrong, it's actually not that bad.

"Mommy!" Brooklyn shouts.

"I'm Nana," Patricia says absentmindedly as she sips her tea. "Mommy will be back soon."

"No, Nana. That's Mommy."

Patricia perks up, glances around the house, wondering what she's missed. "What's Mommy?"

Brooklyn bounces on the couch, jarring Patricia's leg with her excitement. If she was all exclamation points before, now she's multiple exclamation points.

"Mommy is on TV!"

Patricia looks at the television, trying to understand what Brooklyn is talking about. There's a commercial for some sort of odd new pro wrestling, but instead of large men with greasy hair, there are all sorts of people cavorting across the screen in a brightly lit ring. One man looks like a ghost, a handsome one looks like a banker—*if Chelsea was smart, she would've married a man like that,* Patricia can't stop herself from thinking—another woman looks like a hula girl.

And then there's a close-up of a blond woman screaming, her blue eyes lined in black and piercing, and Patricia feels as if someone has grabbed her heart and squeezed it out of a fist like those tomatoes Rosa used to put in her famous spaghetti sauce.

The woman on the screen—Florida Woman, by name—looks an awful lot like Chelsea.

"I don't think that's your mother," Patricia says, rubbing Brooklyn's shoulder as consolation.

"Yes it is," Brooklyn says, no exclamation points, completely adamant and certain as only a child can be, her hands in fists and her little brow drawn stubbornly down. The scar on her forehead shines like a pink star.

"Your mother doesn't know how to wrestle," Patricia gently reminds her. "And I don't think she's the sort who would want to be in the spotlight."

A memory brushes up against Patricia's certainty, though—Chelsea in some strange costume with a half mask and tuxedo, Chelsea telling her about a play she can't attend because she's on the schedule to work at the diner, Chelsea asking to borrow pantyhose for a choir event because all hers had runs in them—and Patricia turning her down, stating that if she won't take care of her own things, she can't be expected to care about someone else's.

"That's. My. Mommy."

Brooklyn says it like a bull about to charge, like a bomb about to blow. Patricia doesn't think the Violence can be triggered by actual rage, but she doesn't really know.

"I guess you're right, then," she says.

"We have to go find her. This is why she didn't come get me."

Patricia doesn't have the heart to tell her—well, everything. How a simple request and too much pride has landed everyone out of reach.

How she wishes she hadn't turned Chelsea away, hadn't struck her name from the list at the neighborhood gate. She'd wanted to teach her daughter a lesson, a little humility. Instead, she drove her away and . . . to this.

When Brooklyn is safely asleep on the couch, Patricia limps to her laptop and does several searches.

She learns that yes, scientists do believe that emotions, especially rage, can play into sparking Violence storms. And Brooklyn is right—her daughter has gotten herself oddly wrapped up in some big, dangerous TV stunt.

Patricia stares at the shiny images of Florida Woman, screaming her rage at the camera.

That's how Patty used to feel inside, too.

It's like looking in a mirror that shows what's really there.

Good for her, Patricia thinks. *Good for her.*

45.

David may be out of jail, clean and well dressed with a good hair-cut again, but his entire life is still a goddamn mess. He thought he would come home to find his wife desperate and scared and suffering, ready to get back in his good graces, but the house is empty. He has no idea where his family is, he hasn't heard from Huntley in days, and he's fucking furious.

The tracker on Ella's car is still pinging in the same garage, but he's driven by that house multiple times and even got out to bang on the door and peek in the curtains, to no avail. It's locked up tight and doesn't seem lived in at all. When he called the police to file a missing persons report on his daughter, he went into an endless phone chain system in which a cheerful woman repeatedly told him he would receive help but he never did. He still can't get into Patricia's neighborhood despite approaching various guards with threats, promises, and bribes.

And Huntley needs to fucking call him back.

He feels like an idiot, sitting around with nothing to do.

Well, except go to work, because you can't make money without money. All the other guys at the office already have their vaccines, and David tells them he has his, too, and never wears a shirt that would allow that part of his arm to show. Brian said he would set it up, but then again, Brian said his recent investments were a sure bet. Even with David's emergency cash and savings, he has nowhere near enough to pay for it, but he's been tested by the county twice and is staying away from mosquitoes, so he should be fine.

And even if he isn't—shit, not like anyone's doing anything about it. His wife—the murderer—is still on the loose, and literally no one cares. There hasn't even been a follow-up news story. It was just five minutes of entertainment, only interesting and different from the other thousand murders that day because of the bloody Yeti cup and the old guy covered in cow shit, and because Chelsea is a hot little blond piece instead of some methed-up guy with no teeth.

If he had more money, David would hire a private investigator to find her. And if he could get his father-in-law to answer his fucking phone, he would get into that neighborhood, or at least get answers. But Randall is just another name on a long list of people not taking his calls. David's life is just one giant shitshow right now, and it's all her fault.

At least no one is there to give him dirty looks for drinking too much, no one is there to piss him off. Even the crappy little dog is gone. No more shit on the floor, no more piss on the corner of the sofa. No more crayon drawings on the fridge or waxy streaks on the table. Everything at home is finally exactly the way he likes it—quiet and clean.

And yet.

He doesn't like it.

Everything here reminds him of Chelsea.

And not of the good old days when she was fun, not of the sex.

Every time he passes the bathroom door, he has to see those marks from the baseball bat he dropped while he was being Tased. Every time he sleeps in his bedroom, he remembers that last night, Chelsea curled up in his bed with the girls, smirking before she goaded him into exploding. She did it on purpose; he can see that now. She did everything wrong just to push him over the edge.

She's smarter than he thought.

He hates that, too.

There's got to be a way to find them—all his girls.

He knows Ella is on the run, but he doesn't know if she's with Chelsea. His daughter has blocked him on her phone, and she's not in her car. Which one of them has Brooklyn? Or are they all together?

He wants to see their faces, when he finds them.

Wants to see the surprise, guilt, and fear.

Wants them to know what's coming.

They ran away from him, and they need to know that was a mistake. They belong to him.

His phone rings. It's Brian.

"Hey, man," David says. "Any news on the vaccine?"

"Forget the vaccine. You hear about Huntley?"

David puts the beer down. "What about him?"

"He's dead. I just found out."

"How?"

Brian sighs. "Looks like the Violence. He must've been after a perp, and the perp got him. They found him in some old lady's house, just beat to hell with a crystal candy dish. His patrol car was parked in the garage. There were prints all over it, but there was no match in the system."

David goes very still.

"Where? Where'd they find him?"

A pause, the keyboard clicking on the other end of the line.

"Huh. Near you. The neighborhood next to yours."

". . . you mean the neighborhood connected to mine?"

A sad chuckle. "Man, I don't know. But it's nearby. What's in the water over there? His memorial's next week. They cremated him."

"Email me the info, will you? And if you've got the address where they found him, I'd appreciate it."

Another pause. "Why?"

Even though they've been best friends for decades, Brian doesn't know David's dark side like Huntley does, so he needs a decent lie. "If it was in my neighborhood, seems like something I should know about, if we have some sort of psycho around here."

"Well, the cops would've searched the house. Whoever did it is long gone, and unless a match turns up in the system, there's no telling who did it."

"Thanks, man," David says, eager to end the call.

"See you at the memorial, brother."

As soon as he's hung up, David's already googling Huntley's name for more information. There isn't any; he's lucky Brian gets the real news. When the email lands in his inbox, it confirms what he thought: Chad died at the same place where Ella's car has been, all this time. But did Ella get him, or was it Chelsea? He knows Chelsea has the Violence; shit, everybody in the country knows that now, thanks to that news story. But does Ella have it, too, and are they even together? And if so, where's Brooklyn?

Everything about this situation is infuriating.

He hates not knowing things.

He hates not being in control.

He hates that some part of him wants to cry over Huntley. He would stomp that part to bits, if he could, grind it into nothing until it was as broken and bloody as the dead guy outside of Big Fred's Floors.

He doesn't have time for this shit.

He searches for Chelsea's name again and reads the main story as if he's going to find some new bit of information in an article that's weeks old. He nearly knows it by heart, now, but every time he reads it, it confirms what he's known all along: His wife is a stone-cold bitch, and somebody needs to find her and put her in her place.

The fact that the news story calls her Florida Woman never fails to amuse him.

His meek, joyless wife does not fit that nickname.

But as he scrolls through the story, one of the clickbait articles at the bottom catches his eye.

FLORIDA WOMAN TO FIGHT THE KILLER CUBAN IN VFR SHOW-DOWN, it says. On one side, a man in a luchador mask bares his teeth. On the other, a blonde screams, her lips blood red and her eyes thick with makeup.

David goes to click away, but something calls him back.

He stares at the image.

She's so familiar.

Florida Woman.

That's the name in the article, and now it's the name of some new wrestler, apparently.

Blood rushes out of David's head like he's about to get in a fight or fuck.

He knows her. He knows her better than anyone.

He googles "Florida Woman" and "Violence Fighting Ring," whatever the fuck that is.

He clicks on Florida Woman's page.

He finally knows how to find his wife.

PART IV

46.

After Harlan tries to kiss her, the rest of the party doesn't feel like a party at all. Chelsea keeps waiting for Arlene to sneak up, take her aside, and explain that she's being let go, that the VFR doesn't need Florida Woman anymore. Or for Harlan to come back and . . . she's not even sure. Some deep, reptile part of her brain can picture him leading her away, shoving her down, forcing her to do things— because David's apologies were always segues into allowing her to win back his favor through subjugation. Another part of her mind can imagine Harlan trying to reason her doubts away, sweet-talk her into sleeping with him—or gaslight her into believing it never happened.

She wishes she could get her hands on the paperwork she signed when she got hired and see what it says about something like this, but she never got her own copy. At the time, it didn't seem like an issue as long as there was a roof over her head, food in her belly, and the promise of enough money to live on and an eventual vaccination. Now she sees that she's always been too trusting of any authority figure that wasn't her own mother, whom she's never trusted.

No one else seems to have witnessed what occurred around the corner of the RV, or at least they're not being weird about it. The rest of her co-workers are all in fabulous moods, drinking Harlan's liquor and eating Harlan's snacks, scrolling through their splashy new pages online, grateful that the gambit is paying off. As soon as the first woman yawns and peels off for bed, Chelsea follows. With only half the bunks occupied and voices still murmuring outside, she can't sleep. She would give anything for what seemed like the most basic of technology at home—an old tablet and a Netflix account and enough Wi-Fi to watch a show, something stupid to take her mind off the seriousness of real life. She still remembers during the Covid pandemic when she and Ella binged all of *Gilmore Girls* in a couple of weeks as David kept stubbornly going into work, living his life quarantined in the spare bedroom upstairs, furious about how much the daily death toll impacted his clients' investments—and equally furious that Chelsea wouldn't get within six feet of him.

That should've been a red flag, right there. The man has no empathy, no semblance of feeling for anything beyond himself. With her current distance from him, she can't believe how much she'd been ignoring or repressing the horrible things he did, turning away with a bright smile when he didn't seem to give a shit about the girls when they were upset or refusing to tip delivery drivers during the pandemic because he was "already being price-gouged for groceries."

For hours, she lies in bed on her back, feeling her bruises and sore spots from what might possibly be her first and last match in the VFR, thinking about every goddamn thing she's done wrong.

The only thing she's proud of since her high school grades is being a mother. If David was cold or cruel, she was the flowered umbrella over their heads, protecting them from the violent storms of their father.

She was a good mother.

Is a good mother.

And the only reason she would ever leave her children would be to avoid hurting them, which is why she's here instead of somewhere else. She might not have Ella's number or her mom's, but she's going to get a phone and get in touch with them as soon as possible.

That is, if she hasn't gotten herself fired, in which case the greasy cash in her pocket is all she has in the entire world.

She falls asleep—well, how the hell would she know when? She doesn't have a working phone and she doesn't have a window in her bunk and time no longer has any meaning. But she wakes up the next morning to Arlene's alarm and rubs her eyes as she waits her turn for the tiny bathroom, stomach grumbling and mouth fuzzy from last night's wine.

What would it've been like to kiss Harlan Payne? Even if it was something she wanted, which she doesn't think it is, the scent of beer sickens her these days, and the tang of cigar is even worse. It brings back memories of David's barbecues, after his friends had all gone home drunk, their tipsy wives chauffeuring them, when David tottered into their bedroom and clumsily woke her up and bullied her into sloppy, whiny sex.

She does not want to kiss Harlan Payne. The thought doesn't give her those flutters she used to get in her tummy, back when she was just a girl.

She wonders if anything ever will again.

David once gave her those flutters, and now she has to question if her body has any goddamn sense at all.

"You went to bed early," Amy says on the way to breakfast.

"Tired." In no way a lie. "Did I miss anything?"

"Nah. Nobody drank too much—not with training going hard core. Are you excited?" Without waiting for an answer, she keeps talking. "I hate that I didn't get to go last time—it was like when you wait in line for three hours for the roller coaster and then it breaks down right before it's your turn, you know? It looks so exhilarating. Like it'll make your heart pound. Nothing ever feels that way, once you're past your twenties. Even roller coasters. Even skydiving. Everything is just . . . *Ah, so we're doing this. Okay. We did that.* Right?"

Chelsea felt that kind of exhilaration when she was giving birth, but knowing what she now knows about Amy, she's not going to bring it up.

"Pretty much," she agrees.

"Chelsea, can I borrow you for a minute?"

It's Arlene, her eyes big and apologetic, her hand on Chelsea's arm.

This isn't a flutter or a pounding heart—this is a feeling that definitely doesn't go away with adulthood. A sinking, dark, thick feeling, a stone in her stomach.

Something bad is going to happen, and nothing can stop it.

Chelsea knows this feeling intimately.

She pastes on a fake smile that doesn't reach her eyes and says, "Sure."

Arlene nods and leads her away, toward Harlan's RV. Chelsea jerks back a little, tripping over her feet, but Arlene's hand is there to steady her. Arlene isn't going to leave her alone with Harlan, is she? Chelsea's heart is definitely stuttering now as they near what is by far the nicest of the RVs. This one doesn't have an awning and tarp and grill outside. This one is for the big boss alone, and to her knowledge, no one outside of Harlan and his lieutenants, Chris and Arlene and maybe Sienna, has been in there.

"I'm going in with you," Arlene says as if reading her mind, firm and warm as always. "I'll go in first."

With a smile and a pat on the arm, Arlene knocks on the RV door, and when Harlan calls, "Come in!," she steps in first. Chelsea follows, although what she really wants is to turn and run away. She isn't sure where she would even go, but she has always felt this instinct around David and has never been able to follow her body's yearning. This time she forces herself to keep walking. Not because she's afraid of Harlan or wants to please him personally, but because she sees now that the VFR is real, that it's going to be wildly successful, and she wants to stay a part of it and grow along with it. If Harlan pays them in kind, doing this will get her vaccinated and back with her daughters much faster than delivering pizza will.

Inside, the RV is outrageously sumptuous. It reminds her of pictures of the Rock on a private jet. Creamy leather, gleaming wood, shining metal. Harlan sits at a booth-style table wearing his usual costume, his scarf a quiet gray. He's sitting up straight, his face neutral. It's odd, seeing someone so vibrant and alive trying to mute himself.

Arlene scoots into the booth across from him and pats the leather seat beside her. Chelsea slides in, too, noting the neat stack of stapled paper in front of her seat, along with a silver pen—no plastic bank pen here.

"I'll be acting as arbiter," Arlene says, sounding like she's in court. "Chelsea, have you read the agreement you signed when you accepted employment with the VFR?"

Heat floods her cheeks and she looks down. "No. I was . . . pretty desperate."

Arlene exhales through her nose. "See? I told you. They must receive their own copy, or it isn't fair." She says this to Harlan in a scolding voice, but now she turns to Chelsea, her voice softer. "Well, here is a copy for you now. You can read it yourself, but please allow me to condense the part that's important today. Is it correct that Harlan here made a pass at you last night?"

Chelsea looks at the table, glances at the paper, fiddles with the cool silver pen. She does not want to lose this job, but she also doesn't want to lie or lose any protections the papers in front of her might offer.

"Kind of."

Arlene nods. "That's what he told me."

"It wasn't . . . aggressive, or predatory, or . . ." Chelsea struggles for the word. "Indecent? It just seemed like an honest mistake. We were talking about an emotional subject."

Across the table, Harlan holds himself so carefully, his lips pinned shut. It's a revelation to Chelsea, as she would expect a man in his place to talk over her, to offer excuses, to say she was asking for it, to write it off as a joke. That's what David and his friends would do, and they're the only men Chelsea has been around in almost twenty years.

"That doesn't make it okay," Arlene says gently. "So I need to ask you. Do you wish to continue employment with the VFR? I can tell you now that we would very much like you to stay with us, and that you will not be put in this position again."

Chelsea looks up then, in surprise. Harlan looks sorry, like a little boy who accidentally hit a baseball through a window. Arlene looks like the teacher who caught him doing it but knows he didn't mean any harm. And that would normally leave Chelsea feeling like the window, but this time . . . she feels more like the person who owns the window.

"I'd like to stay on," she says softly. "If it won't be weird. Am I in trouble?"

Arlene turns to her swiftly, puts a hand on her wrist. "Honey, no. Of course not. You did absolutely nothing wrong. You did a fine job in your first match, and your quick thinking and courage in helping that poor woman who was storming saved lives on the floor and brought us a great deal of positive publicity. Make no mistake: We want you here."

Even though it takes every ounce of self-control she has, Chelsea forces herself to look at Harlan, right in the eyes. "You're not mad?"

Harlan huffs a chuckle. "Ms. Martin, you're the one who should be mad. What I did was very much against workplace ethics."

"I'm confused. I thought we operated outside the law?"

"There's us dealing with the government and their post-Covid rules, and then there's us acting as an employer of a growing number of people, who may or may not be listed as contractors instead of with their real titles. Point being, you'll get a 1099 and pay your taxes, even if some of the numbers are fudged." Harlan's big finger points at the papers in front of Chelsea. "This protects the VFR, but it also protects you. After seeing what Rayna went through working her way up to the ring, I swore I'd never let a woman be preyed upon in any business I was tied up in. Even if I was the one causing the problem. So we're going to make this right."

Arlene puts up a hand. "Let me handle this part, please, before Mr. Big Heart owes you an RV of your own. How would you like to move forward?"

Chelsea sucks in a breath. "What do you mean?"

"What are your demands?" Harlan asks.

Arlene warningly aims a finger at his face and he moves back from it as if she has superpowers.

"The paperwork you've signed promises a safe working environment. If this were a different kind of business, you could go talk to HR, file a complaint, possibly take us to court."

Because a man who could have nearly any woman he wanted tried to kiss me? Chelsea thinks but definitely does not say.

"But since we're here and I'm basically the HR department, we'd like to know how we can make your working environment more agreeable." Arlene's eyebrows rise, and a small smile plays around her mouth. "Within reason."

"I need a phone and phone service," Chelsea says first, because that's the thing she thinks about constantly. "Today. It doesn't have to be fancy, but I need phone, texting, email. And I'd love to be able to watch a show at night on a tablet or something."

"Okay," Arlene says, nodding. "A work-issued phone seems very reasonable for an upcoming star of the VFR. Anything else?"

Chelsea's mind is going a mile a minute, weighing the various benefits and drawbacks of asking too much, asking too little, and considering how awkward it would be, seeing Harlan every day. Judging by this RV and his previous career and the capital it must take to get the VFR up and running, he's a very wealthy man—or maybe he has great investors. Still, she likes this job, and she doesn't want any bad blood.

Really, there's only one thing she really, truly needs more than anything else.

"I want the vaccine. Soon. And to be able to support my girls. If we do well enough one day, I'd like to bring them along with us, if this is a long-term thing, but the main reason I said yes to this job was because I can't be around my daughters until I'm safe."

"We're working on it—" Arlene starts.

"I don't have the cash yet," Harlan admits, deadly serious, which is a relief as she was worried he'd laugh at her. "I have investors I have to pay back. The last year has drained me, and I can't sell my dumb Miami mansion in this market, and . . . well, I flat out don't have the money. But I have feelers out, and I assure you that the very first thing on my list when the VFR hits even bigger is not a new truck or a private jet for myself. It's to vaccinate every one of our fighters as thanks for taking this chance on me and my dream, just like I promised from the beginning."

"Then I want better security. And a raise," Chelsea says, amazed at her own audacity and at the firm command of her voice. Over the past few years, it began to feel as if all her sentences ended on question marks, because it's easier to take back a question than a statement with a man like David.

Harlan holds in a laugh. "I've got two security guys for the talent starting this week with more to come. But honey, you don't even have a salary yet."

Chelsea shrugs, playing it cool. "So give me a salary, and then raise it. And then take me back to Target so I can buy some more clothes. And, you know, access to more than one washer and dryer per twelve people would be nice."

Harlan can't help himself; he throws back his head and laughs. "Hot damn, Florida Woman. That's some moxie right there! Arlene, does that sound reasonable to you?"

Arlene cocks her head, her eyes probing. "It's not about how I feel. It's about how Chelsea feels. You can still sue, if you like . . ."

"But the courts are a madhouse right now," Chelsea finishes for her. "My stepfather is a judge. And . . ." She doesn't want to minimize what happened, now that it's borne ripe fruit, but she's also not going to set herself up as a diva, as someone who's more trouble than they're worth. "I didn't take offense. I'm just glad I still have a job. No harm done."

Harlan stands—or tries to. The booth is awfully small for such a large man. He scoots out, hunched over, and then stands, his head nearly brushing the ceiling. He smiles at Chelsea, and she realizes her audience is over. She slides out and stands, then makes room for Arlene, who moves behind her. When Harlan holds out his hand, she takes it and shakes, feeling like a child shaking the hand of a bear.

He's a good man, she realizes. And not because anyone is watching. He just is.

"On behalf of the VFR, thanks for all that you do," he says.

"It's a tough job, but somebody has to do it," she responds drily, making him laugh again.

"I'm surrounded by crazy people," Arlene says.

"I'm so glad I met you in rehab, Arl."

Arlene playfully swats his arm. "That's confidential!"

"Only for you. Me? I can say whatever I want." Harlan bobs his head at Chelsea. "Sorry I got to let TJ kick your ass tomorrow."

"All in a day's work."

And it could go on like that, awkward ripostes ad nauseam, but Arlene says, "C'mon, let's get you back to breakfast," and then Chelsea is waving goodbye and stepping down from the cool breath of luxury and back onto the heat-cracked Florida parking lot and thick summer air.

"You did good," Arlene says as they walk back to the breakfast trailer.

"That was the weirdest thing that's ever happened to me in my life," Chelsea admits, glad to have her original assumption about Arlene's skills as a therapist confirmed. "Did that just happen?"

"It did, but you should've asked for your own car. When he feels bad, he'll do just about anything to please the people he likes."

Chelsea can't help grinning. She thought she was going to get fired for turning her boss down, and instead, she got most of what she needed.

Apparently standing up for yourself and asking for what you want actually works when the other party's not a narcissistic asshole.

47.

The world moves in slow motion as River pulls out their laptop and shows Ella the webpage for the Violence Fighting Ring. They click on the lurid image of Florida Woman, and Ella recognizes the mother she's known all her life despite the over-the-top makeup and costume. The location of the next VFR match is several hours away, which means Ella's mom is several hours away, but it feels impossibly far. Can her mom really have been that close all this time, while she's been running and fighting and starving and trying so hard to make it on her own? Has her mom really just created a new life for herself while Ella's been slowly losing herself in someone else's abandoned home, malnourished, terrified, alone? It can't be possible. In her imagination, her mother was across the country, across the planet, maybe on Mars.

So much has happened. Ella is a different person now. Washing blood off your hands will do that.

But then again, her mother is probably a different person now, too. She killed Olaf. She killed Jeanie. Maybe she killed someone else.

It doesn't matter. She's still Mom.

"When can we leave?" Ella asks.

River and Leanne exchange a troubled look.

"We can't," Leanne says softly. "We're on a schedule. People are signed up to donate, to get vaccinated. Most important, at each stop we have a rendezvous with someone with lab equipment who can spread the cure themselves. We're meeting a doctor in Zephyrhills tomorrow."

"So we can drive over now, and—"

River shakes their head. "Nope. We don't take chances. A six-hour round-trip journey on the highway means we could pop a tire or get in an accident or get pulled over and arrested. Having a lab in the back of your camper doesn't generally look too good, especially when half the equipment is stolen."

Ella looks to Leanne, tearing up and shaking. "Please. You guys could give her the vaccine. She's already got the Violence. I watched her kill the dog. Please."

Leanne leans forward in her chair, eyes brimming with sympathy. "You don't need us to give her the vaccine. It's easy. We'll give you a vial and a needle, and you can vaccinate her yourself. And a few people more, besides. And I'll print a copy of the vaccine instructions so if you find anyone with the right background, they can spread it, too."

Ella glances around the RV. It's funny—a few hours ago, she was so anxious to not be in here that she accepted the fact that she'd rather kill someone than get herded up the steps. And now she doesn't want to leave it. It's like home—a small, portable home where no one is cruel to her—and she likes Leanne and River, likes their easy energy, likes knowing that there are still people in the world who will heat her soup for her and put a folded napkin beside it.

She assumed she would go back to Mr. Reese's oven of a house after this, but ever since she woke up on the RV floor and understood what was really going on, she's nursed this tiny, sweet vision of traveling with Leanne and River, helping people, knowing that if something bad happened to her, someone would care. And they do care. But they care about a lot of things, and people are counting on them. They've made commitments, and what they're doing is, in the long run, a thousand times more important than what Ella is doing.

But to her, there's nothing more important than being reunited with her mom and getting Brooklyn back.

"Maybe you could postpone it a day?" Even as she says it, she hears the whiny little baby in her voice.

Leanne shakes her head again. "We can't. But look: It's going to be okay. Okay? We'll give you the vaccine, you've got your groceries, you've got a working car. You leave here and you'll see your mom in just a few hours. No big deal, right?"

Ella takes a shuddering breath, tries to connect with the ground under her feet. There are probably alternate universes where it's no big deal, where she could just hop in her car and drive three hours as part of a fun road trip on spring break with her girlfriends.

But she doesn't have girlfriends anymore, and there is no spring break when all the beaches are closed because people keep bludgeoning one another to death with umbrellas.

In this world, she's never driven that far. She's never driven more than thirty minutes away from the house, really. Doing it all alone, on new, big highways, not knowing how she's going to get to her mom when the show is sold out and everyone will probably be trying to get in? It's crazy. If she had just one person with her, she would feel better.

"Maybe one of you could come?"

Oddly, it's River who puts a hand on her shoulder. "Look, kid. I know it's scary out there when you're alone. My parents kicked me out at seventeen. Didn't even wait until it was legal. Just dumped all my shit on the driveway in cardboard boxes. And I was terrified, right? But I found people. Made connections. When you go out in the world with a pure heart, the right things happen."

"Eh," Leanne interjects. "I think that's kinda crap? I mean, what your parents did was one hundred percent bullshit, and Florida is known for its child trafficking problems. But I think it takes more than a pure heart to find your place. This isn't a videogame, with a carefully planned character arc. It takes actual determination. And tenacity. That's what got us both through." She meets Ella's eyes. "And you've got determination and tenacity already. And you know where you're going and why. That's more than most people know. You just have to keep going for a little while longer."

"I've been telling myself that for weeks," Ella says, although it's actually been years. Living with her dad was a different kind of fight.

"So maybe you just have to keep going for another day," River says.

Ella stands up. They've said no. To everything.

She has to do this alone.

"Okay, then."

"I mean, you can sit down and hang out a while," Leanne says with a smile. "The fight is tomorrow night, right? So watch some TV. We can get some fast food or something."

"Pizza," River adds, not looking up from their phone.

"Pizza," Ella repeats dreamily. She hasn't had pizza in forever. You can't have pizza delivered when you're squatting in someone's supposedly empty house.

"Pizza it is. And you can shower and then sleep in my bunk if you want. This chair reclines, and I sleep here a bunch anyway."

So that's how it goes. They turn on Leanne's soap opera, which is over, but now a new one is coming on that's just as bonkers. Leanne goes back to work on her vaccine every now and then, River spends most of their time on the laptop, and Ella charges her phone and dreams about pizza. It's funny, how she's only known Leanne and River for hours, but she's clinging to them like a life raft.

Because they've been nice to her. It's been so long since anyone was nice.

As afternoon turns to evening, the new drugstore security guard shows up for the night shift and walks around the RV and car, peering suspiciously into Ella's windows. They get the hint and drive to the Walmart parking lot, which conveniently has a Little Caesars pizza in an adjoining strip mall. Soon they're watching awful sitcom reruns and stuffing themselves and laughing, and Ella is happier than she's been in forever.

No one wants anything from her. No one expects her to babysit. No one is mad at her. No one actively dislikes her. No one is primed to explode like a hidden land mine.

Is this what it's like in normal families?

Probably not.

There probably aren't any normal families, just families fucked up in different ways.

She gets her bag out of her car and takes a much-needed shower and changes into borrowed pajamas and washes her face and brushes her teeth and stands in front of Leanne's lower bunk, unsure about occupying such a personal space. River is sitting in the corner of their upper bunk with headphones, brow furrowed as they work, and Leanne is in the lab, doing something she explained but that Ella didn't understand about purifying samples.

"Go on," River says when they finally notice her hunching there. "It's just a bed."

It's not the most comfortable bed she's ever slept in, but there's airflow and the sheets smell like flowers and even though her body feels like it's permanently tensed, she focuses on relaxing. She's been so alert for so long that she's not sure how to be anything else. Ever since leaving home, she's been staying up all night, walking the tightrope of anxiety, before falling asleep after midnight and sleeping in until noon. She doesn't know how to sleep like a normal person anymore. At least Leanne has a huge stack of gossip magazines, which are just the right sort of nonsense but addictive enough to keep her turning pages.

"Can't sleep?" Leanne asks some time later.

"It's always hard," Ella admits.

"That's what she said," River murmurs from somewhere overhead, and they all dissolve in laughter, remembering the episodes of *The Office* they watched earlier.

Leanne digs around in the bathroom and holds out a bottle. "Melatonin. They taste like candy. They'll help you sleep."

She pours a gummy into Ella's hand, and Ella stares at it. "My mom says kids shouldn't use chemicals to sleep."

Leanne's mouth twitches. "Is she a doctor? A scientist? Hell, is she here? Nope. I'm two of those things, and I'm telling you that it's perfectly acceptable to take a melatonin when you can't sleep, you're an absolute mess, and you're going to wake up and drive three hours to do something scary. You shouldn't deny yourself sanity when it's within reach. I've been taking it since I was ten. And I medicate for my ADHD. And I'm fine. So there."

Ella considers it for the briefest moment before eating it. If she was anywhere near functional, she would've googled "sleep remedies" back when she stopped sleeping, but the thing about living with constant anxiety is that you can't break free of the loop to look deeper or even separate what's wrong from what you're worried might be wrong. If she'd typed "sleep remedies" into the search bar on her phone yesterday, she would've landed on WebMD and decided she was currently dying of four different diseases including cancer and lupus.

She doesn't fall asleep immediately, but she does fall asleep, and that's all that matters.

In the morning, she wakes up groggy, and for a moment she can't tell where she is. The light is strange, and someone is moving around, crunching plastic and jostling silverware.

Ah. Yes. The RV. Leanne and River.

They eat breakfast together like it's totally normal. River offers Ella three different kinds of cereal and two different kinds of milk. Leanne is pleased with whatever's going on in her lab; the vaccine is going to work fine. Sometimes, apparently, it doesn't. Ella is glad she didn't know that part; one more thing to worry about. It should be ready in a few hours—the small dose they're making just for her.

While they wait, they go into Walmart, where Ella helps River record a vlog in which they set up giant girl dolls and then aim to knock them down like bowling pins, except instead of a bowling ball, it's River riding a child's tricycle. It makes a big noise and mess, and then they hide and struggle not to laugh. Ella is scared, a little, but River explains that it's not actually illegal, and no one can really do anything, and even if they did they would go after River because Ella fits their heteronormative assumptions. Which doesn't really make Ella feel any better, but by then they're across the store picking up fried chicken for lunch. River pays for everything, and Ella thanks them, and they shrug and say, "Bless my patron saints, ad revenue and Patreon."

As Ella finishes her lunch, she starts to look around and notice little things. The way Leanne won't eat her chicken off the bone but has to scrape off all the meat with silverware first. The tiny tattoo River has of a stylized frog on their middle finger. The way the light shines in through the little kitchen window and almost makes it seem like a real kitchen instead of a really big van. There's a hollow feeling in her chest, knowing she has to leave this comfort and strike out on her own into the unknown. She has a bad feeling about what's to come, but she doesn't know how to put it into words in a way that wouldn't make her seem like a big, superstitious baby.

Finally, she can't pick over her lunch anymore, and her drink is down to ice. When was the last time she had ice? She dumps her trash in the garbage and briefly wonders where the garbage in the RV goes, and as she's standing there, staring into the trash can, River says, "It's going to be okay. You know that, right?"

"It really is," Leanne adds. "It's bound to be better than where you've been."

Ella's throat locks up. She doesn't want to cry again. Even if the whole reason she's here is because she started crying in a drugstore and these two people, out of all the people in the whole world, stopped to give a shit.

"I know," she says, a choked whisper.

"You're going to have a nice drive—make sure you've got a good playlist lined up or a podcast or audiobook or whatever—and you're going to drive right into that fairground parking lot and find your mom, and everything is going to be okay." River pulls their wallet out of their back pocket and puts a twenty on the table. "That's for parking and incidentals."

Tears well up in Ella's eyes as she takes it. "Why are you guys being so nice to me?"

They exchange a wry glance, but it's Leanne who answers.

"Because we were both lost and fucked up when we were your age, and if just one person had reached out, it would've meant the world."

"And we weren't even going through a pandemic decade," River adds. "Life was borderline normal then."

"You shouldn't have to be out on your own."

"But—" Ella starts.

River jumps in. "Okay, have you ever seen, like, a really cute dog just walking down the road, and it's got a nice collar and is well cared for, and you know that it's not an abandoned dog, you know somebody really cares about it and is missing it, and you just want to catch the dog and call the number on the collar?"

Ella sniffle-laughs. "I'm that dog, huh?"

"You're that dog," they confirm.

"Woof woof."

Ella barking breaks up the tension, and they all laugh, and then things move way too quickly. They have her sit down in the recliner while Leanne vaccinates her, narrating the entire process so that she can repeat the process. It's actually kind of anticlimactic, after everything else. Such a small, simple procedure, and soon, she won't have to worry about accidentally killing anyone. River puts a bandage over the tender spot and gives Ella two more Oreos, and then they're hugging her goodbye outside her car. Leanne hands her a big ziplock bag full of neatly organized medical supplies and papers and explains again how to administer the vaccine and reminds her to never share needles and to always take precautions and refrigerate any remaining vaccine. River gets Ella's social media handles and makes her promise to stay in touch, and then she's in her car and tuning up the podcast River recommended, and the RV pulls out of the Walmart parking lot and onto the road, headed in the opposite direction.

On her way to the highway, Ella passes Big Fred's Floors. It's a beautiful morning, and she dreads every time she has no choice but to drive past this haunted hellhole, knowing full well that in the best of times, what she saw there made her furious on behalf of women, and in the worst of times involved a corpse. Much to her surprise, the corpse is gone, and a woman in overalls is painting flat white paint over the place on the wall where the stain was. There's a work van parked by the building, and the dismantled LED sign sits beside the open rear doors. A new sign sits in front of the tiny building, the end-posts sunk into satisfying piles of sand surrounded by pots of marigolds and impatiens.

SIMPLY ELEGANT REMODELING BY GRACE, the sign reads in stark black script, refined and modern, with sketches of a kitchen sink in front of a window.

Maybe the woman with the paint roller is Grace. Ella hopes it is.

Just seeing that woman out there, painting over the bloodstain, dismantling the horrible sign, maybe turning this nasty little shed into a booming business—it brings Ella this odd lift of hope. She'd forgotten that, much like a hurricane, the pandemic would eventually run its course, that there is always a promise of sunshine at the end of all the rain. That's one nice thing about Florida—the worst thunderstorms bring the most beautiful and surprising rainbows.

She zooms away from the intersection, noticing for the first time in a very long time that she's breathing, that her body is moving, that she can take a full breath, if she focuses. Ella has never driven more than thirty minutes from home. She's never navigated a new highway by herself. And now she's following the map on her phone to a place she's never been, where she doesn't know what will happen.

Her biggest fear isn't that she won't be able to find her mother.

It's that she'll learn that her mother doesn't want to be found.

48.

I t takes a lot to wake Patricia up in general, but especially when she's had both Percocet and a sleeping pill. She's been holding herself carefully, with Brooklyn around, trying to stay alert should the child storm and need to be controlled, but tonight . . . well, she's in pain and can feel her body struggling. She locks her granddaughter in the closet and takes both pills with only a little guilt. Her sleep is a deep and echoing chasm, and then . . . there are noises—so many noises— and something reaches deep within and pulls her up out of the sticky swamp of dreamlessness, bringing a rising tide of panic with it. She bolts upright, eyes nearly glued shut, ripping the Velcro open on her elastic mask to reveal the pitch-black room around her.

"What?" she rasps. "What's wrong?"

"Mommy!" Brooklyn screams. "Mommyyyyyyyy! Help!"

It's not a call, not a shout.

It's the throat-tearing scream of terror that children are generally taught to save for kidnappings and incidences that will require an ambulance.

And it's coming from her closet.

The child isn't storming, though. In the throes of the Violence, there is only silence, not even animalistic grunts. Patricia knows that personally, now. She throws off her weighted blanket and rolls out of bed, her spine cracking audibly. The alarm clock suggests it's some time after four. She hurries to the closet, feeling her way in the dark. Her hand fumbles for the chair wedged under the doorknob, and then the door is open and Brooklyn is pressing her wet face into Patricia's stomach, the tears dampening her shirt.

"Mommy, it's the dream. I can't get away. He keeps chasing me and chasing me, and he grabs me with his big monster hands and turns me around and I can feel it, I can feel his arm around my neck and I can't breathe, and I hate the monster, but he won't let go."

It all comes out in one rush of breath that ends in a shrieking sob, and Patricia wraps her arms around her granddaughter, holding her close. She wants to sit down and drag the little thing into her lap, but her stitches are hot and pulsing and it might be time to admit that women of her age can't just topple over anytime they want to without repercussions. She can't pick Brooklyn up, either, for the same reason. Instead, she inches backward, until she bumps into the big velvet chaise in the corner. As she sits, she drags Brooklyn into her lap, and Brooklyn willingly climbs in and latches her arms around Patricia's middle, hanging on for dear life.

Her little body can't stop shuddering as she gets out all her tears, and Patricia doesn't know what to do other than rub her back and be there.

"Mommy, I want the monster to go away."

Patricia draws a breath and doesn't know what to say. Is it better, in the dark with a half-sleeping child, to remain silent and let her think her mother's much-needed arms are shielding her from the world? Or is it better to speak and remind the child that even if her mother is gone, there is still someone present who cares for her? Without the lights, Patricia can't tell if Brooklyn's eyes are open or closed, if she knows where she is and what's happening or if she's caught in that strange twilight of childhood where the mind simply accepts what it wants over what it can't see for certain.

"Will it ever go away?"

Patricia is fairly certain that the monster haunting her poor granddaughter is a he, not an it, and that it's doing everything it can to claw its way back into the child's life.

"Shh," she croons, rocking a little. "Shh."

Brooklyn goes still and pulls away, her body tense.

". . . Mommy?" she asks, suspicious and full of dread.

"It's Nana, but I'm here and you're safe. I won't ever let the monster get you."

Brooklyn shudders again but doesn't move farther away. She feels like a horse, skin twitching, muscles tight, deciding whether to run.

"Do you know how to get rid of a monster?" Patricia asks Brooklyn in a normal voice that suggests everything is exactly how it should be.

"No." Brooklyn snuggles in the tiniest bit closer, listening.

"You stop believing in it."

Brooklyn pauses, considering this statement.

"I don't think that's true, Nana. Some things . . . they don't care what you think at all."

Patricia pulls her in closer, nestles the child against her chest as she leans into the chaise. Her back is tensed up, but that's nothing new. Brooklyn allows it and arranges her legs more comfortably as if they're setting up for story time. Patricia is surprised she hasn't asked for a light, but then . . . maybe really seeing that she's not at home, that her mother and sister are gone, is worse than letting darkness mask the truth.

"In my experience, monsters feed on fear," Patricia says, idly wondering which part of her is talking, as she feels half asleep and knows Patty is close under the surface these days. "Monsters need to know that you see them and are frightened of them, that they're bigger and more important than you. If you run or cry, they like that. But if you stand up to them or—even better—don't care about them, they falter."

"What's *falter?*"

Patricia's lips purse that her granddaughter doesn't know the word before she remembers that at this age, she didn't, either.

"To falter is to hesitate and lose strength. To doubt. A monster wants to make you feel that, not feel that itself."

"But what if he . . . if he doesn't care about you at all? If he's just plain mean?"

Well, that is the question, isn't it?

A question asked by millions of women around the world and, yes, surely some men as well. What do you do when you're chained to a monster that isn't particular about what it destroys?

"Then you escape. Maybe you can't do it when you're very small; you just have to stay out of the way and learn how to be . . ." She racks her brain for a way to talk about such things that's appropriate for a five-year-old, because she remembers when Mama had man-friends over, and how she felt, then. "You have to learn to be like a bunny."

That gets Brooklyn's attention. "How? Bunnies are nice and soft."

Patricia's eyes go unfocused in the dark as she strokes the child's sweaty hair away from her face. It's funny—when Brooklyn first attacked her, she was scared of having the child so close. But now she feels certain that keeping her close is the right thing to do.

"Bunnies are nice and soft, yes. But bunnies are also clever. They can hide and blend in and be silent. They can sneak and find little hidey-holes. They can run and jump. And then, when a bunny is cornered, that's when the bunny knows the only recourse is to fight. Very fierce, are bunnies."

If Brooklyn asks her how she knows all this, she will not say that it's because she read *Watership Down* in tenth grade and was deeply affected.

"So it's okay to be small and hide?"

Patricia nods fiercely. "Oh yes. Whatever gets you to the other side is what you need to do. Because one day you'll be big, and then you can go away from the monster forever and do what you want instead of what the monster wants."

Brooklyn sighs and collapses against her chest. Patricia puts her chin atop the child's head, feels Brooklyn's tiny fingers running up and down her arm.

"I can be like a bunny," she finally says.

"I can see that."

"Did Mommy go away because she got big enough and didn't want to be near monsters anymore?"

Ah, that's a different question altogether.

Patricia knows David is the real monster, but Chelsea didn't leave because of him. She left because of Patricia. The question makes her wonder how much Chelsea has told the girls about her relationship with her own mother. Does Chelsea think her a monster? Is Chelsea's meekness, her weakness, her own version of playing the bunny so Patricia will finally stop attacking? Regret peals in Patricia's heart, a muted chime hindered by years of rust. She held Chelsea away, tried to make her daughter strong, but she's accidentally engineered a relationship in which she is the perpetual goddamn monster.

Everyone wants to be the hero—yet there always has to be a monster to fight, doesn't there?

She's the one who locked Chelsea out, who forced her to leave. When she was a young woman, she leapt into David's arms just to get away from Patricia, and now she's left because Patricia closed the gate.

And now Chelsea is fighting on television, taking on a crazed, feral countenance for fame.

It's definitely not what Patricia thought would happen when she told Homer to strike out all those names from the clipboard at the gate. She thought Chelsea would go home, stew a bit, and then call to apologize, like a rational person.

She was very, very wrong.

"I think Mommy went on a grand quest," she finally tells her granddaughter. "An adventure. I think that she, like so many heroes long ago, went out to win her fortune and one day return bearing gold and gifts."

When Brooklyn speaks again, her voice is a tiny breath in the darkness. "Then why didn't she take me with her?"

"Because she wanted you to be safe, and adventures are rarely safe."

Tiny fingers play up and down her arm, a soporific, thoughtful rhythm.

"What about Ella?"

Patricia flinches.

Yes, that one is her fault, too, and there's no way she's going to tell this tiny, frightened, abused blessing of a child the truth.

"I think Ella is on her own adventure. She's a big, grown-up girl. All big, grown-up girls have to go out and seek their destiny."

"Will I do that one day?"

Patricia resists the urge to hug the child so tightly that it would make her yelp. When her own daughter was this age and older, she dreamed of the kid finally being out of the house, of having enough space to be her own person again, of enjoying a simple meal without a single request or complaint or taking a shower without finding a wet towel and the last of the shampoo gone. Patty counted down the days until Chelsea was no longer her responsibility, and even if she disliked David from the very start, she was relieved when her daughter chose her own exit strategy.

Yes, she told Chelsea she didn't approve of David, but she never told her why. Never told her how she'd seen a million men like him, Mama's man-friends and her own diner customers, men who sized up women as if looking at a car they might buy and run into the ground, a thing to be entered and exited at a whim, allowed or denied proper maintenance depending on the time and resources required, trotted out or hidden, crashed to smithereens and called an accident or an act of God and left behind to rust. Patricia never told her daughter that David made a pass at her once, when she was younger, telling her she and Chelsea could be sisters and he could barely tell them apart, a knowing gleam in his eye and his thumb playing over her bare shoulder.

Worst of all, a sin she's done her best to bury and forget, she remembers that time a newly married Chelsea came to her, tentative and hunched over, and danced delicately around the topic of . . . how did she put it?

"Did you ever know someone who was like a different person when they were drunk? And they say horrible things, and the next morning, they don't remember it?"

That's what Chelsea asked her, arms wrapped around her waist as she stared unseeingly out the window at the bird feeder.

And Patricia was preparing for her first wedding, and she was nose-deep in the guest list, and she could feel the enormous can of beans that question threatened to open, and instead of facing her daughter and looking her in the eye and telling her the truth, instead she tapped her pen on the list and said, "Everyone does stupid things when they're drinking, you included, I'm certain."

Chelsea never brought it up again. There was more conversation, but it veered away from tense topics, and then Patricia was free to return to her guest list. She didn't regret it then.

She does now.

But what was Brooklyn's current question?

Ah, yes.

"Well, do you want to go have an adventure one day?"

She likes that Brooklyn stops to consider such questions before speaking.

"I want to go away," the child says slowly, but as she speaks, her words pile on. "I want to go to Hawaii. I want to be a dancer. I want to be a puppy doctor. I want to live at Disney World. I want to meet Elsa. I miss Olaf. Mommy said he ran away, but I think he might come back. Do you think he'll come back?"

Even on the mind-muddling meds, Patricia can put two and two together there. One desperate mother with the Violence plus a missing dog suggests that Olaf will not be coming back.

"Maybe he's having an adventure of his own," she says.

Brooklyn's hand lands on her nose, then moves to her cheek, patting gently. "Nana, you talk a lot about having an adventure. Did you ever have an adventure?"

Patricia feels tears prick her eyes. What she'd like to say is, *No, precious child, I didn't. I was date-raped by the preacher's son, and then I found out I was pregnant, so my mother kicked me out, and my entire family shunned me, so I used men and jobs like Tarzan uses vines until I landed in a place that felt a little like safety, and then I dreamed of what being free might feel like, and then I had everything I ever wanted except love, and then I lost it all, and here I am.*

She does not say that. Doesn't say anything like it.

What she does say surprises her, too.

"Not yet, but I'd like to." She stares off into the easy darkness, grateful for it, for all the sins it can hide. "Shall we take off on our valiant steed to find your mommy?"

49.

This time, Chelsea can already hear the crowd. Instead of the back of the semi, they have a real greenroom, nothing fancy, all concrete blocks and bright lights, and she can hear the audience laughing and booing and screaming from down the long, dirty-gray hallway. She stares at herself in the mirror, her eyes alight with the round bulbs lining it, and can't help remembering that night in high school when she gave up one thing for another, not knowing how permanent it would be. Not knowing that maybe she was giving up the wrong thing.

And it's not just that she gave up theater and chorus for David. It's that she gave up her friends, her interests, her passions, all for the *idea* of David. She wouldn't trade her daughters for all the world—she's doing this for them, after all—but if she could go back in time and stand in that greenroom, before that mirror, surrounded by those lights, she wouldn't choose David.

She would keep her Phantom mask and her borrowed vampire cape.

She would choose herself.

"You ready?"

TJ appears beside her. They're one of the last matches, but they have to be ready for anything. She's wearing an official Florida Woman T-shirt, artfully torn, plus her ripped jean shorts and boots, and she looks like an actor, whereas TJ looks like some sort of elemental spirit. It was his idea, The Killer Cuban. He thinks it's hilarious because luchadores are Mexican, not Cuban, and he's personally half Brazilian. His eyes are heavily surrounded in black because they have him fighting in that glittery mask so they can do a big reveal one day, and his head is always shaved down low. He brought his own clippers with him, Matt told her once, and treats shaving his head like a religious experience; not the loud church kind, but like a monk going through a holy ritual. The black around his eyes makes their brown pop, and he's got a loosely zipped hoodie over his shaved chest, per Harlan's pronouncement that somebody's got to wrestle topless and it might as well be the guy who can fight off anyone who has something to say about it.

"Ready as I'll ever be. You?"

He cocks his head and considers her, side by side in the mirror. "My last match went a little cattywampus, as my grandmother would say. I don't even know what I did to set Joy off like that, but I guess I'm just hoping that—"

"I won't screw up your career permanently?"

He smiles and nods. "Something like that."

Chelsea leans in to unclump her eyelashes. "We'll be fine. I think she's one of those people who's always looking for a fight, you know?"

"Hm. I would say she actually sees everything as a fight. As a threat. That happens when you grow up without enough."

"Enough what?"

He shrugs. "Enough of whatever you think you need. You scrabble for what's there, defend what you have, and see everyone else as the enemy. If you're a hammer, everything looks like a nail. But if you're a starving bird, every bit of plastic looks like fruit, and you'll fight to the death for it."

Chelsea's breath catches. What he's saying rings so true—but not about her. David is the hammer, her mother is the bird. "Yeah, I've known people like that. Do you think they'll ever be able to change? Because they seem miserable. Both kinds."

A smile tugs at the corner of TJ's mouth, a rare sight. He's always serious, always aloof, like a cat. "The thing about changing is that first, you have to want to change. And change is uncomfortable. To decide to change and then follow through with it and then maintain it is the work of a lifetime." He nods. "But I do think it's possible. More for the bird than the hammer. See you in the ring."

"Oh my God," Amy says from the other side of the mirror where she's been quietly eavesdropping while pretending to scroll through her phone. "He's like the freakin' Dalai Lama, right?"

"Then I guess it's okay that I have to lose to him."

Amy chatters on about her first match, how glad she is that she gets to win, how she's already getting fan mail even though she's never been out in public yet, but Chelsea spaces out. What TJ said—it's scratching at the door of her mind.

The thing is, she always thought that David's cruelty arose from her, from the fact that she wasn't what he needed or wanted, that she wasn't doing her part in the marriage, that she wasn't enough. After growing up with a single mom who was rarely home and when she was, spent most of her time sleeping and reading and making it clear that her daughter was an annoyance, she decided early on that she would fully commit to her marriage and her children, that she would succeed where her mother, she always assumed, had failed.

Those years in student housing, David was gone a lot, in class or studying or partying with friends or doing—well, he never really went into detail about all the time he spent away. College stuff. She didn't see him a ton, and when she did, he was tired and always in a bad mood, and she assumed he was working so hard—and, yes, partying so hard—that he didn't have any energy left for her. And then she got pregnant, and he was always annoyed because she was the tired, grouchy one, and because, as he put it, she was ballooning up. He said pregnant bodies were gross on purpose, to protect the baby, and that was the end of their physical relationship, a dry stretch that lasted until after Ella was born and Chelsea had shrunk back down almost to her regular size. Then he grew hungry for her again, which was a relief. She felt loved and cared for again.

The first few years of a marriage are hard; everyone says that. Pregnancy and babies and toddlers are hard; everyone knows that. But she thought it would get easier after those speed bumps, that once he had a good job and they were in their first little house and he no longer had twenty college demands but one work demand, things would be sweet.

But they weren't.

He was still gone from dawn to dusk. He was back to partying with his friends. He didn't want to spend time with Ella or help with feeding or diapering or middle-of-the-night crying jags.

"That's your job," he told Chelsea sternly. "You chose this. You have your job, and I have mine."

She kept stretching herself to take care of everyone, to do everything David asked, memorize how he liked things, and keep the house nice so that when he came home the daily tornado was all tidied up and it didn't even look like they had a child.

He started erasing Ella when she was a baby, Chelsea sees now.

He started erasing Chelsea even earlier.

The realization crashes down on her like hot summer thunder:

She could've been anyone.

What David wanted wasn't Chelsea, it was a cute wife who would shrink or stretch to suit him. What he did to her, whether he did it on purpose or not, was horrifically impersonal. Any blond girl without a backbone would've suited—or any girl who could be negged into bleaching her real hair. She's just the first fish that took the bait.

The years fly past in her head, remembering how easily she gave ground.

Theater and chorus? Gone. Friends David didn't like? Gone. She wanted the purple Honda but he said it looked weird, so he leased the white car with the better resale value. She liked the little bungalow house with brightly colored walls, he preferred the McMansion painted in shades of beige with a patio for his grill. She wanted to go back to work, maybe get her own college degree, but he stressed how much a good wife and mother needed to be home. Even down to neighborhood Bunco nights or drinks with the other moms at preschool—she shouldn't go, her life was at home, it was stupid, the women were too this or too that.

She just needed to stay home and take care of her family.

He's been hacking off bits of her for years until she couldn't run away. Until she couldn't even go out and see what she'd been missing.

Until she decided that things had to change.

Until the Violence gave her an excuse.

It hurts, to see how dispassionate his abuse has been.

To see how, again and again, she's said yes to it without saying anything at all until there was nothing left of her. She simply drifted around the house like a little ghost forgetting herself.

And it could've been anyone.

He could've simply put an ad on Craigslist.

Wanted: Broodmare, doormat, and punching bag. Free room and board, but you'll pay for it with pieces of your soul.

Chelsea blinks and comes back to herself, staring into Florida Woman's face floating in the mirror, a still spot amid all the movement and energy and excitement.

Craigslist.

Craigslist!

She's been racking her brain on how to find Ella, but just a few hours ago, Arlene gave her a brand-new iPhone, and even if she can't call or text or email her daughter, even if Ella has never shared her social media handles and they're not under her real name, she can still try Craigslist.

Because she's tried to use it for years to find Whitney and apologize for the talent show, and Ella knows that. And Ella thinks Craigslist is ancient and stupid, but . . .

Ella also knows that when Chelsea is trying to find someone unfindable, that's where she goes.

Maybe . . . maybe Ella already tried it.

Whipping out her new iPhone—the newest model, thanks to Harlan's guilt—she goes directly to Tampa's Craigslist and searches the Missed Connections posts. Even if she should be getting her head in the game, going over the end moves for the match, she won't be able to think of anything else until she's scrolled all the way back through to the date her mother stole her children. Back, back, back, all the way to—

Wait.

There.

Smella looking for her favorite Swamp Momster.

Momster.

That's her.

That's her.

She opens the post, her heart flooding with need and relief and fear, and there's an email address. Thank God for autocorrect because she's typing the email so fast it barely makes sense. She tells her daughter how much she loves her, how much she misses her, where she is and how to find her. Most important, she gives Ella her new number and begs her to call or text as soon as she can.

"Chelsea, you okay?" Amy stands by her side in the mirror, looking concerned, her long hair wavy and topped with a green wreath.

"Yeah. Sure." But Chelsea doesn't stop clutching her phone, staring at the screen, begging it to ping a notification.

Amy puts a hand on her shoulder. "You're shaking."

Chelsea turns to her and smiles, tears in her eyes. "Yeah, but it's for a good reason, I promise. I think I found my daughter."

Tears start to well up in Amy's eyes, her lip trembling. Of course this is a very sensitive topic for her, but Chelsea is so overrun with emotion that she can't think of someone else first, just now, and she hopes Amy will understand.

"That's so great," she says, trying to smile.

"Amy?" Sienna calls from the door, headset on and clipboard in hand. "We're waiting on you."

Amy gives Chelsea the quickest of hugs, careful not to smear anyone's makeup or damage either costume.

"Good luck out there," Chelsea says.

"Shouldn't you say break a leg?"

Chelsea has to laugh. "Yeah, not when actual fighting is involved."

With a wave, Amy heads out the door, leaving Chelsea to stare at her phone.

The world is dangerous now. David is surely out of quarantine. Patricia is at best cold and at worst sadistic. Sickness is everywhere— Chelsea knows that better than anyone. The Craigslist posting is weeks old, with nothing more recent, no more attempts to find her. She can only hope and pray that her daughter is still able to reply.

50.

Patricia had forgotten how hard it is to help a child pack for a trip. Children have no clue about the difference between necessities and frivolous junk. Brooklyn packed two dance dresses, all her shoes, and no underwear, then forgot her toothbrush.

If this was a younger version of Chelsea, Patricia would snap at her, call her an idiot, and tell her exactly what to pack, slowly and with the implication that she's doing the listener a favor and won't repeat herself. But that was then and this is now, and she is done being someone's monster. Instead, she simply gives Brooklyn a gentle smile and says, "I think you may have forgotten a few things. Let's finish packing together. Nana is an excellent packer."

It's late morning now, and last night's revelations feel like something that happened long, long ago. They both fell back to sleep in Patricia's big bed. She was just too sleepy and exhausted and drugged up to let herself contemplate what would happen if the child stormed again. Luckily, nothing happened, other than a little drool on her pillow.

The sun shines in the spare room windows, landing on Brooklyn's clothes spread all around on the floor, along with a few garbage bags opened up to expose Ella's abandoned things. Patricia helps her granddaughter find tops and matching bottoms, socks, and plenty of undies, calmly explaining her choices and showing her granddaughter how to roll her clothes up to prevent wrinkles and save space. Brooklyn does not pay complete attention, but she's amenable and does her clumsy best to roll up a tiny T-shirt and skort. They add toothbrush, toothpaste, and hairbrush, plus some bows. Chelsea never let her put bows in her hair, but Brooklyn is all for it. Patricia wishes she'd known this sooner; she would've rained down bows for every holiday. It's nice to learn they have certain tastes in common.

She takes more time packing her own things, unsure how long they'll be gone or if it's even worth coming back to an empty house from which she could be evicted at any moment. They're pretty much out of portable food, but she takes care to bring all her first-aid supplies, including the Percocet, plus hydrogen peroxide in case her wounds get fussy. The bigger one is still a bit red and achy, and she's been dousing it with peroxide, but at least she doesn't have a fever. She's bringing the thermometer, too. Maybe there's a less pricey urgent care out there in the middle of nowhere, where she can get a prescription for antibiotics, if she hasn't been tagged in some awful system for nonpayment.

Patricia is anxious to get on the road, and yet she can't help noticing that she's dragging her feet. She's taken one last tour of the house at least three times as if something necessary might pop out from under the bed like a lost cat. She's looking for—what? Some surprise cache of cash or jewels that she's conveniently forgotten and Diane, or whoever stole her bag, benevolently left behind? She knows now, after a bit of internet sleuthing, that the jewelry she still has on hand is basically worthless, as the only jewelry rich people buy during pandemics are enormous gems, not someone else's cast-off engraved anniversary band. She's combed through every inch of Randall's study, opening books and running a knife blade around promising cracks, but no convenient secret door has presented itself. Life, it turns out, is not a game of Clue. Sometimes there's nothing left to find.

Chelsea's next—ugh—fighting match is this evening in Jacksonville, and Patricia has used a discount website to secure a room at a nearby hotel. It's the grubbiest place she's stayed at in decades, but it's all they can afford, and whatever Chelsea is up to, Patricia is completely certain that she doesn't have a guest room and even if she takes Brooklyn back on the spot, an older woman with failing eyesight that Lasik can no longer touch up can't be driving on the highway at midnight. If Chelsea has a plan, Patricia has decided she'll be open to it. If Chelsea wants nothing to do with her, she'll drive back tomorrow alone and go stay at the Herbert house for the foreseeable future. If she's there, the police can't find her, and there will surely be food, plus all the utilities. Randall can't divorce and evict her if he can't find her.

The thought of him selling this house, her house, makes her want to bare her teeth and bite.

Some stranger entering this space she's carefully crafted, this life she's built, judging it and deciding on some innocuous color to paint it, some cheap tone of taupe. They'll take down anything personal, leaving a blank slate to attract the next owners.

Patricia isn't ready to give up, but she's also not willing to fight for what's left.

The Herberts will be gone for quite some time. And when she runs out of food or they return, there's always the Houcks.

Her neighborhood is a ghost town.

She is a ghost.

She shakes her head.

No good being morbid when there's more to do.

She's survived worse, after all.

Her sedan is packed as tightly as a tin of sardines. The trunk, the backseat. She assumed Brooklyn would sit up front, but the child balks at that and stands firm that it's not safe for a highway drive. Finally Patricia relents and repacks everything, making a space behind the passenger seat for her granddaughter to nestle in with pillows and blankets. She finds it odd that the child still insists on wearing a seatbelt and continues asking for a car seat. At this age, Chelsea would make a bed in the backseat for any trip over an hour, lying the full length of whatever beat-up station wagon they were puttering around in that year until they drove it into the ground.

The last thing she does on her way out is reset all the security codes, even going so far as to call the security company and change the secret password.

Someone will come to lay claim to her home, and they will be greeted by shrieking alarms. She should've done this sooner. Much sooner. Before Randall and Diane stole her last Tarzan vine.

As the grand gates open and she drives through and Brooklyn hums along to some inane cartoon theme song, Patricia recalls the first time she saw this house, when Randall's real estate agent drove them here in his black town car. They were sipping champagne because that's how they used to do things, and they pulled up in front of the palm-lined sidewalk and she felt this lift in her chest, like a bird long held captive finally flying free. This place—she saw it as her Barbie Dream-House. The sanctuary she'd always wished for and never gotten. The pony that never arrived for her birthday. She told herself it was the thing she'd always wanted, the only thing she needed, the last thing she'd ever want.

She was wrong.

The house didn't satisfy her for long. As it turns out, what she really wanted was freedom from worry, and the house merely brought along a new cadre of worries. When it rained hard, she didn't smile to be somewhere safe and dry and warm—she listened for leaks and flooding and looked for water damage on the walls. When it was sunny, she didn't lie on a float in her pool, luxuriating in the warm kiss of the sun and the absolute languor of a private oasis—she noticed her dimpling thighs and the brown spots on her hands and wondered if she needed to have more sprinklers installed or tell Miguel to fertilize the grass that was a shade less green than the neighbors'. And she told herself she didn't love Randall and if he chose to spend time elsewhere, that was his right, but she eventually got sick of dining alone when she'd thought their arrangement might provide some kind of comfort or companionship.

The castle became a cage, as castles tend to do.

She's sorry to leave it behind, but she's not as devastated as she thought she'd be.

For lunch, they stop at McDonald's again. Patricia is beginning to remember that when you don't have much money, it's the little things that make life bearable. Hot fries eaten from a paper bag make her happier than her thousand-dollar high heels, these days. She can't quite remember why those shoes became so important to her. She'd rather throw one at Karen and Lynn than pick out a new pair. She left them all behind, opted for comfortable moccasins and a pair of flip-flops and one pair of sneakers, in case she needs to . . . what?

Run?

Yes, because she's done illegal things, and she might have to actually run.

"This is a good adventure, Nana," Brooklyn says between bites of chicken nugget.

How pleasant it must be, to possess that sort of naïveté.

When she was Brooklyn's age, Patricia was already a tiny adult.

She thinks of the child's spark like a tiny, sputtering flame, and now it's up to her to keep it burning, to tend it, no matter what. She may have failed in that job once before, but she won't fail again.

Patricia doesn't know what will happen when they find Chelsea. She's fairly certain that there will be a place for Brooklyn with her mother; no one would deny a mother her child, and surely Chelsea told her new cohort about her situation. It's Patricia that's the problem. Her daughter has every right to hate her, not only for what she's done recently, but perhaps, she's beginning to see, for what she's done all along.

She has never been a woman who apologizes. She's never been a woman who needed to.

She is, she can admit to herself, a bit of a bitch, but then again, a bitch is just a woman who doesn't do what you want and then refuses to feel bad about it.

All the way to Jacksonville, Patricia practices in her head, the same way she used to practice for her big speech to open the auction.

The opening line is the hardest. "Chelsea, I'm so sorry . . ."

51.

Ella is in the slow lane doing fifty-nine in a sixty-five, hands at ten and two, the only car on the highway. The Miata may have been built for speed, but Ella definitely was not. She's running late because there was a semi truck accident, and she got lost on the detour. According to her map app she should still get to the fairgrounds in time to see her mom, or at least find someone who knows her before the fights are over. Now all she has to do is get there safely.

Headlights appear in her rearview mirror, getting closer much faster than they should. Her eyes bounce from the road ahead to each mirror, and panic begins to creep in. She's not in the fast lane, not bothering anybody, so this guy should just go around her, right?

He's nearly caught up, and she holds her breath as she waits for the car to zoom around her, rocking the little Miata. But instead, he slows and turns on his high beams. She can barely see now, and she'd like to shield her eyes, but she can't take her hands off the steering wheel or she might lose control. She wants to slow down, but if she does, she knows he'll hit her. He revs forward and backs off, revs forward, and backs off. He gets so close that she can't see his headlights, can't see anything but the flash of streetlights on tinted glass. It's a sedan, but it's so much bigger than her car. One tap, and he could send her skidding into the guardrail.

Whoever he is, he won't let up. He lays on the horn, and she winces. Her speed has gone down, below fifty now.

He must enjoy this, the absolute turd. Must love knowing he's scaring someone to death.

Somehow, she instinctively knows it's a man. She'd bet her life on it.

"Just pass me," she growls. "You goddamn asshole, just pass me."

After a few more honks and flashes of high beams, he finally does, screeching around her and hurtling off into the night at what's got to be at least a hundred miles an hour, maybe more. When his taillights are so far ahead that they look like dying stars, she slows and guides the tiny car onto the shoulder under a streetlight, feeling like she's driving an aluminum can that nearly got steamrolled. Her entire body is shaking, her hands clenched on the wheel, her feet and fingers freezing cold.

"He's gone," she says out loud. "It's okay. He's gone. I can do this."

She's almost got her breathing back to normal when her phone buzzes. What she sees there sends her heart back into overdrive.

It's an email.

From her mom.

She has to reread it three times before it sinks in.

Her mom didn't want to leave her.

Nana closed the gate on her.

Just like she closed the gate on Ella.

Her mom isn't hiding—she wanted to be found, at least by her daughter.

Ella isn't particularly surprised by what Nana did, but still. How rotten does your heart have to be, to throw your own blood to the wolves like that?

And the old bitch still has Brooklyn. It chills Ella to the bone, thinking about Brooklyn waking up from a nightmare and finding grim, disapproving Nana standing there, hands on her hips, mouth puckered up like she's sucking on a lemon, commenting that nice girls don't scream in the middle of the night.

But that's not the focus now.

Mom finally found her message and explained everything. How

Nana had her stricken from the clipboard. How she went home to figure things out. How Jeanie offered what felt like a good chance at making money, and Mom jumped at any opportunity to get vaccinated and get her girls back.

And then, what happened with Jeanie . . .

Knowing is one thing, hearing it firsthand is another.

It's a huge weight off Ella's chest, knowing that her mom wasn't ignoring her frantic texts for some dark reason but instead lost her phone weeks ago when she also lost her car and all of her belongings. She wonders if maybe there's some officer with a desk full of confiscated phones, keeping them charged and checking them regularly for updates that might lead to arrests. If so, they've definitely gotten a wide range of emotions from Ella over the past few weeks as she vented her fears and frustrations into the ether, hoping every moment for an answer that would suddenly bring this new world into focus.

Now she has that answer.

She immediately texts the number Mom sent in the email, her hands shaking and her thumbs as sloppy as a numbed tongue after a root canal.

Dear Mom,

It's okay. I understand now.

I'm on my way, tonight. Should be there in twenty minutes.

Please tell me how to get to you. I miss you so much. We have to get Brooklyn back.

Love,

Smella

She stares at the phone for several minutes, keeps running a thumb over the screen to keep it glowing, hoping for an instantaneous response. It doesn't come. She glances at the car's clock, as if that will add some additional magic the phone clock can't provide. Of course nothing changes. Because the event is starting, and her mom's match is probably going on soon. Or maybe she's getting ready and doesn't keep her phone with her. Her outfit is pretty skimpy, after all—it's the kind of thing that, just a few months ago, really would've bothered her, the thought of everyone on earth seeing her mom's thighs and boobs, but now she doesn't care what her mom is wearing or how stupid she's acting, she just wants the solidity of that hug, the surety of those arms pulling her close. She told her mom years ago she didn't like being hugged, but really, it was always more of a dare.

She gives it five minutes, staring at her phone, willing any ounce of magic she's ever possessed to provide an easy answer to all her problems. *Of course, my darling daughter, here's the secret password, meet me in my fancy tour bus and everything will be fine.*

When the five minutes are up, she reluctantly brings up her map app again and places the phone in the cup holder and puts the car back in drive, checking the rearview mirror before pulling into the slow lane. There's not a single set of lights behind her, no more terrifyingly murderous assholes, so she gets back up to the speed limit, almost. Before, it felt like she was running from something, but now it feels like maybe she's running *to* something. Against her better judgment, her eyes constantly flick to her phone, praying that an email or text will light up and block out the map that's leading her to the closest thing she has to home.

Maybe ten minutes later, her phone buzzes with a text, and her heart skips as the car swerves sideways, jumping with her hands. She checks her mirrors and slows, risking a glance down.

IMPORTANT, is all she can see before the bubble disappears.

"Shit," she murmurs, pulling off the highway for a second time. She hates how the shoulder grinds under her tires, as if actively repelling her. Once the car is stopped, hands trembling all over again, she checks her texts. But the message isn't from her mom. It's from Hayden.

God, to think: She'd almost forgotten about him.

IMPORTANT

I'm going to kill myself.

Ella, I'm really going to do it. The world has been too cruel, and I know I'm not perfect, but I don't deserve this. I thought you cared, but it's clear now that you're just another shallow, out-

for-herself bitch. I've bled my heart out for you, and you won't condescend to answer.

"God, who does he think he is? Hamlet?" she murmurs, pretty certain that anyone who begins a message this long with **IMPORTANT**: I'M GOING TO KILL MYSELF isn't going to. Probably.

Not a single answer as I spill my guts. Which tells me that you're worthless, and that it's your fault that everything that happened, happened. I didn't even tell you the worst of what they did to me in quarantine, the things the older boys did after dark, when the guards thought we were asleep. You can't begin to imagine it. I have been subjected to things that I can't even

That's it.
Hopefully it's over.
But then the phone buzzes in her hand, the next part of the message.

begin to describe. I thought I could confide in you. Trust you. I thought you were special. You're the only person I talked to during that hellish time. I hacked the system just to get to you! But no, you're stuck up and cold, an ice queen, and you have no heart, and you won't even answer me. So I'm going to do it, and when it's done, it'll be your fault.

"Weird flex, but okay," she says to the quiet of the night.
Because this . . . doesn't read like a suicide note. Or, at least, it doesn't read like the ones she wrote after her dad choked her, when she just wanted to escape, to stop being scared all the time. Those, she wrote and burned with a forbidden candle and dumped in the toilet. She did not send them to people she wanted to make feel terrible. This is just some new kind of manipulative bullshit, and she doesn't have time for it.
This is the very reason she's never answered any of his missives.

All this, and not a single iota of care for her.

At no time during all his letters has he asked how she is, if she's okay, if anyone in her family has been afflicted. It's always about him.

Just like her dad.

Don't you have anything to say to that? Are you even capable of feeling anything?

Her thumbs hover over the keyboard.

What she'd like to say is:

Dear Hayden,

It's funny how you emotionally manipulated me, pawed at me, made me feel guilty for not being into it, physically abused me, and then suddenly discovered your emotional depths when your vile behavior was captured on video by a third party and displayed for the public to see. I'm certain that your time in the quarantine camp—to which you sent yourself, with no input from me—was not pleasant. Although you haven't asked, my time has also been less than agreeable. After my dad beat up my mom and she turned him in for the Violence, she actually came down with it herself, and I had to watch her stomp my dog to death.

Have you ever heard a dog being stomped to death, Hayden? The way its yelps go quiet in a fit of crunching? I'm guessing not.

Even in the nightmare of quarantine.

Then my grandmother kidnapped my sister and me. And then she kicked me out.

And then I scraped up dead cats I used to feed and killed a man I was taught to call my uncle.

And then I lived like an animal for several weeks.

Perhaps, learning this brief history, you will understand why I have not tenderly crafted responses to each of your kind, informative missives about your ongoing emotional pain. I have in fact been dealing with my own emotional pain and have not had the bandwidth to care about you.

Sorry about that.

What I have learned in our time apart is that it's not you, it's me.

By which I mean it IS you, and everyone like you.

Everyone who thinks he's a great guy who deserves everything good but doesn't want to provide support in kind.

Everyone who thinks the word no means "maybe."

Everyone who thinks he's a victim when he creates victims.

You probably shouldn't kill yourself, or at least, you shouldn't kill yourself for the shitty, selfish reasons outlined in your text message. If you do go through with your cunning plan, please do it to rid the world of someone who appears to be, on all counts, a piece of shit who will only bring pain to whatever poor trophy wife he manages to ensnare and persistently shrink and belittle.

Good day, sir.

> *Signed,*
> *Ella*

P.S. You are a terrible kisser. It was like being attacked by a piece of escargot.

Instead, she simply types, *New phone. Who dis?*
And keeps on driving.

52.

Chelsea is about to go onstage, and she can't stop shivering. She gave her phone into Arlene's safekeeping, briefly explaining the importance of guarding it. Arlene nodded solemnly and now cradles it in her hand like a baby bird as she stares out the door, waiting for Harlan's cue. Chelsea is grateful that there's someone in this world she can trust. She didn't have that, before the Violence.

She told Arlene that Ella is here, that all the security guards need to know her name, need to let her through. There is nothing more important to her in the whole world, and because Arlene has been with her through this journey, she understands that.

Her heart held in Arlene's hands, Chelsea stands at the door beside a masked, silent TJ, waiting for the cheers to stop. They don't. The hall is full, packed to the gills. The incident with the Violence at the last match didn't deter a single person. The lights go out, and they keep cheering. They're . . . really into it. Whether they're pro wrestling fans trying to scratch their itch or something new, well, it doesn't matter. They're here, they paid for seats, and they're already wearing shirts they bought at Harlan's merch booth. Even though she can see only a tiny sliver of the crowd, Chelsea can already see her face on a woman's boxy black T-shirt. She needs to talk to Harlan about women's sizing and the importance of a slimmer fit.

It's funny how little thoughts like that float past when the stakes are so much bigger.

The lights come on, shining on the ring where Harlan stands in another softly gleaming silver suit, his tie the color of wet blood. He holds the mic, wired for old times' sake, and announces the match.

"During our last event, if you saw it online . . ." He pauses, grins out at the crowd. "Who's seen it?"

The crowd roars back, the walls seeming to bend in response to their power.

"Good, good. Glad to hear it." Harlan gives the tiniest nod. "Then you know what Florida Woman did to Steve Nissen. We got any Club Nissen members out there tonight?" Portions of the crowd roar back, and there's a brief chant of *Steve-n Steve-n Steve-n,* but then Harlan flaps a hand at them, rings winking on his fingers. "Yeah, well, sorry to say, your boy lost. Are you here tonight hoping to see retribution against Florida Woman?"

Chelsea startles at the crowd's responses, half booing, half cheering. These people . . . feel things. About her. Their hearts are beating together, the air is full of their cries. They care.

To her, what she does is, well, silly.

But to them, it's *real.*

She's not just a mom wearing too much makeup and skimpy jean shorts, rolling around on a mat.

She's Florida Woman.

And whether they love her or hate her, these people feel deeply.

It's a revelation.

She never understood what people got out of pro wrestling, but now she does.

The understanding sinks into her bones, and her hip pops out. Her mouth quirks. Her eyes light up. It takes over her, possesses her.

No matter what Chelsea Martin wants right now, Florida Woman just wants to party and mop the floor with blood.

"So I'd like to introduce the man who wants to take her down, The Killer Cuban!"

Spotlights flick to the empty space just outside their door. TJ winks at her mischievously through his luchador mask, jumps up and down in place a few times, and slaps his own face before stepping out into the puddle of blinding light, raising his arms and roaring behind the mask. Chelsea is grateful she doesn't have to wear something like that—anything that feels remotely like strangling or choking makes her nearly have a panic attack, these days.

The crowd howls, but not as much as they did before. TJ stalks down the aisle, lunging and growling at fans and shaking his upraised fists. He's a good actor, Chelsea'll give him that—and Arlene and Chris are wonderful at bringing out whatever latent melodrama some- one might be holding tight in their chest. TJ reaches the ring and climbs up to the top rope, doing a front flip to land on his feet beside Harlan.

"So, how do you feel about Florida Woman?" Harlan asks him, holding out the microphone.

But of course The Killer Cuban doesn't speak. He reaches into his waistband, pulls out a glossy photo of Chelsea—that's so weird! Where did they get that?—and rips it in half again and again before throwing confetti on the crowd. They lunge for it like dogs fighting for scraps of kibble.

This event, this match . . . it's become so much more than it was last time.

For a moment, Chelsea believes it herself, that this masked man wants to tear her in half.

But no.

It's just TJ.

TJ, the straight-edge guru martial artist.

He won't hurt her.

That's his job—to look like he's hurting her without leaving so much as a bruise.

It's the opposite of her former life.

As Harlan asks TJ another question, Arlene's cool, dry hand lands on Chelsea's wrist. "Your daughter texted. She'll be here tonight. Do you want me to—"

Forget the show, the theatrics, the fight. Chelsea's entire body is alive and shaking now.

"Just get her in. Keep her safe. Please."

Arlene nods, smiling warmly, her hand still on Chelsea's wrist. She squeezes lightly. "I will. We'll keep her back here. She'll be proud."

"Thank—" Chelsea begins.

But down by the ring, Harlan has no idea of the very real drama playing out in Chelsea's life behind the curtains, so he has no compunction about interrupting. He wouldn't anyway, she's fairly certain. He might be a caring person, but this is his dream, his life, and he wouldn't put it on hold for a text message.

"And now, fighting The Killer Cuban, may I present your hometown heroine, or at least object lesson: Florida Woman!"

Arlene gives her a strong nod and pulls her hand away, and Chelsea steps fully into the open doorway, into the blinding hot white of the spotlights. Her body is made of energy, a lightning bolt, a live wire, and she feels it in every pore, sizzling in every muscle, igniting every bone. Her stance is animal, her hands red-lacquered claws as she throws back her head and howls.

The crowd goes berserk. She rides it like a wave—the screams, the garbled words, the low, hooting boos. Love, hate, it's all the same, and it's better than indifference.

That's what these people need, in the age of the Violence, after Covid, after keeping their distance from one another and what they love and what they want for so long: They need to care, to feel, to have any emotion burning when they thought they'd given up or lost too much to ever feel again. After so much trauma, this is part of their healing—going back to that dark cave before humans were humans, when they were just animals united, jeering at the moon.

Her throat is shredded as she lowers her head, bangs bouncing in her blinded eyes. She—God, what even is the word for the way she walks—unapologetically wide-legged, swaggering and primal, unafraid and angry and heavy? She has never walked this way in real life, has never taken up this much space, has never allowed herself a single atom of ugly, if she could help it.

But something about wearing Florida Woman like a second skin turns her entire being into something else completely, an idea, a thing, a creature, an archetype. She's some minor, forgotten goddess who pays no heed to mortals, who sucks in every sound from every throat, tender offerings laid at the tips of her wrestling boots. At the ring, she slithers in under the lowest rope, rolls over with an almost sexual energy, writhing across the ring until she's on her back by Harlan and TJ, who stare down at her, curious, until she does a kip-up to land on her feet in a near-squat, glaring at TJ like she's a living beam of light who just really needs, on a primordial level, to either fuck him or fuck him up. She grins, baring her teeth, hoping the cameras are catching it.

She has never felt more herself, for all that this isn't herself.

Or maybe it's some lost part of her she buried long ago.

"Florida Woman, are you ready?"

Harlan leans in with the mic, but not too close, like he's scared of her. Good.

"I'm gonna beat him like he's my ex-husband shopping with his side bitch at Walmart," she growls.

The crowd barks their laughter, screams their hunger for the fight.

Harlan says something else, and then he's backing out of the ring with his mic. TJ rounds on her, likewise moving into readiness, up on the balls of his feet, hands up, eyes snapping.

"You ready for this?" he whispers.

"Born ready," she replies, right as the bell rings.

The glittering chalk cloud descends, and they throw their heads back to faux inhale and then refocus with a new, deeper level of animalistic threat. Chelsea is supposed to go first, so she does, tucking her head and ducking under his armpit, pulling him into a full nelson from behind. TJ allows it because they've practiced it, and at the last possible moment he slips out and goes for his own hold. What they're doing is some strange intersection of fighting, poetry, and surgery, real and violent but artistic and melodramatic and yet also extremely careful and practiced. Chelsea gets into the zone, fully immersed in the fight but also flowing through it like water, like liquid mercury, dancing with TJ as if doing the flamenco in a spotlight. The crowd recedes, the overhead lights burn like the sun, and the only time there's anyone else in the world is when one of them pins the other and waits for Pauley to dive in and count down to two before they kick out or otherwise remove themselves from the perceived trouble.

They're nearing the end of the match, and it's gone by so swiftly that Chelsea is startled to hear Harlan announce they only have thirty seconds left. She has to get into a position for TJ to finish her off with his new token move, the Cuban Sandwich, which is really just a modified version of Rampage's signature pin. She acts stunned as she waits for him to spring, and he takes her down with a gorgeous combo. He's so delicate and precise that she barely feels it, even as she lands on the springy ring. But as he pins her and Pauley runs in to count, she realizes that . . . she doesn't want it to go down this way.

Her baby is here.

Watching.

Her daughter, who spent her entire life watching Chelsea get taken down a peg nightly, who watched her take abuse, suffer cutting comments, accept whatever bullshit remarks David doled out about her body, her clothes, her food, her work.

She doesn't want Ella to see her lose.

"TJ, I know you're supposed to win, but my daughter is here," she whispers in the quiet, dark tent of their bodies, their faces hidden from the crowd as Pauley counts down slowly from ten to maximize the drama and the crowd screams encouragement. "I haven't seen her in months. Any chance you'd let me have this one?"

His breathing is labored as he says, "I don't mind, but will Harlan?"

"Who gives a shit?"

He pauses, panting.

"She watched her dad beat me up, TJ. I don't want her to see me for the first time in months with . . . with . . ."

"With you as a victim again," he finishes with that familiar, calm cunning. "Kick out and pin me."

He loosens his grip—she feels it happen—and she kicks out dramatically, doing a back roll and immediately throwing herself on top of him, yanking his arm behind his back in a way that's got to hurt, but he has enough self-control and chivalry to only gasp.

"A shocking reverse for Florida Woman!" Harlan shouts. "Ladies and gentlemen, this is indeed a surprise as the ref counts down an incredible kick-out. Boy, The Killer Cuban must be feeling that . . ." Chelsea loosens up her hold a bit.

Pauley counts down to zero and slaps the ring, and Harlan is there, grabbing her arm and hoisting her to her feet, her fist up in triumph as she feigns momentary confusion, like she's just waking up.

"You saw it here live! Florida Woman strikes again! Believe what you read in the news and don't put anything past her. She'll surprise the hell out of you."

Chelsea does a circle of the ring, pumping her fists and screaming along with the crowd, drinking in their adulation and delight and devouring their fury and disappointment. Behind her, TJ dramatically drags himself up from the ring floor as if he's been pulverized. He hasn't, but he's a great actor. She owes him one, definitely.

She scans the audience, hoping against all odds that her daughter will be in the front row, that their eyes will meet like that moment in the movies when life changes forever for the better, when the music swells and everyone takes the deepest breath and feels their heart crack perfectly open for just a moment.

Ella isn't there.

At least not where Chelsea can see her.

These seats originally sold for fifty dollars and got scalped for upward of a thousand, or so she heard. Of course her daughter isn't here.

But she doesn't let her mask waver. Florida Woman doesn't do hangdog.

She doesn't do disappointment.

Florida Woman chews people up and spits out their bones while throat-kicking gators.

She climbs up the ropes and gives one last fist and pelvis pump before Harlan shoos her out like a lost rattlesnake, and then she's marching up the aisle in the spotlight, meeting gleaming, energized eyes and slapping the sweaty hands that strain for her. Some kids hold out glossy photos and a Sharpie, and she signs with an uppercase FW and a big, shiny star, which Arlene and Harlan suggested would keep her from accidentally using her own signature, signing her real name. Arlene pulls her back through the door, and the sudden calm is like being slapped in the face by a fish, cold and still and dead, compared with what came before. She collapses into a chair, drooping like a cut flower.

"What the hell was that?" Arlene says, standing over Chelsea as

Sienna moves to take her place at the door with a disapproving frown. Not as disapproving as Arlene's frown, though.

No point in playing dumb. They both know what she did. And they both know it wasn't TJ's doing, which is why he's tearing off his mask and digging for an iced Gatorade in the cooler instead of sitting in this plastic chair like a kid in trouble with the teacher.

"My fault," Chelsea manages to wheeze, just now realizing she's out of breath. "My daughter."

She doesn't have to say anything else—Arlene understands immediately.

"Couldn't let her see you lose, huh? Of course TJ was down for that. I swear, y'all got to learn to do what you're told. Harlan knows best."

Chelsea raises an eyebrow. "Gonna fire me?"

Arlene's mouth twists.

They can't fire her. She's hugely popular; she lost count of the Florida Woman shirts she saw out there, but there must be hundreds of shirts, hundreds of posters, thousands of fans. Even if they managed to find a woman who looked exactly like her and was willing to live on the road with no real resources, they couldn't get her trained in time for the next event. And Chelsea has gathered up enough self-esteem to believe that no one else could do exactly what she does.

"I'm not gonna fire you, no. Harlan will definitely have thoughts, though."

Chelsea grins, knows it's lopsided and smeared with cheap red lipstick after the fight.

"Sorry not sorry?"

Arlene rolls her eyes and shakes her head. "That's between you, the boss, and your accomplice. Go get some Gatorade." She tries to look stern as she waves Chelsea away and turns to find whoever is up next.

Over at the cooler, TJ hands her a red Gatorade, the sides sweating down his hand. He's got his fluffy robe back on, his mask turned inside out on a nearby prop table.

"So that was interesting," he says.

"I owe you one."

He doesn't acknowledge that. "So where's your daughter?" He

looks around the greenroom like someone is hiding a teenager here, and Chelsea heaves a sigh.

"I don't know. We made contact right before the match, but I gave Arlene my phone." Her heart revs up as she remembers there could already be another message. She scans the room, but Arlene must've stepped out to direct someone in the ring or fix something for Harlan. Sienna is at the door with Matt, her hand on his wrist as she whispers in his ear. He's shaking, but that's just how he is before matches, like a greyhound ready to run.

Chelsea jogs over and waits until Sienna looks up.

"You all good?" she asks, eyebrows drawn down a bit in acknowledgment of Chelsea's earlier blunder.

"Did Arlene give you my phone?" she asks. "Or do you know where it is?"

Sienna shakes her head. "No, but she said to tell you that when your kid shows up, everyone knows to send her to the tour bus."

"So I'm good to go?"

Sienna, like Arlene, can't help smiling at her, even though she's in trouble. After all they've been through, everyone knows little pieces of her story, and she suspects the management team openly discusses such things. "Go on, honey. You did well. As long as Harlan's not too mad, I think the results will be worth it."

Chelsea bobs a nod and heads to the mirror. No time to wipe off the layers of makeup. Her daughter will recognize her, even under the paint. She jogs out the back door and down the hall toward the tour buses, feeling lighter than air, her heart singing.

Finally.

Finally.

53.

Patricia hates forking over twenty dollars for parking, but what are they going to do, park in the cheap field a mile away and walk? Not on her leg, not with the skin around her stitches gone red and puffy, weeping pus.

She pulls in beside an El Camino, and Brooklyn bounces in her seat.

"It's like Disney World, Nana!" she burbles. "Do they have balloons?"

"I do not think they have balloons," she says grimly, softening it with, "but they might have candy."

Brooklyn doesn't entirely understand what's going on, but then again, she doesn't really have to. Patricia knows her granddaughter is the key to finding Chelsea, and so here they are in this great throng of burly men and fierce women, the child's small, sticky hand clutched in hers. She couldn't afford tickets, but she didn't know what else to do. They're sold out, the cheapest scalped tickets still up in the hundreds. This is not a place where she can offer a diamond ring in exchange for a seat like they're the plucky protagonists in some old, sepia-toned musical.

At the gates, she hunts for the most sympathetic-looking ticket taker, an older woman whose eyes are creased with smile lines. "I'm looking for my daughter," she tells her, pulling Brooklyn close. "Chelsea Martin. She's Florida Woman. This is her daughter, my granddaughter. We lost track of Mommy. Can you help us?"

The woman's face crinkles up like a prune, and she shakes her head. "Sorry, honey, we're by the hour. I don't know nobody with the crew. Maybe try Security? Or go around back to the buses?"

Patricia nods and thanks her, feeling like some filthy groupie as she drags Brooklyn away. She doesn't like anything that smacks of official authority these days, so she leads her granddaughter around the side of the large building toward a long line of fans with signs standing in the puddle of light around some RVs and tour buses. Not the newest and shiniest of vehicles, but not too shabby. She tries to make her way through the crowd, to edge closer to the buses, but every time she tries to slide past with a murmured, "Pardon me," someone hip-checks her or turns and frowns in a menacing fashion. Her head is pounding, and the heat is making her feel dizzy, and all the shoving isn't helping. Good Lord, do these people think they're lining up for Mick Jagger?

"Nana, what's wrong?" Brooklyn asks. "Where's Mommy?"

Patricia looks up ahead at the thirty people blocking her from reaching her goal. She looks down at this tiny, adorable child dressed all in pink with her chipped plastic tiara.

"She's on the other side of these people," Patricia says, leaning over so her lips are right near Brooklyn's ear. "I'm too big to get past. Are you ready for your adventure?"

Brooklyn takes the question very seriously. "I . . . I think so."

Patricia nods. "That's because you have a hero's heart. Do you think you can dance past all these people using your vampire ballet?"

Brooklyn's face lights up. "Oh yes! Like a vampire! Or a ghost! What do I do?"

Patricia smiles, her heart breaking.

Why is her role as an authority figure always to push these tender souls away?

It's a cruel joke.

"Get past these people and tell that large man that your mother is Chelsea Martin, Florida Woman, and your old, sick nana is back here.

He'll take you to your mama, and then you can bring her back here to collect me. I'm just going to sit down by that wall over there. Okay?" She points to a deeper shadow against the huge metal building, which seems like it might offer some respite from the way the asphalt just here has absorbed a day's worth of blazing sun. Or perhaps that's her fever talking.

Brooklyn nods and throws her arms around Patricia's waist.

"I love you, Nana! Wait here! I'll save you!"

And then she's gone.

The last thing Patricia sees before she turns to hobble to the patch of shadows and sink to the hot, hot ground is her spunky, clever granddaughter bypassing the crowd entirely and crawling under a tour bus on hands and knees.

54.

Ella has been to a few concerts, but she's never been the one driving, and this concert parking lot shit is bananas. She nearly gets in
three accidents before pulling into a space, and losing that ten-dollar
bill hurt, passing it over as if for nothing. Surely her mother has
money. Surely her mother will take care of her. Surely she won't have
to find her way in the world with only seventy dollars to her name.

Outside, the heat beams up off the cracked asphalt, the gabbled
voices laughing and carefree in a way that she can't even approach.
She follows the crowd because they know where to go and she doesn't.
People in green vests use lit-up lightsabers to guide them toward
gates like they're airplanes going in for a landing. She doesn't have a
ticket. She couldn't afford one. But she knows what to do. Chelsea
told her what to say in her email.

"Can you please direct me to Security?" she asks an old woman
with a face like a withered apple.

The woman's face crinkles down. "What for? What's wrong?" But
then she shakes her head before Ella has to come up with a lie and
points. "Doesn't matter. Girl asks for Security, you send her to Security. Go knock on that door."

Ella thanks her and heads for a thick metal door with, rightly enough, a sign reading SECURITY taped to it. She knocks, and a huge bald dude glares out. When he sees her, his face softens.

"You okay, honey?"

Normally, Ella hates it when people call her honey, especially men. But just now, she'll take any kindness she can get.

"My mom is Florida Woman. Chelsea Martin. I'm supposed to meet her. She said you would have my name. It's Ella Martin. And she said if there's any problem with that, you can radio Arlene or Sienna and they'll set you straight."

The guy flinches at mention of those names. "Hang tight for a few." He gently closes the door, and a few moments later it swings all the way open, letting out a puff of cold, mechanical-smelling air. He smiles. "Come on in."

Ella steps into a room that looks like some kind of crisis center. There are several big dudes in SECURITY shirts, a teen guy looking at a bank of monitors, and lots of little radios.

"I'll take you back to the tour bus," the guy says. "Arlene said your mom was real excited to see you."

He leads her down a long, cold hall, all white concrete blocks going gray with dirt. Their footsteps echo, and Ella realizes that she probably looks like some kind of animal, that her hair is a mess and she never put on deodorant today. She crosses her arms as she walks. "Yeah, I haven't seen her in weeks. Months. I didn't know she was here."

The guy chuckles, but not in a mean way. "Your mom's a star. Guess that was a big surprise, huh?"

"Yeah."

At the end of the hall, he opens another heavy metal door, and the humid, hot air makes her draw back. They're outside in a loading zone, where several RVs and buses are lined up. There's a riot of voices, people laughing and talking. Sounds like a party. Her head jerks around as she looks for her mom, but all she sees are fans, lined up like groupies.

"It's this bus," he says, guiding her around the group. "Arlene said you could make yourself at home."

A teen girl in the driver's seat opens the door, cocking her head at Ella with curiosity, a hardback book splayed in her lap. "So you're Ella," she says. "You look just like your mom."

But Ella stops before stepping up into the air-conditioned bus, which feels like a cool, calm, safe space, a space where she's expected and wanted, two things she hasn't felt in forever.

Something . . . she heard something.

Her name?

"Ella! Ella!"

She turns, and there, running up the asphalt, impossible and magical and wearing her broken tiara, is her little sister, Brooklyn.

55.

Chelsea runs down the grimy hallway in her VFR-branded robe, heart pounding harder than it did in the ring.

Her baby is coming. Her daughter.

Ella.

She shoves out the big metal door into the humid twilight fug of the parking lot beyond, the asphalt lit by sick orange streetlights, and much to her surprise a small crowd of people is standing there in the dark. A few heads turn, someone starts whispering, and it only takes a moment before they all focus on her like sharks smelling blood. They screech and wave and hold up signs, screaming, "Florida Woman, oh my God, it's Florida Woman! I love you!" They surge toward her, but the security guys hold them back, and still hands press out toward her like she's a guru who can offer blessings. She gives the crowd a single, frowning up-nod, trying to stay in Florida Woman character until she's past, then jogs for the tour bus. It's chugging in place, right where she left it earlier today. She stops in front of the door, her heart going a mile a minute, the makeup melting off her face, her lungs bursting.

The tour bus door swings open, but Indigo isn't sitting in the driver's seat. Chelsea turns her head to the left to ask what's up, and that's when she sees him.

David.

It's like seeing a ghost, some hideous monster from her nightmares, and she's stepping back outside in slow motion, the world running slow as honey when she hears a familiar voice from inside the bus cry, "Mommy!"

Ah. Shit.

He has Brooklyn.

She freezes.

"Come on in," David says, looming over her as she stands on the bottom step, a wall of heat and groupie energy behind her. "The water's fine." His smile is a slow, cold thing, an alligator crawling up from the blackened depths. When she doesn't step up fast enough, he raises his eyebrows and shows her the evil black gun in his hand.

She steps fully onto the tour bus that has become her safety, her sanctuary, her healing space, and he jerks the lever that closes the door behind her and locks it. The sound of the crowd goes utterly silent; that's the beauty of a tour bus. It blocks all sound.

Well, most sound.

She's pretty sure that if he shoots his gun, someone will hear it. But considering the close quarters, by then it would be too late.

"Mommy?"

Her inner lioness kicks in, overriding her current fear, and she pushes past David in the narrow aisle, past all the bunks to the sofas in the communal area in the back where . . .

Dear God.

It's not just Brooklyn.

It's Ella and Patricia, too.

All of them, here at once.

What the hell has David done?

It doesn't matter. She and Brooklyn tackle-hug each other, and she digs her nose into her daughter's hair and inhales that sweet perfume every mother knows, her baby's head, her entire body flooding with a heady mix of love and terror and whatever makes a cat's claws come out. Brooklyn smells like someone else's shampoo and has a new star-shaped scar on her forehead that Chelsea wants to ask about.

"Mom?"

Her head jerks around, and there's Ella, biting her lip, looking like one of Peter Pan's Lost Boys. Chelsea holds her arm out, and after the briefest of teenage pauses Ella launches herself to join them in a tight, perfect, wonderful hug. Chelsea sneaks a sniff of her head, too, smells more unfamiliar shampoo and a sort of world-weary stench. Ella has been through something Brooklyn hasn't, Chelsea can feel it on a gut level, her Mom senses tingling.

Much to her surprise, Patricia stands and hobbles over—is she hurt? What's wrong with her? Why is her skin so hot?—and inserts herself awkwardly into a hug that was very natural before she showed up and is now uncomfortable and stilted. Chelsea wishes she could freeze and rewind this moment, just put her arms around her daughters and feel that burst of genuine love and relief again, but now here's her goddamn asshole mother forcing herself into a moment that's not hers, as always, and Chelsea wants to tell her to fuck off, but . . .

"Just survive, little bunny," her mother whispers, and she sounds dazed and sad and absolutely nothing like herself at all.

Chelsea looks up from the hug, over her daughters' perfect, sleek blond heads, and there's David, watching them, gun in hand, disgusted and full of hate, blocking the only way out.

"Are you done?" he says, sneering.

"Go sit down," she whispers to her girls. "Far back. Ella?"

Ella meets her eyes and nods, and there's a new and terrifying understanding there. Whatever her eldest daughter has been through in the weeks since Chelsea left has not been good. She's too thin, skittish as a wild animal. Ella puts an arm around Brooklyn and pulls her to the couch all the way in the back, the one right by the toilet.

"But why—" Brooklyn starts.

David points the gun at them—at the girls.

"Sit the fuck down and shut up, for once!" he growls.

Ella pulls her little sister into her lap and murmurs, "Shh, Brookie. It'll be okay."

Patricia, left standing alone, hobbles back to the nearest sofa and collapses onto it, slumping a little. She's not well, but it's clearly not a Violence thing, nor could it possibly be a Covid thing. But that's a problem for another day—if there is another day.

Now only Chelsea and David are standing. She's in her costume still, the heavy black mascara framing her view, her robe coming un-done. At least she's wearing a T-shirt today, not the skimpy tank top that shows deep cleavage. David is wearing a Florida Woman–branded shirt that hangs too low, her own face staring back at her. He's lost a little weight and a lot of muscle, but that doesn't lessen the threat he presents—he's holding a gun, after all. An older version of Chelsea would cower, would kowtow, would ask him if he's okay, ask him what he needs. An older version of Chelsea would pretend to care.

But that version of Chelsea is gone.

"What do you want?" she asks, her voice flat.

He snorts and shakes his head like she's a little kid who keeps writing her *E*'s backward.

"What do I want? Are you shitting me? I want to reverse three months and forget what it's like to shit in a public toilet surrounded by criminals after eating expired government food. I want a wife who didn't betray me and destroy our life, destroy our family."

So melodramatic.

And of course, it's all about him.

"I can't change any of that, David. I'm asking what you want right now. What will it take for you to leave us alone?"

David's eyes bug out of his head. "Leave you alone?" he splutters. He advances, taller, looming, the gun held down at her head at an angle from bad 1990s gang movies. "Bitch, I don't want to leave you alone. I want you to fucking apologize!"

She glances back at the girls to remind him to watch his language. Brooklyn is in Ella's lap, her eyes as big as the Disney princess she thinks she is. When Chelsea glances outside the bus's heavily tinted windows, she doesn't see anything comforting or helpful, no one ap-proaching. Even the security guard is out of sight. And Indigo isn't in the front seat.

"Looking for help? Too fuckin' bad," he says. "The driver's locked in the bathroom without her phone." When he smiles . . .

God, it makes Chelsea shiver.

To think that this . . . thing . . . was inside David all along, and she invited him into her life. It was bad enough as she learned, bit by bit, everything she'd given up for him, but she never thought that underneath all his demands, his gaslighting, his cruelty, he was this monstrous. She thought maybe he was just callous, self-absorbed, distracted. Emotionally disconnected at best, narcissistic at worst.

Now she's learning he's a stone-cold psychopath.

That changes things.

She can't lean into tears, into pleading, into anything emotional.

Because any man who threatens his own children with a loaded gun can't be reasoned with.

Her mind shifts, slides sideways like she's an animal caught in a pen and working her way out. She refocuses on David.

"Now," he says, bellying up to some sort of evil-villain speech that he probably sees as a hero's monologue. "I'm going to put this away so we can just talk." The way he says *just talk* suggests that Chelsea will do no talking other than saying *yes, David* or *I'm sorry, David* when appropriate. He holds up the gun with a smug, idiot grin before placing it on the counter he's leaning against, in a place none of the women could reach. "The way I see it—" he begins.

But Chelsea has heard enough.

She lunges.

56.

Ella watches, frozen, her fingers clutching Brooklyn's arms so hard that she'd probably yelp if they weren't both so fixated on what's going on. Their dad is clearly insane, and if their mother isn't careful, she's going to get everybody killed.

Because if there's one thing that's utterly clear, it's that their mom has changed.

She's not meek, cowering, apologetic, making herself small.

She looks . . . bored.

Unimpressed.

A snake preparing to strike.

Her hip is cocked, her hands loose and open as she watches Dad strut around. Every time the gun waves in their direction, Ella clutches Brooklyn to her and curls around her. Ella doesn't want to die, but this is what her body does, an instinctive urge to wrap around Brooklyn and protect her no matter what.

If her dad will point a gun at Brooklyn, a little five-year-old kid, someone on whom nothing can be blamed, all bets are off. And Ella already knows he wouldn't mind hurting her, the older, rebellious, sulky, more annoying sister. He's done it before, and she's seen it in his eyes—the wanting to.

He wants to silence her, and he's now in a position to do it.

When he walked onto the bus, he didn't rush to his daughters. He showed his gun to the girl in the front seat, broke her phone, and shoved her in the bathroom, promising to shoot her if she made a single noise. And then, gun still in hand, he looked to Ella.

"Stay out of my way," he told her. Not Nana and Brooklyn, just her. Like it's Ella's job to make sure no one interrupts his—fuck. Whatever this is. Monologue.

It's funny how time runs when someone is thinking about killing you.

It stretches out. Things slow down. She's frozen only because there is no move to make.

Can't escape.

Can't fight a gun.

All she can do is watch, helpless, as her mother makes it clear that her father is boring her with his threats.

His threats to kill everybody.

C'mon, she shouts telepathically. *Apologize! Make him stop!*

But her mom does not apologize, doesn't say anything comforting or placating, doesn't beg Dad to let the girls go, doesn't promise to be good. She's acting out in a way that Ella was never allowed to, and Ella feels a slow, steady fury start to build like an oven warming up.

How dare her mother pick this moment to defy him?

Out of all the moments when she could've said no, could've walked away, why now?

Finally, Dad puts down the gun, and Brooklyn sags in Ella's arms like a puppet with cut strings. Ella feels a tiny lift of relief, but she's all too aware that Dad barely has to lean over to have the gun right back in hand again. Plus, there's a knife on his belt. It's just a trick.

It's always a trick.

He starts talking, and maybe, just maybe, he'll give them a way out, make some offer, reveal some tiny crack that will let light shine in and clear out all the terror.

There has to be a way through this.

There has to.

And then, out of nowhere, her stupid goddamn mother attacks him like a goddamn idiot.

There's no sound, no clue that it might happen. Dad is mid-sentence, and Mom tackles his legs, knocking him to the ground. He falls in the aisle between the bunks, the curtains rattling as he grabs for some kind of purchase. His head bangs off the floor with a bouncy thunk that stuns him, and Mom straddles him, her legs pinning down his arms.

"Chelsea, you'd better—" he growls.

Her mom yanks something out of the lowest bunk and—

Jesus.

Jesus.

Hits him over the head with it, bringing a blocky, pinkish something down on his forehead with both hands, with all the power in her body.

Again and again, she hits him in the head with it—

Ella sees it now.

It's a Caboodle.

A fucking Caboodle.

A pink plastic makeup case, all rounded edges, now all splattered with blood.

Bash. Bash. Bash.

Not a sound from her mother, not a word or a grunt or a pant.

Complete silence but for the *goosh, goosh, goosh* of the plastic slamming into her father's head and, sometimes, his head bouncing off the carpeted floor. Just like with the two boys at school, like when Thomas had the Violence in the cafeteria, but this time no one is running to stop it.

"What's happening?" Brooklyn asks, her voice muffled.

Because while Ella is watching the horror unfold, her body has wisely tucked Brooklyn against her side, wrapping her arms around her sister's tiaraed head so she can't see what's happening.

Ella's focus shoots to Nana. Her grandmother is watching the scene as if it's a boring TV show, her eyes glassy and unfocused, her smooth, tan skin an uncomfortable, hammy pink.

A high fever, she said.

Ella shakes her head. Too much to take in.

She looks back to Mom and Dad on the floor.

That's not—

She can't—

His . . . head . . .

Her mother rises, silent but for the lone pop of her knee or her spine, some random bone's complaint.

She drops the makeup case on Dad's chest.

Dad's chest isn't moving anymore.

His face looks like a dropped cherry pie.

Ella turns her head, feels her gorge rise.

Nothing but acid.

Acid. Acid. Acid.

Just like with Mrs. Reilly's cats, just like with Uncle Chad.

She's an emptiness that will never be comfortably filled again.

It's been years since she ate soup with Leanne and River.

Her mom is walking toward her, still silent, her hands bloody to the wrist, her Florida Woman shirt's fake blood spatters proven all the wrong color by the real blood spatters layered over them. For the longest moment, Ella thinks maybe her mother is still under the spell of the Violence, that she's going to hurt someone else. But no. That's not how it works.

Her mom is awake. The storm is past.

Her mom has to be okay.

But wait.

She looks to her mom's eyes.

Her pupils are nearly normal.

She . . . doesn't look confused.

Ella remembers what it feels like to wake up from the Violence.

It's like waking up from the middle of a dream—you don't know where you are, what you're doing, what happened.

Her mom doesn't look like that at all.

"Mom?" she says, voice shaking.

Mom sits on the sofa beside them, prim. She holds out a hand, glances at it, gets up, washes both hands at the tiny sink, dries them off on a roll of paper towels, leaving pink streaks. She shrugs out of her bloodstained white robe like a snake shedding an old skin. All this time, she says nothing. Then she comes to her place on the sofa.

"Sweetheart, I'm here. It's okay. You don't need to be afraid anymore."

She holds out her arms, and before Ella can really process what's real, Brooklyn slides into her mom's lap, her thumb stuck stubbornly in her mouth. "Oh, Mommy. Oh, Mommy," she says, over and over again. Mom strokes her hair with blood under her fingernails. Some of them are torn. She meets Ella's eyes. The look on her face is blank and calm with the smallest hint of a smile, but also like she's not quite in her own body.

"Mom, I have the vaccine," Ella says, stumbling over how to make words. "I have enough for you and Brooklyn. If I'd gotten here sooner, this wouldn't have happened, you wouldn't have—I—"

Mom reaches over, pulls her into the hug.

"It wouldn't have mattered," she whispers.

"Yes, it would," Ella insists, wishing she'd found Craigslist earlier, wishing she'd driven here just a little faster. "It's a therapeutic vaccine—"

Mom pulls her closer, puts her lips to Ella's ear. "That wasn't the Violence," she says, so softly no one else can hear. "That was me."

57.

The wonderful thing about working for Harlan Payne is that Chelsea doesn't have to run away and hide what happened here today. Her steps are measured, her smile as cool as the *Mona Lisa*.

She knows this floaty feeling.

Dissociation.

Like her mind is a balloon, bobbing just behind and above her body.

She has faith that they'll be reunited soon.

It's not as scary because it's happened before, and because her babies are safe now.

But she still has work to do.

"Can I borrow someone's phone?" she asks, hating that she never got hers back from Arlene.

Ella holds hers out, her hand trembling, and Chelsea takes the cracked screen and faded cover like she's being handed something precious.

"Go let Indigo out of the bathroom," she says, because Ella needs something to do to stop the shaking.

Chelsea goes to the front of the bus, where a Post-it is taped to the dashboard with all the pertinent numbers on it. The world outside is dark now, and the groupies stand and shift in the puddles of orange light like a school of fish, unaware of the sharks that have swum past them tonight. Sitting in the driver's seat of the bus for the first time, Chelsea makes a group text for Arlene, Harlan, Chris, and Sienna. No point in leaving anyone out.

It's Chelsea. Husband came to tour bus to kill me and my girls. Need your help. NO POLICE. I stormed.

Only one of those things is a lie, but she's not about to admit in any traceable way that she is responsible for killing David.

She . . . killed David.

She's imagined it multiple times while sitting through his abuse, but not in any way that was concrete, nothing like what actually happened.

She was there for every second of it, and she also wasn't. She felt like a portal to something else, some deep, boundless pit of simmering rage that could no longer be contained. She welcomed that connection, was glad to let it move her hands, to bring them down, firmly, with conviction, to disallow any sort of pause or consideration.

When she was little, Ella got a horrible stomach virus once, and Chelsea spent days sleeping on the bathroom floor with her. When she puked, it was like a fire hose from hell, a pressure and volume and sound far too big for that tiny little body.

This feels like that, but like hell was trying to help her.

Chelsea shakes her head and hits SEND.

Strange thoughts for strange times.

As she sits in the driver's seat, staring out at the light glimmering on groupies smiling and waving at her from some other world, her hearing comes back, first a loud buzz and then complete words.

"Mom, do you have any ibuprofen? Nana's got a really bad fever."

Chelsea glances back down the long line of the aisle between the bunks. This place felt so safe only a few hours ago. She won't be able to sleep here again. Maybe no one will. All these strong, brave women reclaiming their lives don't deserve to be haunted by some asshole like David.

Ella is by Nana on the couch, Brooklyn still clinging to her older sister's orbit. Patricia looks terrible. To get to them, Chelsea has to step over what's left of her husband. She . . . doesn't even remember doing that to get up here. Human brains are so good at creating holes where terrible things dwell.

"The cabinet above the kitchen sink. Glasses for water on the right."

Her voice comes out strained and husky, as if she's been silent for decades and is learning to speak again.

Part of her feels that old, familiar tug of expectation and duty. She shouldn't make her child do this work alone. She should get to the other side of the bus and check her mother's temperature and find out why she's so sick. But there's a definite weakening in the chains that bind her to obedience just now.

Ella can hand someone pills, fill a glass with water.

Chelsea herself needs to sit here until she knows help is in view.

She looks down at the phone in her hand.

She didn't even notice it buzzing.

There are messages.

Arlene: *On the way. Hold tight.*

Chris: *Is he still a threat?*

Sienna: *Is Indigo with you?*

Nothing from Harlan, but he's probably still by the ring or otherwise on camera.

She fumbles to text Sienna, to let a fellow terrified mother know her child is safe.

A sharp rap on the glass door draws her attention.

It's Chris, looking deadly and furious in a way she's never seen before.

Why doesn't he—

Ah, yes. The door. David locked it.

Chelsea reaches out, noting the red speckles up her arm, above where she washed her hands, and unlocks the door.

Chris steps in and up and past her, a small black gun as slender and hard as a blade pointed forward in both hands.

"It's okay," Chelsea says.

The words aren't quite working right, but Chris must see David on the ground. Anyone who takes one look at what's left of his head knows he's not a threat.

Chris slides his gun back into a hidden holster in his waistband and turns to Chelsea.

"Did he hurt you? Is anyone hurt?"

Only for the last twenty years, she wants to say. But she just shakes her head.

"He left his gun on the counter," she adds, wanting to be helpful. "It's loaded."

"Chelsea?"

Now Arlene is standing at the bus door, already stepping up. Arlene doesn't ask any questions. She glances inside, sees Chris, and envelops Chelsea in a hug.

"It's okay," she croons. "It's over. You're safe."

Chelsea gulps a weird little laugh.

It doesn't feel okay. Nothing is ever really over. She doesn't feel safe.

"He found me," she whispers to Arlene in this new, husky voice, as if she's torn her throat without a single scream. "He cornered us here. He had a gun."

"I know. I know. This is not your fault."

And those five simple words are the ice pick that pokes a hole in the dam of her emotions, and the balloon floats back to her shoulders, uniting body and mind, and Chelsea draws a screeching, animal breath and lets out a tremendous, shaking sob. She's gulping for air between jagged moans, fat tears already drenching her twice-bloodstained shirt.

"Mommy, are you okay?" Brooklyn shouts from the back of the bus, but she can't get here to hug her mommy because her daddy is dead on the floor and Ella is surely doing her best to shield Brooklyn from the worst parts of it all because she's a good, noble, selfless, wonderful girl who learned from a young age to sacrifice herself. Just like her mother.

"Your mama's okay," Arlene calls back, still holding Chelsea's head to her shoulder and rocking back and forth. "Everybody's got to cry sometimes."

There's movement, too close, and Chelsea startles like some tender forest creature, but it's just Chris. He always looks compact and competent, but now he looks dark and crafty, too.

"I put a sheet over him. We should wait for Harlan. We'll need hotel rooms tonight."

Arlene looks up, her hand still gently cupping Chelsea's skull like she's a baby, but her voice is hard and certain. "Sienna can do that. Have TJ keep everyone in the greenroom once it's over. Tell him to order pizza."

"Got it."

Chelsea allows herself a small smile through the receding tears. Of course Arlene is the one in charge, at least once it's clear that no one is still in physical danger.

Pulling away, Arlene inspects Chelsea's face, asks her what day and year it is, watches her pupils as they follow Arlene's finger back and forth and up and down.

"Can you tell me what happened?" Arlene says softly.

"My girls," Chelsea whispers.

They're back there, alone, cornered by a corpse. She needs to go to them, comfort them.

"They're fine. Let's worry about you for a minute. Are you hurt?"

Chelsea explains what she can, as best she can, as quickly as she can. She doesn't know what happened before she got here, only that when she did, David already had a gun out and pointed at her daughters and mother. She's remotely curious about how it all came to pass, whether he brought them all here as some sort of sick audience or as a backup plan, knowing she wouldn't run away if they were present, or if they somehow all ended up here independently.

And when she gets to the part about attacking him . . .

"Was it the Violence?" Arlene asks quietly.

"I . . ." Chelsea doesn't want to lie to this woman who has done more for her psyche than anything else in the past twenty years. But the steady, probing look Arlene is giving her tells her that what she says next is important, and that there's more at stake than the truth. "It was."

"Such a horrible disease," Arlene says, patting her arm. "Now I have to ask you something before Harlan gets here, and he's on his way." She leans in close. "How do you want this handled? Because we can call the police, make it official, but then they'll want to take you in, maybe put you into one of those awful camps, and I know you just got your girls back. It might be better if . . ."

"If we handle it ourselves," Chelsea finishes.

Arlene nods slowly, knowingly. "I'm not gonna pretend that we wouldn't get shut down if this went public. And I'm also not gonna pretend that you'd have a chance of staying with your girls. But it's up to you."

Chelsea stands on numb feet and wobbling legs, looks down the long aisle, her brain skipping right over the navy-blue sheet draped over a lump on the floor. There's Ella, holding Brooklyn, who's eating a Moon Pie they must've found in the cabinets. There's Patricia, leaning back against the wall, face strained and eyes closed, red as a boiled ham as Indigo puts a compress on her forehead.

"Arlene," she says urgently, turning back, "I want—"

"I'm so sorry I wasn't here," Harlan Payne says, squeezing up the stairs. It's a tight fit, but he makes it. The groupies outside are screaming his name, screaming for Rampage, the flash from twenty cameras blinding Chelsea. He frowns and yanks the door shut and clasps her shoulders in oddly gentle hands. "Are you okay?"

Chelsea nods, he asks her all the same questions Arlene has asked her, Chelsea explains again using even fewer words. It's exhausting, being forced to live it over and over again. Arlene must sense that, as she interrupts.

"I have all the information. Let's not make Chelsea talk about it again. We need to get the bus far away from here, get all our people into a hotel, and do some cleaning up."

Harlan gives Chelsea a sharp, cunning look. "No police?"

Chelsea shrugs. "What's the point? I don't want to end up in a quarantine camp, and you don't want to lose the VFR."

"But what do *you* need, from all this?"

It's oddly put, but she appreciates the question. How does she want to move forward?

Funny to be asked this question twice in as many days.

"Do I still have a job?"

Harlan Payne, pro wrestling star, seven feet tall and clad in a five-thousand-dollar suit, honks a chuckle like a little kid who just farted.

"Honey, do you think I'm gonna fire you for getting rid of some abusive asshole who threatened to kill your kids? Who probably found you because I plastered your face all over TV and the internet? No fuckin' way. We're gonna toss this piece of shit in a swamp and keep on fighting. If you want your job, it's still your job."

"But the tour bus?"

He waves a dismissive hand. "I'll tear out the carpet, put in new, sell it, and get a new one." He winks. "I got money now." He cocks his head at her. "But I got to ask you again, you plan on suing me?"

Now it's Chelsea's turn to splutter a laugh. "Sue . . . you?"

"I said I'd protect you, and I clearly failed at that. Now, it's not written down somewhere, but this is . . ." He glances down the aisle of the tour bus, rubbing the stubble at his throat. "This is beyond the pale."

Warmth rushes into Chelsea's chest.

"Let me keep doing this. Just let me bring my girls along, too. They can share a bunk. They—"

He puts a hand on her shoulder, but not like David used to, not like he's holding her down. Like he's steadying her.

"Done. I'll just get you a little motor home. Nothin' big like mine, mind you, but a little one. You okay to drive something like that?"

"No, but I can learn."

"Good girl." He looks around the bus again. "If you're out of this particular bus, I can just replace the carpet and keep using it, save a few thousand. But you got to promise me: This is between us. You won't tell anybody what happened in here. And your little motor home—we'll just say your bank account finally unfroze and you bought it yourself."

The knot in Chelsea's chest unfurls, and her whole body feels as loose as soft serve. She flops back in the driver's seat, suddenly acutely aware of how uncomfortable it is, how much her arms hurt, where every new bruise from her match with TJ is forming into a purple smudge.

Which reminds her.

"You gonna yell at me for convincing TJ to throw my match?" she asks. It seems like such a small thing, comparatively, but small things matter, too.

Harlan grins. "Yeah. This is me yelling. Don't throw my matches. Next time, you're gonna lose. To Matt. And it's gonna be embarrassing. And you're just gonna take it. Got it?"

"Got it."

He nods decisively and puts his hands on his hips, his elbows awkward in the small space.

"Then we'll just drive this bus the hell away and get you ladies somewhere more . . ." He stares at David's corpse. "Comfortable. I heard there was gonna be pizza."

"Pizza?" Brooklyn shrieks.

Harlan looks back at the little girl, who's standing on his tour bus sofa in her tiara.

"Whatever you want, Princess," he says.

EPILOGUE

They're on the road again—they've been on the road for two months—and Ella sits at the small kitchen table, finishing her homework and making sure Brooklyn stays mostly on task with her workbook while Mom drives the motor home. It smells comfortably of lavender potpourri, a vast improvement over everywhere else she's stayed since leaving the house she grew up in.

She doesn't know what else happened that night, after Mom killed Dad. Chris drove the tour bus to a hotel and helped her and Brooklyn and Nana get over . . . the lump . . . as if he were chivalrously whisking them over a puddle. She didn't look down, didn't breathe, just jumped and hurried away, following Brooklyn off the bus and into a clean, pretty lobby with free chocolate chip cookies. They got an adjoining room with Nana, who took a couple of pills and fell into a deep sleep. The next morning, Arlene took Nana to an urgent care, paid her bills, and got her the antibiotics she needed. Nana came out of her fever almost a different person.

She's funny and sharp. Even her voice has changed, like she has a country accent now. She walks differently, actually sees her grand-daughters instead of basically looking through them to her next hair appointment. Ella is starting to kind of like her. Brooklyn loves her and is attached to her, which blows Ella's mind. A lot happened between them, while she was living at Mr. Reese's house. Part of her is glad to share the burden of being Brooklyn's nanny and playmate and best friend and nighttime comforter, but part of her feels so threatened at losing something. She's not even sure what's being lost. She just knows that Nana has gone from some weird caricature of a country-club queen to a real person. And she also knows that Nana is dating Steve, the VFR wrestler who looks like a banker, and actually seems to love him.

Life with the VFR is pretty sweet. They have their own motor home, and yeah, Ella sleeps in a tiny bunk bed over the cab, but it's her own bed, and her dad didn't die nearby and it doesn't smell like dead cat, so she can't complain. Nine women—who have no knowledge of that night—still sleep in the tour bus where it happened, but she made it clear she'll never set foot in there again, even if it has brand-new carpet.

They travel, and Harlan's built extra days into their schedule so the fighters can rest and they can enjoy whatever city they're in or spend time at a nearby beach. She's seen more of Florida than she ever did in her previous life, and none of it with the ominous storm of her father sitting just a little offscreen in every photograph, ready to explode at a moment's notice.

But the coolest thing is that now that the VFR is popular, Harlan is loaded, and when he found out she had the vaccine recipe, he made a few calls and bought the right machinery. Ella emailed Leanne for some names, and now Tara and Pedro travel along with the VFR in their own motor home and vaccinate as many people as they can, as many people as want it. Everyone in the VFR got the vaccine first, of course—Ella was so proud to be the one holding the needle.

Like Leanne and River said, there are still people out there who cling to their disease, who carry an illegal baggie of pepper, knowing that as long as they want to roam free, they'll be safe from whatever previously threatened them. Ella doesn't blame them. Not everyone's monsters have been exorcised.

It's actually been nice, letting the past go. Ella has a new phone with a new number. She has a new email account. Nobody back home knows where she is, how to find her, if she's alive or dead. Olivia and

Sophie probably don't even notice that she's gone. Hayden sent her one more email titled I MEAN IT FOR REAL, and she logged out of that address and never looked back.

She has Brooklyn and her mom and Nana. She has everyone in the VFR, which is like a family. She has Indigo, who's become the best friend she's ever had, and who somehow finds all the best music and knows exactly which taqueria to visit in whatever city they're in. And she has Arlene and Chris and Sienna and Harlan, who's like some magical combination of grizzly bear, movie star, and rich uncle.

And maybe the weirdest part is that Ella has a paying job now. She helps Sienna cook all the food, and she gets a real wage, and she's got her own bank account without her dad's name on it.

No. Wait.

The weirdest part is that her mom is basically a famous pro wrestler. The VFR is expanding, selling out bigger and bigger venues. Celebrities pay to stop by the greenroom, and Ella has pics of herself with her mom and Guy Fieri and John Oliver and Nicki Minaj, although not all at once.

Things are, impossibly, good.

The Violence is disappearing, whether because of herd immunity or heavy mosquito spraying or the fact that the vaccine is spreading, slowly but surely, thanks to an army of secret volunteers. The expensive one that rich people pay for? No one needs it. The guy who bought it went under in some insider trading scam. The government never actually developed one. The president is being impeached— again. The world is righting itself.

And they never talk about Dad.

Like, ever.

There aren't a ton of good memories, and the last one set everything else on fire.

Even Brooklyn doesn't ask about him, although Ella's pretty certain that one day, when she's older, she's going to have questions.

Ella kept her shielded the whole time, and she's pretty sure Brooklyn didn't see anything. After Chris covered him up, Brooklyn asked what the lump was, and Ella said it was dirty laundry, and Brooklyn seemed to believe her. By all rights, the kid should be completely messed up, but she still dances through life in mismatched socks and a tiara, although Harlan bought her a couple that aren't chipped and cracked, which won Brooklyn's love forever.

Living in the motor home with her mother, grandmother, and sister, everything came out, bit by bit, all the words Ella never thought she'd say or hear. Each one of them had a story to tell, and there were so many apologies made and accepted, so many tears, so many hugs. Ella isn't sorry for anything she did while she was out there, alone in the world, and her mother doesn't want her to be. Nana is sorry for pretty much everything, but hearing from her and Brooklyn about what they went through together—it made her go from hating Nana to maybe possibly understanding her. People call her Patty now. Chelsea calls her Mom, but with a lot more warmth than she used to. It's the happiest Ella's home life has ever been, which seems like an odd thing to say after a pandemic and the death of a parent.

Which isn't to say she's not totally messed up.

She is.

And she has a counseling session every Thursday with Arlene where they work through it, and at first she was resistant, but it really does help.

Arlene told her that trauma doesn't mean you're broken, doesn't mean that things will never get better again. That it becomes a part of you, and if you can face it and shake hands with it and find a way to move on together, you'll always be better off than people who shove theirs down or, weirdly, people who've never had trauma at all.

"Your trauma is part of what makes you a survivor," Arlene told her one morning. "It wired your brain to always be ready, always be thinking, and when you needed to act to stay alive and protect yourself, you were ready to do it. You didn't hesitate. You're a survivor. And you're not alone. Everyone here is a survivor, too. Even Harlan. Even me."

That helped. Ella had always imagined that she was the only person at school who didn't have a perfect home life, the only one who cried herself to sleep at night with a chair wedged under the door. Turns out she was never alone, but everyone else was hiding their pain, too. She hates that she feels better now that her dad is dead, but . . . she's just glad she feels better.

And today? Well, she expects to feel pretty great today.

As the caravan crawls across Florida, she can't help checking the clock on her phone. When she's about to burst, her mom calls back from the driver's seat, "Smella, what's your plan for today after home-school?"

She fights a huge grin as she looks up. "Gosh, Mom. I don't really have anything to do until the show tomorrow. Do you know something we could do?"

She can hear Mom struggling not to laugh. "Hmm. I don't know. I mean, we're in Orlando. But what is there to do in Orlando?"

Brooklyn looks up from her handwriting workbook, sunlight limning her golden hair as she bends over the kitchen table, pencil in hand.

There are benefits to the fact that six-year-olds never pay attention to state maps.

"We're in Orlando?" she squeaks.

"Yeah, but I hear it's pretty boring," Ella says. "Big yawn. Nothing to do here."

"But Disney World is here!" Brooklyn shrieks. "Oh my gosh, Mommy, can we go? Please? I have ten dollars from my birthday, and I'll pay for everything, and—"

"Did someone say they were paying?"

Nana pokes her head in from the back bedroom, grinning knowingly.

Brooklyn nods enthusiastically. "Yes! Nana, we're going to Disney World!"

"Well, now, we never agreed to that—" Mom starts, trying to prolong this glorious moment for as long as she can.

"Pleeeeease?" Ella says.

"Please?" Brooklyn shrieks.

"Pretty please with sugar on top?" Nana adds.

"Well, okay, I guess it's all right, then."

Brookie jumps up from her workbook and does a fantastically chaotic dance merging ballet with jumping around like a fool, and Ella jumps up and takes her hands and joins her, and when Brooklyn holds out a hand, even Nana joins them, briefly shaking her hips and doing some old-fashioned disco moves.

This moment—Ella wants to distill it so she can take a sip whenever the darkness creeps in, whenever her heart hurts, whenever she wakes up in the night from an unknowable nightmare, eyes hot and tingling, unable to breathe. Everything that happened led to this.

They survived for this. They fought for this. They killed for this.

And maybe it's not perfect, because nothing is ever perfect. But they're exactly where they should be.

ACKNOWLEDGMENTS

To my editor, Sarah Peed, for championing *The Violence*.

To my other editor, Tricia Narwani, for passing it on to her.

To my agent, Stacia Decker, for seeing the promise of this story and selling the hell out of it.

To David Moench, Alex Davis, Alex Larned, Keith Clayton, Nancy Delia, Liz Carbonell, and everyone at Del Rey who made this book happen.

To my husband, Craig, for spending the last twenty-four years as my unofficial therapist. I'm so grateful that when I say, "I'm broken; please fix me," my partner and best friend is happy to talk about my feelings.

To Rhys, for the healing laughter, and to Rex, for the healing hugs.

To Betsy the therapist, who told me it wasn't my fault.

To Ms. Wolfe, Dr. Huntley, and Jan Gibbons, who helped me navigate high school life while I hid the fact that I was a complete mess from my peers.

To Dr. Bryan Heit, for helping me figure out how the Violence works. If I got anything about the disease and vaccine right, it's thanks to him. If I got anything wrong, it's completely on me.

To the friends who got me through the pandemic: Kevin and Chuck, bringers of Friday Cocktail Chat, and Cathy, bringer of Oops, Now I Love Mountain Biking.

And to my mom, who got us both out of there alive. Living well is the best revenge.

ABOUT THE AUTHOR

DELILAH S. DAWSON is the author of the *New York Times* bestseller *Star Wars: Phasma,* as well as *Star Wars: Galaxy's Edge: Black Spire, Mine, Minecraft: Mob Squad,* the Hit series, the Blud series, the creator-owned comics *Ladycastle, Sparrowhawk,* and *Star Pig,* and the Shadow series (written as Lila Bowen). With Kevin Hearne, she co-writes The Tales of Pell. She lives in Georgia with her family.

delilahsdawson.com
Twitter: @DelilahSDawson
Instagram: @delilahsdawson

ABOUT THE TYPE

This book was set in Caledonia, a typeface designed in 1939 by W. A. Dwiggins (1880–1956) for the Mergenthaler Linotype Company. Its name is the ancient Roman term for Scotland, because the face was intended to have a Scottish-Roman flavor. Caledonia is considered to be a well-proportioned, businesslike face with little contrast between its thick and thin lines.